**HEIRS TO THE SPLENDOR AND
CEREMONY OF THE OLD SOUTH,
THEY MIGHT LOSE EVERYTHING
WHEN THE DREAM ENDED. . . .**

MIRIAM RAPHAEL—She was too proud to be a
demure chattel, too honest to ignore the wrongs
around her. The first sin made her an embarrassment
. . . the second might make her an outcast.

DAVID RAPHAEL—Stubborn and dangerously out-
spoken, he pursued justice beyond rebellion—and into
treason and exile.

EUGENE MENDES—In the cloistered world of
Crescent City he was the ideal husband—rich, domi-
neering, and as brutal to his wife as he was to his
slaves.

GABRIEL CARVALHO—He had worshipped Miriam from childhood. Now that love demanded the ul-
timate sacrifice.

ANDRÉ PERRIN—Witty, dashing, he introduced
Miriam to temptation—and to a turbulent love that
might sweep her world away.

CRESCENT CITY

"Moves along briskly. . . . With each new novel
Plain demonstrates increasing skill at integrating atmosphere and detail into seductively readable romantic sagas." —*Publishers Weekly*

Other novels by Belva Plain:

EVERGREEN
RANDOM WINDS
EDEN BURNING

CRESCENT CITY

BELVA PLAIN

A DELL BOOK

Published by
Dell Publishing Co., Inc.
1 Dag Hammarskjold Plaza
New York, New York 10017

Dell ® TM 681510, Dell Publishing Co., Inc.

ISBN: 0-440-11549-3

Reprinted by arrangement with Delacorte Press
Printed in the United States of America
New Dell Edition
September 1985
10 9 8 7 6 5 4 3 2

To the memory of my husband,
companion of a lifetime.

AUTHOR'S NOTE

In the course of this novel many names of people who actually lived are briefly mentioned. These, with the exception of historically important characters like Lincoln and Davis, are the following: Valcour Aime; Judah P. Benjamin; Dyson, the schoolteacher; Rabbi Einhorn; Manuel García; Louis Moreau Gottschalk; Jesse Grant, father of the general; Rebecca Gratz; Rabbi Gutheim; Henry Hyams; Rabbi Illowy; Manis Jacobs; Gershom Kursheedt; Isaac Leeser; Rabbi Lilienthal; Rowley Marks; Penina Moise; Father Moni; Eugenia Phillips; Baroness Pontalba; Rabbi Raphall; Ernestine Rose; Seignouret; Rabbi Seixas; Slidell; Pierre Soulé; Judah Touro; Rabbi Wise; Dr. Zacharie.

All other characters are completely fictional.

1

Toward evening of a spring Saturday in the year 1835, a traveling berlin made a sudden appearance at the crest of a rise above the village of Gruenwald— midway between the Bavarian Alps and the city of Wurzburg in the province of Franconia. Its varnished yellow wheels were grayed with dust and the four massive horses who drew it were weary. It had evidently come a long way. Peasants, ending their day in the fields, straightened their rounded backs and gaped in dull wonderment, for visitors seldom came to the village and those who did traveled either on foot or in some lumbering farm wagon to trade. For a moment the berlin stood in bulky outline against the windy pink-streaked sky, halted on the brink of the descent as though someone within had wanted, before descending, to get a bird's-eye view of the village below. Then, swaying and creaking on its leather straps, it disappeared from view beneath a cover of budding linden leafage. A minute or two later it emerged at the bottom of the hill, traveled down the short length of the single street, and turned into Jews' Alley.

The watching peasants shook their heads. "Well, now, what do you make of that?"

Inside the berlin the single occupant was also shaking his head in wonder. He was a sturdy young man,

still in his thirties. His rich dark hair encircled a good-
humored face with inquisitive bright eyes and a soft
loose mouth.

"Judengasse," he murmured to himself almost in
disbelief. "It hasn't changed"—although why it
should have changed or how it could have changed
materially in the eight years since he had seen it last,
he could not have said.

The same cramped, narrow houses which had been
new three centuries before still stood on either side of
the alley, tilting over it as old men quarreling lean
toward one another. The last weak evening light
winked on little window-eyes under the brows of a
medieval second-story overhang and glossed the criss-
crossed beams that seamed the ancient faces.

Between the butcher's and the Inn of the Golden
Bear, halfway down the alley—there, there in another
moment *the* house would loom! And a wave of sickness swelled up in the young man's throat. Again that
dark doorway, the terrible cries, the vicious laughter—
yes, there had been laughter—the running feet, and
the blood of his young wife spilled on the steps—With
a violent effort he steadied himself.

"America," he said aloud, not knowing that he said
it.

The Sabbath had come to a close, and the double
doors of the old wooden synagogue were shut, the
high steps deserted. When the berlin jolted to a halt in
the yard of the Golden Bear, the last worshipers were
just straggling home in their Sabbath finery. So a little
crowd of them gathered quickly. What the young man
saw as he leaned forward, readying himself to step
down, was a pale blur of faces, collectively startled
and hopeful of some novelty. They were like people
coming to the circus or a play. Nothing, after all—not
counting intermittent disasters—ever really happened

in this place. Aware of himself as the focus of attention and having no wish at the moment to be recognized, for he was in a hurry, he lowered his head.

What they saw, then, was, first, a pair of leather boots extending from the vehicle's open door; next, a walking stick with a silver knob; and finally, a velvet-collared broadcloth coat and a top hat of the same fawn color. A stranger sight, though, which diverted their attention, was the pair of coal-black human beings, who, descending from the box where they had been almost hidden by the coachman's flounced cape, now revealed themselves as half-grown boys in bright blue breeches and waistcoats with gold lace cuffs.

The traveler, with his back to the onlookers, instructed the coachman, "Get a room for me for the night. And see that these two are well taken care of. They don't speak the language." He clapped the two black boys on the shoulders.

"Maxim! Chanute!" There followed some words in French to which the pair responded with cheerful nods. Then, looking neither right nor left, the traveler strode out of the yard and down the street to the home of Reuben Nathansohn. There he rapped on the door. When it was opened, he disappeared inside.

Astonished eyes rested on that door. "Now, who the devil would he be, coming to see old Nathansohn, do you suppose?"

"A foreigner, a Frenchman. You heard him."

"Some dignitary?"

"Dignitary! Not in a hired coach!"

"A banker. A foreign banker, or a merchant maybe—"

"A Jew. Couldn't you see? He was a Jew."

"How could I see? A rich foreigner looks like a rich foreigner. You think he wears a sign 'I am a Jew'? or 'I am not a Jew"? Foreigners don't have to wear our badges."

An old woman cried out with shrill scorn. Her gold earrings swung in her excitement. "You don't know who that is? You didn't recognize him? It's Ferdinand Raphael."

"Ferdinand the Frenchy!"

Voices crossed in midair, interrupting each other.

"He wasn't French, he was Alsatian! He'd just come from Alsace when he married Hannah Nathansohn."

"I remember when—"

"It can't be! He went to America after the troubles."

"Yes, and what's to prevent him from coming back? He's here to fetch his children."

"Well, anyone might figure that out."

"You think so? But high time if it's true. The girl's already eight."

"Nine. Miriam is nine."

The woman who had spoken first moved to the front. "Miriam is eight," she said decidedly. "I was there when she was born. Didn't I see her mother give birth and die all in a minute's time?" Her voice rose, chanting. "Oh, a miracle it was! A miracle that the child could live at all—"

There came an instant's respectful, grieving silence. Then a young woman spoke. "Wasn't she killed when the students—"

"That was before your time here, Hilda. Oh, yes, when the fine young gentlemen went mad, tearing through the village on their great horses straight to the Judengasse. . . ." Now the voice became a dreamy monotone, as if the speaker were unwilling, and yet compelled, to repeat the horror. "Windows smashed, doors broken in, all of us running, running . . . The

stones they had! So big, hurled in two hands. Oh, God!
I was with Hannah, two steps ahead when they hit—"

"She was struck on the head, Nathansohn's
Hannah, young Raphael's wife, right at the front door,
at that door over there. We carried her inside."

"The baby took her first breath as the mother took
her last."

Once more silence fell, the hideous recollection
making a single entity of the little group.

Then someone said, "He left right after that. Left
for America."

"A man would want to get as far away as he could,
wouldn't he?"

"Well, now, it seems he must have made his American fortune and he's come back for his children."

"He'll have his hands full with the boy, that's sure."

"Why so? He's a fine, bright boy as far as I can see."

"Oh, smart, yes, but stubborn as an ox. And not
such a boy, either. He must be fifteen."

So they waited in the alley, reluctant to miss any of
this extraordinary happening. Full darkness came. The
crowd began to dwindle. A few fetched lanterns and
waited. But there was really nothing to be seen other
than the rump of the cow feeding in the byre next to
the Nathansohn house. After a while the last lingerers
went home.

A file of green-painted storks circled the tile belly of
the stove in the corner. As the night grew colder, the
listeners drew closer to the stove. When Ferdinand
held his hands toward the heat, a round sapphire on
his finger bloomed out of the shadows.

"Not used to this northern climate anymore," he
said in his soft French-accented German. He looked
up, smiling.

"So you remember your father a little, David?"

The boy had not taken his eyes away from his father. There was something judgmental in those rather
somber eyes.

"Yes," he said. He spoke shortly, decisively, as people do who do not speak for the pleasure of hearing
themselves. "And I remember my mother, too. I remember everything."

"Of course you do. You were a very smart little boy.
But why not? Brains have never been in short supply
in our family. Never."

And Ferdinand smiled again, since it was his nature
to intersperse his remarks with smiles. He received no
smile now in return, however, only the steady regard
of those thoughtful eyes. He felt uncomfortable. And
he passed his hand reflectively over the sleek beaver
nap of the hat which still rested on his knees, smoothing and smoothing the brim, absently perhaps, or else
to reassure himself by the feel of it that he was who he
was.

This shadowed room—had he actually lived here
once? Dank and spare it was, at any season of the
year. The stove and the great oak cupboard rearing in
the opposite corner like some forest beast were its only
substantial shapes. The table and chairs were mere
spindly sticks, little better than firewood. The floor
was bare and chilly. Ferdinand shuddered. Wretched,
everlasting poverty! Here in this place one could forget
that wine was fragrant and fruit luscious, that laughter
was music and music made the feet dance. One hardly
knew in such a place that a man could have the means,
the comforting means, to let himself savor all those
things and sleep well through the night.

They were staring at him, waiting for a fuller explanation of his presence, as if they were hostile to it. He
must seem a stranger—was a stranger now. And Dinah had her own special bitterness: She'd been an old

maid already when he'd married her younger sister, gentle Hannah, so dark and dear, when Dinah had been dried up. Dryer than ever now, gone pasty yellow, forty years old, with a disgusting stain on her Sabbath skirt and nothing to wait for, nothing but the old man's death, which would, by the look of him, be coming soon enough. On his cot Opa was coughing and shaking while he pulled the shawl around his gaunt neck. To grow old, to die, in this gloom! And Ferdinand was soft with pity.

Miriam's was the only face in the room that answered to his, that gave what he wanted to receive. She had her mother's opal eyes, tipping upward at the corners, with a kind of gaiety about them even when their owner was in a serious mood, as she was now. Like her mother's, too, was the short upper lip, channeled between nose and mouth by two delicate ridges, while the upper lip barely closed upon the lower. It was a tender mouth, too tender, he thought penitently, for this house, for the poor querulous old man and the spinster, who must, he suspected, have her own forms of petty tyranny. So he was painfully moved by the discovery of this little daughter, by the elegance of her narrow feet, crossed at the ankles, and the grace of her thin fingers, now stroking the small, silky dog on her lap.

"I've got some nice things for you, Miriam," he said. Tears gathered at the back of his throat, and he swallowed. He wanted so much to give, to give out of love and sorrow over the irretrievable lost years. "I bought things in Paris and left them there to be shipped home."

And he thought of the marvelous things which were already on their way to New Orleans: a Pleyel piano, boxes of gold and blue Sèvres porcelain, yards of Alencon lace, embroidered shawls, ruffled parasols, painted

fans, and fine leather-bound books for the boy. Then it
flashed through his mind that to speak of these things
here on the Judengasse would be a cruelty. There
would be time enough to show what he could do for
his children when he had them home.

So he said only, "I've bought you a doll with golden
hair. It's in my portmanteau at the inn, and I'll give it
to you in the morning." Then a moment later he could
not help adding, "Also a suit for you, David, and a
traveling dress for you, Miriam. They're in this box.
You must wear them tomorrow so you'll look nice on
the journey."

"And now you are going to take my children
away." The grandfather spoke reproachfully, accusingly.

"Opa, I know how it must be for you, I know. But
I'll take you, too, if you'll come. And you also, Dinah." Instantly Ferdinand was dubious about his offer:
What if they were to accept? Well, then, he would just
have to take them!

"I have a wife, a good woman, Emma. A widow
with a family. Two daughters. One was married last
winter. Pelagie, a lovely girl. And I've a fine large
house, as grand as anything you've ever seen in Wurzburg."

"Naturally. Gold lies about on the streets in America. We all know that," Dinah said.

Sarcastic as of old, she had to let him know that she
was impressed neither by his magnificence nor his mu-
nificence.

The sharp tongue of the unmarried woman, the un-
chosen, he thought, pitying her, too. For her condition, one had to admit, was only in part her fault.
Young Jewish men were either penniless or leaving for
America. In addition, there was the heartless *matrikel*

to be reckoned with—the state permit granted only to a few at best. No, not altogether her fault.

He answered quietly. "I didn't find mine lying in the streets. I had to work very hard for it."

The old man coughed violently, painfully, spitting blood. David brought a cup of water; with gentle patience he held his grandfather's hands steady on the cup.

Suddenly, almost forcefully, as though he had with strong effort willed himself to break his own silence, the boy addressed Ferdinand. "Tell us about America. Tell us what happened after you left here."

Although he must have told this story a hundred times or more, it pleased Ferdinand to tell it again now.

"Well, after your mother died—I had been thinking for a long time about America—I made up my mind. As you know, I didn't own very much, so I just took what I had, wrapped it up in a linen bag, and tramped westward. Before I reached the Rhine, I had worn out my shoes, so I traded two days' work picking apples for a pair of old boots. Luckily they fit. Then I journeyed part of the way on a Rhine boat. In Strasbourg I had some distant cousins who let me rest for a few days and gave me some good meals."

They were all listening in that attitude of motionless attention which encourages a tale. The boy was rapt. He can't wait to go, too, Ferdinand thought. And he went on.

"I got a ride on an empty cotton wagon as far as Paris. . . ."

Paris then and Paris now. Revolting, smelly alleys. Flowering chestnut and long, wide avenues. Two different cities, depending on the money you have or have not got in your purse.

"I reached Le Havre at last and sailed from there. It

took two months and cost me seventy American dollars, all I had in the world. . . . The sea is like mountains crashing toward you. You can't imagine it. I was at the bottom of the ship where the immigrants go. I was so sick. Some people even died of seasickness." He looked up, a smile spreading again across his face. "Don't worry, it won't be like that for you. You'll have nice cabins, high up, with plenty of fresh salt air. You should see the cabins! Teakwood and polished brass. Fine quilts and linens. Well, anyway, I crossed the ocean, got to Baltimore, and went to work. It was very hard. Sometimes I wonder how I did it, how anyone ever does it. But they do, and I did. Got to New Orleans in the end, too."

"Is it very far," David asked, "to New Orleans from that place, Baltimore?"

"Oh, far! Miles and years between the two. Although, to tell you the truth, in my case the years have been surprisingly few. I began on a farm in Maryland. I'd never farmed before, as you know, but when you have your health and a strong will, you can learn to do anything. I learned English fast. I've an ear for languages. It wasn't bad there. They were decent people, a fat man and his fat wife, silent, hardworking folk. They'd sit at meals and there wouldn't be a sound but chewing and forks clattering. They fed me well, I will say that, yet they were stingy with pay. When the time came for my wages, he only gave me half of what he'd promised. Said he'd had a bad year, which wasn't true, because the crops were good. We'd had the best weather, enough sun and enough rain, and I'd gone with him to market and seen him sell his corn. It was just that his big fist didn't want to let the coins go loose. Well, I said to myself, I'd promised to stay two years and he'd promised to pay, but he'd broken his promise, so I had no qualms about breaking mine. I just got up very early one morning and slipped away out of the barn where I slept."

Fall. Fall of the leaves. Such golden, rosy leaves! Sour-sweet apples lay rotted on the grass. Dawn was cold; in a few hours the sun would be hot and the warmed air humming with bee buzz in the apples. By that time I would be far down the road, any road, as long as it was going west.

"This time I had a plan. I'd met a peddler who came by every few months with knickknacks for the farmwives: cotton cloth and thread, needles and toothbrushes. I saw he could do pretty well for himself. So that's what I did. Got a pack full of stuff with the money the farmer had paid me, and I worked along the road from farm to farm all the way to the Ohio River. And this wasn't a bad life, either, walking through the country with the coins jingling, growing heavier in your pocket. Or riding the riverboat, turning and curving, wondering what's around the next curve. . . ."

After a hundred hills and valleys, remember the debarkation at the spot where the Ohio rode into the Mississippi; the green shimmer of just-beginning spring, the smell of grass and all the vast space, the vast silence. Remember how one threw one's hat off and alone there, unobserved, flung oneself into a crazy dance just for the joy of freedom, of answering to no man, of being young enough to feel one's own strength and no longer being afraid of anything, not having to be afraid of anything anymore.

"After a while I was able to buy a horse. It was such a poor thing, all worn out and sick with saddle sores! I could have afforded a better creature, but I felt sorry for it. So I let it rest awhile and get its strength. We made friends, he and I, and went on together. In and out, back and forth, inland and back to the river. At

the wholesalers' in the towns I replenished my sacks.
Sometimes I'd get back onto the riverboat for ten or
fifteen miles to the next landing."

Ferdinand, in the telling, was living it all again, telling as much now to himself as to the others.

"I saw great plantations on the riverfront, grand
columned houses, hundreds of black slaves, miles and
miles of cotton fields. I saw poor settlements, three or
four log houses in the woods. There are no forests like
those in Europe, no . . ." He thought for words.
"You can't imagine the distances, the wildness of those
forests. Sometimes it startles you to think how seldom
a human foot has been there before you. Often it is
hours between settlements. You will see a cluster of
men in deerskins, women and children in ragged
woolen. You wonder what brought them, what keeps
them in this primitive, hard life."

*Forest and swamp and trail. Darkness falls under the
pines and the thorny underbrush, pressing across the
path, whips at your face so that you must protect it with
your hand. Your footsteps crackle. Then comes the
fright, the old terror out of childhood, everyone's childhood; something is following at one's back. In another
instant it will spring forward, it will grasp. And you
force yourself to steady your mind toward common
sense. You will yourself not to turn around and look
behind.*

"Lonely, empty—"

"And Indians?" David had gone tense with interest.
With finger to forehead he twined loose strands of
curly hair.

"Oh, yes, Indians! The Choctaw tribes. And wolves.
It was because of the wolves, though, not the Indians,
that I got a rifle. The Indians never bothered me."

"A rifle," the boy repeated. What was left of the
child in him was enthralled, Ferdinand saw. Three-

quarters man, or maybe more, he was; the rest was the remnant of the child. And with these adventures the father was reaching that child.

He nodded to his son. "Yes, but fortunately, I never had to use it on anything except a rabbit. After a while I was able to afford a wagon for the horse. I remember my first wagonload. Ten trunks, I had, stuffed with every kind of cloth from bombazine to madras. I had brass clocks and gold watches, lisle stockings, paisley shawls, kid gloves, and gimcrack jewelry, everything for master and servant both. Once I had the wagon, I had to stay on traveled roads." He laughed. "Traveled! Why, you could go a whole day there, too, without meeting another human being! Sometimes I'd come upon another peddler, another European Jew, most likely. After a while I began to feel the loneliness of the life. Still, you know, if you've an idea in your head, a thought that goes along with your steps, you're not entirely alone. I wanted to settle down in one place and open a store, that was my thought. After all, I knew how trading is done; my father bought grain for Napoleon's army. Well, after two years or so I had saved enough to set up a trading post. Wasn't much more than a big square shed with shelves all around. But the location was right, on the way to the Chihuahua Trail, supplying caravans on the way to Mexico. Everyone who passed that way, from planters to Indians, came to me. And things moved fast. They moved fast in America."

The candles were almost burned down. Dinah got up and kindled another. To burn candles so late into the night was still a luxury, an extravagance, Ferdinand knew, as it had always been and as it would always be. Here in these European villages, nothing moved.

"So—where was I? Oh, yes. I prospered, you see,

because a community sprang up around me in no time
at all. The next year I sold my plot of land for three
times what I had paid for it and made my way
downriver. What a river! One of the greatest in the
world. So wide that in some places you can't see the
opposite shore. With bustling cities all the way: Memphis, the big inland cotton market, Baton Rouge, going south, always south into the heat. New Orleans
was what I'd had my eye on from the beginning. The
Queen City, or sometimes they call it the Crescent
City, at the mouth of the river."

*Ah, New Orleans! The jewel in the river's crescent,
the slow green bayou water, the slumbering afternoons,
the glittering nights—*

"I fell in love with it as one"—he was about to say,
"as one falls in love with a woman," but a man does
not say such things in front of his daughter—"as one
would expect to fall in love with such a place. Almost
at once I struck up a friendship with a very fine man.
His name was Michael Myers. He was a Jew from the
northern part of the country near New York. His father had served under George Washington in the
American Revolution. Do you know anything about
that, David?"

"I've heard about it. It was a fight for freedom from
England."

"Exactly. You've done some reading, I see. So, now.
This Michael Myers had been in New Orleans for
twenty years and had built up a thriving import-export
business. But he wasn't young, and he'd been looking
for a partner, someone younger and stronger who understood the business or who at least could be taught
and trusted. It happened that he found that man in
me. He never had any reason to regret his choice, I
can say that with confidence. I not only caught on fast,
but I was able to add a few touches of my own. For

instance, I made friends—I make friends easily—with some of the ship captains you meet in the cafés. And through such contacts alone, I was able to get hold of a profitable line of goods appealing to the ladies—jewelry, shoes, linens, and such. Luxuries, delicacies. I always had a good eye for delicacies. Yes, my partner never had reason to regret his choice in the short time we were together."

The grandfather had been paying close attention. "Short time?"

"Yes, unfortunately my partner died of yellow fever a year ago. Most people leave the city in the summer, but for once he didn't do it, and he caught the fever. Terrible thing."

"So now you own the business?"

"Yes, he left it to me. His widow and daughter are otherwise provided for with a fine home in Shreveport. I did promise to look out for them if ever I should be needed. The girl, Marie Claire, is a little older than Miriam."

"Marie Claire," Dinah remarked. "A strange name for a Jewish girl."

"Well, customs are different in New Orleans." Yes, different, he reflected, wishing himself back there now and suddenly aware of how far away it was. "My business soon will be one of the largest in the city, if it isn't already. Last year I finished my house. All brick, built around a courtyard"—his arms swept the air in a large, enthusiastic gesture—"ten times the size of this whole house, with stables and quarters at the rear, built in the square. All the houses are built that way, it's actually a Mediterranean style."

"After the Roman atrium," David said.

"You do keep surprising me, David!"

The old man's thin voice quivered with scorn. "This

boy's head is full of things that don't concern a Jew. Roman atrium!"

"Opa." David spoke patiently. "Opa, you never understand. People aren't content anymore to live behind closed doors. We want to know what's been happening in the world outside. That doesn't mean we must lose our faith."

Opa rose on his elbow. "Listen to him. Oh, they may not be content, but they'd be better off if they were. I've seen enough in my lifetime not to be tricked again. Napoleon came: we were all free. Napoleon left; back inside the wall with us!" The skeletal hands clapped together, making a wall. "Here's where we are. There's where they are. And I don't need to know a thing about what's happening on their side of the wall because I'm never going to live on their side of the wall. It will never be different. Let a war come or a financial panic, or God knows what, and it'll be our fault again. It always has been."

Ferdinand spoke quietly. "With my respect to you, Opa, David is right. If you could only see how we live in America! In my city nobody asks what religion you are, or even whether you have any religion. Anyone who can afford the cost is free to move in the highest social circles."

"It seems to me," Dinah remarked, "you were always telling us the same thing about your family in France when Napoleon was emperor."

"And so I did. There were great days. If he had lasted, things would have been different all over Europe."

"But he didn't last," the old man interrupted. "So it's just what I've been saying. Must I tell you—you of all people—what happened when the Hep Hep boys swept through half the towns in Franconia? Massacre in Darmstadt, in Karlsruhe, in Bayreuth—Hep Hep," he said bitterly. "I keep forgetting the words it stood for, something about Jerusalem—"

"*Hierosolyma perdita est.* Jerusalem has been destroyed. That's Latin."

"Latin or not, it was blood to us. Hannah's blood."

There was a somber silence. Ferdinand lowered his head. The eyes—his son's, his daughter's—were unbearable to see. They were Hannah's eyes, her sweet eyes, which, during these years since he'd lost her, he had almost forgotten.

"Yes," the old man resumed. The terrible subject had poured a few minutes' worth of energy into his veins. "Yes, back where we were before! No equal rights of citizenship. No public office. Wear a badge so the German will know who you are when he passes you on the street. Your few pfennigs taxed away. And *matrikel* resumed—"

Ferdinand was stifled. The weight of all this affliction, which he had for so long been trying to discard, now fell back upon him. And he tried with feeble levity to remove it.

"So you'd have to pay to get married here, David. Think about that!"

"I don't want to get married."

"You'll change your mind in time. A pretty face will change your mind."

"Smile it away if you can," the old man said, "but you can't get away from the truth. All through the horror, did anyone do anything to help us? The clergy, for instance? No. Nobody did anything and nobody ever will."

"You're right," Ferdinand said softly.

"Then what are we arguing about?"

"I don't know, Opa. I've forgotten how this all began."

"You were saying," David reminded him, "that it's different in America."

"Yes," said Opa, "and I was saying you will see it will be the same there, too."

"No," Ferdinand insisted. "You never will. What do you know about America? Oh, I agree that Europe is finished. Away with it, then, as far as I'm concerned, away with its rotten bigotry and its rotten wars! There's no future here for the young. Not for our young, at any rate."

The room closed in. As the night deepened, the space grew smaller, and this very smallness made the world beyond the walls grow larger. They were isolated on an island in a menacing ocean. Suddenly Ferdinand was exhausted. Sorrow and fear exhausted him as he had not thought they could: all the years of his children's lives that had been wasted! Patiently they sat, the little girl now drooping with sleep, while the boy was poised on the verge of new thoughts.

Suddenly the boy spoke. "I've often wished"—he hesitated, glancing at his grandfather, then back at Ferdinand—"I've often wished—I should like to be a doctor. It would be impossible for me here." His outspread palms with their simple gesture described the life of the house.

"Quite possible in America," Ferdinand said.

The boy—his son!—was pathetic in his outgrown jacket. People always looked pathetic in clothes that didn't fit.

"The Medical College of Louisiana was founded just last year. You could go there or anywhere. And I'm not forgetting you, Miriam. We have fine schools for young ladies."

"I'll come with you," the child said. "But only if Gretel can come, too."

"Gretel?" Then Ferdinand understood that she

meant the dog. "Of course. She's a beauty, an aristocrat, isn't she? A King Charles spaniel. Wherever did
you get such a dog?"

"I found her on the road when she was a puppy
only a few weeks old, Aunt Dinah said. We think she
must have fallen out of someone's carriage." The
child's arms tightened around the dog.

"There is an anecdote about them," Ferdinand remarked. He was fond of anecdotes. "They say that
Marie Antoinette had a King Charles spaniel hidden
under the folds of her skirt when she went to the guil-
lotine. It may or may not be true, of course."

The old man was not to be diverted. "So you will
take the children away," he repeated. "Now at the
end, you will all leave me."

This appalling selfishness offended Ferdinand. Opa
would actually keep these children here if he could! He
would deprive them of their future. In one swift flash
Ferdinand saw their future: David a respected doctor,
an authority. Miriam married well in a fine house, perhaps even married to a planter owning wide acres. But
then, he thought, who knows what I'll be like when
I'm old and sick? So he answered kindly.

"Consider, Opa. Here is a boy, a young man with a
long life ahead, and a girl who in a few years will be a
woman. What is here for them? New Orleans, even
with yellow fever, is better than this."

"What sort of religious life will they have in that
place where you're taking them?" the old man interrupted.

Ferdinand hesitated. "The truth is, not as much as
here."

"Well, that never bothered you, as I remember. But
I hate to think that Hannah's children will forget what
they are."

"There's no reason why they should forget, Opa."

"They have been brought up in this house to observe the laws. Like their mother, they are faithful
Jews."

Ferdinand looked at his children. Much good it had
done their mother! He stood up, drawing a gold watch
from his pocket.

"I've kept you all too late. It's almost midnight, but
I delayed so as not to arrive here before Sabbath sun-
down."

"You traveled on the Sabbath all the same," Dinah
said.

"Ah, yes. I'm sorry! I've grown careless about
things like that. My New Orleans ways again. I shall
have to mend them," he said soothingly.

Long before dawn the two who were to depart from
the house rose from bed in their attic rooms, wakeful
with excitement, a little fear, and some sadness. From
their separate windows they watched the roiling black
sky fade to gray, to melancholy lavender, then blaze
into a sudden silver over the arc of the emerging sun.

David, leaning on the windowsill, closed his eyes
against the spreading light. Papa boasts, he thought.
He wants to show how important he is. Did I seem
sullen to him? I didn't know at first what to say. I
suppose I'll admit I'm angry that he went away and
left me—left us. Still, that's not fair: What could he
have done with a little boy and a baby? And he was
young. When he married my mother he wasn't many
years older than I am now. The queer thing is that he
still seems very young, while I feel maybe older than
he is—though that's ridiculous. But I've always felt
old. It has something to do with a picture that I've got
in my head. It's been painted there. Nothing wipes it
away, no matter how I force myself to cover it with
cheer. I can't wash it away. Chalk-scrawls on a door:

Jude verreck; Jew, die like a beast. Laughter and marching boots. Hep Hep. A woman with a swollen belly arches her back and screams and screams. Yes, yes, that's how it was: a flurry of skirts, women's long flying skirts and a door that banged and slammed; behind the door something terrible was happening. Then weeping and the long skirts in a surrounding circle, the women's faces bending down: poor little boy with no mother, poor little boy.

Blood sickened him. Yet if one wanted to be a doctor, one must be able to look at blood. But that was different. It was the *violent* blood that sickened him. For a period, only a year or two ago, he had discovered he could not swallow meat. It stuck in his throat. A slice of chicken on the plate took life again: flapping, fluttering, feathers, spread wings, squawking, running on skinny fragile legs from the slaughterer. That period had passed. He had willed it to pass, as he had willed himself into the longing to be a doctor.

Downstairs now someone stirred and a chair scraped. Poor Opa, cranky, good old man! Surely he must know he was dying. Terrible to be old, to have no strength, to pass each day knowing that one was dying. Papa, now—he had strength, you couldn't help but see that and admire it. To have done what he did, to have marched out into the world alone and made a place there for himself! Yes, you had to admire such vigor and will, even if he did boast about it.

A piece of cracked mirror hung on the wall: He had found it in someone's household discard. And David examined himself. No, there was no resemblance between his own habitual half-scowling face and his father's pleasant twinkle. Only the dark curly hair was the same. Papa's determination, though: That I have. I know I have it.

How wonderful for Miriam to get away from bitter,

mournful Dinah! He would send her to school, Papa
said. She was a bright little thing. David had taught
her to read and sometimes she even tried his books,
borrowed from the rabbi, the "modern" rabbi, against
whom Opa railed. Naturally, she wasn't able to understand them, but she tried and, surprisingly, here and
there caught on to a sentence. Curious, she was. Quick
to laugh also, as well as quick to cry. Sometimes he
felt almost fatherly toward her. Well, now her real
father could take over and care for her in the proper
way.

He shut his eyes, swaying a little as one did in
prayer. Then he opened them, wanting to keep in ear
and eye this place that he was leaving, wanting to remember the risen light and a distant voice, and the
hollow rumble of a farmer's cart.

In the other attic room the little girl was stroking
the skirt of her new dress. It was her way to describe
things to herself in terms of the natural world; so the
material was soft as new grass, it was butterfly-blue, it
was warm and light as goose down. She had no mirror, and it was only by craning over her shoulder that
she could see a whirl at her back where the plump
corded ruching of the skirt swayed above her ankles.
Holding her hand up, she let the fluted cuff fall back
over her little wrist. What a wonderful dress! Better by
far than Aunt Dinah's synagogue dress. Better by far
than any she had ever seen. And there were to be more
like it, for Papa had said so. It was a pity they were
going away so early this morning, for it would have
been a fine thing to walk up and down the street in this
dress and let everyone see it.

She ran to the window. Nobody was out yet; there
was no sign of life except for the caged bird hung
outside the shuttered window of the shop across the
way. The sight of this bird bothered the child; it al-

ways had. The cage was too small. The poor thing
could not even spread its wings. Was it to hang there
drooping, silent, every day and every night of its life?

Opa had said once, "Your mother never could bear
the sight of a caged bird, either."

Your mother. Miriam knew the story of her mother,
had known it long before she was supposed to know it,
having overheard the voices. *She is so like Hannah.
Think of it. A life going and another coming at the
same time. Horrible. Horrible.* And having heard this
so many times, she had begun to feel a certain distinc-
tion, a certain importance about herself that other
people, those born in the ordinary manner, could not
have. On the other hand, the knowledge had also
given her nightmares.

Some said she ought never to have been told. But it
was too late for that. Like her brother, she had made
mental pictures, engravings not to be eradicated. In
these pictures her mother was always wearing a plaid
shawl: Why? No one had ever mentioned a shawl.
And her hair would have been worn high, piled on her
head. No one had ever told her that, either, and she
had never asked.

Now, taking her own two braids, she twisted them
into a black silk coil on the top of her head, elongating
her face by sucking in her cheeks, which produced a
serious, adult expression—and immediately broke into
laughter, flouncing the skirt and scooping up the little
dog, which had been looking at her with a dog's equiv-
alent of amazement.

"Gretel, we're going to America, and you are, too.
Did you think I would go without you?"

She became sober again. "I shall miss Aunt Dinah.
When she's not scolding, she can sometimes be so
nice. I think she will be lonesome without me. And my
friends Lore and Ruth—but still it will be wonderful

on the ship. And David will be there, so it won't really
be very strange. Besides, I like Papa, I love him already. He has such a good smile. The doll has golden
hair, he said."

And it seemed to the child that the sun had never
risen so brightly and with such sparkle as on this
morning.

They stood downstairs saying their good-byes. Ferdinand took out a purse. Smooth, fat coins, gold flo-
rins, slid into a puddled heap on the table.

"This will do for now," he said. "I have instructed
my banker in Strasbourg to send you the same every
month for as long as either one of you lives. And this
bag here—this is a donation to the synagogue. Make it
for me in Hannah's memory."

The old man and the aging woman were overawed.
There was something in their speechless awe, in the
wetness of their eyes, that made David ashamed. That
any human being should have to be so grateful to another was wrong somehow. It was humiliating.

"And don't worry about the children. They will
have perfect care in my home. My wife Emma is the
kindest woman. She is looking forward to them."

Aunt Dinah wiped her eyes. "David is too daring
for his own good, too bold and careless. Headstrong.
When he gets a thought in his head, you can't dig it
out. So stubborn. But such a good boy all the same."
David looked at her in astonishment. Never, never
once that he could remember had she called him a
good boy.

"Yes, he knows what the world should be and
thinks he can change it. When you learn not to say the
first thing that comes to mind, David, it will be better
for you," Dinah concluded.

The old man had something to add. "Last year he

got us into trouble with the neighbors. The father over there was beating his young son for stealing potatoes, and David shouted at the man: 'That's no way to train a child!' he told him. 'You ought to know better! The Torah instructs you to teach a child, not beat him.' Imagine! A boy just past Bar Mitzvah telling a grown man how to rear his son! The man was angry, I can tell you that."

"But David was right," Miriam remarked suddenly.

"His shadow," Dinah said, embracing the child. "She is her brother's shadow. Anything he does is right in her eyes. Isn't it, Miriam?"

Ferdinand laughed. "Well, I can see my life will be more interesting from now on, anyway."

Now the moment had come, the hardest of all, the final moment when there is nothing more to say than a farewell, which must be said with some restraint and dignity lest the last memory be of total grief. There must be a severance, but not a ripping.

David took Dinah's hand and then the grandfather's, kissed them, and without speaking turned away. Moved by the boy's intuition, for in another moment the old man would have broken down in tears, Ferdinand took those same hands in his. Then with his arms upon the shoulders of his children, aware that the two left behind were closely watching, and that the sight of this affection would be a consolation to them, he led them down the alley to the yard of the Golden Bear, where the coach was already waiting to take them on the first leg of the long journey home.

2

Five weeks out of Le Havre the brig *Mirabelle,* carrying cotton goods, wine, and passengers, had left the iron-gray North Atlantic behind, had taken on fresh food and water in the Azores, and was now moving southwestward into summer. Between blue and blue it sailed, the dome of sky merging with the indigo swell of the sea. Turquoise and lapis lazuli and azure, the waves raced with the ship. Where the wake followed, splitting the surface of the water at the stern, the blue was so pale as to quiver into silver. Caught by the trade winds the tall sails whipped and the ship gathered more speed; its festive pennants crackled and the carved, aristocratic lady on the prow stretched her long neck toward the western hemisphere as if she, too, were impatient to reach it.

For Miriam, who had never traveled more than a few kilometers between identical villages in a horse and cart, who had never seen anything more impressive than the rather mediocre summer residence of the Graf von Weisshausen—and that only glimpsed from a distant road at the end of a long cypress allée—who had never seen anything more exotic than a traveling coach such as the one in which her father had arrived, the voyage was miraculous and would have been an end in itself had it led nowhere at all.

For David, who had traveled in books across the world, it was miraculous, too, but in a different way. His eyes were alert. Nothing escaped him. He had great expectations.

Having been told that French was the spoken language in New Orleans, he had immediately set himself and his sister to learning it. Among the small company of passengers—a pair of Paris bankers with their fashionable, vivacious wives, and a group of nuns on their way to a convent in New Orleans—were a father and son returning from a European trip to their home in Charleston. The father, Simon Carvalho, was a physician. Gabriel, the son, was David's age. He was an attractive boy with even features and a reserved manner. Unlike David, he moved deliberately and slowly. Yet he had been friendly enough to suggest that he teach French to the Raphael pair. David was greatly in awe of him and his knowledge.

"He knows so much. I'll never catch up with all that Latin and science. And he's six months younger than I am, too," David complained to Ferdinand.

"Well, with the advantages he's had, no wonder. But you'll catch up, I'm confident you will."

Ferdinand had found out about the family on the first day of the voyage, almost before they had left the harbor.

"They're Sephardic Jews. Came to South Carolina from Spain via Brazil generations ago. In 1697, I think the doctor said. He has a married daughter living in New Orleans, Rosa and Henry de Rivera. People of substance. Accustomed to wealth. Quiet in their tastes, although they own the best of everything," he concluded with satisfaction.

It pleased his father, David saw, to be acquainted with important people. This bothered David. He saw it as a sign of weakness, and he didn't want to see weakness in his father. At the same time he was ashamed of his own disloyalty for having such a thought.

"You're making good progress with Gabriel, so I see, or rather, so I hear," Dr. Carvalho remarked to David one day. "Pretty soon I won't need to speak in German to you anymore. You seem to understand almost anything I say in French. Perhaps you could persuade my son to start you on English, too."

"Oh," Ferdinand said, "they won't need English in New Orleans. We've twice as many French speakers there as English speakers. It's considered rude to speak English at home, even when you know how."

Dr. Carvalho replied, "That will change. It is already changing. My daughter tells me the city is fast filling up with Americans."

"I thought everybody there was an American!" David exclaimed.

"That's just an expression," Ferdinand told him. "It refers to people from other parts of the United States. Creoles have French or Spanish ancestors. And, socially speaking, they're the summit. A so-called 'American' of my acquaintance told me that the proudest day of his mother's life was the first time she was invited into a Creole home."

Dr. Carvalho responded politely. "Is that so?"

"Yes. She was invited for *café noir* one afternoon and she understood she was being honored. Creoles prefer to keep to themselves, among their own."

The other man smiled. "Artificial differences."

Again David felt the quick heat of embarrassment, as if the doctor's remark, mild as it was, had been a reproof to Ferdinand. And, troubled, he looked away, out to the placid sea, which was at the moment barely moving, slowly tilting like liquid in a cup. The sight of it was soothing. The rigging hummed in the wind, vibrating like a violin.

Ferdinand rubbed his hands together. "It won't be long before you'll be home in Charleston, Doctor. After that, it's down the coast for us, into the Gulf and home." He took a deep, audible breath. "Ah, glorious! Glorious! This freedom you feel on the ocean! Who could believe we left Europe way back there only a few weeks ago? It's hard to remember that Europe exists at all!"

From the lower deck came a babble and rumble of voices. Everyone looked down to where a mass of humanity had gathered on the open deck below. They were mostly young men—immigrants, with here and there a clustered family: restless children, fathers in peasant clothing, women carrying infants. They were taking their allotted daily hour of air. Those above watched in silent curiosity; those below did not once glance up.

"Poor creatures! I hope," remarked the doctor, "they don't carelessly set fires with their cooking down there. I worry about that."

"It gets cold below," David said. "Either that or hot as a stove. I could hardly breathe in the heat one day when I was there."

"You were down there?" Ferdinand asked sharply. "What were you doing?"

"I brought them something to eat."

"To eat! They have food."

"It's not fit to eat, Papa. Even their water smells foul. Last week their meat was maggoty and they had to throw it overboard. It's not fair, you know! The captain promised these people decent food, but he makes them buy potatoes from him when they run out. They're thirsty and hungry. Up here in the cabins

we get fresh meat and oranges from the Azores. It's
not fair."

Dr. Carvalho murmured gently, "A great many
things in this world aren't and never will be."

In earnest protest the boy's forehead wrinkled.
"There's no reason why they shouldn't be!" he cried.
"I asked one of the sailors how many people there
were down there in that little space. Four hundred!
They're all crammed in. Two double rows of bunks,
one above the other. There's a narrow aisle between.
You can hardly squeeze through. And the space is
only five and a half feet high. If you're tall like me, you
have to stoop to walk."

Ferdinand interrupted. "You're not to go down
again, do you hear? They've got rats and dysentery.
God knows what diseases you might have caught or
given to the rest of us."

"Your father is right," Dr. Carvalho said. "Where
the air is fetid, fever breeds. That's well known."

David was distressed. "But I promised to bring
some oranges! I've had them every day; surely I can
share a few, can't I?"

"Lower your voice before you bring disgrace on
us," Ferdinand said, for David's voice had risen. The
French bankers and their wives were staring.

"I haven't said anything disgraceful. I was only saying what I believed."

With conspicuous tact Dr. Carvalho moved away.
And Ferdinand continued, "Your manners need
mending. Jews especially need better manners, and it's
time you learned some, David."

Anger mounted; the father's face flushed and his
lips quivered; the son faced the father.

"Jews? Why should we especially cringe?"

"I'm not asking you to 'cringe,' as you put it. I'm

only asking you not to make a spectacle of yourself and of us."

David persisted. Something in him wanted to avoid his father's anger. Something else drove him to goading. "But why? Why should just Jews have better manners? You still haven't told me."

"Because." Ferdinand spoke in a low, agitated tone. "Because to be Jewish is to be judged, to be a victim. Heine—you've read Heine?"

"Yes, I have. I've read his poems."

"Well. He himself said that to be a Jew is a misfortune. Heine said that. Read it for yourself."

"And you agree with him, Papa?"

"Certainly I agree. Look around you. It's only common sense."

The boy felt as if he had been bruised. "Yet you gave money to the synagogue at home."

Ferdinand shrugged. "For old times' sake. For your mother's sake. I never go to the synagogue."

"You're a Christian, then?"

"Certainly not. I would never convert. What do you take me for? It's simply that—it's just that—none of it means that much to me. None of it. And least of all that foolishness of the dietary laws; you think God cares what you put in your stomach? That any man who eats pork is an evil man?"

"I don't think that at all, Papa. For myself, I obey because it's a reminder of who I am. It's hard to explain—"

"Well, don't try," Ferdinand grumbled.

David turned frowning into the western sun. He stood for a long time at the prow. A line of gulls which had been following the ship past Bermuda rode with the wind over the phosphorescent, gleaming sea. A flying fish sprang upward, flashing silver, then curved back into the water.

God is a great strength, the boy thought. We move with Him. The gulls move through the air and the fish through water, but we move with Him. We feel large then; we feel proud.

But his father had made him feel small and ashamed. Tears came to his eyes. He saw a chasm opening between himself and his father.

Miriam, in her childish way, was troubled, too. She had heard it all. Oh, how shocked Opa would be to know what Papa had just said! Still, why did David make Papa angry? He couldn't possibly win, so why start? This was like being home with Aunt Dinah's complaining and Opa's snapping at her to be quiet. One could hear their quarreling voices even with a wall between. She had such dread of angry voices. When they fought at home, she'd pick Gretel up and hold her close. The soft, licking tongue, the small warm life, were such comfort against angry voices.

Now, leaning over the rail, Miriam pressed the dog to her chest. "Ah, Gretel, little Gretel, you and I— Gretel! Gretel! Oh, God!" she screamed.

The scream tore the air. All faces turned to her, all feet rushed to her, not knowing, not understanding, until she pointed.

Far, far below, the dog's head bobbed in the water.

"David!" It was to him, not to her father, that she turned. "She only wiggled a little, slipped away! Oh, David!"

"Good God!" Ferdinand cried. "The boy's gone mad!"

For David had on the instant stripped off his jacket, climbed over the rail, and, feet first, plunged overboard. Sailors shouted from the rigging as, helplessly, the boy thrashed in the swelling sea. And with sudden comprehension, Ferdinand screamed in horror.

"He can't swim!"

Two sailors raced down the deck with a rope ladder and began to climb down, but before they had gone a quarter of the way, young Gabriel had also gone over the side, diving in an expert arc to where, only a few feet away, David's head had already gone under. The cheering, frightened, fascinated watchers on the deck saw the boy grasp David's shirt, saw the sailors pulling, hoisting David up the ladder, and saw Gabriel pluck the dog up to safety.

It had all taken no longer than five minutes. Of such minutes eternities are made.

Retching and gasping, David lay stretched on the deck. Whirling through his descent, he had fallen flat upon the water and his belly was tight with pain. He lay unspeaking. Nobody expected him to speak. From his supine position he could see Miriam clutching the bedraggled dog. Legs loomed above him, his father's and Dr. Carvalho's on either side. The nuns in their heavy black skirts glided past as if there were no legs inside the skirts. The French ladies were chirping admiration at Gabriel, heroic Gabriel.

The only difference between him and me is that he knows how to swim. I look like an idiot.

After a while he was able to sit up, and Ferdinand, immensely relieved, attacked him at once.

"You fool, David! What did you think you could do down there? And this warm ocean full of sharks, too! Don't you ever think before you speak or act? Don't you ever think?"

"She loves the dog," David muttered stubbornly.

"She may love it, but is a dog worth your life? I don't understand you. And your friend, young Carvalho, he risked his life for you. He's a hero. At least he can swim, and he was risking himself for a human life, not a dog's."

David was silent. Ferdinand paced up and down.

When again he stood over David, he had calmed himself.

"Yes, it was good of you to think of your sister. I shall try to look at it that way. A big, impulsive heart. Not a bad thing to have." He tried to smile. "But, my God, you would have died if it weren't for Gabriel. The sailors were too slow and Maxim and Chanute were belowdecks."

The incident had darkened the afternoon. Quietly, as if chastened, people stood like the wooden lady on the prow, looking out to the west.

Someone brought a stool for Miriam, and there she sat, facing westward like the rest, with Gretel, now fastened by a chain, beside her. Shock silenced her. David had almost died. And the other boy, too. How brave they had been, both of them. And Gabriel only a stranger.

He had gone to sit with David. Catching her look, he waved to her. Had she thanked him enough? Could one thank him enough? He looked so nice like that with his hands clasped around his knees and his hair ruffled in the wind. She wished David would be quiet like him; not that David wasn't gentle and sometimes quite silent; but when he had an idea, he was so excited, he wouldn't be still, would just go on arguing and never give up! He had been like that at home with Opa and it was plain he would go right on being like that with Papa.

"Your father doesn't get angry at you the way mine does," David was saying to Gabriel.

"Today, you mean? Well, he did scold me a little in the cabin when I was changing my clothes. But he was proud of me all the same." Gabriel spoke almost shyly.

"When I think about it, I see that it was wrong of

me, but I would never admit that to my father. Never. And do you know why?"

"Tell me."

"Because I don't like the way he talks to me about —about things. It's because he doesn't understand."

"Understand what?"

David hesitated. "I just feel that he is too different from me, and I from him."

"But you hardly know each other. Why don't you wait to find out more?" Gabriel asked.

David leaned over and whispered. "In the morning, when I take out the phylacteries, he looks scornful and walks away. Do you think that's right?"

"Well, no," Gabriel answered doubtfully. "But then, I don't know much about—"

"I forgot. You don't do it, either."

"But we are Jews as much as you are. Our customs are only—well, newer, that's all."

David thought, The "customs," which is what he called the Laws, have been fixed once and forever. It is absolutely forbidden to change. . . . And his indignation simmered.

"Newer? So you must find the older ridiculous?"

"Not at all. If you believe in something, you have to follow it all the way, with all your heart."

Gabriel's frank sympathy made David ashamed of his momentary indignation.

"My trouble is, and I know it, that I'm not patient, Gabriel. Anyway, regardless of anything else, I owe you a debt for my life. And my sister owes you for her dog."

"She's a pretty little girl."

"You think so? Her nose is too big," David said affectionately.

"My father says she has the look of an aristocrat."

"Oho! She can be a nuisance. Anyone who has a younger sister can tell you that."

"I don't know. My sister's so much older. You'll probably get to know her in New Orleans."

"Is New Orleans as wonderful as my father says?"

"Of course. Why do you doubt it?"

"Because he exaggerates things."

"Oh, you will have to stop suspecting him all the time, David."

"Do you know, I think you're probably a very good influence for me. I wish you were going to live in New Orleans."

"But I'll see you. We'll stay friends. I'm sure to visit my sister again. And in the meantime we'll write to each other. You'll write in French." Gabriel laughed. "And I'll send back the corrections."

"I'll write in English, too. No matter what my father says, I plan to learn English."

So they talked with the simple honesty of the young who have not yet learned to choose friends for advantage, prestige, or any reason but honest liking, one for the other.

From across the deck Ferdinand was observing his children. The girl was very quiet, clutching her dog. Poor little thing! And he understood that the animal was a link between the unknown and all she had ever known. However, she was a cheerful soul. There would be no trouble with her, and a good deal of pleasure, he was certain. Yes, he thought, Miriam will be a brightness in the house, which has had no child.

Ah, but David! David is another story. So righteous, with those penetrating eyes, as if he were examining me, looking inside my head! If one were to judge him by his righteous talk, one would have to say he was an obnoxious young prig. But prigs don't do the things he

does, bringing food belowdecks, making himself a part
of the misery down there, and God knows, and I
should know, how miserable it is! Oh, a kind boy, yes,
but still, it's not his business to interfere with those
poor people. There's nothing we can do about them,
nothing. A few oranges don't help their wretchedness;
they may only make it seem worse. He wouldn't understand that. Such indignation in him, as if he were
ready to explode! That frown: two deep-cut lines
across the forehead, and the Adam's apple bobbing in
his skinny neck. He's got down on his upper lip, feels
himself a man, no doubt. It's not going to be easy
living with him. I hope he won't make too great a
difference in our lives, poor fellow. I hope he won't
talk this way around my wife. She won't like it.
There's no grace in the way he looks, either. All those
new clothes I bought for him before we sailed! And yet
he's always rumpled, he looks as if he'd slept in them!
Oh, I should have taken him with me when his mother
died and taught him *my* ways. But he was too young. I
never could have survived or done what I did with
him along. I had to keep him safe until I had something to offer him, didn't I?

Well, now I've got something to offer. What would
he be in Europe? A peddler, probably. A peddler till
he got too old to drag himself from place to place. In
Europe peddlers don't turn themselves into commission merchants. Now he can be a doctor or anything
he wants. He'll have everything young Carvalho has.

And a smile of satisfaction touched Ferdinand's soft
mouth. David was smiling, too, now, talking to his
friend, the Sephardic aristocrat. My son has a beautiful smile. If he would just learn to use it more! One
thing—he's not like other people.

An evening wind roughened the sea and began to
chill the air. Ferdinand moved away from the rail to

seek shelter inside. He would remember this day.
When this voyage was far in the past, this one day
would stand out. It was always so. Out of long forgotten years, here and there, a single day blazes, a day on
which portents are given, unrecognized at the time,
but clear and undeniable when, years afterward, one
looks back.

The air was tropical, clinging like damp silk to the
skin. In the Gulf dolphins reappeared, racing with the
ship, rising and plunging in some vigorous aquatic
game. The southern sunset came abruptly; with a
sweep of a dark brush, all pink, all gold and violet,
were wiped out of the sky and the thick night came
down.

Now that the voyage was almost over, the passengers, both eager to arrive and already regretting the
end of their easy days, began to feel a troubling restlessness. The Carvalhos having left the ship in
Charleston, Miriam and David were surrounded by
adults and feeling the same restlessness. The nuns,
who throughout the voyage had seldom looked up
from their murmured prayers as they paced and told
their beads, now scanned the west as if they, too, were
anxious about what awaited them. Even the bankers
and their vivacious wives grew quiet.

But Ferdinand exulted. "Home!" he cried every
morning as he emerged on deck. "Home! It won't be
long now."

And so, on one of these mornings, they came at last
to the mouth of the great river. Everyone came early
on deck to look.

"See there," Ferdinand said, "how the water
changes color. It's the river mingling with the Gulf."

A long brown ribbon ran, wavering and blurring,
into blue. In the river's open mouth a hundred tiny

islands had been scattered. Turning and curving among them, the *Mirabelle* began to move upstream.

Bayous and creeks led into darkness; uprooted trees lay crumbling in the swamps, where shredded moss hung from standing cypress; water stood motionless on land. And over all lay an intense and gloomy silence. David strained to hear and see. Yes, it was as his father had said, primeval and wild; nowhere in the farthest countryside of Europe was there anything like this.

"Oh, look! Oh, look!" Miriam whispered.

A great white bird with a swan neck stood on one long leg in a patch of sunlight between the trees.

"That's a heron," Ferdinand told the child.

"Oh, the beautiful thing!" she cried.

They passed lakes and a pale sandy beach. In the cypress swamp an ibis with a beak like a red scimitar fed on fish. Then came more bayous, more lakes, and finally a stretch of wide water.

"See there, that's a pelicans' nest. There's the male bird. . . . This is Barataria Sound," said Ferdinand. He put his arm around David's shoulder, speaking rapidly in his excitement. "That island's Grande Terre. We've only ninety miles more now. Over there in the cove—you can't see it from where we are— there's a whole town! I went there once out of curiosity. Neat little houses with gardens and flowers. You'd never believe it was a pirates' town."

David drew in his breath. "Pirates!"

There's the child in him again, Ferdinand thought, pleased to see enthusiasm for the things that one might normally expect to interest a boy.

"Yes, Jean Lafitte was one of the deadliest pirates in the West Indies or the Gulf. He had a sumptuous house, all furnished with stuff stolen from the ships he waylaid. But let me tell you something you'd not ex-

pect. About twenty-five years ago there was a war between the United States and England and the British
sent a fleet of fifty warships to capture New Orleans.
They offered Lafitte thirty thousand pounds—that's
English money and a huge amount—if he would guide
their troops up to the city." Now Ferdinand pointed to
the swamps. "You can imagine one might need some
guidance to get through there! Well, Lafitte pretended
to accept the offer, but actually he went to the other
side and guided the Americans so they could surprise
the British. For that the President of the United States
pardoned his piracy."

David was fascinated. "What happened to him
then?"

"Oh, he opened a fine shop on Royal Street." Ferdinand laughed. "But I don't think he gave up piracy
even then."

Hour after hour the ship plowed northward. The
swamps and the waterlogged forest slid behind it; on
either side the cleared land bloomed in white.

"Cotton," said Ferdinand.

"Like snow," said Miriam.

After a while Ferdinand gave orders. "Go change
your clothes. We'll be there soon and you must make a
fine first impression." Fondly he regarded his daughter. "Wear the lavender dress with the lace collar. And
take your parasol, the one that matches. It will be
terribly hot when we land, as soon as we leave the
river breeze. You will get used to carrying a parasol.
All the ladies do."

Among the gathering traffic of steamships and cotton ships coming and going, the *Mirabelle* slid toward
the city.

"You know," Ferdinand said, "the city is five feet
below sea level. The levees are twenty-six feet above.
And that's cotton in those bales on the levee. Could

you ever have imagined so much of it? Miles and miles of it, enough to supply the world, which it pretty nearly does," he said with satisfaction. "And over there in those hogsheads, that's sugar. We almost do supply the world with that, too. Well, not quite. But we could if we had to. See all these wharves, all those market boats? The commerce of the world passes here. Tobacco, whiskey, hemp, anything and everything. There's only one city in America that's got more shipping, and that's New York. See that brigantine? That's Captain Ramsay's *Gloucester Breeze*. He's probably got a shipment for me. Comes twice a year from Liverpool. . . ."

David took Miriam's hand. The long dream of the voyage was over. Now feet were about to touch land. It came to David, sobering his excitement, that they were about to touch reality.

The father's voice struggled against the rising din and scream of whistles and bells. "Look there, that's a load of furs from way upriver arriving for export. Over there on the right, that's the village of Algiers, right across from the French Market. Ah, it's good to be home!" he cried, standing on the tips of his toes, waving and pointing. "Look there! That's the Cabildo, the Spanish built that, and the Presbytère, that was a priests' residence, there on the other side of the cathedral. They built the St. Louis Cathedral over a hundred years ago, you know, but a fire wrecked it and they had to build another. . . . Can you see, Miriam? Want me to raise you up? Beautiful, isn't it? Named after the patron saint, Louis IX—"

"Where is the synagogue?" David asked quietly.

"Oh, it's on Franklin Street, a small place. You can't see it from here." Ferdinand took a deep breath. "Smell the sweet air! I always think I'm smelling sugar in the air, though probably I'm not. You know, I'm a

city man. I survived the wilderness, I'll survive anywhere you put me, but I'm a city man at heart." He
drew himself up. Not a tall man, he could make himself appear taller than he was. "Yes, a city man, a New
Orleans man."

The ship nosed into the wharf with a shudder and
thump. There were a rattle of ropes and shouting from
the dock. The gangplank clattered into place.

From the height where they stood at the prow, the
passengers looked down on a jumbled, animated bustle: drays, carts, wheelbarrows, crates and boxes, stray
dogs, children, workmen, horses, carriages, coachmen,
parasols, and high silk hats all moved among an astonishing mass of black faces. Ferdinand searched the
crowd.

"There!" he cried out. "There they are! On the banquette, on the other side, standing by the two white
horses. See them? I see them!"

"Banquette?" asked David.

"Where you walk, at the side of the street. That's
Emma in the yellow dress and Pelagie's with her. Her
husband's come, too—how good of him! A nice chap,
Sylvain is. And there's—oh! they see us." Ferdinand
waved his hat. "The gangplank's up! Let's go!"

as though you were part of the empty air. Unless, of course, he went on a rampage—for God only knew what reason—and killed your mother on the doorstep of her house. . . .

And his mind traveled back to that old dwelling, to the dim, low rooms, the sour smells of age and damp, the memory of sudden death, traveled back to the old fear, and forward again to this, as he tried to make a sane and plausible connection.

He stirred the food, moving it around his plate. Never had he seen such quantities of food, too great for even his young appetite. So much of it was forbidden anyway! There had been suckling pig, which of course he had recognized when it was carried to the table on an enormous silver platter, with its skin all crackled to a crisp. They had stuck a pipe in its pitiful snout: poor, filthy little animal, with its scanty eyelashes and its dead eyes! Then there had been something called *vol-au-vent,* a kind of pastry filled with oyster stew; this he had tried, not knowing what it was, and found it very tasty. But he had laid the fork aside as soon as he had been told what it was. At least there were quantities of vegetables. One could live very well on them alone if one had to, along with the good hot breads which were always on the table. Also, there was wine. Even at breakfast there was wine. But one had to be careful of overdoing that, especially in this smothering heat. A Jew must never be drunk.

Miriam was eating shrimp in a spicy red sauce. David had refused that, too. He no longer had any authority over his sister, however; from now on it was evident his father and his father's wife would take charge of her. She was their child. Permissions would be granted or denied by them. He watched her now as she scraped the last of the sauce from the plate, licking her fingers when she thought no one was looking. She touched his heart, small as she was in the ornate high-backed chair, with the pleated lace collar almost engulfing her frail, childish neck.

Observing everyone around the table, missing nothing, he was aware that every woman there wore lace somewhere on her person. Aunt Emma—they had been instructed to call their father's wife "Aunt"—Aunt Emma's ruddy cheeks bloomed over a foam of black lace. He marveled that she was already on second helpings and yet had hardly stopped talking since they had sat down. The lace quivered under her chin.

"Yes, Sisyphus is a gentleman, an exquisite gentleman. Why, he taught manners to all my brothers when they were hardly old enough to walk."

Sisyphus, an aging Negro with hair like a gray woolen cap, stood at the sideboard with a folded napkin over his arm, directing the young maids.

"Yes, Sisyphus is a faithful servant," Aunt Emma went on as if he weren't there at all. "Much more than only a butler. He has a talent for landscape gardening; he actually laid out the rose gardens at my father's house. Have I ever mentioned that to you, Ferdinand? My brother Joseph would love to have him in Texas, but he can't have Sisyphus, I won't give him up! Joseph may have his fifty thousand acres of cotton, but he won't get my Sisyphus."

The resonant deep voice ran on uninterrupted. David's ears closed themselves to the rush of words. Again he looked around the table as if to analyze or to memorize all the nuts and candies in their filigreed silver dishes, the candelabra, the flowers, still so fresh that one could see glossy drops of water on the stems. But most of all, as always, he watched faces and people. Never had he sat down to eat among so many. In this house the dining room was filled at every meal. Even at breakfast there were guests.

Now, catching David's eye, Ferdinand gave a satisfied nod of acknowledgment, asking without words:
You see? Isn't it just what I told you? Everything I
told you? How do you like it?

Across from David sat Pelagie, a soft young woman
with a timid, curving, constant smile. Her thick hair
swept back from her forehead; her eyes were turned
always toward the husband who sat beside her. "Isn't
that so, Sylvain?" she asked after every observation,
every slight remark: "Isn't that true, Sylvain?" To
which Sylvain, a severe young man with prominent
features, a fashionable cravat, and perfect linen, would
nod his approval. But then, David thought, she never
says anything one could disagree with!

And he amused himself with silent appraisals as his
eyes moved down the row. That bored old man, now,
he was someone you would like! He twinkled. The
woman in blue looked as if she had been crying; no
doubt her husband was nasty, he looked it. Eulalie,
Aunt Emma's elder daughter, now, she—no, I don't
care about her at all. She had angry eyes, two black
lumps under a high forehead rounded as a dome. Her
dress was hideous; he knew nothing about clothes and
cared little, but he could feel color in his soul, and the
violent green of this woman's dress was terrible. A
lumpy necklace collided with her collarbone. Catching
his concentration on her, she stared back angrily so
that David had to lower his eyes. He rested them on
her white, bony knuckles. We do not like each other,
he thought, but it's she who began it. I might try to
like her if she would try, but she will not. He had
known that on the very first day, in the first hour in
that house. He didn't know why; he had done nothing
wrong. Was it because she did not like Jews? Naturally, that was the first thing experience had taught
one to think of.

It was astonishing: He had never in his life been in the company of so many people who were not Jewish. To be exact, he had never sat down to eat with anyone who wasn't Jewish, not even once. The peasants at home never invited you into their houses, and he knew no one else. The man and woman between whom he now sat were the only other Jews at the table. They were Henry and Rosa de Rivera, she the sister of his friend Gabriel from the *Mirabelle*. Papa had invited them to this Sunday dinner.

Beneath the louder flow of Emma's voice Rosa de Rivera murmured, "You're very like my brother, I think, a serious young man. Old for your age. Although, I don't know, I haven't seen Gabriel for three years." She had a lively, amused expression and the familiar, vivid, heavy-lidded eyes of her people. Amber jewels swung from her ears and glistened at her wrists. "So thoughtful. Of what are you thinking this minute, may I ask?"

"How strange all this is. I don't know what to say to these people, what they expect of me."

"Expect? Just smile and mind your manners. They don't expect anything more than that."

"But," he stammered, "I've lived in a different world, so small, shut in—"

"Then, this will be good for you. Just be yourself. You're very keen. You'll get along."

"You and your husband are the only Jews here. . . ."

"There's Marie Claire Myers, the little girl sitting with her mother. They're visiting from Shreveport."

"That's her mother? But she's wearing a cross."

"Her mother is a Catholic."

"Then she can't be Jewish."

"She's Jewish."

"She can't be! That's the Law and has been since Moses," he protested.

"I know. But it's different here."

How many more times would he be told that things were different here?

"Her father, although he married her mother in the cathedral, wanted their children to be reared as Jews."

David regarded the girl. Three or four years older than Miriam, she had a long freckled face and a mass of pale curly hair. He felt confusion. A Jewish girl whose mother wore a cross!

"We've had to make our own rules here," Henry de Rivera explained. "Our synagogue's only ten years old, Shanarai Chasset, Gates of Mercy. Thirty-four of us men got together and started it. Manis Jacobs—he was the first president—had a Catholic wife, but he didn't want his children excluded, so he had the synagogue's constitution read that no Israelite child should be barred on account of the mother's religion. No one minded, because most of the men were married to Catholics, anyway."

David shook his head. "Strange."

"Not as strange as it used to be. Remember, we had no trained rabbi and still haven't got one. We're a thousand miles away from any center of Jewish life like Charleston or Philadelphia. We've nothing at all like that. Why, we only needed five thousand dollars for a building, yet you can't believe how hard it was to raise it! There were so few of us."

A question came to David's lips. First he swallowed it down, then asked it. "My father—did he give?"

Henry de Rivera smiled. "He gave. Rather more generously than some, although I must admit he never did set foot in the place after it was built. But," he added, "that's a man's privilege if he so chooses. And there are many in this city who do so choose."

He will commit himself to no opinion, David thought. He's a lawyer, and prudent, risking no offense.

Rosa spoke. "New Orleans is not a religious city for Christians, either. Oh, the women go to church, but the men don't really care much. There's easy living here, as Henry always says. One makes money quickly, one wants to spend it. . . ." She shrugged. "Anyway, you must come see us. You may go to the synagogue with us if you like. And Miriam must come. We have two baby boys. Little girls always like to play with babies."

"You're not eating anything, David." Emma's voice, interrupting her own monologue, rang across the table.

"I'm eating what I want. Thank you," he answered, remembering to be gracious.

"It's this heat. You're not eating because of the heat. Monroe, move closer to M'sieu David with that fan."

A black boy in bare feet approached with a large palmetto fan. David recoiled.

"No, not for me. I don't need it."

For an instant Emma looked vexed, then as quickly her small frown vanished. She is a woman who doesn't want to be troubled, David thought.

Her husky voice, a proper voice for a fat woman, resumed. "M'sieu Ferdinand is ready for his coffee, Sisyphus. Have some of Serafina's marvelous little cakes, Miriam my dear. *Langues de chat*, cats' tongues, they're called. Ridiculous name for anything so delicious." Emma's mouth lingered like a cat's tongue on the syllables of "delicious." "Do move closer to me with that fan, Monroe, I'm perishing with heat." And indeed her color had gone from pink to deepest plum. Circles of sweat darkened her dress as she raised her arms to smooth the lace at her neck.

"I'm perishing with heat," she repeated, not ill-naturedly.

"Never mind, you will soon be at the Pass," Ferdinand consoled her, explaining to Miriam and David, "Pass Christian's our seaside place. Wonderful breezes, good bathing and boating. We're late starting this year because of my traveling to Europe."

"The best people go there. You will see the best young people," Emma said, addressing her husband's children. "Don't you think, Mr. Raphael, that David in particular ought to be meeting young men of influence?" And without waiting for Ferdinand's reply, "We have such a delightful house there. My first husband's father, Mr. Leclerc, built it years ago. Of course it's nothing compared with some you will see, but very nice all the same."

Rosa whispered to David, "The Leclercs were enormously rich! The grandfather came here before the Louisiana Purchase and made a fortune!"

Emma was saying, "He used to go to Paris every year—every year, mind you! And brought home such marvelous things: tapestries, gold plate, and—"

"Some say he was involved with a bit of piracy," Sylvain interrupted, his mischievous tone unfitted to his strict bearing.

Emma dismissed the comment lightly. "For goodness' sake, they say that about half the population of the city!"

"And it's probably true about half the population, too," Sylvain retorted.

He must be very rich, David thought, fancying his own shrewdness, or else he would never dare speak to his wife's mother like that.

Since early childhood David had observed and weighed the life around him. One of the facts he had first learned was that the possession of wealth allows liberties which are denied to people who do not possess it.

Yet he liked Emma. He saw that she was boastful and foolish, but she was also kind. Sylvain made him uneasy, he did not know why.

"Well, I can't tell about other people's ancestors, but I know about mine, and there were no pirates among them, just honest German country people," Emma said. "Lived on the German Coast just north of here. Farmers, you know, and very poor, didn't even own a cow, they say. Oh, how they worked, those people! Then they married among the French and died out. French blood is strong, you know. They even changed their names to sound French. Yes, it's a long way from the corn husk mattress and the Acadian farmhouse. Sisyphus remembers, don't you, Sisyphus? He was only a child when he came with my mother and two or three other servants, all she had brought with her when she married my father. My mother came from a much simpler home, you see. Simple, but refined, the best stock. *De la fine fleur des pois,* the first blossom of the sweetpea, we call ourselves, we old Creoles. The best blood. Blood tells, I always say."

Blood, David thought. Blood and money. That's all they've talked about since we sat down to eat. He stared uncomfortably, wanting to get up.

Miriam was yawning. She had brought the yellow-haired doll to sit with her. Now she was fingering a narrow gold bracelet, given by Emma as a token of welcome. It would be good for the child in this house. She would be safe here, cared for, cherished.

At last chairs were pushed back and everyone stood up.

Emma asked brightly, "Shall we have some music?"

"Perhaps Marie Claire will sing for us," Ferdinand suggested.

One passed through folding doors from the first parlor into the second. In the first the blinds were always drawn against the sun. Now, in the evening, a grave blue light came through the slats, touching gilded chair frames and yellow silk, crystal bric-a-brac and mirrors, enhancing their dignity and worth. In the second parlor the piano, the harp, and the bookshelves made a more lively setting.

"Pelagie, will you play for Marie Claire? Marie Claire has a wonderful voice," Ferdinand explained with kindly pride. "I'm told that her singing master has great hopes for her. . . . But look here, David, I don't know whether I've pointed out Emma's picture. It's by Salazar, the famous portrait artist."

Between two doors in an oval frame hung a painting of a slender young woman wearing a thin white shift gathered under small breasts. Pensively she contemplated a spray of lilacs.

"Of course, the Empire style was ridiculous, although I must say one did feel free, almost naked! But it's a good likeness, don't you think so?" Emma asked eagerly.

"Very," David said, not seeing even the remotest resemblance to the lady beside him.

"Well, now." Ferdinand rubbed his hands. "Shall we begin? What have you two decided on?"

Pelagie had taken her seat at the piano, while Marie Claire stood in its curve.

Pelagie answered. "We'll start with some Irish songs, we thought. 'Kathleen Mavourneen.' It's quite new and very popular."

Her hands moved on the keyboard with a caressing touch, so that the notes lingered like sobs. The sound was sentimental, like Pelagie herself. But the girl Marie Claire sang without sentiment. Her unadorned, pure emotion caught at David. He knew nothing about either music or voices, yet he was certain that this was a woman's voice in a child's body. He was totally absorbed in the sound and in the radiance of Marie Claire's plain face, when Emma leaned toward him to whisper.

"Do look at what Eulalie's doing. It's called macrame. She has such talent with her hands, she made those portieres."

Obediently he looked to where the somber one—for he had mentally bestowed that name upon Eulalie—was making elaborate motions with a length of string.

"Very nice," he murmured, smiling inwardly at his own newfound suavity. I am learning, he thought, returning to the music.

After a while his mind began to wander. His eyes moved from Pelagie's floating skirt to the carpet's arabesques, then to the red silk draperies, splashed pink by candlelight. Down the depths of the house, across the hall, he could see the dining room, where servants were still clearing the long table. Beyond that, he knew, stretched a verandah from which one stepped down into the courtyard, the garden, the stables, and the kitchen, where the true life of the great house was carried on. There in the cellars, the washhouse, and quarters the work was done. His room faced in that direction, and last night he had heard servants' voices talking and arguing, heard shrill female yapping and resonant male rumbling. He had heard singing, too, rich, passionate song, different from any he had ever experienced, and it had touched him as he lay in bed, touched him with a strange nostalgia, a strange yearning. But yearning for what? Nostalgia for what? Surely not for home. He never wanted to go "home."

Ah, such confusion in his young heart! That the comfort of this room, at this moment, with the chairs so soft, with stomach so filled, and the gauzy light, the drowsy fragrance—that these should seem so wrong! There was a surfeit in them. Something cloyed in this house. There was too much food, too much silk, too many flowers—

Sisyphus, entering on soundless feet, was murmuring something to Emma. He caught the words "Blaise and Fanny." Emma stood up just as the music was coming to a close and the evening ending.

"David and Miriam, come with me. Blaise and Fanny have arrived," she explained as they climbed the stairs. "I've sent for them from the country, or rather bought them from a dear friend of mine who has no need of them anymore. They are sister and brother and very well recommended, naturally, or I wouldn't have taken them. Well, here we are."

In the upstairs hall a young girl waited. She was possibly twelve or thirteen years old. Her skin was almost white; her black hair, straight as Miriam's, hung in two braids down her back.

"This is Mam'selle Miriam, Fanny."

Fanny curtsied.

"And this, Blaise, is M'sieu David."

He was a boy of David's age. His light-gray eyes were startling in his dark face, so many shades darker than his sister's.

"Of course," Aunt Emma said, "it would have been better to begin your association at first. That's the custom and it's very nice to have a servant who goes straight through life with you," she explained to Miriam and David. "But still, you're all young and you'll have many good years together, I'm sure. Fanny, you will sleep on a quilt at Mam'selle Miriam's door in case she should need you for anything during the night. But I'm sure you know that already." Emma smiled encouragement. "And Blaise will do the same

for you, David. As soon as you start school, he will go
with you to carry your books and packages or do any
errand you may have. Well, again, no need to go into
that, Blaise knows what's expected. Now, if ever you
have need of extra help for any reason, David, your
father will lend Maxim or Chanute. Otherwise, they
already have plenty to do around the house. I'm told
you are both very good-tempered, Blaise and Fanny,
and I'm glad to know that, because that's just what we
want." She paused, as if waiting for some comment or
question, but since there was none, concluded the in-
terview with "Well, I can't think of anything else,"
and started downstairs. Halfway down she called
back, "They will be good for your French, David and
Miriam, since they speak nothing else."

The four young people now faced one another, none
knowing how to begin. Then Fanny, somewhat bolder
than her brother, smiled at Miriam. Blaise stood with
downcast eyes, while David, flushed with embarrassment over his own awkwardness, as well as for other
reasons not yet quite clear to him, struggled for something to say. But at that moment Pelagie came upstairs
with Eulalie and dismissed the servants.

"We'll call you when we're ready to retire. The men
are still playing dominoes," she told David, "but I'm
too tired. Shall we sit out on the balcony awhile?"

They passed through a series of bedrooms. "Mama
must get a *lit de repos* for you, David, so you don't
ruin the bedspread when you take your afternoon
nap."

"But I never sleep in the afternoon!"

"You will here. Everyone does. Our afternoons are
so languid," Pelagie said, drawing out the syllables.

Unconsciously she smoothed a rising bulge above
the circle of her skirt, and Miriam, observing the ges-

ture, inquired directly, "When are you going to have your baby?"

Eulalie drew in her breath. "What can the child be saying?" she cried over Miriam's head.

"Oh, I know Pelagie's going to have a baby," Miriam said wisely. "I can tell. I've seen that at home. When are you going to have the baby?"

"In November. I should like to talk about it," Pelagie said softly. "I'm so happy. But my sister thinks it's shocking to take notice of it. I'm sure I don't know why, when Mama had nine after us, counting all the ones who died, that is." And she went on in a kind of quiet defiance of her sister, who was already halfway out of the door. "My baby will be born right here in my room on the borning bed. The napping sofa has more than one use, you see."

There was a gentle silence among the three until the young woman spoke again. "I hope you're feeling a little bit better about being here, David."

David flushed. "I feel fine, really I do."

"You weren't happy at all the first few days." When he did not deny that, Pelagie continued, "You didn't know this wasn't a Jewish household. I understand."

In the next bedroom through the open door, David could see the altar, or what the family referred to as the altar: a table covered with a lace cloth on which stood a vial of holy water and some small white plaster statues. His eyes traveled from these to the floor, which was covered with a summer matting of cool straw.

"I think your papa should have told you beforehand."

He laughed shortly. "I'm just as glad he didn't. Opa would have fought our coming here, and who knows, he might have won."

"But on the voyage he should have said something

—still, it's over and done. But if there should be some questions you want to ask me . . ."

For a moment the awkwardness and the stammer came back. Yet for some reason David had to ask—not that the answer would make any difference now—but he had to ask: "How did my father marry your mother?"

"Where, do you mean? It was in the cathedral. The vicar general gave a dispensation because of the difference in religion. And Father Moni performed the ceremony. Oh, it was beautiful! I always love the cathedral anyway. Even a funeral is beautiful." And Pelagie, rapt, made a pyramid of her fingers. "I was only a little girl when they held the memorial service for the Emperor Napoleon. Everything was draped in black, so solemn, and there was wonderful music, a French chorus. It was as if God Himself were there."

It had gone quite dark outside. The three faces were blurred against the mild glow of the lamp in the adjoining room, so that one could only imagine the expression on Pelagie's face as she half whispered, "But then, of course, God is everywhere, isn't He? I always think it doesn't matter which way you worship Him in your heart. I know some priests say our way is the only way, but I don't think that can be true. If only you take Him seriously. Too many people in our city don't, I'm sorry to say."

"That's what Mrs. de Rivera told me tonight," David answered.

"Rosa? I'm very fond of Rosa. She tells me you met her brother on the voyage."

"Oh, yes, and we liked each other. But he's going to college in the North when the time comes, so I shall probably never see him again."

"Yes, the Anglos send their sons to William and Mary or even Harvard. Of course, we Creoles send our sons to Paris, but maybe you'll go north to college, too."

To that David made no reply. The possibilities were confusing, almost alarming.

"Or perhaps you would like Paris, too? You and Miriam? I was at school in France for a while."

"No," David said. This was more alarming. "I don't want to go back to Europe. And I don't want Miriam to go, either," he added firmly.

"Oh, Miriam can go to school here. It really doesn't matter for a girl one way or the other. She'll be married young, pretty girls always are. I was sixteen. I met Sylvain when I was fifteen, and we were married the next year. Oh," Pelagie cried, "I only hope you'll be as lucky as I am, Miriam. But you will be." And taking the child by the shoulders, she turned her toward the lampglow. "Look at those eyes! You'll put your hair up here, like this, with a curl over each ear. And I'm sure your papa will buy some diamonds for your ears, you have good little ears. Oh, yes, you'll be a beauty, darling."

She prattles like her mother, David thought; that is to say, like a silly child. But she's good all the same. He liked the tender way her hands touched Miriam.

"You have to come see us in the country. We live with Sylvain's father, but Sylvain has promised me to buy a house in town so that we can have a place of our own for the social season and the opera. I do so love the opera. . . ."

The prattle ceased when Sylvain appeared and took his wife off to their room.

Blaise got up from his pallet on the floor when David entered his own room.

"I'm sorry if I woke you, Blaise."

"No, no, I've been waiting for you, M'sieu David."

"You go back to sleep. I'll come in a minute."

"Where are you going, M'sieu David?"

"Call me just David, will you, Blaise? I'm going to the *olla* in the back hall for water."

Blaise was dismayed. "Not that one! It hasn't been clarified yet. Serafina put alum in it not an hour ago. Besides, I'm always supposed to get things for you, M'sieu David."

"But I'm used to doing things for myself, Blaise."

"Not here, M'sieu David. Not here."

Blaise's bare feet slapped the steps as he descended; his slender shadow wavered on the wall.

David went out to the rear gallery overlooking the courtyard. The moon had risen and in the luminous night he could see the ragged outlines of massed banana leaves; a wind passed briefly and they rustled. He heard the purl and ripple of water, and remembered that there was a fountain at the end of the garden. A fresh fragrance, faintly tart, lay in the air; he remembered being told it was from those syringa bushes banked like snow against the farther wall. And a restless bird called out one startled, poignant note. Sweet night! Like no night the boy had ever seen. So sweet so troubling!

Perhaps I came too late, he thought. Perhaps even fifteen is too late to make a change like this. I don't know. I want to do right. I will do right. But I just don't know about this place.

4

"Well, now you've seen the U.S. Mint," Ferdinand said as they swung together past the foot of Esplanade Avenue. He put his arm around David's shoulder. "You don't know what it means to have my son here with me! My one regret—I can't say it often enough—my one regret is that it took so long, that we've lost so much time. But enough of that. You're here," he said cheerfully, "so let's get on with the present. What was I telling you? Oh, I was saying I do a great many other things beside merchandising, you know. It's not enough to work for money. Once you've got it, you have to make it work for you! So you see, I've been branching out. I transact business all over the country. I hold a good many mortgages and I'm a broker for planters who need advances on their crops. It seems they always do need them, too. Well, they live high. . . . David, would you like to try a *cala?* They're a kind of rice pancake, awfully good."

In front of the cathedral a Negro woman in a starched white apron was cooking over a small fire. Ferdinand hailed her. "How are you, Sally? This is my son. I want to buy him a *cala,* but he's not hungry. She makes the best in the city," he said as they walked on. "Used to belong to a friend of mine, but she bought her freedom. You can always tell a free woman of color by the *tignon,* the handkerchief knotted on top of her head. Some of them are marvelous cooks. At night they come out with hot sweet-potato cakes. You'll have to try one."

And suddenly, as they rounded a corner, they came upon a bustle of life; never had David seen so much color in motion or such a crowd converging on one place. All his senses tingled. Voices swirled, flower-fragrance merged with river smells, and his eyes were dazzled by the burning light. He stood, astonished.

Ferdinand was delighted with this effect upon David.

"Surprised?" He laughed. "Yes, it's quite a sight, the French Market."

Nestled below the levee, the stalls were strung out in a long line. Freshly watered vegetables were arranged like bouquets. In the fish stalls, on beds of ice, the fresh catch glistened silver, black, and mottled gray. Live crabs, green as new grass, crawled alongside lobsters. An aged Indian woman squatted behind a pile of leather goods. Ladies, protected by parasols and followed by maids, moved from stall to stall, or took their beignets and coffee at small tables under a shady roof.

Silent and marveling, David walked up and down, in and out, seeing and remembering as though he were a painter marking a preliminary sketch in his head.

"Like a *café noir?*" urged Ferdinand. "No? I suppose you've seen enough for today, then?"

They went out beyond the stalls. At the far end a dentist's chair, surrounded by a band of loud musicians, stood on a platform. A small crowd lingered there, watching a hapless man having his teeth pulled while the band's noise covered his cries.

"The fellow pulling teeth has a brother at the Medical College. Fills the chair of Materia Medica. I know

him pretty well. I know plenty of others, too. In any
case, you'd have no trouble being admitted. I'll take
you soon to visit, but there's really no hurry. You have
a few years' work ahead of you first. The Americans—
you know, I must give them credit—have really been
agitating for education. I hear they're bringing in a
man who worked with somebody called Horace Mann
up in Massachusetts—that's way north of New York
—setting up free schools. They say we're going to have
free schooling here in a few years. Well, it'll be a good
thing; Lord knows, I never had much schooling in
Europe and I've felt the lack of it ever since. The lack
of it makes a man feel a little shy at times, although I
hate to admit it. Yet I've certainly done well enough
without it, haven't I?" He laughed. "But I want you to
have all you can get, David. Fortunately, you won't
need free public schooling. People in our class here
have private tutors or send their sons to private
schools."

David recalled the previous night's talk with Pelagie. "What about Miriam?" he asked.

"Oh, there are plenty of little schools around here
for girls, run by gentlewomen usually, women of good
family, very refined, who need the money. I don't
know how much the girls learn, but they learn enough,
all the niceties. What does a girl need, after all?"

Eager little Miriam, curious, quick and fanciful!
Surely that mind was the equal of David's own? It
occurred to him that a girl's mind might be wasted
just as much by idle luxury as by the meager poverty
of their European village. He was about to say so
when his father resumed his explanations as they
walked along the river's edge.

"Yes, these ships are my lifeline to the world." He
looked around, lowering his voice so as not to reveal
any private affairs to strangers. "Last year, David, we

brought in thirty thousand dollars' worth of specie from Mexico alone."

Four and five deep, ships lay in tiers along the river. On foot and on horseback, in fashionable carriages and overloaded wagons, traffic surged through the streets. The city was fat and glossy with prosperity.

"You can see any type of humanity you can think of on this riverfront," Ferdinand mused. "Every kind of confidence man and swindler. You will see a laborer shoot dice for a few cents and a rich man bet thousands on the boat races. On the river steamers, of course, you've got the professional gambler. You have to watch out for card sharps going up the river. Many a planter's been fooled by one of those gentlemen. I've seen a man lose the profits of a whole year's crop in one hour's poker game. Thousands and thousands of dollars."

They crossed to walk on the shady side of the street under triple tiers of iron-lace balconies. Someone above them, watering a pot of hanging ferns, sent an instant's worth of pungent fragrance into the sultry air.

"That's the Cotton Exchange, corner of Royal Street. Maybe I'll take you there tomorrow and introduce you to some of my friends. Sure there's nothing you want before we go home?"

David thought of something. "I'd like to buy some books in English."

"Still insist on English? Well, all right, there's a bookstore down this way. We've got about nine bookstores in the city, you know."

At the back of a deep narrow shop sat an old man wearing a skullcap. He stood up when they came in.

"English books? Over here. Poetry, novels, history, grammar. All here." He stood watching curiously while David examined the shelves. "If you want a grammar, young gentleman, I recommend this one."

"I want to teach myself to speak English," David explained, speaking in French.

"The grammar will not be enough, then. You should acquaint yourself with the literature. Then the language will come alive for you. Do you like poetry?"

"I've not read very much, and that in German. But yes, I like it."

"Then try Lord Byron, a Romantic." The word was savored and repeated. "Romantic. A young man's poet. Not for me any longer, but certainly for you. And for novels, Sir Walter Scott. He'll hold your interest. There's nothing dry about him."

"My son can have as many books as he wants," Ferdinand said. "On education I don't stint."

The old man bowed. "And most wise of you, sir."

When a pile had been assembled and paid for, the proprietor shuffled back to the shelves and handed David a thin leather-bound volume.

"When you have finished all these others, you will have learned enough of the language to appreciate Jonathan Swift, the greatest writer of them all. He was a satirist. You know what a satirist is, young gentleman? No? I'll tell you. He is a man with sharp eyes and a sharp tongue, or, I should say, pen. He sees the evils of the world. He ridicules and scolds."

"I should imagine that sort of thing to be way over the head of a fifteen-year-old lad," Ferdinand objected.

The old man shook his head. "Not this boy's. I see by his eyes that he will understand. Here. Take it."

After they left the shop, David asked why the old man had given him a present.

"That's called *lagniappe*," Ferdinand explained. "Merchants here always add something in proportion to what you buy. And we did buy a bundle. We should have sent Maxim or Blaise to carry them home."

"Papa, I don't need a servant to carry a few books. You know, I liked the man, didn't you? He's Jewish, isn't he?"

"I believe so. Yes."

"The People of the Book," David said deliberately. He didn't know what made him say it, what it was that made him keep leading his father back to the subject that only brought discomfiture to them both.

For a moment Ferdinand made no comment. Then he said, "You know, David, I understand you, even though you may not think I do. Your religious feelings are entirely natural at your age. At fifteen one likes to feel virtuous! Even I did, though I must say for a much shorter time than most." He spoke with a kind of amused tolerance. "You'll outgrow it, very likely, now that I've gotten you away from village life. But if you don't, that will be your affair. If only for the sake of your mother of blessed memory, I shall never interfere."

"I will not outgrow it."

"Well, time will tell. As I believe I told you once before, Heine himself said that Judaism is a misfortune. Why do you think that in the last ten years alone under Friedrich Wilhelm III more than two thousand Jews were baptized? Because it's the only road to survival under an oppressor, that's why. Fortunately here it's not necessary to convert, and as I've also told you, I never wanted to. All I want is to be let alone."

"If they will," David said.

On Chartres Street Ferdinand exchanged bows with a stout young man in a rich black suit.

"That was Judah Benjamin," he whispered, "one of our rising young lawyers. A Jew, too, but he doesn't keep to it, either. And here's the St. Louis Hotel. Very

good dining here; I'll take you to lunch one day soon.
And they've got the biggest auction exchange in the
city. You can buy anything from a ship to a house, a
houseful of French furniture, or a thousand acres of
land. Anything."

A placard on the wall caught David's attention. He
stopped. Carefully he spelled out the words.

"Young Negro boy, not yet twenty, excellent gentleman's valet, speaks English and French, can do some
tailoring, honest, good appearance."

Something drew him on, a vague and dawning comprehension which at the very same time repelled him.

"I'd like to go in," he said.

"Now? To watch the auction? All right. We have an
hour to spare."

Chairs in concentric circles surrounded a raised
platform on which stood an energetic man wearing a
bright shirt. Ferdinand squeezed his way through rows
of hats perched on broadcloth knees, nodding and
greeting as he went. Men stood clustered in the aisles;
conversation buzzed as at the theater before the curtain rises, or as at some village fair, David thought,
before the start of the entertainment, the jugglers or
the dancing bear. It was only when he was seated with
a clear view of the platform that he saw the true nature of the event. Even with the handicap of language
and in spite of the auctioneer's rapid veering between
French and English, he understood.

They were selling human beings! A small assem-
blage waited at the side of the platform, waited
mutely, like horses at those same village fairs. And
David strained to see: a humped old man; three strip-
ling boys; some fat women, one of whom wore a
strange, ingratiating smile; a young woman, very light
of skin—three-quarters white, he estimated—crying

without a sound. His eyes went to the man whose lively voice boomed out over the crowd.

"Gentlemen, gentlemen! Quiet! We're doing business, we can't hear. How much am I offered for Lucinda here?"

His hand rested on the shoulder of a handsome Negress in a neat green cotton dress. Tall and quiet, she stood as if oblivious to the hand or the voice. Her own hands were clasped at her waist. Her head was high. She seemed to be looking far beyond the spectators.

The demand was repeated. "How much am I offered for Lucinda here? Who'll start the bidding? She can launder, she can cook. The only reason she's available is that her master died without heirs and the estate has to dispose of her. Come, now. Who'll start?"

"Six hundred," someone called.

"You can't be in earnest, sir! Why, I could never let this woman go for that!"

"Pretty long in the tooth," the man objected.

"Old, sir? You're not talking about a woman of sixty. Why, she's hardly a day over forty. She's strong and well-behaved and healthy. None of your rebellious, inferior Kentucky stock, either. She was born and raised not fifty miles upriver from here." He swung his head to the other side of the ring. "What am I offered?"

"Seven hundred."

"Eight hundred."

"Eight hundred, I've got eight hundred. What am I bid?"

Down the back of his neck and under his arms, David felt the gathering sweat. The sweat was cold even in that crowded hall. His hands were cold. He thrust them into his pockets.

The woman Lucinda still stood looking into whatever lay beyond this place and this room. It seemed to

David in his horror that only her body was present, indifferent and patient; her spirit had removed itself.

"A thousand."

"One thousand fifty."

"Eleven hundred."

"I have eleven hundred. Does anyone offer eleven fifty? Eleven hundred once, twice, three times. Sold for eleven hundred dollars. Lucinda. Next, please. Come, come, bring them up, step up. We've a long list and the day's already half over."

Next a pair of boys mounted the steps to the platform. Not more than twelve or thirteen years old, they faced the crowd with darting eyes in which fear and childish curiosity mingled.

The auctioneer became enthusiastic. "Now, here we have a fine pair, two brothers not yet full grown, it's true, but there's plenty of work in them. Their owner is really reluctant to part with them but he finds himself overstaffed. He'd like to sell them as a pair, if possible. They've grown up together—"

"Chanute and Maxim came together, too," Ferdinand whispered. "They're cousins, though, not brothers."

"So the owner is willing to concede on the price to anyone who'll buy the pair—"

On the platform the younger of the boys suddenly reached for the other one's hand. And David felt a knocking in his chest as if he were going to be ill. He stood up, bumping against his neighbor, who glared at him.

"Let's get out of here! I have to get out of here, Papa."

Ferdinand followed him to the street. "That distressed you so much?" he asked curiously and added, "Yes, it can be distressing the first time you see it, until you understand how the system works. It's really not as cruel as it seems, or the way it used to be at all, you know. Goodness, in Jean Lafitte's time they put caufles and iron collars on the Africans when they brought them in! Lafitte had a blacksmith shop on St. Philip Street where he used to forge the chains. Well, that's long since gone.

"Today the Negro is part of a respectable business structure. Our biggest corporations, the railroad, the gas plant, all of them use Negroes."

"Own them," David said.

"Oh, yes, they train them in every kind of work you can think of, anything from carpentry to catering. All the skills. Train them and treat them well."

On the other side of the street a young man with a black beard tipped his hat to Ferdinand.

"That was Eugene Mendes. Originally from Louisville. You must wonder that I know so many people. I wouldn't be surprised if he were to settle here permanently. He's been buying property, one nice piece on Canal Street only last month. He deals in merchandise sent on consignment from the North. Would you believe he's not much more than twenty? Twenty-two at the most. I daresay he got an inheritance to start him off. But there's something in knowing how to handle an inheritance, too, you know. Yes, there are great opportunities in the city for a young man who looks sharp about him. It's a great place to be young in." He patted David's shoulder. "I expect big things from you, David." And as if he were trying to urge out of his son an enthusiasm to match his own, he seemed to examine David's face for some sign of encouragement. None was given.

Hasn't he noticed that I've scarcely said a word all the way? David wondered, as they came to the front door. In sadness and anger he thought: My father will be disappointed in me. I am not what he wanted.

In the evening Sylvain Labouisse was there. David
went to the library with the men after dinner, while
the ladies took the air on the verandah. By mid-eve-
ning Ferdinand and Sylvain put the chessmen away
and in the heat of conversation were setting the *café
brûlot* aside, too. A sharp scent of citrus peel and
burnt brandy rose from the cup.

"Fanatics." Sylvain spoke angrily. "Coming here
into a peaceable country. Abolitionists and fanatics."

For the last quarter of an hour David had been listening to the agitated conversation. Now he asked
what abolitionists were.

"People who come down from the North with some
idea of stirring up the Negroes and setting them free.
'Free,' " Sylvain repeated contemptuously. "Free to do
what? To roam unfed and unclothed like children
without parents or a home?"

"What do the abolitionists do when they come?"
David wanted to know.

Sylvain uncrossed his legs. He was tense with energy and indignation. "Do? Why, spread terror, that's
all they do. They'd have us all murdered in our beds.
We had an insurrection last year not ten miles from
my father's place. Some half-crazed Negroes were
whipped up wild, but fortunately we got to them in
time. I kept my horses saddled for two weeks afterward in the stables, ready to leave at a moment's notice. That's how long it took to feel sure that everything had been quieted down."

"Sylvain doesn't tell you that the governor ap-
pointed him a colonel of militia last year," Ferdinand
said. "The right man for the job, too."

"Let me tell you," Sylvain added, "through it all,
while I was away, my own Negroes guarded our family faithfully. I put total trust in them and it was justi-

fied. So much for your abolitionists!" He snapped his fingers.

"Obviously," Ferdinand said, "they're well satisfied with their lot. Having kind masters, they know when they're well off."

"And are all masters kind?" asked David.

"No," Ferdinand answered mildly. "No, any more than all men are just. But most are, wouldn't you say so, Sylvain? After all, none of us has ever whipped a Negro. I'm certain no one I know has done so, either. Most people are decent. At least, that's been my experience."

Sylvain turned to David. "I'll tell you something interesting. Did you know that almost any Negro would rather be owned by a white man than by a free person of color? If you want to see cruel treatment, there's where you'll see it. Right in this city, where the FPCs keep house servants and treat them abominably."

David got up and fetched the newspaper. "I read something in the *Bee* this afternoon. Here it is." And he read aloud: "Xavier Barthelemy will give a thirty-dollar reward for the return of his boy Caesar, about sixteen years old, light-skinned, light eyes, may still be wearing part of fine uniform, gray jacket and matching pantaloons, silver buttons. Ran away last Thursday." He stopped.

"Well?" asked Ferdinand.

"A boy my age! A year older," David said slowly. "A boy like me."

"Not like you. He's he, and you're you." Sylvain spoke with exasperation. His eyes, which had tended to look past David, now fastened themselves on David's eyes. David thought: We are like two strange dogs, circling warily, waiting for the attack. Sylvain was first to look away.

"You have to remember how few ever try to leave their homes. When they do, it's because an overseer is harsh, and oddly enough, nine out of ten overseers come from the North. Most of those who want to be free can earn their freedom far more pleasantly than by running away, I assure you."

Deeper and deeper David was being drawn in, almost against his will. He had to know more. He had to know.

"And how does one buy his freedom?"

"Well," Ferdinand began, "someone who has a trade, a barber, let's say, or a nurse, can hire himself out. He pays his master a certain amount every month for the privilege and saves the rest up till he has enough to buy his freedom. It works out very well."

"For the master," David said.

His father was startled. "What do you mean?"

David spoke deliberately, fighting disgust. "I mean that it's unspeakable and horrible to own another human being. It's not"—he sought a word—"not civilized." And vividly into his mind came the picture of the woman Lucinda: the impassive face, the dignity, the resignation.

Sylvain gave a short, unpleasant laugh. "Allow me to say you really don't know enough about it to have any opinion, David. It happens that the system is eminently civilized. It frees the white man's mind from petty concerns, frees him for higher endeavors. And certainly it civilizes the African, who was nothing but a cannibal in Africa. Here he's supported, he learns religion and refinements. He acquires a conscience." Sylvain paused. "And as to conscience, let me tell you, I feel much safer on the plantation among my Negroes than I would living in some northern city with angry mobs of unemployed factory workers at my gates, even though they're white."

"But you said a while ago that you kept your horses ready all those nights—"

Uncomfortable and embarrassed, Ferdinand glanced at Sylvain, then back at his son. "Sylvain is right. You really don't know enough about it, David. It's stupid to talk about things you don't understand."

"What I saw today wasn't hard to understand, Papa."

"He was at the St. Louis Auction," Ferdinand explained, "and he—"

David interrupted. "I've been thinking of it every minute since. I've been remembering the things you always said about the way we were treated in Germany, and why you left and why you wanted us to leave." And as he spoke there came again that old fast memory of screaming terror, the dark doorway and running feet and his mother's bloodied skirt. "And it seems to me this is the same thing. Just the same."

Now Ferdinand's anger flared. "Same thing! Nonsense! Ask Sisyphus what he thinks about that! Sisyphus who goes to the opera and the concerts of the Free Negro Group and travels to the seaside with us! Take a look at Maxim and Chanute next Sunday! Why, they have better clothes than you had when you lived with your grandfather, than those people had on the ship, those people you were so sorry for. Look at your own Blaise—"

"He's not 'my own Blaise.' I don't own him. I don't want to own him."

"You're being ridiculous, David. You're talking like a child. . . . Well, after all, you are a child, aren't you?"

"I'm talking like a Jew. 'For we were slaves in the land of Egypt.' So we should have all the more pity, shouldn't we?"

"You're mixing the issues. The one thing has nothing to do with the other."

"But I think it has," David answered. He was being pushed; some tide was turning, and its vast waters rushed to engulf him.

"You know what I think?" Ferdinand demanded. "I think this talk has gone far enough. David, your father orders you to drop the subject."

Sylvain tactfully studied his fingernails. The shadow of a smile touched his well-shaped lips, conveying a silent opinion: Go on with your quarrel if you will; it's really not worth my interest.

For that superiority alone, David despised Sylvain.

And he cried out passionately, "This isn't what I imagined America to be! I thought—" Then he stumbled. Even if he had been more fluent in the language, he would have stumbled. "I thought it would be all clean, all different. . . ." Romantic images filtered through his head: spruce forests, virginal and aromatic; heroic new cities, all of them possessed of some vague virtue and gladness. He scarcely understood himself what it was that he had expected, only that it was certainly not what he had found. He would have liked to explain his sensation: that things were closing in on him, that he could not bear to live where life was stratified and each man had his "place" forever and ever. But instinct told him that neither of these men would understand. Worse yet, they would mock. Already Sylvain's subtle smile had broadened to frank amusement. The sardonic eyebrows raised themselves into perfect semicircles of disdain.

"America isn't what you expected? What do you want to do? Go back to that mudhole in Europe? Damn you!" Ferdinand cried, he who almost never cursed.

"I don't want that, either," the boy said vehemently.

"Well, what do you want? Make up your mind! You're fifteen years old, a young man. You ought to know what you want, dammit!"

"A minute ago you said I was a child."

"What are you trying to do, trip me up? I won't stand for this, David. I haven't said this before, but you might as well know: You've been a trial to me. I've tried to overlook things and build something between us, but you seem bent on preventing it. It's sad, I tell you, terribly sad, when all I wanted was to bring us together, and now all you seem to want is to quarrel with me."

"I don't want to quarrel, Papa. It's just that I feel— I feel that I won't ever fit in here!"

"Will you lower your voice! You'll upset the women. Look, you've frightened the child already with your shouting."

For Miriam now stood in the doorway, looking from one to the other. And stricken, David remembered how she feared loud, angry argument, how she had used to stick her fingers in her ears and run from the house.

Pelagie drew her outside again. "Come away, Miriam. It's nothing. Just men talking. It's nothing."

"Maybe it would be bearable," David said, "if you at least saw how wrong you are and would try to change things. Let all the servants go free and join those—what did you call them, abolitionists?"

Sylvain coughed and looked at Ferdinand. His look said: He's your son, are you going to permit this?

Ferdinand stood up. "Fool's talk! Ignorant and dangerous! Dangerous! Keep opening your mouth like that and none of us will be accepted in any respectable house between here and Richmond, Virginia. Now,

get this in your head, David, I'll have no more of it.
You'll have to promise me that there'll be no more of
it, or else—" The father trembled and finished, "Or
else you can't stay here."

David also trembled. But the great tide swept over
him, pulling him with it. "Then, I suppose I can't stay
here," he said very low.

Ferdinand paced. He smashed his fist into his open
palm. "Was ever a father so bedeviled?" he demanded
of Sylvain, who did not answer. He whirled upon
David. "What do you want? What's to become of
you?"

"I can work. I can go north where the abolitionists
are. Yes, I'll work. I'm strong."

"Work? What in blazes can you do, do you think?"

"I don't know. I can find something. You did."

"I did, did I? You want to do what I did? Tramp the
miles with a bundle of gewgaws for sale? Is that what I
brought you from Europe for, so you can begin all
over again? No, dammit, you'll start where I left off!
You'll go to school or you'll go back to Europe! As
sure as I'm standing here, you will."

"Papa, I'll go north to study. You said I might." A
lump formed in David's throat. A lump of anger and
fright. With enormous effort he swallowed it. "That
boy Gabriel Carvalho said he'd be going to Columbia
in New York. I'd like it better in New York, I'm sure,
and I'd be out of your way. It would be better for us
both."

Ferdinand walked to the end of the room. His fists
were clenched at his sides, his head bent. Reaching the
fireplace, he studied the bronze mantel clock as if it
might hold the answer to his perplexity. When suddenly, on the half hour, it chimed its treble note, he
started as if indeed an answer had been given.

"Yes, by God, I think it will be better. Maybe you'll

get some sense in your head so I can leave you my money when I die and not have it squandered in some crazy renegade cause."

"I don't want your money when you die. I don't even want it now," David said stiffly. "I told you I can take care of myself."

Up past Ferdinand's collar the flesh turned red. "Don't want my money? You'll take my money and like it! And you'll make something of yourself. When you're away from here maybe you'll come to appreciate what you've got here and come back and shut your mouth and let people who know more than you do run things! Yes," he shouted furiously as David fled from the room, "yes, run! You don't want to hear me now, but the time will come when you'll remember what I've said. A mule!" he cried to Sylvain. "A Goddamned mule! And only God knows what will become of him!"

The carriage which was to take David to the train waited beneath Miriam's window. When the child drew the curtains back, she could see the hot glisten of the leather seat, which would be broiling to the touch. Maxim's round black head was turned toward the front door. In another second or two David would emerge from it; his hurrying feet were almost at the bottom of the staircase now. There was such heavy sorrow in her small chest! All morning she had been pleading.

"Take me with you, David! I won't be any trouble. I'll go to school, I'll be quiet while you study, please—"

Her hands, her whole body, had implored him. But his hands had only stroked the hair from her forehead.

"No, no, *Liebchen*. You stay here. It will be much better for you."

"But why?" she had cried. "Why will it?"

"Because. Listen to me. You're a woman, a little woman, and women need to be cared for. Here you'll have everything. You'll be safe."

And then he had kneeled down to her level so that she could see into his eyes where green-gold flecks swam through the brown, and could also see the thickening black fuzz on his cheeks. Suddenly he had become older and determined, someone different from her familiar brother.

"You'll go to school and learn lovely things, music and poetry, and you'll learn to keep a house so that you can marry and have children and take good care of them." Then he had stood up. His voice had changed. Something had come into it that was perhaps like laughter, a queer sort of laughter with a little twist of anger. "Someday, heaven knows when, women will know more and do more. Maybe then I'll even send for you. . . . But it's not time yet, and this is best right now." So he had kissed her and left her.

She watched him walk to the carriage. She saw Maxim reach for the portmanteau, saw David refuse the service, bringing the heavy case up by himself. Then Maxim mounted to the box and the horses moved away. The street was still with the sultry quiet of late morning so that the slow clop of the horse rang clearly. At the far end of Conti Street a passing vendor cried once, "Melons! Sweet melons!" and subsided. Two agitated sparrows attacked each other on the piazza railing. Dropping the curtains, the child let them fall back to dim the room and put her head on the sill —not crying anymore, just very tired and empty. The dog plucked at her skirt with a questioning paw, but receiving no answer, curled up on the floor and went to sleep.

For long minutes Miriam knelt there until something buzzed in the room, circling, angrily buzzing. And she knew it was one of those swollen blue-green flies that cluster in horse droppings on the street. Shuddering, she raised her head. Fanny had swooped on the fly with the swatter. For a moment the two girls stood facing each other; then Fanny's arms opened and Miriam came to rest on a knobby young shoulder that smelled of freshly laundered gingham.

"I know, mam'selle, I know. I was sad, too, when I came to this strange new place. But I'm over it, and you'll get over it, too. You haven't even been here a month."

"You think so, Fanny?"

"Of course, I do. You'll go to school and have friends and parties and dresses. You'll have everything a young lady like you is supposed to have. Oh, you'll like it here! Maxim was telling Blaise and me how nice it is. It's really very nice. . . ."

5

On Miriam's eleventh birthday they gave her a diary
bound in white satin with gilded edges. For every day
there was a page, and in the corner of each page a
flower, an orange blossom, violet, or rose, along with a
verse appropriate for young ladies.

> May! Queen of blossoms,
> And fulfilling flowers,
> With what pretty music
> Shall we charm the hours?

Every day after school she sat down at her rosewood desk while Fanny moved on sliding slippers,
putting clothes in the wardrobe, folding petticoats,
drawing the blinds against the western glare, and with
small thuds, stacking the school books on the shelf.

Miriam's pen ran over the silky paper in the round
American script which now replaced the pointed
script she had learned in her earlier life, inscribing her
dutiful daily lines.

Years later she would read her words with a certain
wistful amusement at the simple sentences, often trivial and sometimes charming, those intimations of a life
turning from childhood into girlhood as gradually as
morning slides toward noon. And through the words

she would recall the event: *Yes, that was the summer we went to Pelagie's, that was the day I won the elocution prize.* But the real life, the true life of the moment when the hand was stayed on the pen and the mind went spinning, would not be found upon the paper.

"It is two years today since David went away. It seems much longer, and much longer since we crossed the ocean.

"When they wrote that Opa was dead, I tried to remember his face. His beard was thin and gray; veins crawled on his bare head and on the backs of his hands. I squeezed my eyes shut, but that was all I saw; I didn't see *him* at all.

"I tried to remember the place where we lived. Here in this city the yellow sunshine covers everything like paint; over there the world was gray and brown or in summer a dark, wet green. I know it was like that but I can't really *see* it."

"David and Papa don't write to each other, not any more than Papa's sending money, and David's sending thanks.

"In the beginning Papa said angry things about David, but I think he was really more sad than angry. I think he is a man who doesn't like being angry. He never is for very long. Aunt Emma says that's why people take advantage of him. Papa hardly ever mentions David anymore.

"Aunt Emma says I am doing very well at school. I heard her talking downstairs, having coffee in the afternoon.

"Aunt Emma's voice is rich and satisfied. 'All Miriam's French is perfect,' she says. 'All children learn languages with no trouble at all. She doesn't do badly at the piano, either, or at flower painting,' she says. 'Only her needlework—well, she will never be like my Eulalie, that's certain.'

"I hate Eulalie. She is never without some kind of needle in her hand, crocheting, tatting, embroidering baby clothes for Pelagie's children.

"Aunt Emma always says: 'Poor Eulalie! Unfortunate girl! She has so many virtues. It's so hard that her younger sister should have everything. Just yesterday it seems we had Pelagie's wedding, and to think she's expecting her third in another month. How fast the years go. Why, I was saying to Mr. Raphael only the other day, sooner than we think it will be time to find a husband for his Miriam. She's already going on twelve.'

"Grown-up women say such stupid things!"

"I had a letter from David yesterday. He has finally had a long letter from Papa, who sent him a lot of money to buy books. I am so glad.

"Today Papa sounded a little hopeful, even a little proud of David. At least he spends for books, Papa says. He's no wastrel like so many of them, away at school, spending too much and drinking too much. Columbia, Aunt Emma says, is in a fine neighborhood. The best families, she saw once when she was in New York, live on Chambers and Murray streets. They will be a good influence. She says he will grow out of his foolishness and come home. When he is finished at the medical college, he will come home, you will see, she says. And Papa says yes, perhaps so.

"I do not think so."

"David wrote that he is happy I visit Rosa's house every week. It is a Jewish home.

" 'What,' Emma says, 'You do not call her "Mrs. de Rivera" or at least "Aunt Rosa"'? She is shocked. But

Rosa asked me to, although I do call her husband Uncle Henry. Aunt Emma does not understand that Rosa is like that; she doesn't care much about rules. The house is jolly. The boys are such pretty little boys; they break everything, but it doesn't seem to bother Rosa. She scatters things around, too. I laugh a lot when I am there. People laugh in their house. The boys are named after their father and their uncle. Jews aren't supposed to name after the living, but the de Riveras are Sephardic, and that's different. The family takes me to the synagogue, the Gates of Mercy. Sometimes when Marie Claire is in the city visiting, we take her, too.

"I wish I had a talent like Marie Claire's. Uncle Sisyphus says she might sing at the opera someday. She is surely not pretty except when she is singing. Then she is almost beautiful. I have quite a silly thought about her, that we will be connected in some way when we are grown up. I don't know why that should be, we hardly know each other."

"The Scroll of the Law is full of holes; this synagogue is a poor place, but it is better than nothing, Uncle Henry says.

"I wish Papa would go with us, but he will not. It is too bad. Aunt Emma says that he is pleased that the de Riveras take me, they are a fine family. They are rich, that is what she and Papa mean. I am beginning to understand things that people don't think I understand.

"Sometimes I sit at the services half asleep because it can be very boring, but I don't mind, because I know my mother is glad I'm there. I feel her warm breath on my neck. Her shoulder touches mine. She is wearing the plaid shawl that she always wears when I think of her. I remember her death and I know for her sake I will never be led away from what I am. Never. I am what I am. New Orleans is a mixed-up place."

"What a good thing it was that Papa was not with us last week on Yom Kippur. Manis Jacobs, who isn't really a rabbi anyway, said right out in the middle of the service that he was going home to eat and we should all go home, too, and eat, because fasting was ridiculous. And now this morning he is dead. I said to Papa that was perhaps God's punishment and Papa said that was superstitious nonsense. He said it kindly, though.

"Now we shall have Rowley Marks to lead the congregation, and I think he knows even less than Manis Jacobs knew. Rosa says he got his name because he plays old Rowley in *The School for Scandal*. He is a part-time actor and also a captain in the fire engine company.

"But he doesn't pretend to be a scholar of religion, Uncle Henry says, and he keeps saying it will all come right in time, you have to give credit where it's due. These men are trying to keep our people together in the absence of anything better. At least they are not turning their backs on their own people. Like Papa, he means, and so many others."

"I wrote to David and asked him why he can't study medicine here next year. But he doesn't want to. He says he cannot live in a place where human beings treat other human beings so cruelly.

"One would think that people here sat around thinking up ways to torture their servants! Aunt Emma and Papa are always so kind. They gave a wedding for the cook's daughter last month, with a white veil and a big cake. All the people in the house are very fond of them. They buy beautiful new clothes for

Maxim and Chanute, who are always joking with each other. If they were so miserably treated, would they always be joking?

"I asked Fanny whether she was happy and she said she certainly was. She likes the dances in New Orleans. You know, colored people love to dance, she said. And she was so pleased with the hat Aunt Emma gave her for Easter. I asked her whether there was any place she would rather be and she was quite alarmed. 'You're not going to send me away?' she asked. 'Of course not,' I said. 'I am going to teach you to read.' I go over my own lessons with her on the upper piazza after school. She is learning quickly, she is very smart, I think."

"I got a letter from David in which he says he met Gabriel Carvalho.

New York, November, 1841

Dearest Sister,

I do not know why you have been in my mind more than ever today. I am sitting here in front of my lamp and a pile of textbooks, three big, fat ones, to be exact, and I cannot open them without first writing this to you.

Oh, I do know why you've haunted me all day! Last night I met Gabriel Carvalho—we don't see each other much—the law school and the medical school are on different planets—but when we do, it's always so good. We have some gay times in New York, theater, dancing, interesting people. Last night we went visiting on Washington Square. That's where "old" New York lives, very elegant, a little bit like your Place d'Armes, but not much. The houses all have "stoops," a high

flight of steps up to the front door. Gas lights, of
course, and fires in every fireplace—it's terribly
cold here, the way it was in Europe. Can you still
remember how we shivered?

Anyway—I'm wandering, it's past midnight
and my half-sleepy thoughts come crowding—
anyway, there was a young girl in the house who
looked so much like you, or the way I imagine
you must look now that you're almost fourteen,
and it's because of seeing her that I've been missing you all day. Gabriel, too, remarked on the
resemblance. I was surprised that he remembered
you so clearly after all this time, but he did, and
we talked about the day Gretel fell overboard and
how you cried and thanked him so prettily.

Sometimes it seems as if all that was yesterday,
so I must remind myself that you are no longer
that eager little girl. I suppose they will soon be
getting you ready for marriage. Whoever the man
may be, I hope he will be exactly right for you, a
kind man with the right thoughts.

You will at once interpret that as meaning the
"right politics," I'm sure, but believe me, I am
realistic enough to know that would be expecting
too much, living as you do, where you are. So I'll
merely hope you will love each other well, and let
it go at that.

As to politics, you would be astounded—at
least I always am, although I should be used to
things here by now—at the number of people who
talk like southern planters and have never been in
the South at all. One finds them mostly among
the Washington Square and the stock market
crowd. In the medical school there's a mixture of
opinions, ranging all the way to fiery New En-

gland abolitionism, with which, you must know, I find myself most at home.

Funny thing—when I'm with Gabriel, I hold my tongue about politics most of the time, and he does the same, because we don't want anything to come between us. I hope nothing ever will, but I don't know. In my dark moments I seem to see the country sliding toward conflict. God knows, I hope not.

Oh, why do I bother you with all this? It's only my middle-of-the-night mood, and missing you.

Besides, I'd better get to the books. It seems there's no end to what you have to memorize to become a doctor. But I still love what I'm doing and can't see myself being anything but a doctor.

Write and tell me everything about yourself, about school and the holidays and even your new dresses, everything.

> Your loving brother,
> David

"And Rosa got a letter the same day from Gabriel telling how he had met David. Rosa is very proud of her brother. 'He is the spiritual one in the family,' she says, 'not like me.'

"And then she said, 'Do you know he would make a fine husband for you?' Which was very embarrassing because of the way she looked at me, as if she were measuring me like yard goods. After all, I am only thirteen—well, almost fourteen. Papa, I'm sure, would be very pleased if I were to tell him. The Sephardim set the standard with their culture, he says, in spite of being a trifle haughty. But Rosa is not haughty. And Gabriel wasn't, either. I liked him. He wasn't fun to talk to, the way David is, though. He was too quiet, I

thought. Papa said he will be a handsome man when
he's grown up. Anyway, I think it was very silly of
Rosa to talk like that."

"We are all going up the river by sidewheeler to stay
at Plaisance for the christening of Pelagie's new baby,
her first boy. Just think, she had no children when I
first saw her, and now she has four!

"Aunt Emma says it is the duty of a wife to have a
large family, as many children as she can. Rosa says
Aunt Emma is the typical Creole. 'Make no mistake,'
Rosa says, 'these women may not appear to, but they
really run things. They are the matriarchs. It is the
secret power of women.' Rosa tells me interesting
things about the world, but I do not always agree with
them. I think, from what I see, having all those babies
cannot mean you run things. What secret power is
that?

"So many of them die! What can be the joy of that?
One of Aunt Emma's children died when it was just a
week old, three of them died in the fever epidemic, one
was bitten by a rattlesnake. How horrible! And some
others died of second-summer sickness. It is such a
dangerous time, the second summer. Oh, I should feel
terrible if any of Pelagie's babies died! I don't know
how Pelagie would bear it, she is so tender. She cries
so easily. Over nothing, sometimes."

"The house at Plaisance looks like that engraving of
the Parthenon that hangs in the upstairs hall outside
Papa's room. It belongs to Pelagie's father-in-law, Mr.
Lambert Labouisse.

"Pelagie has to live there even though she doesn't
want to. Sylvain's father scares me, he is so formal,
with such cold eyes. You feel as if he'd have your head
off if you were to laugh too loud or spill something. He

is all starched, without a wrinkle; he kisses your hand and bows his head like a king with such a charming smile that does not go with the rest of his face. Pelagie says he can be charming, but when he has rages, then everyone, even his son Sylvain, is afraid of him.

"David and Sylvain didn't like each other. David has such strong opinions about people, the way he liked Gabriel and still writes about him. Yet I must say Sylvain is very kind to me. He gave me the most thoughtful present for my birthday, a basket for Gretel, who is growing old. But everyone here is very kind to me except perhaps Eulalie. I think she doesn't like Jews, but I wouldn't tell anyone I think so. She sometimes makes remarks that have a certain meaning, I'm sure. 'Oh, it's your holiday,' she'll say with a queer expression, as if she didn't think much of it. Rosa says people nurture hatreds when they are miserable, they need something or somebody to scorn. I suppose that makes sense."

"What a grand place this is! One could fit our house inside it six times over. Every room is filled with relatives and all their children with their nurses. The children are everywhere on the stairs and in the halls, the white children and the servants' children, running and playing. I have never seen so many servants. The chef was an apprentice to one of the best chefs in Paris, they say.

"There are four thousand acres at Plaisance. It was a wedding present to Sylvain's mother when she married Lambert Labouisse. Most of the servants came with the place, born and buried here. It's like an enormous family. They have riding horses, I am learning to ride. There are carriages for everyone, whenever and wherever you want to go. Such splendor!

"I suppose Pelagie doesn't like it because it isn't her

own, or won't be until Lambert Labouisse is dead, which I don't think will be very soon, he seems quite strong and not so very old."

"The christening is to be on Sunday. One of the Labouisse aunts is to be *marraine,* the godmother, while Papa is to be the *parrain,* the godfather. Godfather to a Catholic child! Papa laughed. 'I told you,' he said, 'in this wonderful place it doesn't matter.' His gift has to be a silver cup. It is the custom. He is a lovely baby named Alexandre.

"This morning Sylvain told Pelagie that now she had given him a son, he hoped she would give him many more. Can she really want more babies? She is getting too fat and after a while she will look like Aunt Emma, which will be a shame. She was and still is so pretty. I don't understand it. Can't she say no? Is there no way? Does he force you if you don't want to? Does he rip your dress off? Suppose you said no to whatever it is that is done—and I'm not quite sure, I think I know what it is, but it's not clear and there is no one to ask, not even Rosa. She will talk about many things, but not that. Once I said something to Fanny, but she only looked scared and told me I mustn't ask such questions, it wasn't fitting for a young lady like me."

"After the christening I went outside by myself. I felt quiet, not exactly sad, although sometimes I do feel sadness. No, it's not that exactly, it is only that a person can be so alone, especially when there is a crowd.

"So many strangers talking at once, talking *at* each other, not *to* each other. As if all the talk were a way of saying, Look at me, listen to me, I'm here, I'm important, am I not important? Those are the times I feel scared, because there really isn't anybody who can understand the way I've been feeling lately. Not Papa, who would tell a joke and buy me a present the very next day. Not Pelagie, who would say something kind about how fortunate I am, which I already know. Not Rosa, who would just insist that I stay for a 'nice dinner.' Maybe David would, but he is not here and probably never will be.

"When I feel this way I have to go outside into some green place, even the courtyard at home for lack of anything more green. So I walked down to the bayou and I sat there on a flat rock.

"The slope is covered with wild iris of the palest lavender with moist, thick stems. There are swarms of white butterflies, small as moths; one sat on my hand, I didn't move, its wings kept opening and shutting as if on hinges. David says all life is one, which means that those transparent wings are made of the same stuff that I'm made of.

"I heard somebody come up behind me and I jumped. It was a man, older than David—I compare everyone with David—but not old. He had on a fashionable straw hat with ribbon ends hanging down the back of his neck. He said his name was Eugene Mendes and he knew I was Ferdinand Raphael's daughter. 'How do you know? You don't know me,' I said. 'Because I saw you—I've just come from the party,' he said. He sat down next to me. 'I'm waiting for my servant to row me home,' he said. 'It's easier than going by road.' Then he wanted to know what I was doing here by myself. I told him I liked the stillness. 'You can hear the stillness,' I said. He asked me how old I was and I told him I will be sixteen next birthday. I did not want to say I had just turned fifteen last week. He said, 'Then the young men will come to the family box at the opera to be introduced.' He smiled. His teeth are square. He has watchful eyes, he never took them away from me. I'm not sure whether he was admiring me or not. It feels strange to have a man's eyes so close. When his skiff arrived and his servant hailed him, he stood up. He is so tall that he stoops a little. He seems very strong. Rosa would say he is handsome, I know her taste, and it is not for a slight, weak man like her husband, I know that much.

" 'Don't sit here too long,' Mr. Mendes said. 'Alligators come out when it starts to grow dark.' I jumped up at that and quite suddenly he bent over my hand and kissed it. His lips were wet. When he raised his head he had that smile again. He has strange eyes, the color of tea. 'I'll see you at the opera,' he said, 'when you are sixteen.'

"Why do I write this down? I don't know why. I don't know what I want. When I am sixteen I shall be a woman and my life will really begin. I should be eager for it, they tell me, and sometimes I am. But I puzzle myself. I puzzle the family, too. Aunt Emma will never understand why I would rather read than pay calls with her. Those endless calls! A lifetime of that! Visiting cards and coffee and gossip and coffee, the roasted chicory fragrance as you come through the front door. 'Novels,' Aunt Emma says—she makes a little snort through her nose when she says it—'novels are quite indecent for young girls. Even the newspapers are better left alone, if you ask me.'

"What is there left? To be married, of course. Everyone knows that's what life is for a woman. Even the old-maid teachers at school know that. They are supposed to teach us how to be better wives and mothers. But how can an old maid possibly know?

"Rosa is wrong when she says that the power is in women. The power is in men. There is so little one knows about men. What are they like under their broadcloth and linen? I don't even know how they look. I shiver inside when I think about it and then I feel so warm. I'm ashamed of some of the things I imagine. Am I imagining crazy things, or are they true? If they are true, they must be wonderful. Still, I am so ashamed.

"I want to love somebody, that's what I want. Still I'm afraid. I don't want to be like Pelagie, I want to be free.

"I don't know what I want."

6

"No, I don't like that fan. There's too much yellow, the dress, the bouquet, and the ribbons. I do think the ivory is much better. Besides," said Emma, "this is the one Pelagie carried when she made her first appearance at the opera, and she wants you to have it. She is so fond of you, Miriam, I hope you realize it."

The pier glass reflected four women grouped around a fifth in the foreground: Miriam, on this day becoming a woman; Fanny, kneeling to fluff and perk six rustling petticoats; the hairdresser, Emma, and Eulalie. The latter had come in spite of herself to witness the preparations and stood now holding the bouquet of baby hyacinths and golden iris. Emma beamed. In a sense this evening was hers as substitute mother, and Miriam's triumph was to be her creation. So, wearing royal-blue satin and a pearl collar, Emma gave instructions.

"Yes, that's right, the fan must hang on its cord around your wrist. Open it from time to time after we are seated, flutter it gently, but remember not to hide your face behind it. Hold it like this. Oh, that dress is really a triumph, my dear, your father will be so proud."

Miriam's cheeks were hot. A dozen candles were blazing in the room. She stared at the stranger in the glass; the stranger who wore diamonds in her ears, whose naked white shoulders rose out of a foam of pastel ruffles.

"In your other hand you will carry your shoe bag, of course. You can change into the silk shoes when we arrive. I must say Scanlan's makes the most marvelous dresses! The work is as fine as French work any day. Your father says when the time comes for your trousseau we must order it from Paris, though for my part I have always been more than satisfied with Scanlan's or the Olympic."

Fat women couldn't wear French dresses. Aunt Emma, growing wider every year, had to be fitted at home.

"Fanny! I do believe," Emma said impatiently, "you've got the petticoats reversed. The double taffeta goes underneath so it won't crush the muslin. Raise her skirt, that's it, and reverse them." Emma was mildly exasperated. "Oh, I do so miss my Monty! I had to part with him just before you came to us, Miriam. He was the most marvelous dressing maid, never made mistakes, understood clothes to perfection. Unfortunately, I couldn't keep him past fourteen, he got too old to wait upon a lady. Yes, that's it, Fanny, that's it."

In the evenings, Miriam thought, young men will call. They will play cards with Papa, but they will have come for me. There'll be soirées on Sunday nights downstairs; we shall dance; like hens in a brooding house, the old ladies will sit in a row watching. Tonight at the opera in the family box, in the front row, people will look over, whispering, "Yes, that's the little Raphael girl, how charming she is, I wonder who will marry her. . . ."

And the world was radiant, revolving slowly to enchanting music in a dance of its own with Miriam at

the center. Everyone was so kind, everyone loved her.
Eulalie had admired her new earrings. No one need
ever be angry at anyone else; people were good; really,
one ought always to be happy.

"How nice for you that it's a premiere!" Emma
cried. "And so fitting that it's Halévy's *La Juive!* My
cousin saw it when it opened in Paris. Terribly dramatic, so sad—but then so many Jewish themes are
sad."

This very night, maybe, he would see her and come
to her. But who would he be? Suddenly Miriam veered
to panic. What if no one came? What if there was no
one at all, not tonight, not ever? It happened! You had
only to look at Eulalie to know what can happen. Eulalie, of course, was homely; yet there were others—
and mentally Miriam made count of the unmarried,
the unwanted—Marcelle's sister, really not homely at
all, or Amy's cousin, who lived with them, and all the
school mistresses. Mam'selle Georges must have been
lovely once with that red-gold hair, and what had become of her?

Then something of Ferdinand's optimism, her chief
inheritance from him, submerged the panic. No, no, it
was impossible, it wouldn't happen like that! And she
had a vague anticipation of glowing eyes, of a dark
head bent over her hand and a fervent voice. But who
was he? Who?

"There," Emma said. "That's perfect. Now hurry,
your father is already waiting downstairs. Sisyphus
will walk with us, he has been reading all about the
opera and is so proud whenever there is an American
premiere in New Orleans. It's astonishing what that
man knows about music. Good heavens, it's begun to
rain! Don't open the umbrella in the house! Miriam,
it's terrible luck, do you want to bring disaster on us?"

They walked through a fine warm drizzle, picking

their way toward dry spots. But Miriam walked through a silvery gauze curtain; it hung between her and what was to come; suddenly on this night the curtain would be drawn back and a dazzle would be revealed. These streets where she walked every day and the theater itself, which she so often passed, where the crowds were now converging, where an old Negress was selling gumbo at the door, all of these were waiting for her. She was the star of some great play, the lines of which she had not yet studied, but which would somehow come clear.

She was aware of greeting and being greeted as she mounted the stairs between Ferdinand and Emma and took her seat in their box. Yes, all was falling into place; one had only to sit with head up, smiling, patient, and wait for the great thing to happen. She was conscious of the hard, steady thrust of her heart.

"Look," whispered Emma, "that's Louis Moreau Gottschalk's father. One of the best Jewish families in the city. The son's a musical genius, you know. He's been sent to Paris to study. And there are your friends, the de Riveras. She does manage always to look so smart, she must spend a fortune on her clothes."

Miriam asked about the screened boxes opposite, the inhabitants of which were invisible to the rest of the audience.

"Those are the *loges grillées*. Women in mourning and ladies who are—expecting—can see in privacy without being seen."

Ferdinand leaned across Emma. He winked at Miriam. He was proud of her, of her dress, and the diamond earrings which he had brought to her that afternoon in a black velvet box. And she was sure he was remembering, as all at once she remembered, that first night in Europe when he had sat by the stove and promised her great things. Now they were here.

"After the performance, of course, we'll go to Vincent's for pastry and chocolate," he said.

The curtain rises now on a stony square in front of the cathedral, far larger and more grand than the one on the Place d'Armes. The music rises with the shimmering of angelic voices; the man's throbs like the lowest notes of a cello, the woman's is firm and pure as birdsong. The story unfolds, an old story of love and hatred, of pogroms and death. There is a Passover feast: *O God, God of our fathers,* they sing. So familiar and yet so strange and sad! How can they make an entertainment about death? And yet they can. The music soars and trembles, it thunders and weeps.

Miriam looks about in the darkness and wonders whether anyone beside herself is moved to tears. In the next box people are whispering, not hearing the music; they have come for other reasons, to see and be seen—which is why she's come, isn't it? But no more, not now. She is transported. Her heart breaks over the love, the passion, the death.

During the intermission people come to the box and are introduced. She has barely had time to wipe her eyes, and hopes that her nose isn't red. She bows politely, but does not remember any names, she has forgotten why she is here.

"Rachel." A man's voice speaks. He seems to be speaking to her, but she does not understand.

Her father recalls her to reality. "Mr. Mendes called you, Rachel. He pays you a compliment. He thinks you resemble Halévy's heroine."

She comes back to the present and thanks the man. She knows she has seen him somewhere before.

"You don't remember me," he says.

The tea-colored eyes seem not to blink, so steady is the gaze. They are the most important feature of this face; they are what one would remember about it.

"I said I would see you again when you were sixteen, Miss Miriam." His voice has authority, it is intense and commanding, like his eyes.

She remembers the afternoon at the bayou and the look of him swinging down the bank, his hand raised in a slight wave as he moves off in the skiff.

"You have grown even more beautiful than I expected you would, Miss Miriam."

Of course she is pleased. It is the first time a man has spoken to her like this. Yet she finds his words extravagant. She has quite shrewdly analyzed herself: She is supple and graceful, her features are very pleasing, but she is not a beauty. One has only to look over at the adjoining box where the Frothingham sisters sit, they with their masses of golden hair, their Valkyrie faces, to see beauty.

But she smiles in polite acknowledgment just as the curtain is about to rise again. Papa has barely time to remark, once Mr. Mendes is out of hearing, "A distinguished young man. He will go far."

Fanny said, "If you count all the gray horses you see up to a hundred, you'll be sure to marry the first man you shake hands with after that."

Miriam laughed. "That's silly, Fanny. Who told you such a thing?"

"Miss Eulalie told me, but everyone knows it anyway."

Beneath the window where the streetlamp threw a circle of fuzzy light into the spring mist stood an open carriage drawn by a gray horse.

"Can you count the same horse over and over or must it be a hundred different horses?"

"You laugh, but it's true," replied Fanny, evading the question. "And he's so tall. I like a tall man."

Eugene Mendes had been coming to the house for

two weeks past, ever since the night at the opera. In
the front parlor he played dominoes and drank port
with Papa. Or else, when there were other men present, they played cards. In the back parlor the women
played bezique or did macrame. Then over coffee the
two groups joined briefly and ended the evening.

"I had a tall boy once," Fanny said. "I was only
thirteen. But he was for me. Then I lost him."

"That must have been when you came here."

"Yes, they sold me away, me and Blaise. But I was
glad to go, more glad than sorry." Suddenly Fanny
seemed compelled to talk. "My father was a white
man, a bachelor, and my mother was a maid in the
house. A grand house, too, all brick. But when my
mother died my father married a lady, and she hated
having me and Blaise around, so she made him sell us.
But that was better for us because she was mean. That
was one mean woman."

"Why haven't you ever told me all this before?"
Miriam had thought she knew everything there was to
be known of Fanny's simple life. Fanny was just always there, someone who was kind and to whom you
were kind in return.

"Because. You were too young, too innocent. Innocent white child."

She felt now almost as she had felt at *La Juive,* a
piercing sorrow over human pain.

"But that's so terribly sad, Fanny. To leave your
home and your father—"

"He never was a father and the house wasn't mine.
How could it be, how could it be?" Fanny frowned.
Then she brightened. "Anyway, they were all Baptists
there, and Baptists don't allow music, they have no
dancing. It's much better for colored people to be
Catholic. Blaise doesn't like being Catholic because
the priests don't allow shouting in church, but I do.

There, your hair's done. You'd better go downstairs. It's time."

As always, Miriam was to spend the first night of Passover at the de Rivera house. Each year Ferdinand received his proper invitation, and each year he found a plausible reason to refuse. Tonight he had not had to stretch his imagination for an excuse, since it was Emma's birthday.

"Very kind of Mr. Mendes to be calling for you," he said now as he came upstairs. His eyes sped over his daughter from head to foot.

"Yes," she said. "Very kind."

"He's a religious man. A benefactor to his fellow Jews."

She thought ironically, And you forgive him that?

Her father kissed her. "You're a lovely girl, Miriam. Always feel sure of that."

"Thank you, Papa."

"Enjoy yourself."

"I will, Papa."

A varied group encircled the table. Gershom Kursheedt, black bearded, with serious eyes, was a biblical figure, an ascetic prophet, if only in appearance. The red-haired Jewish merchant visiting from France with his fashionable, vivacious wife was a figure of worldly assurance. The poor German Jew who taught Hebrew to little boys for a living wore a shabby jacket and an innocent smile. Two Catholics were neighbors and old friends. There were prosperous cousins and lonely strangers, invited because it is required that those who have share with those who have not: "Since we were strangers in the land of Egypt . . ."

And there was Eugene Mendes, sharing with Kursheedt the center of attention. Miriam was relieved and also disappointed that he was at the other end of the table. It would be worrisome to make conversation with him all through dinner, holding the conversation exactly right, amusing and witty, yet not too much so. Emma always warned that men don't like prattling women. Of course, the married ones prattled all the time, but by then probably the man was used to it, or was perhaps so busy talking to other men that he didn't even hear. So that was a relief. On the other hand, had he not told her, was he not the first and only man who had said: "You are even more beautiful than I expected"?

The ceremony of the Seder moved in orderly progression, for *Seder* means *order*. The host's amiable face smiled on the company while candle flames made spots of light dance on his spectacles.

"We praise you, O Lord our God, King of the Universe," he prayed. "You have kept us alive, sustained us, and brought us to this season. Amen."

The blessings were chanted and everyone raised the first cup of wine. Always at this point came a feeling of warmth, of closeness and peace in this ancient community of Miriam's people. Thoughts of her mother were interwoven with thoughts of Eugene Mendes. An outstanding citizen . . .

Rosa whispered, "I met your Aunt Emma on the street. She mentioned that Eugene Mendes has been calling."

"He has been calling on Papa."

"But surely you must have talked to him. Do you find him agreeable?"

"I hardly know him." She took a sip of wine.

And the service proceeded. "Let all who are in want come and celebrate the Passover with us."

Two candles stood tall in the old Spanish silver menorah. The Seder foods, the charoseth, the bitter herb, the shankbone, and the greens were set forth on silver.

Rosa whispered again. Like Aunt Emma she was unable to hold her tongue still for more than a minute.

"We are lucky to have Gershom Kursheedt and to have got rid of Rowley Marks. Such a disgrace. You know Kursheedt is a great admirer of Mr. Mendes. He has great respect for him."

She wished Rosa would stop whispering. Raising her eyes over the rim of her wineglass, she met Eugene Mendes's glance. He was talking to the Frenchwoman who had also been looking at Miriam. What could they be saying about her? She looked down at her dress, to the red velvet neckline above her breasts. There was nothing wrong. She touched her earlobes where the little diamond buttons were still safe. No, there was nothing wrong.

Little Herbert, the younger of the de Rivera boys, had now got safely through the Four Questions. The host broke off a piece of matzoh and held it up to lead the blessing. "We praise you, O Lord our God, King of the Universe. You have sanctified us through your commandment that ordained that we should eat unleavened bread."

Through the general murmur of prayer the voice of Eugene Mendes was distinct, not louder, but vibrant and full, a voice one would remember. And Miriam, taking another swallow of wine, felt her head grow light.

"*Schulchen aruch.* The table is set," Henry said. "Dinner is served."

Two servants brought in a great tureen and began to ladle out the soup.

Rosa had turned to people on her other side. "Yes, I came overland from Charleston as a bride. It took four weeks by carriage and horseback. Oh, it was a great change, coming here. My family founded the temple in

Charleston, you know. I had so many friends, such deep roots," she sighed.

"And admirers," Henry said, overhearing.

"Only one that I ever cared about until you came along, Henry. But he was a Christian," she said frankly. "And of course I would not marry him. I am like Rebecca Gratz. Her closest companions all her life were in the Christian community and the man she loved was a Christian. But she always said that the members of a family should be of the same faith, and therefore she would not marry him. She remained an unhappy spinster. As for me, I am glad I did not remain a spinster."

"Thank you, my dear," Henry said. "I am glad, too."

"Rebecca Gratz," Miriam said shyly, "isn't it said that she was the inspiration for Rebecca in *Ivanhoe?*"

Eugene Mendes caught her question. "Yes, Miss Miriam," he called out. "It was Washington Irving who told Sir Walter Scott how kindly she had nursed Irving's fiancée when she was ill." His smile praised Miriam. "And did you know that Rebecca Gratz warned her brother when he went to New Orleans that it was a godless city, that we Jews here had all lost our faith? But it wasn't quite true, as you see."

"Certainly not true of people like yourself, Mr. Mendes," Gershom Kursheedt affirmed.

Eugene replied, "You do me too much honor."

"I was referring to your valiant efforts to get Judah Touro to do something for our people, Mr. Mendes."

"They've not come to very much so far. But one tries. He's an interesting man, at any rate."

"He would be even more interesting," Kursheedt observed, "if he would return to his beginnings. You've all heard, I suppose, that he's bought the Christ Church rectory on Canal Street? Gave twenty-five thousand dollars for it, far more than it's worth. He might as well have made an outright contribution and been done with it. This in addition to the thousands he gives to the Presbyterians."

"And when you think," remarked Henry, "that when we were organizing Shanarai Chasset, he gave practically nothing. And what was worse, didn't even join."

Like Papa, Miriam thought, feeling a flash of shame.

"Well," said Eugene Mendes, "no one denies it's a fine thing to give charity to all. It's his not giving to his own as well that rankles." And he went on, "He's had quite a history. Arrived here from Boston in 1802 with nothing in his pocket. New Orleans was under Spanish rule then and still under Bienville's Black Code. Catholicism was the only religion to be tolerated in Louisiana."

Miriam was engrossed. This conversation was so much more absorbing than Aunt Emma's trivia at the Raphael table. All heads were turned with respect toward Eugene Mendes, who spoke well in rapid, sparkling sentences.

"Got his wound under Andrew Jackson at the Battle of New Orleans in 1815. The man's been a fighter from the start. Worth a fortune today, of course. Shipping, West Indies rum, tobacco, horses—there's nothing he doesn't touch."

"You're describing yourself, too," the host said graciously.

"No, no, I'm hardly in the same class. A long way from Judah Touro."

"It's an old story," Mr. Kursheedt remarked. "When Jews rise to great prominence there comes a temptation to take the easy social path and forget one's heritage. Touro is not the only one. Take Judah Benjamin."

"I knew him when he came to the city," Henry observed. "I was invited to his wedding in the cathedral."

"He's buying a plantation twenty miles south of here, Belle Chasse. Very grand," said Eugene Mendes, adding ironically, "It's got silver-plated doorknobs, or so they tell me."

"But you have a fine place of your own," Rosa told him.

"Oh, you can't mention it in the same breath as Belle Chasse. It's merely my quiet retreat from the heat and the fever."

"Don't you believe it," Rosa whispered as they left the dining room. "It's a splendid place. It's just that he doesn't like to talk about himself."

If it were Papa, Miriam thought fondly and ruefully, he would be telling everyone how many rooms there were and what it had all cost.

"I suppose you would call Mr. Mendes a modest man," she said then. "A simple man."

"Simple?" Rosa laughed. "That is the one thing I would never call him." She regarded Miriam, her eyes narrowing. "It's a lucky girl who will get him, I can tell you. And I wouldn't be a bit surprised if you were that lucky one."

"I don't really . . ." Miriam murmured and, stopping, saw that Rosa was mistaking a mixture of pride and fright for modesty and joy.

"Oh, I'm almost sure of it!" Rosa cried, squeezing Miriam's hand. "It couldn't happen to a sweeter girl, either, or more deserving! Such an attractive man . . ."

They were caught in a crush at the door, and Rosa

was swept into the parlor, leaving Miriam for a moment alone with the echo of her words.

Such an attractive man.

If everyone else says so, Miriam thought, then I ought to think so, too. Shouldn't I? Yes of course, I should.

On the following morning a servant bearing a note and requesting an answer knocked at the Raphaels' door. Almost immediately after he had gone away, Fanny came to say that Mrs. Raphael wanted Miriam downstairs.

"We have a visit to make this afternoon, Miriam my dear. Mr. Mendes sent his boy just now to ask whether we will call on him." Emma's smile was sprightly, almost mischievous. "He pays me the compliment of admiring my taste and asks my advice on the decoration of his new house. Do wear your new coat. I don't think we need ask Odette to do your hair, do you? The curls are still quite tight. Perhaps Fanny could go over them a bit."

Once more Miriam stood before the pier glass. Just the week before the mantua-maker had finished a bottle-green silk coat with taffeta bow knots. She had not worn it yet. Her boots of gray cloth and black patent leather were also new. Gray kid gloves and a bonnet heavy with roses waited on the bed while Fanny brushed her hair. For an instant their eyes met in the mirror before Fanny's, quickly lowered, hid themselves under her lashes. Fanny knows, Miriam thought. Servants know things before they happen. She may know better than I do what I'm feeling, too. I wish David were here to tell me what I'm feeling, because I don't understand myself, and he would understand.

I'm racing downhill, running so fast I can't stop,

scared that I'll crash. Am I perhaps imagining things that are not there at all?

"You look beautiful," Fanny said, fastening the last hairpin. "Now the bonnet. Back on the head a little more. Yes, that's it."

In the carriage Emma echoed Fanny. "You look lovely, Miriam. I must remind you, though, to be more careful about wearing a veil when you're outdoors. You do want to keep your complexion so no one will ever get the idea you've a touch of the tarbrush. Not that there's any danger of that, you having been born in Europe." She laughed. "I so envy you your hair. It's like black silk. Enjoy it while you can before you have to start covering the gray with coffee."

The carriage rolled down Esplanade Avenue. "I'm really eager to see the inside of Mr. Mendes's house. It was built by Parmentier, a very wealthy auctioneer—before he lost his money, that is. Gambling," Emma said disdainfully. "It's one thing to make money and another to hold on to it. He came of poor stock, though; French, but *Chacalatas*, back-country people, not my sort. That's why I was never in the house. Well, here it is."

Stone cherubs held up the gallery, across which ran an iron-lace balcony in a pattern of acorns and twining oak-leaves. At the side of the house a brick wall surrounded a large plot of ground, which almost certainly contained a spacious garden.

Eugene Mendes waited at the top of the steps. He looked taller than Miriam remembered. As Rosa had said, he was an imposing man. His hands reached down to help the women mount the steps. Miriam had a queer thought: He can get anything he wants.

Addressing Emma, he asked now, "Would you like tea, madame, or would you rather see the house first?"

"Oh, since you are kind enough to want my advice, let us see the house first."

It was a fine building in the Greek Revival style, finer and larger than the Raphael home. A clean breeze traveled through the tall windows, rippling the curtains. Lofty, shady rooms, twin parlors, a music room and a ballroom, were separated by double doors carved in panels of magnolia blossoms. At either end of the long back verandah was a cabin-size room.

"The cabiniers, for the boys of the house," Mr. Mendes explained. "The previous owner had many sons."

"Well, he was fortunate in that respect, anyway," Emma observed, adding with a daring, almost coquettish air, "You are well prepared in this house for whatever life may bring you, one sees."

The host smiled slightly, and the little procession continued through the rooms. Mirrors tossed their reflections back and forth, Miriam following in silence while Mr. Mendes courteously bent his head toward Emma's chatter.

"Think how many hundreds of hours of labor in that!" she exclaimed over an Empire sofa covered with flowers in needlepoint.

Miriam realized that this friendly stream of trivial remarks did serve some purpose. It covered silences that might otherwise be dreadful.

In front of a painting of a Renaissance noble whose velvet hat drooped over a dissipated face, Emma paused. "Is that not from the collection of the Duke of Tuscany?"

"You are most discerning, madame. Yes, like your husband, I am a founder of our National Art Gallery of Painting." For the first time Mr. Mendes spoke directly to Miriam. "You may be familiar with our undertaking. A group of us here in the city bought the

Duke's collection and we're hoping that the Gallery will take it. If not, we shall keep these for private homes. Do you know as much about paintings as you do about literature?"

"I know very little about either, I'm afraid."

"You have read *Ivanhoe,* at any rate." And turning back to Emma, "Shall we go upstairs?" he asked. "It's really in sorry condition without carpets or hangings. I've had some furniture sent on approval from Seignouret. I should like to know what you think of it, madame."

"You couldn't do better than Seignouret, Mr. Mendes."

"Nevertheless, I should like your opinion. If you have other ideas, do be frank. And you, too, Miss Miriam. After all, I am without mother or sister to advise me."

Massive armoires of rosewood and mahogany stood with huge four-poster beds canopied in tufted satin.

Emma spoke approval. "Most elegant! And, so wisely, he has used marble tops on the tables. He knows our climate."

"Yes," agreed the host, "dampness does the veneers no good."

A half-opened door revealed a little room at the rear of the hall. Miriam, pausing, saw a bare, shining floor, a narrow, plain bed, and a cypress wood chest standing between two white-curtained windows.

Mr. Mendes apologized. "That's just a spare room. A catch-all for some old things from my grandparents' country place."

Something in the spareness of the little room appealed to Miriam and she exclaimed, "Oh, but I like this best! It feels comfortable and peaceful."

"Then, you admire simplicity," Mr. Mendes said.

"Miriam!" Emma cried reproachfully.

And Miriam, aware that she had made a mistake, amended at once, "Of course, the other rooms are beautiful, they're very different, very grand. . . ."

"Oh, but I like your spirit," Mr. Mendes said. "You expressed your true feelings and you are right. There is a special beauty in simplicity. Shall we go down again? So you approve, madame? Now I need only to increase my plate service. I shall be entertaining rather a good deal now that I am permanently settled in the city. I suppose I ought to have two dozen settings?"

"Oh, indeed. Perhaps more, if you wish. Mr. Raphael frequently brings guests for lunch. It is nothing to find twenty-four in our house at two thirty in the afternoon."

"Then I shall put in my order tomorrow. Would you prefer refreshment in the garden, madame? It's very cool and pleasant, I think."

A bench encircled a round table in the gazebo, where cakes and coffee had been set out. Emma immediately praised the cakes.

The host acknowledged the praise. "My cook Grégoire was trained at the best eating house in Savannah."

Emma reached for her third. She admired the camellias espaliered against the wall, the jessamine and the daylilies; she loved the peal of the cathedral bells.

"We can barely hear them at our house. This is a perfect location here in every way."

"Yes, it is," he replied.

He was paying only partial attention to Emma. His eyes were on Miriam now. She was uncomfortably conscious of his stare.

Some distance away on the garden wall a plaque marked the spot where someone had been buried in the garden. She strained to read. "AIMÉE DE—" The surname was concealed by a branch of hibiscus. "AI-

MÉE DE—, DÉCÉDÉE LE—FÉVRIER, ÉPOUSE DE—" A
young wife, died in February. Of the fever, or in child-
birth? Had she gone singing through this house?
Would it be a happy thing to be a wife in this house?

"You are very thoughtful, Miss Miriam."

Now she was forced to look at him. "I was admiring
the statue."

A small stone figure of Aphrodite stood above a
two-tiered fountain. Into a little pool the falling water
splashed and doubled like flounces on a skirt. The city
was so far away, beyond that wall. One might think
oneself in a forest, in a grove, all green, and but for the
quiet splashing, all still.

"What do you think of it?"

She hesitated. "It's a happy thing to have in one's
garden. With the doves and the flowers. She was a love
goddess."

"You know something about mythology, then."

"Miriam is a reader," Emma explained. "But not a
bookworm, thank goodness! If there's one thing," she
said meaningfully, "that you men despise, it's a blue-
stocking female, isn't it?"

"And do you like my house, Miss Miriam?" Mr.
Mendes asked, not replying to Emma.

"Oh, yes. I hope you will be very happy in it," she
said with the courtesy that was expected of a guest.

"Thank you, I expect to be." He turned back to
Emma.

It was strange how different he seemed from what
he had been at Rosa's yesterday. Today there was
something too intense about him. He is so very strong,
she thought again. He can manage anything. Under
the tight gray coat was a body muscled like those of
the Greek gods and Roman warriors in the engravings
upstairs in that room. There had been a flowered china
pitcher and a bowl where he must wash and shave in

the mornings. From the mosquito bar on the bed the netting hung like a veil, a bridal veil. In one of those large carved beds, probably in the red room—she didn't know why, but it seemed that he would select the red room for himself and his bride—in that bed, the girl whom he brought there would be . . . She would be different in the morning. The mysteries! Perhaps if David were here she could ask him. But no, of course not. He, too, was a man, even if he was her brother. What would she ask him, anyway? She wasn't even sure.

She was stiff and tense on the bench. Her hands were so tightly clasped on her lap that the fingertips went red. Mr. Mendes's hands were hairy. But they were clean. His fingernails had white rims. That was good; she liked his being so clean. But his forehead was too high. It was like a dome. Someday probably he would lose his black hair and be bald.

"You're shivering," Mr. Mendes said. "Are you cold?"

"A little. There is a chill in the wind."

"Is there? I don't feel it. Shall I get you a shawl?"

"She's in the shade," Emma said. "Move over into the sun, Miriam."

Now her skirt almost touched Mr. Mendes's knees. Why was she so afraid of being that close to him? She had admired him yesterday. Such a gentleman. So well thought of. And this fine house. What was there to be afraid of? And besides, he hadn't asked her, might not even want her, despite what Rosa thought. And she embarrassed herself with her own thoughts.

But he will ask you, Miriam. And you will say yes. You will be expected to. Any girl would say yes to him, wouldn't she? But it will be wrong if you do. But a girl has to be married. But it will be wrong. And she had a terrible sense of dread.

The blood pounded in her neck. She had never fainted, but she felt so queer. It was unbearable to sit there any longer. She prayed that Emma would get up and leave.

Presently Emma did.

On the way home in the carriage Emma spoke with a satisfied sigh. "I'm almost certain he's going to speak to your father about you, Miriam. Tomorrow, I shouldn't wonder. Of course that's why he wanted you to see his house."

"I'm sure he only wanted your advice about the decorations, Aunt."

Emma laughed. "Nonsense! How innocent you are! Not that that isn't very becoming. To tell you the truth, your father and I have already discussed it. Your father is delighted. And why shouldn't he be? We both think you're a very fortunate girl. New Orleans is scarcely filled with eligible Jewish men, and while, as you have seen, many Jews and Christians marry each other, we understand that you wouldn't do it. And certainly it's your privilege to have a husband of your own faith."

Miriam did not answer. The blood still pounded in her neck.

"And since it's so important to you, you must consider: How many are there like Eugene Mendes? He's educated and a man of taste, as you have just seen." Emma spread her chubby fingers apart, counting. "He has a prosperous business and they tell me his country place is delightful. Beau Jardin, it's called. Yes, you will have everything you want, a position in the best society of the city. I have inquired, you see, as if you were my own daughter, my dear." And she laid her hand on Miriam's arm.

Yes, she has been good to me from the beginning, Miriam thought. No one could have been better.

"It must seem like a fairy tale to you sometimes, all that's happened since you came here. Why, what is it? You're not crying?"

Miriam turned her head away. "I don't know. I'm not sure how I feel."

"Well, you're young, and this is very sudden. Although you're certainly not too young. I was married at fifteen and my Pelagie was sixteen, like you. You see how happy she is, don't you? Only my poor Eulalie . . ."

Now the lament would come, as it always did whenever any girl of Emma's acquaintance became engaged. Yes, if Eulalie weren't married by twenty-five, all hope would be over. From that time on she would wear a hooded bonnet with chin ribbons and she might never wear a velvet dress, something that seemed to Miriam to have no relevance to anything whatever. Well, Eulalie had better get all the wear she could out of her velvet dresses; she had only two months to go before turning twenty-five.

"Eulalie was never admired," Emma mourned for the thousandth time. "I don't understand it. She's an excellent housekeeper, comes of a fine family, and certainly we had a good dowry for her, some forty thousand dollars, Miriam! Why, there were at least a dozen young men on neighboring plantations who would have been suitable. Goodness knows they knew us all for generations; our families had played together as children, so they knew there could be no danger of the tarbrush. You know, so many of the FPC are so white you can't always tell. Some of them have a lot of money, too. One has to be very careful of bloodlines. Well, there was never any fear of that with Eulalie, so I just don't know." The mother sighed. "So, she'll just be another old auntie, a *tante*, that's all. She can help

Pelagie with her children as the family grows larger. Help with yours, too, Miriam."

Not with mine, Miriam thought fiercely. Not with that sour temper.

"But you don't have to worry, Miriam. You have your future before you now. And your father will be very generous with you, I know. Of course," Emma said, "you're thinking there's more than that. A young girl dreams of love. That's ideal if it's there. But if it's not there at the start, it will develop."

It will develop. What a terrible life never to have love! Not to be loved, not to love anyone but some other woman's children.

And suddenly Miriam remembered something. "It was the same in Europe, in the village. When I was very little, Opa wanted my Aunt Dinah to marry a man who had the best house on the street. But he was fat and ignorant, and she wouldn't. She wouldn't do it. So he asked my Cousin Leah instead."

"And did your cousin marry him?" Emma inquired with interest.

"Yes, and they had four of the most beautiful babies when we left."

"Ah! You see? It all worked out, didn't it? I should imagine your aunt is sorry now. A girl should listen to her elders. It's the same the world over. But you don't have to worry about that!" Emma laughed. "Mr. Mendes isn't fat and he certainly isn't ignorant. He's a fine-looking man. And ten or twelve years older than you, that's good. A man is more steady when he's older."

It all went very quickly. The engagement was celebrated at a formal breakfast, the *déjeuner de fiançailles,* with the giving of the traditional ring, a ruby in a setting of flat gold. The wedding date was set for a

Saturday night in spite of Emma's protest that Saturday was common and the better people always married on Monday or Tuesday night. Eugene Mendes wanted Saturday.

"We can fit three hundred in here at home with no trouble at all," Ferdinand said. "We'll need that many. I'm on so many boards and they'll all expect an invitation. Let's see, there's the City Bank, the New Orleans Gaslight and Banking Company, the board of the Western Marine and Fire Insurance Company, and the Chamber of Commerce." His cheeks were pink with anticipation.

Suddenly Miriam had become of chief importance. Before, she had been merely the daughter of the house, cherished and admonished; now she was an object of respect and envy. First among her friends at school to be married, chosen by none other than Eugene Mendes to be his wife.

Even Fanny was tremendously affected. She was to go along into the new life as a wedding gift to Miriam with the dowry, the pearls, and the silver service. Excited and proud, she fluttered through the house, running up and down stairs as gifts arrived. With as much delight as though they were her own, she sorted through the Dresden shepherdesses, embroidered linens, lace mantillas, and silver trays.

Eulalie alone remained apart. She sniffed. "You could put enough punch in that bowl for an army. And so ornate. Those people always manage to overdo things."

"What people?" Miriam asked, although she knew quite well.

"Rosa and Henry de Rivera—isn't that theirs?"

"No." Miriam took satisfaction. "No. It's from Mr McClintock at Papa's bank."

Eulalie flushed. "Well, I'm surprised at him, then. *He* ought to know better, I'm sure."

Caterers came to arrange for little round tables and gilt chairs. Florists came with estimates for orange blossoms. In the kitchen fruitcakes high as hats stood soaking in brandy. Dressmakers rushed their samples, strewing the beds and chairs with lengths of Irish dowlas and Swiss lawn, of muslin and calicoes for morning wear, gauze for dancing, of bombazine and velvet.

There had been no time to get the wedding dress from Paris as Ferdinand had wished, for the bridegroom was in a hurry, unwilling to delay the wedding for half a year in order that a dress might be brought from abroad. This seemed sensible enough, Emma and Ferdinand agreed, especially since there was a dress Miriam could wear, a family heirloom which had been worn by Pelagie and by Emma before her.

She was to wear her diamond earrings and a pair of narrow gold bracelets which had arrived in the mail along with a letter from David.

"These belonged to our mother," he wrote. "They were all the jewels she owned, Aunt Dinah said when she gave them to me. I was to keep them for you and give them to you when you married. Dear Miriam, wear them on your wedding day. They come to you with so much love that they should warm your arm. I wish I could be there with you, but it is so far. . . . Yet in a way, I shall be there. I am always with you."

She could have repeated from memory every word of that letter. He had written also: "You have not told me much about the man you are to marry. I understand it must be hard to put your deepest feelings into words on paper. But I know you must love him very much, and I am so glad for you. . . ."

Aunt Emma reminisced, "Oh, you should have seen

me as a bride. I was married—I speak of my first marriage, naturally—on the plantation. There were five hundred guests; my father chartered steamboats to bring them, along with the hairdressers and all the confections which came from the city."

Pelagie clasped her hands in her typical gesture. "My wedding was so splendid, Miriam. Of course you'll be invited to a cathedral wedding sometime and then you will see. The Suisse seating the guests, he in his scarlet coat and gold lace and his plumed hat, and the bells all ringing like mad! Oh, it was splendid! Then home for the supper and dancing. But except for the cathedral," she said hastily, "yours will be the same. Little Miriam! I remember going down to the ship to meet you. You were holding a doll. And here you are," Pelagie cried. "And here you are!"

So, on a tide of generous enthusiasm, Miriam was swept along. Never once did it occur to her that she had not spent a single hour alone with the man she was to marry—although if it had occurred to her, there would have been nothing that she or any other girl in her position could do about it.

Roads were crossed and points were turned in this upstairs room, in the corner where the pier glass stood in its tall oval frame. When Miriam awoke, the afternoon sun had already gone round the corner of the house, but the tilted glass still shone, reflecting the couch on which she lay and the dog on the floor with her nose between her paws in an attitude of watchfulness, as though she, too, knew that the day was to mark a change in their joint lives. Lifeless objects on the table and chests now took on life, announcing the hour; the veil, the white gloves, the fan, the diamond locket and lace handkerchief, waited in the basket, the *corbeille de noce,* the bridegroom's gift, to be worn for

the first time on this day. She sat up as Pelagie, followed by Fanny, came into the room.

"It's almost five o'clock. You've had a good nap,"
Pelagie said. "I wonder that you could sleep at all. I
was much too excited on my wedding day."

Fanny laid a wreath of orange blossoms on the
dresser. "Maxim is bringing hot water for your wash
in a minute. I'll just move these things and make room
on the bed for your dress."

The two women bustled lightly as they prepared the
bride. Pelagie chattered happily.

"I've just been in the kitchen and everything looks
beautiful. They've brought mountains of ice from the
ice house on Chartres Street. Papa must have ordered
a hundred bottles of champagne, I'm sure. We mustn't
let people drink so much that they stay all night,
though I don't suppose it matters if they do. At midnight Mama will take you upstairs anyway and help
you into your negligée. I'm sure she's told you—"

Emma had, several times. She had explained how
she would go down to inform Eugene that the bride
was ready, and how they would then stay five days in
the bridal chamber. Miriam had been astonished. And
Emma had laughed.

"Oh, honey, the servants will bring food. Is that
what you're thinking about?"

"Imagine," Pelagie said now, "you'll have the same
room where Sylvain and I began."

Through the partly open door Miriam could see the
bride's traditional tester bed, refurbished with fresh
sky-blue silk and glossy gilded cupids, from whose
twining hands pink ribbons fell. Important, ceremo-
nial as an altar, the bed waited.

Fingers fumbled at her back, fastening the buttons
which ran from neck to waist. Her own fingers
smoothed and smoothed the two fine gold hoops on

her wrist. Her mother's fingers might have smoothed them so. David had held them for her all these years! And she felt a sudden wash of loneliness, chilling and sorrowful: If only he were here! This minute, now, to say, in that positive way of his, that she still remembered: Yes, yes, this is right, this is good! And then to smile encouragement, with that smile that she remembered so well, too.

She straightened her shoulders. She mustn't look for her brother or for anyone at all to lean on; she must stand with her own strength. Of course this was right! Her fleeting doubts had been only natural! Hadn't Emma assured her that all brides were fearful? Why, even David had written how pleased he was with her marriage to a serious man of their own faith!

From the hall below now came the sounds of arrival and greeting.

"They're here!" Fanny cried. "Come, look!"

Pelagie warned, "She mustn't be seen until Papa brings her down."

"You can peek," Fanny urged. "Nobody'll see you. Stand here on the gallery."

The courtyard was illuminated. Under a canvas ceiling a floor had been laid. White roses on the bridal canopy were opalescent in the descending dusk.

Pelagie pointed out the first arrivals. "There's Pierre Soulé. They say he'll be in the Senate soon. And there's Rosa, there in the striped silk; what a handsome dress! And Henry—it does seem so odd, the men keeping their top hats on! Mama has got a separate table with kosher food for your Mr. Kursheedt and the others. The rest of us will have lobster salad and fried oysters and venison and chicken salad."

She spoke hungrily. Pregnant again, Pelagie was always hungry. And Miriam laid her hand tenderly on Pelagie's.

"My, your hand is freezing, Miriam! Come on, let's
look over the banister and see what's happening. Oh,
look what Maxim and Chanute are bringing inside!"

A bride and groom of nougat, a *pièce montée* almost
two feet high, was set upon the table and wreathed
with more roses.

"Isn't that too beautiful, Miriam. Quick! Quick! Get
in here, that's Eugene coming in. He mustn't see you,
not even the hem of your dress. It's terrible bad luck.
Oh, but he looks so solemn—"

"Good heavens!" Emma cried, rushing upstairs.
"You haven't got the veil on yet! Come, it's almost
time."

Reverently, as though crowning a queen, the
women set the veil and the coronet of orange blossoms
on the bride's head. Clouded in white, the bride stared
with blank eyes at the girl in the mirror.

Someone knocked at the door. "Now, now," said
Emma, opening it for Ferdinand.

Along with his dark suit and satin tie, Ferdinand
wore his triumph. "Mark my words, the *Picayune* tomorrow will say this was one of the most magnificent
weddings the city has ever seen!"

Miriam took his arm. "I'm ready, Papa."

They moved toward the stairs. Stately music flowed
toward them as they descended. The feet in the satin
slippers moved with courtly rhythm. Not my feet, she
thought. Not Miriam's feet. All this is happening to
somebody else.

None of her imaginings had prepared her for the
reality. Neither apprehension nor those most secret
and suppressed, most embarrassing and ravishing
imaginings had prepared her. For this was the most
ugly and terrible thing that could happen. The impressive gentleman in gray broadcloth who could quote

the classics and the Bible, who brought proper gifts and paid compliments—this gentleman was—he was an animal. His touch was a horror.

Were all her nights to be like this? The first one had been especially humiliating. A tumultuous racket of cowbells, drums, and horns had gone on for hours in the street beneath their window. Miriam had been appalled, but Eugene had been merely amused.

"An old custom," he said. "The *charivari*." They wouldn't do it after the first night. Why did she let it upset her so?

She could not have told him it was because it seemed to her that they knew what had been happening in their room and were laughing at her—which was not true, and she knew it was not true, but was sick with shame nevertheless. And she covered her hot face with her hands.

Yet, perhaps all men were like that; perhaps it was supposed to be like that. Or maybe it would change in time and he would be different, or she would be different.

Now on the fourth morning she woke to see a lake of sunshine on the floor, which meant that it must be nearly noon. Under the sky-blue canopy her husband still slept with little puffing noises coming from his open mouth.

She got up quietly. The house was still and she understood that out of consideration for the bridal couple, the servants had been instructed to make no noise. On the table the wilted wedding bouquet lay in its frame of paper lace. Emma had offered to have it dried and framed. On the table also lay the *ketubah,* the marriage contract with its graceful Hebrew letters running across the page like bird tracks on sand. She picked it up. The thick parchment, the important signatures, the words which she was unable to read, all

filled her with a sense of awe and gravity, a conviction
of permanence. It was as if she were holding a tablet of
the Law between her hands. Actually she was holding
her own life, two lives. And she felt the terrible weight
of it.

But at the same time something else said desperately: You're young, you're sixteen, what can you
know? Nothing. Or not very much. Much is yet to
reveal itself. Surely this can't be all there is ever to be?

From her basket in the corner the dog Gretel raised
her head. Miriam picked her up, laying her own head
against the warm hair and the delicate bones of the
little skull. And her mind traveled through this link
with the past, back to the road where the dog had first
been found, to the village, the house, and her unknown
mother. How far away and long ago! Maybe a mother
would be able to explain—

"You're deep in thought. What is it?"

Eugene was sitting up in bed. Wide awake and curious, he might have been observing her for some minutes.

Flustered, she answered, "Nothing, really. Nothing."

"Come, now. One doesn't stand without moving in
the middle of a room and think about nothing."

"I was thinking about—yes, thinking about God,"
she said suddenly.

His eyebrows moved, giving his face an expression
of amusement or faint mockery. In the confinement of
this room she was already becoming familiar with his
gestures and expressions. This one was habitual, she
saw; the eyebrows moved, they slid on his forehead
like black caterpillars. Strange that she had never noticed them like that before; otherwise perhaps she
would have had courage enough to refuse him.

"Religion is certainly respectable and I have no

quarrel with it. But now is hardly the time or place. Come back to bed."

"It must be almost noon. Shan't I ring for breakfast?"

"Later. Come back to bed. Come now."

"Please," she said. It sounded like a whimper. She despised the helpless sound of it.

"Please what?"

"I want—not—"

Eugene got up and moved toward her. Naked, he seemed twice as tall. He threatened her, although surely he had done her no physical harm and she had no fear that he would. Her pain was deep inside, a pain of the spirit. She closed her eyes. It was easier when she did not look at his nakedness; she could pretend she was not there at all.

She lay inert. Yes, this was happening to somebody else. Her pretense, if he could know it, wouldn't matter to him; it seemed as if what he was doing was only for himself anyway. Besides, a woman was not supposed to show pleasure, nor supposed to feel it, if she was a decent woman. Everyone knew that. It was only a pleasure for the man. Therefore it did not trouble her that she had no pleasure.

Yet it seemed fairly sensible to assume that she was not supposed to feel loathing, either. Surely one was not supposed to loathe one's husband. But if one did, if one hated "it," how far was that from hating him?

7

From the bluff northwest of Lake Pontchartrain one saw the bronze shimmer of the great muddy river as it moved slowly toward the Gulf.

"Get out of the carriage. We'll walk the rest of the way," Eugene said. "I want you to see the view."

The light was green; moved by a wish to see its shimmer on her hand, Miriam turned her palm up into it. The light was tender, a veil on the waving corn, and beyond to a line of sweet gum trees, and beyond to a low rising hill, and beyond . . . To walk there, to keep on walking in an unswerving line through the corn, past elm and hickory, up the hill, to keep on walking, keep going—

"You're not even looking at the house," Eugene said.

Obediently, she turned. There it stood, much as it had been described, perhaps even more imposing than she had imagined. Its brick was rosy. Twenty-two Doric columns upheld the gallery. On the left lay a long camellia garden. The oleander hedges were a mass of pink.

"Beautiful," she said, adding, since one was expected to produce more than a single word of praise, "Beau Jardin. It's well named."

"That beech is a treasure. A hundred fifty years old.

Unfortunately it hides one wing of the house. What's behind it are the garçonnière and a schoolroom. I had that built last year."

And as Miriam had no comment, he continued smoothly. "Over there is the pigeon house. You should find that pleasing, with your love for animals. That's a wine house and that's a smokehouse. Behind the kitchen wing are the stables, the cabins, and the sugar house. But you'll have time enough to see it all after you've rested."

She stood quite still. Where the live oaks were hung with moss, where the ground was sandy, that must be the way to the bayou. There, some afternoon, if you were lucky, you might see a heron feeding in the brackish water.

"Come. Why are you standing there?"

"I was only listening to the silence."

"Silence? But the servants are waiting to be introduced. Come, will you?"

Entering the house, coming from outdoors, she blinked into the dimness. In a blur she saw a two-storied hall, a spiral staircase, black-and-white marble squares, black faces, white teeth, and a bust of Homer on a pedestal. Beau Jardin.

In the heat everything sagged. The curtains were limp and the crystal pendants on the chandelier were cloudy.

"Ah, but it's lovely, lovely." Emma sighed.

"Nothing to compare with the Labouisse place," Eugene responded, choosing to assume modesty. "I've only eight hundred acres here, and fifty hands. But that's all I want. There are so many problems—floods and plant diseases and freezes. Anyway, I'm not a planter at heart. Tell them about our visit to the Valcour Aime plantation, Mrs. Mendes. *There's* some-

thing to see if you want splendor." And as Miriam
hesitated, he continued almost impatiently, "It's mod-
eled after Versailles, but of course you know that. The
parterres, the gardens, the furnishings, everything's
French. My wife doesn't like it."

Miriam said quietly, "Why are you surprised?
You've known I was not intended for grandeur."

"Well," said Emma, glancing uncertainly from one
to the other, "I should think Beau Jardin was grand
enough for anyone. You're a fortunate young woman,
my dear, to be mistress of this place at your age. But
I'm sure you realize it."

She was being wistful, Miriam knew, about Pelagie,
who would not become mistress of her home until the
death of her father-in-law.

"Yes," Ferdinand added, "it's a blessing to see one's
child so happy. The happiness I see in your face is
worth everything to me. The most wonderful time in a
woman's life," he finished, making a tactful oblique
reference to her pregnant state.

The happiness in her face! Blind! Blind! She could
scorn her father's insensitivity and at the same time
pity it; but he had been diminished in her eyes; she had
been diminished in her own eyes. There he sat, unsee-
ing, accepting service from the platter which had been
borne in by the *siffleur,* the pathetic boy who must
whistle all the way in from the kitchen wing to prove
that he was not sampling the food. Behind him another small boy waved a fly brush made of peacock's
feathers. In the pleasant stirring of the air Ferdinand
smiled his contentment. Through his greed he had beguiled his daughter, tempted and coaxed her, using
Emma, willing Emma, to aid with motherly advice.

Then Miriam straightened in the chair, stiffening
her spine.

I despise self-pity.

And blaming someone else for your own folly.

Well, then, stop doing it! You betrayed yourself! Why do you blame your father and Emma and Pelagie and even Rosa and even Fanny? True, they persuaded you, but the fact is, you were yourself beguiled by the dignity of the Mendes name, by the house and the garden, and being the first of your age to be married.

How could you have demeaned yourself so?

Yet people everywhere spoke as though it were the most natural thing in the world for a young woman to desire a proud name and a fine house, and for a young woman's family to seek them for her. So Ferdinand, like a thousand other fathers, had only meant the best for his daughter. It was simply the way things were.

Eugene had warned her against snakes in the bayou area and alligators coming up on the grass at night. The first time she had ever seen him at Pelagie's christening party he had warned her.

And then one night Gretel did not return to the house. Fanny and Miriam went calling round and round the lawns until long after dark, when Eugene, becoming impatient, ordered them to come back.

"I'll sleep on the verandah," Fanny whispered, "so I can let her in. She'll come, she can't have gone far."

She had not gone far. She had gone just to the sandy grove near the bayou, perhaps to flush a red squirrel or on some other errand of importance. In the morning Blaise told Fanny.

"No, don't go, Miss Miriam, don't go," Fanny cried. But Miriam had already gone to follow Blaise, and so she came upon the little tragedy.

It was a horrifying sight. The alligator, surprised somehow before he had completed his atrocious deed, had left the remains of Gretel on the path: a part of the tiny body and some blowing tufts of white-blond hair. There was scarcely enough to weep over, only enough to retch over. And Miriam, after that first look, fled sick and weeping behind a tree.

Shuddering and cold in the heat, she stood with her hands covering her face. She had a flash of recollection: She was on the ship and the trembling wet puppy was placed in her hands; the boy Gabriel had such a tender look on his face—the recollection vanished. She was standing on the lawn with Fanny, Blaise, and Eugene staring at her.

Eugene had followed from the house.

"Take it away, Blaise," he commanded.

"Right away, right away." Blaise turned to Miriam. "Is there any special place you'd like for me . . ." And on the dark face there was a look of extraordinary gentleness.

"Come, now," Eugene said, "it's too bad, and I'm sorry, but let's not go into mourning. Spare me, please. I'll get another dog for you, and that will be that."

As if a dog were a *thing!*

"Don't look so glum," he admonished. "You have other things to think about now anyway."

Her hands went to her stomach, its swelling bulge hidden under the circling skirts.

Fanny had told her how after a while she would feel the new life moving. Her thoughts went then from life to death, to violent death, as if the dog's death were an omen.

Lately she had been thinking of her mother and of her own birth; she could then feel, actually feel, a thrust of pain, even while she knew these thoughts were morbid and unreasonable.

But fear went with her, nevertheless. A looming ghost, it came with darkness. Early in the night, as if on signal, the trill and throb of insects gave sudden way to a foreboding silence. After a while the wind rose, flying and soughing through the Scotch pines on the bayou path where the wet black alligator with the hideous snake-head would be slithering after prey. An owl screeched. The owl's screech is a death sign, Fanny used to say. The house stood abandoned to the night.

Who would tell what lurked beyond the bolted doors? Every night, after everyone was asleep, Eugene bolted the heavy doors.

Often Miriam thought about what lay outside those doors. Much that she had seen on the plantation troubled her. She had looked into the quarters where, on the littered floors, children crawled among fowl and their droppings, while dogs and sheltering hogs rooted under the shacks. She had seen the families taking their evening meal on their doorsteps, eating out of a common iron pot with their fingers or a piece of wood. Friendly voices greeted, "Evening, missis." They were friendlier than the overseer, a sullen Yankee who lived with his family at the far end of the line of shacks. Strange that he never smiled, while those whom he ruled from his tall post on horseback could smile.

"He steals from the master," Fanny told Miriam. "Everybody knows he does."

He got a bonus for every bale of cotton over the fixed quota, and he worked the people hard. Everyone over the age of ten labored from the rising of the sun to its setting. Even children, before they were old enough to cut cane or to pick cotton fast enough to make their three or four hundred pounds a day, worked carrying water to the fields.

So Eugene kept a gun and pistols in the cupboard next to the bed. Eugene, she could have told him while she lay awake, listening to every creak and whisper, Eugene, neither the doors nor the guns will help if they want to get in. She could almost hear the snap-

ping flames whir as they rushed up the chimney and
devoured the stairs.

But there were worse fears. The rounded bulk of
Eugene's back made a deeper darkness in the dark
space of the bed. Her eyes, stretched wide, fixed themselves on the man's sleeping back. A whole life. A
whole life, like this.

He was not satisfied with her. And why should he
be? She could not love him. He wanted what she could
not give. He wanted a wife to please him in return for
his name and his support; that was only what any man
would want. A woman was supposed to please, and to
act pleased, whether she was or not. That, too, was
part of the unspoken bargain.

But I can't do it, she thought; something in me can't
do it. And she felt pity for him because he gave fairly
to the bond called marriage while she did not. They
were strangers to each other, although he would never
undermine his dignity by admitting that he knew they
were, or that she loathed him.

Only in company did his laughter ring. All the long
summer, by carriage and steamer, the guests came and
went, whole families of them, to stay for a day, a week,
or longer. Early in the morning before they clattered
away on horseback to the hunt, the men breakfasted
downstairs. Still in bed, for pregnancy gave her an
excuse to avoid whatever she wanted to avoid, Miriam
could hear them talking over their potted meats, their
salmon and prawns, their claret and sugared brandy.

In the evening after dinner she could excuse herself
again and go upstairs; a pregnant woman was supposed to be delicate. But she was not delicate; her
body tingled with energy. Her feet moved to the sound
of violins, to the mazurkas and quadrilles being
danced below. It was only the spirit, weighted down,
that did not move.

Her mind drifted. To walk downstairs and out of the door! To throw off all these cumbersome skirts, to stride away like some countrywoman in her shift, her cotton or linsey-woolsey with a hole for the head, her cool garments so poor and still so graceful! Yes, dressed like that, to walk and walk through the fields, past the sweet gum groves, up the hill, free, free—Her hand made an arc in the air, a falling gesture of resignation.

Romantic nonsense! Free, free, and over the hill to where?

Late, after she had fallen asleep, Eugene would come upstairs. She would awake to the rustle of his clothes and the creak of the bed when he climbed in; then he would turn and take her by her shoulders. Someday, she thought, someday it will happen. Something inside me that I am holding back will give way, and I shall pummel his back with my fists and scream.

Yet he meant her no harm. He had sought her out and wanted her. She was to mother his child. Would the child make a change? In him? Or in herself? She wanted to ask Pelagie, now pregnant with her sixth child, whether that was so. When Pelagie came to visit she would ask.

"I'm very unhappy, Pelagie," she said.

The blood flowed up Pelagie's white neck and tinged her earlobes.

"I hate it," Miriam whispered. "I dread it."

And she wanted to ask, Is there something wrong with me? Is there any way I can make it better? But Pelagie's hideous blush prevented her.

"If one wants children, it's the only way," Pelagie said. She had not once looked at Miriam. Her answer was no answer.

Pelagie's trailing, wispy hair had not yet been done

that morning. Her hair had gone dead. Her brightness
had flowed away, gone into the children. Thick and
swollen, how changed she was from that girl with the
sweet round face! All those children! All those months
of vomiting, for Pelagie was sick each time. Now, feeling Miriam's gaze, Pelagie looked up. The same sweet
smile came to her face. Uncomprehending and sweet.

"He's a generous husband, Miriam. You must think
of that. Your lovely house and this place. Think of all
the good things. I'm sure you'll learn to be happy,
dear. It's within yourself, you know."

So not even with Pelagie could she open her heart
and mind.

One rainy morning when Fanny brought breakfast,
Miriam saw that she had been crying. Fanny's emo-
tions had always reflected Miriam's joys or griefs,
never her own. This startling realization flashed
through Miriam's head.

"What is it, Fanny?"

The girl struggled. "It's Blaise. The master wants to
send him away."

"I don't believe it!"

"It's so. Master says there's no work for Blaise, not
enough for him to do. Blaise has been crying. We've
been together since we were born, Miss Miriam."
Fanny swept her apron up to hide her face.

"Where does he want to send him?"

"To some friend of his. I don't remember the
name." Fanny's voice was muffled under the apron.
"Somebody moving to Texas, he said. I don't know
where Texas is, but they say it's far."

Miriam got out of bed. "Bring me a dress, Fanny.
Hurry and do my hair fast. Where is Mr. Mendes?"

"In the library he was."

Miriam trembled. She had no idea how she would

do it, but she was certain on the instant of one thing: This was not going to happen to Fanny.

Eugene was reading letters at his desk. He looked up, annoyed at the interruption.

Miriam was still trembling. Nevertheless, she demanded, "What are you doing to Blaise?"

"Doing? Oh, my God, has that Fanny of yours gone crying to you? Don't tell me. I've been wrestling with his tears all morning."

"They have a right to their tears. Do you know what their life has been? What it was until they came to my father's house? Their father was—"

"Don't bother to tell me, please. I've heard these stories a hundred times. Misery, misery. I'm not responsible for their past miseries."

"You could help make up for them, though," she replied, surprising herself with the sharpness of her tone.

The black eyebrows slithered upward. To her further surprise, Eugene defended himself.

"What do you want of me? I treat my people well. You've never seen me lay a hand on anyone. True or not?"

"True, but—"

"But nothing. I'm not running a charity. If I have no use for a person, I have no use. And I'm not going to keep him on, feeding and clothing him, when he's not earning his keep."

"Surely you could find something for Blaise to do. Surely the food he eats isn't going to make us poor." The pain in Fanny's eyes drove her on; she felt Fanny's cause as though it were her own.

"You know they all exaggerate, don't you? When they don't lie, they exaggerate. They're all hysterical. Blaise will have a good home where he's going and Fanny will get over it. They won't die of the separation. They won't be the first brother and sister to be separated. Aren't you separated from your brother?"

"That's different, Mr. Mendes, and you know it is." This mention of David emboldened her further.

"If he were here, David would understand."

She had almost forgotten how, long ago, her brother had been fired by what had seemed an exaggerated anger. Now she remembered that fire.

"David would not do this to them," she said.

Eugene stood up. "Ah, so it's your brother, is it? You're turning out like him, are you?"

"What do you know about my brother? You've never even met him."

"No, but I've heard plenty," Eugene said grimly. "He and his loose-tongued kind don't know what they're talking about. Do you want blood to flow here? Do you want to see the house burned to the ground?"

"I don't understand you. All I asked is that you don't send Blaise away. That's all I ask. Is it so hard to do one simple kindness?"

"One so-called simple kindness after the other. Where's the money to come from? The way I feed my people—"

"Cornmeal, salt pork, and molasses."

"What should they eat, then? They eat what country people eat. Go see what a white farmer puts on his table! The poor are poor everywhere. Can we feed them all from our table?"

That was true: The poor were the poor, as they had been in the Europe that she still remembered. Here, though, the poor whites came to the door, not begging, but demanding. Under their poke bonnets the women's eyes were scornful and Eugene always gave.

"You know I do what I can," he said.

Sometimes when the farmers "got in the grass," when the weeds threatened to choke out the cotton plants, he sent them help to do their weeding and save the crop.

"You know I do what I can," he repeated, and she saw that he was agitated, that in some way she had reached him.

"Do you know how some other people treat their servants? No, I suppose you don't. Well, I'll tell you so you won't think I'm such a monster. Have you never heard of the iron collar? The head enclosed between three iron prongs so that the neck can't turn? Do you know that runaways have been tied naked to a tree and lashed? Or—"

"That's enough! Please."

"Well, then! I treat honorably, I trade honorably, and I don't need interference in my affairs."

She had caught a word. "You trade?"

"It's not my main business, certainly not. But once in a while if a gang should be sent down from Virginia, for instance, and I can make a quick turnover, I do. I've never dealt with smugglers or anything outside the law, and I can swear to that, which is more than some of your most respected families like your Aunt Emma's people can do."

She faltered. "But you're a Jew!"

"I am a southerner, of the South. My people have been in this country for two centuries. We old Spanish families helped to build it. Go to Charleston, to Savannah, and you'll see." He drew himself straight. "I shouldn't have allowed this discussion to go so far, and you should know a woman's place."

A woman's place! Once, perhaps more than once, during the courtship, he had admired her spirit, as on that fateful afternoon when, with Emma, she had been conducted through his house. Now all he expected of her was submission. Anger met shame and burned like fire in her throat.

Then she thought of Fanny's sorrowful eyes. She thought of Blaise, a young man weeping, standing here before the authority of this other man, and weeping. And suddenly she knew what she had to do.

She got down on her knees. When her voice came it was so faint that Eugene had to stoop to hear it.

"Please. I beg of you. Don't send Blaise away. He could . . ." She swallowed. "My time is almost here. If we have a boy you could give Blaise to him. He's a gentleman. He would be a good servant to bring up a boy."

"Get up, Mrs. Mendes, will you, for heaven's sake? Don't be dramatic." Eugene held his hand out to raise her, but she grasped the arm of the chair instead and pulled herself up.

He walked to the desk, turned over a paper, and coughed while she stood waiting.

"Well, to tell you the truth, I had not thought of that. You may be right. He would be ideal for a boy."

"You'll keep him, then? You'll tell them that?"

"I'll keep him only until we know about the child. If we have a son, then, yes, he may stay."

"Thank you, Mr. Mendes. Thank you."

So if it's a daughter, she thought, as she went upstairs, I shall simply have to think of something else. For the time being she had won.

Oh, she thought, I wish I did not know I would have to live out my life in this country, where things like this happen every day and the government allows them.

She was very, very tired, with a weariness and a confusion in the depths of her soul. Best not to think about anything more just now. Best just to close her mind and drift through the days.

Autumn, the season of russet leaves and the turkey hunt, approached. This year there was no cooling of the air; instead, the heat mounted, and in the city the Asiatic choleras appeared, adding to the annual horror of yellow fever. All who could and who had not already fled the city, did so now. But for some it was too late.

Eugene brought in a letter. "This just came by boat. It's from Rosa de Rivera—bad news. Henry's dead of the fever. They ought to have stayed longer in Saratoga. Very poor judgment."

A chill shook Miriam. This was her first experience with death. No one she knew had ever just disappeared, just vanished. Who would sit in Henry's chair at the long table? Kindly, quiet, self-effacing Henry! And poor Rosa! For all her lively, brisk importance, the real source of her strength had come from Henry.

"I shall have to find myself a new lawyer," Eugene said. "Too bad. He was honest and clever. Unfortunately, those don't always go together, either." He tapped the desktop, a habit he had when making a decision. "So. We won't go back as planned on the first of the month. You'll have to be confined here. We'll summon Dr. Roget. He bought a plantation upriver after he retired. Manufactures rum. But I daresay he hasn't forgotten how to deliver a baby."

She was enormous, unable to bend and button her strapped slippers.

Abby, the chambermaid, remarked darkly, "Might be you having twins, missus. I remember my Auntie Flo died birthing twins. Screamed two days and three nights before she died. It was awful, I stopped my ears. Those twins like to tore her in half before she died. You sees my Auntie Flo's boys running round here, two big healthy rascals."

Fanny was angry. "Don't listen to her, Miss Miriam. Didn't the butterfly sit on your arm yesterday? That's a good sign, always a good sign."

She wanted not to be afraid. When Pelagie came to visit, Miriam told her of the newspaper article about Queen Victoria, who had taken chloroform when her last child was born.

"They say it's miraculous. One feels no pain, nothing at all. I wish Dr. Roget knew something about it. No one here does."

Pelagie thought it was wrong. "It's not moral. It's against nature. You're supposed to feel pain. If you weren't supposed to, you wouldn't. Doesn't that make sense?"

No, it did not. How stupid to believe that whatever *is* must be right! Well, that was Pelagie. And yet, to be fair, Pelagie was not really stupid, she was merely unaccustomed to thinking for herself. It came down to that.

Anyway, it didn't befit Miriam to judge Pelagie's reasoning powers. She wasn't above some fuzzy, credulous thoughts of her own, like reading omens in nature's faces. After a gray week during which a melancholy rain dripped steadily from every tree and eave, suddenly one noon the sun pierced the clouds and gray brightened into silver. Not an hour afterward, as if the sunshine had been its herald, David's letter arrived.

> I'm coming home by the first ship that leaves for New Orleans. Now that I've finished and can sign myself "Doctor," I've made a decision that will surprise you and I hope make you happy. I'm coming back to stay.

"I can't imagine," Miriam cried, "what made him change his mind! Do you know it's eight years since we've seen him? Oh, Papa will be so glad! And he must already be on the way. But whatever made him change his mind? He was so against everything here."

"Apparently," Eugene said, "he has acquired some sense."

Immediately she was indignant. "He always had sense. You only know what you've been told about David." She began to worry. "I do hope now that Papa and he will finally get along. Perhaps I should talk to Papa and pave the way, so they'll start out right together."

"You're too sensitive for your own good. You can't take your family's business on your shoulders. They'll manage their own affairs. Besides," Eugene said, "in a few weeks now you'll have another responsibility."

Toward dawn of a foggy autumn morning Miriam's labor began. At first she thought it was the harsh call of crows that had awakened her. Then something twisted, rolling in her tautened belly, and she cried out. Fanny came running and Eugene sent Blaise for the doctor. So it started.

As the sun broke through the fog and mounted the sky, pain mounted with it. It came in spirals, rising and breaking. Closer and faster, faster and closer, the spirals rose. On the descent the rate was slower; she could see yellow stripes of sunlight across the ceiling and her own arm lying weakly on the sheet. Then came the rise again, and the world reduced itself to the pit of the belly, where the battle was being fought. On the descent she saw herself as she was being seen: a shameful thing; above all she must not lose dignity; her cries must not be heard through the house or past the window. She rammed her fist into her mouth: I will not scream, I will not scream, I will bear it.

Eugene's face looked down at her. There were the

eyebrows, the black caterpillars. She screamed. "Get out! Leave me! Go! Get out!"

"She doesn't recognize you," Fanny whispered, apologizing.

They fastened a sheet to the bedpost, making a rope. "Pull! Pull!" Fanny urged. The bed creaked, the very wood complaining of Miriam's strength. Fanny wiped her slippery hands and her forehead. She touched softly, she spoke softly.

Fanny is saying something, but I don't understand the words. Things flash in and out. The doctor's eyes blink, he doesn't know what to do, that's the trouble, he doesn't know what to do. Oh, God, oh, terrible.

The sun goes around the house. It feels like evening. Water, she whispers. Her lips don't move, they're dry, they feel enormous. She feels Fanny's arm around her shoulders; she feels the chill in her mouth and swallows. Pain soars and lifts her high, high, higher, then throws her down. It won't ever end.

She opens her eyes into a blazing light. "Close the blinds," someone says, "the sun bothers her." So it must be morning again. It won't ever end.

She turns, turns on the pillow. At the side of the bed on the table there burns a *veilleuse;* the candle flickers inside the porcelain shape of a lady wearing a ballgown and a powdered wig. Silly lady! She doesn't know anything. But the candle burning? Then, it must be night again.

A man's voice says: Two days now. Is it the doctor's or Eugene's? It makes no difference.

Far off past the window there is a persistent rhythm, drumming and clacking. The man's voice—it must be Eugene's—cries: Tell them to stop that racket, this is no time for a racket.

"Rib bones," she says distinctly.

"She's raving."

No, no, not raving. Rib bones. Over in the quarters they make castanets out of rib bones. Leave them alone. Let them make music. Is she saying it or only thinking it?

Another spiral raises and flings her, crashes and smashes her, against a wall. And again. And again. How long?

The lamp throws a shadow on the ceiling. The shadow runs like water, racing as the candle is moved and is held high. It shines into her face, flickering, wavering, dancing, bobbing. A face looks down on hers, slips into the light and out of it. Eyes come into focus. She strains to see. Eyes in deep sockets, anxious eyes in a white elongated goblin's face, slipping in and out of shadow. David's face. Now I am raving, she thinks quite clearly.

Words come out of the face. "It's David, Miriam. I'm here."

She hears another voice—her own voice?—cracking, whispering denial. "No. Not you. Not really you."

"Yes, dear, yes. Really me. I'm going to help you."

Something passes in swift glimmer from hand to hand, some sharp metal thing. A knife? A sword? What are they going to do with it? She screams. The cords of her neck pull tight with the terror of her scream.

"Miriam. Lie back. Don't be afraid. Just close your eyes."

Something, a hand or a cloth, something light lies over her nose.

"Now breathe, dear. Breathe deeply. Don't be afraid."

A morning light, healthy and clean, washed the room. On white pillows, eased and delivered, Miriam rested. Two swaddled infants lay in twin baskets next to her bed.

"Beautiful, aren't they, David?"

"Very. A handsome pair."

"Eugene and Angelique. I so much wanted to name her Hannah, but Eugene wants Angelique after his mother."

Why not Hannah for my mother? The boy is named after you.

Hannah is an ugly name for a homely girl.

My mother was beautiful.

Aunt Emma said, There's no point arguing with your husband, Miriam. After all, these are his firstborn, he has a right.

His firstborn? Not mine?

Fanny is more clever. Give in, he'll make you miserable if you don't. A name's not worth it.

She had been firm about nursing, however.

"Eugene wanted to find wet-nurses to take back to the city with us next month," she told David now, "but I shall nurse my own. I told him so."

"Good for you," David said. "I'm proud of you."

"Tell me," she said softly, "tell me what happened yesterday. I can't remember anything, it's such a blur. I only know you came in time. I couldn't have lasted much longer."

He did not deny that. "I know. We've chloroform to thank. That's why I was able to use forceps. It's a miracle and a mercy."

"You've learned so much!" she marveled.

He shook his head. "We've a long way to go. This is only a beginning."

She studied his face. So long since she had seen him! And as much as she herself had changed, he had changed more. The fire in him seemed to have died away. He was calm and positive. Wearing spectacles, with deep parallel lines on his forehead and a new manner, he was almost sedate. She concluded that the life in New York and the weight of his profession must have done these things to him.

"You can't know how I have been hoping you would come!" she cried, almost tearfully.

"We had violent storms on the way, ran aground near Mobile. I felt like jumping off and pushing the ship, I was so impatient to get here." David's eyes were wet, too. "Anyway, here I am! And can you guess who's come with me? Gabriel. He's downstairs now."

"I thought he was going to practice law in Charleston."

"He was, but when his sister's husband died, he felt he had to come here to help rear her sons. A southern sense of duty, it seems."

"So he's going to stay and you are, too! I can't believe all this! But you know, Aunt Emma used to tell Papa you would come back, she was sure of it. What made you change your mind, David?"

He got up and stood by the bed, taking her hand between both of his.

"I'd been away from you far too long as it was. Whom else have I got but you?"

"And Papa," she corrected gently.

He smiled at the correction. "You first, always. But Papa, too."

The old worry flared. "You've been talking nicely to him, I hope?"

"Of course I have. Don't worry, everything's just fine. Does anger still upset you so? How it used to terrify you when you were a child!" David was silent for a minute. Then he reflected, "He's been such a generous father. I owe him so much for my education, a whole future opening for me. And for you, too, Miriam. A generous father."

"He gave me more pearls to celebrate his first grandchildren. Gray pearls. They're worth a fortune, Eugene says. He says Papa spends too much. Oh, but I still can't believe you've come home to stay, David! How you hated everything here! You said such things, you wrote—"

"Remember, I was very young when I quarreled with Papa. I'm older and wiser; at least I hope I'm wiser," he said humorously, and as quickly turned serious. "I've learned that I can't change the world, so I might as well get used to it the way it is."

Miriam said slowly, "That doesn't sound like you. And it seems so odd that you've made your peace with the world we have here at the very time I have turned against it."

"Have you really?"

"It's not that I ever actually *approved* before, you know. It's more that I just thought, when I thought at all, that there was nothing one could do about it. It was the way things were. But lately I've thought maybe there are things one could do, although I don't know exactly what."

David took off his glasses and rubbed his eyes. They looked tired. "There's never much that any one person can do. Events take their own course."

"Oh, you astound me, David! It seems to me that's an excuse for doing nothing! If I were a man I'm sure I'd think of something." She hesitated. "It's true that people like Papa and Emma are very kind to their slaves, but still it is not *right* for them to have such power over other human beings, no matter how kind they are."

"It's risky to talk that way. You realize that, don't you?"

"Oh, I know that well enough. And to whom would I talk? Certainly not to Eugene. He belongs to a vigilance committee."

"Does he?"

"Yes, he and Sylvain. They're always at meetings in the city and upriver or downriver."

"Really! Well, people do what they want to do. . . . I'm much more interested in you, little sister. Not so little anymore, now that you're the mother of these two people." David regarded the sleeping infants, then turned to Miriam. "When I think of how you began life and I look at them here, and back at you—what a long, long way it's been! And to see you so well cared for, so happy! You are happy, aren't you, Miriam?"

A rush of words filled her throat and stopped behind closed lips.

Oh, my God, David, I have been so miserable . . . except for these babies, everything has gone wrong . . . a thousand times I've wanted to tell you, but I couldn't put it on paper, I wouldn't have known where to begin or how to explain, and I can't even now. . . . I am so full of sadness.

She said steadily, "Yes, yes, I've a good life, as you see."

"Oh, I'm so glad for you, so glad!"

And if I were to tell you now, there would be nothing you or anyone could do about it. . . .

Now she assumed an air of gaiety. "Well, but tell me about yourself. You're almost twenty-five! When are you going to be married?"

He gave an equally lively reply. "Who would have me?"

"Don't be silly. I'm serious."

"All right, I'll be serious, too. A wife wouldn't fit in with what I intend to do with my life."

"What do you mean?"

"I can't please a woman. I'm restless. I want to work, I'm not domestic, and I wouldn't have enough time to give to a wife and a house and babies."

Eugene was standing at the door. "You'll change your mind. Bright eyes, a head of hair, and a narrow waist will change it."

"I don't think so," David said.

"So, be that as it may, what do you think of my son?" Eugene inquired with a show of simple cordiality.

"A strong fellow. He certainly fought his way into the world."

"Look at his fists," Eugene boasted.

"You don't look at Angelique," Miriam said.

"Of course, of course I do. I've been going over some affairs with your friend Carvalho," he told David. "I may let him do my legal work now that his brother-in-law is dead."

"I'm sure you'll have no reason to regret your choice," David said formally.

"I could go to the top, to Pierre Soulé or Judah Benjamin. Carvalho's very young, but he's impressive, and he knows both languages as well as anyone does, which of course is essential if one is to practice in New Orleans."

"More important, he's honorable."

"Certainly. A southern gentleman. Besides, as a beginner, his fees will undoubtedly be lower." Eugene laughed. "There's always something to be said for that."

David acknowledged that there was.

"Come, join us downstairs. The house is filling up with relatives, mostly Emma's from upriver. And the steamer's just landed a while ago with a load of Madeira and pale ale, fresh from England. Come have a drink."

"David," called Miriam, as they left the room, "remember me to Gabriel. Be sure to tell him I'm still grateful to him for rescuing my brother and my poor Gretel."

"Oh, that dog!" Eugene said. "Came to a terrible end."

"Gretel grew up with Miriam," David reminded him.

"Well, now she has a new son to think about. And a daughter. Come on down."

"How wonderful for you to have your brother again!" exclaimed Fanny, coming in with a tray.

"Oh, yes, I'm glad. To think I'll be able to see him whenever I want to! And yet, I don't know why, I have a feeling that something's not right, that some sort of trouble is waiting."

"Don't you know what that is? Women are sad after birthing, that's all it is. Lasts a few days and passes. Now eat your lunch. Get your strength back. You've been through a hard, hard time."

Sometimes Fanny said foolish things about witches flying over the treetops and such nonsense, yet she also had a lot of plain, good common sense. Eat your lunch and get your strength back. Obediently, Miriam ate the pudding.

The babies stirred, waking each other with small grunting noises. They were hungry again, causing the mother's breasts to tighten with a rush of milk. And she lay there watching the pink waving fists. These two new people were her own! The world must go its way; above all she must care for them. Vague intentions flitted through her mind: that the boy might have gentleness with his strength, that the girl might have strength with her gentleness—and that her life might be different from her mother's.

8

From the tiny courtyard of the house on St. Peter Street, one could look back through tall French windows into the office and the room beyond. The office contained a desk, a shelf of books, and a cabinet with medical supplies: dental instruments, pill containers, and amputation saws. The second room was almost bare of furnishings.

Gabriel's hand, holding a coffee cup, paused in mid-air. "Surely you're not going to leave the place like this? You've been here for months and it looks as though you'd moved in this morning or were about to move out."

"I've all I need. A bed, a table, a couple of chairs, and some bookshelves. What else do people want?"

"Well, let's see. People want carpets, curtains, sofas, pictures, mirrors, many things."

"You sound like my sister. Miriam is constantly after me to 'fix up.'"

"Eugene tells me your father can't understand why you won't let him set you up in a proper office. In short, you puzzle him. You puzzle us all, my friend."

"I do?"

"You know you do. I still haven't fathomed your change of heart. When we were in New York, you used to talk as if we were all poisonous snakes down here. You'd never go back, you said. You even used to talk about bringing Miriam up North."

"I was sixteen when I said that and she was all of nine," David answered evasively.

Something was being held back, Gabriel thought. Since long before they had both left the North, he had sensed something vaguely secretive under his friend's familiar manner. Troubled and anxious now, he waited. Dust motes hovered in a bar of sunshine to settle in a fine soft film on the floor and on his shoes. And David's eyes, cast down, also seemed to be following the dust motes. Suddenly he spoke.

"I came back to change things."

"To change things!"

"Yes. What use am I sitting up North and talking my heart out about the southern system? Talk is easy. Enough steam comes out of talk to drive a thousand machines. So it came to me that I must act instead."

"And how do you plan to act?"

David understood that his friend's calmness was only on the surface. So he said reassuringly, "Don't worry. I won't get anyone into trouble. You can depend on that."

"What about getting yourself into trouble?"

"I'll certainly try not to. But sometimes you have to stand up for what you believe in. Does that sound too noble?" He paused. "I just heard my own voice and I'm afraid it had a pompous ring. But I can't help it, I'm only speaking the truth." Lines of strain and agitation marked David's face.

"You're deluding yourself, you know. You can't change things, David. You are David, remember? They're Goliath."

"Ah, but David slew Goliath. Remember?"

"Well, all right. It was a poor comparison. But listen," Gabriel said earnestly. "Remember when we were boys on the *Mirabelle* and we were in Bordeaux. There were rows of abandoned mansions and warehouses falling apart, all the grandeur and riches rotted away. Why? Because the slave trade had been outlawed. You will see the same here, David. Mark my words. It's only a matter of time and patience. But the time's not yet."

"And it won't be for another century if it's allowed to go at its own pace. The system's too profitable. The cotton gin has increased the value of cotton a hundred times over. The steam engine and the sugar mills have doubled the value of Louisiana's plantations. The upper South produces far more slaves than it needs to work the soil, while down here, and in Texas, where we're expanding, we keep needing more slaves. Why, a trader can double his investment in a matter of days by buying in Virginia and selling in Louisiana! I read a study of that when I was in New York. I have the figures somewhere here to show you."

"So you want to hurry things up? How? With a bloody war? You've got to be out of your head if you want that."

"There's a fascinating book," David said. "I've got it here, hidden away, of course. It's called *The Partisan Leader*, about southern states founding their own government and the war that results. Terrifying, and maybe accurate, God only knows. I'll lend it to you if you want."

"No, thank you, I don't want. And so you're going to be a partisan leader, is that it?"

David nodded. He sat up straighter in the chair.

"Then you are out of your head. You're mad."

"I know. You said that before." David's smile was almost affectionate.

A young Negro man shook a broom out of the kitchen door and closed the door again.

When the door had closed, Gabriel warned, "Servants talk. I hope you know enough at least to keep a good rein on your tongue."

"Lucien won't talk. We're on the same side. He helps me. That's why I hired him."

"Hired him!"

"Yes, he's a free Negro. I pay him wages. Did you think I would own a slave?" And again David's eyes flashed.

A fever is burning in him, Gabriel thought. He asked cautiously, "Does anyone else know about this?"

"If anyone did, do you think I would betray him?"

"You answer all my questions with questions," Gabriel said with some exasperation.

The other laughed. "Don't they always say that's a Jewish habit?"

"David, I'm very serious. Have you ever hinted at this business to your sister?"

"Of course I haven't. Do you honestly believe I would put Miriam in danger? The person who means more to me than the rest of the world put together?"

"Questions again! I can only say I should hope you wouldn't. There are people in that family who would —I can't think what they would do!"

"Believe me, I know that, Gabriel."

"They called a special grand jury here only a few years ago to investigate the abolitionist movement. Sylvain Labouisse was on it. They recommended a permanent military force to protect against an uprising. Sylvain's in that, too. Oh, you're playing with a terrible fire, David!"

"I understand that." David spoke gravely.

"Let me tell you something else. Your own brother-in-law, Eugene—I betray no confidence when I tell you this, because it's a matter of public knowledge—is the head of a vigilance committee to combat sedition. He's a man of great influence, make no mistake. He's already a power in the Democratic party."

"They sicken me, all of them! You can't know how they sicken me!" And David's mouth puckered in disgust.

Gabriel sighed. "I know. But we're not all evil men here in the South, remember that, David. When I was in England I saw more suffering than you will ever see here. Hunger and rags in those cold tenements. . . . And in Massachusetts, all the young village girls in the mills—"

"An accurate description, I've no doubt, but still irrelevant," David interrupted.

"You can't deny we're making progress, either. Take Dyson's school for free Negroes—"

"What do you know about Dyson?"

There was an edge of sharpness in the question that surprised Gabriel. He answered, "Why, nothing that everyone doesn't know! It's a fine thing for a white man to be doing. You see," he explained earnestly, "we are getting somewhere, but it has to be gradual, you can't just turn everything around overnight. Take your own servant—"

"Yes, take him! He had to *buy* his freedom! And even now he can't vote or sit where he wants in a theater! Lucien Bonnet, decent, intelligent—"

Gabriel threw up his hand. "Wait! I'm not arguing, I agree with you. I'm only saying, you're in too much of a hurry, it won't work."

There was nothing new in all this. Too often David had heard these apologies. Time was all you needed before these wrongs would right themselves. Why, not so long ago people in New York City had owned slaves! Why, in Virginia fifteen or twenty years ago even the *Richmond Enquirer* was writing articles in favor of emancipation! And what happened? The abolitionists came in, stirred up all kinds of fury, caused the Nat Turner insurrection, and there you were, with everything set back God knows how long, just because outsiders were in too much of a hurry.

Yes, he had heard all that before, and now was silent.

"So that's not the way," Gabriel said. "Oh, it's easy enough for the North to condemn! Slaves don't fit into the industrial economy! It's easy for Garrison and his ilk to demand an immediate end to the system in the South, but how to do it without ruining the economy here and creating chaos? The slaughter could be terrible, when you whip up passions among the ignorant! You of all people, with your family's history, must understand what mobs are capable of doing."

"I do understand."

"Well, then! Only a few years ago they were plotting slave rebellions in Madison and Carroll parishes. Fortunately, they were found out in time."

"Rebellion is not my intention, Gabriel. Education is. Reasonable, political organization—"

"But it won't stop at that! You'll have clandestine meetings, you'll be found out, there will be terrible punishment, then violent retribution, and it will all come to nothing in the end. No, David, there is no way except to work slowly and patiently within the law. Time and the law will do it."

"Spoken like a lawyer."

"Well, I am a lawyer."

Abruptly David moved on to another subject. "Where are you off to this afternoon?"

Gabriel accepted with grace. "A committee meeting with Gershom Kursheedt. We've come along very well with our new congregation—the Dispersed of Judah, it's to be called. We're going back from the German rite to the Portuguese."

"Too aristocratic to mingle with Germans? Sorry, nothing personal." David smiled.

"Of course it would be ideal if we were all the same. But we're not. All people like to keep their familiar ways, that's all. Especially now that the antisemitic laws in Europe are bringing in so many Germans. However, I must tell you," Gabriel said enthusiastically, "Kursheedt has been doing wonders with Judah Touro. He's got him to subscribe a lot of money for the synagogue and other charities. No one can figure out how he's done it, unless it's a question of timing. Touro's getting old and afraid to die."

"There you are! The power of persuasion toward the right. Isn't that what I've just been talking about today?"

"Not quite, David. Not quite."

Now it was Gabriel who moved away from the subject. "Kursheedt is a sort of disciple of Isaac Leeser's. Now, there's a great man, Leeser. A prolific writer. You ought to read his *Occident and American Jewish Advocate*. It comes out every month, tells you what's going on in Jewish life around the country. He keeps it up even though it loses money regularly. However, he's a bachelor with few wants."

"Like me. A bachelor with few wants."

"David, I came by this afternoon to ask you whether you'd want to work with us in Jewish charities. There are so many committees that need workers. But I can't recruit you if you're going to get mixed up in that other business. You understand?"

"Perfectly. Your meaning's quite clear." David's tone was unmistakably bitter. "I'm not welcome."

"Don't be bitter about it. Would you want to drag others down? Your sister, for instance?"

"I told you a while ago that I wouldn't, didn't I? Yet, I can't help but think: How fortunate for the southern Jew that the Negro exists! He takes the brunt of prejudice away, and now the Jew is freely accepted in the best society."

"That's not fair, David."

"It is fair. Oh, I'll grant there may be some excuse for people like you who've been born into the system and grown up in it, but for those of us from Europe who ought to know better, there can be no excuse."

"We are only doing what the rest of society is doing. We are people like everyone else. We're not all as noble as the prophets."

"We're the People of the Covenant. A greater sense of justice is required of us. Examine our history—"

Gabriel rose to leave. "I haven't made your deep analysis," he said with slight stiffness.

David went with him through the house to the street. "Don't be angry with me. Must we think alike on everything to be friends?"

"No, not at all. I'm not angry, either, only distressed. Take care of yourself, David."

For a few minutes David stood in the doorway watching Gabriel go down the street. Salt of the earth, he thought. Steady. You could trust him with all you had or ever hoped to have. A fine mind, a scholar, with deep warmth beneath the austerity. But slow, too slow, not a man to accomplish things. More's the pity. He sighed.

The afternoon's talk had tired him. He was too tired of late, but it was no wonder. Talk of burning candles at both ends! All the organizing, the planning, and the tension of utmost secrecy, while keeping all the time a "normal exterior," which meant a minimal social life for the world to see.

Often he wished that the social life might be more

than minimal, that he might allow himself more than a
dance or casual chat with one of the delightful girls
who were so eager to welcome the young doctor, the
son of Ferdinand Raphael. And he smiled to himself,
with a certain wistfulness, this "eligible young man"
who was not really eligible at all: Marriage to him
must eventually bring cruel disaster to any young
daughter of the South. So, in all decency, he must keep
his distance and, when any young woman seemed to
be especially charming, must be careful to stay away.

He was wearying beneath many pressures. The
practice had grown rapidly. It had begun one night
when a midwife who had somehow or other heard his
name had appealed for help with a hard delivery. And
he had gone down to the Irish Channel, stumbling
over goats and drunks, and in a shanty behind the
slaughterhouse brought a life into the world. What
stench, what misery! In the North he had heard the
diatribes of the Know-Nothing party and seen signs on
shop doors: NO IRISH WANTED HERE. They were condemned for being shiftless and unclean. When people
were ground down they were blamed for every plague,
as were the Jews in Europe.

Never, never did he see cruelty of any kind without
thinking of his mother. And David burned with furious conviction. Things ought not—the world ought
not—people ought not— His anger choked him.

How was it possible that his father had no such
burning?

I try to understand. I do understand more clearly
than I could have when I was fifteen. He's had his
struggle and used up his ambition; now he wants only
to enjoy what he has. How glad he is to have his son
back! And inevitably I shall bring him pain again. I
shall be sorry when it happens.

He's a good man. No one could be more generous

than he with his overflowing house: Emma's Georgia relatives, flocking to new land in Louisiana, as the value of Sea Island cotton sank, all stayed first with the Raphaels. Her extravagant relatives from upriver, living the reckless life of wealth even when they had no wealth, spent their winters during the opera season at the Raphaels'. Such was Ferdinand's bounty.

David turned back into the house. Lucien, cooking the plain supper, sang. Of course, this frugal house, this single servant, baffled Ferdinand. He wanted his son to live well. He wanted his son to make a splendid marriage with the daughter of a powerful family.

At least his daughter had done so. Only a few nights ago David had dreamed of Miriam, such a strange dream, jumbled with some recollection of a deer. Last fall at Beau Jardin Eugene had shot one, a soft fawn-colored thing. He'd flung it down on the grass where it lay with its eyes wide open, sightless before the bright day and the bright woods in which it had been running with the wind when it was brought down. Miriam had turned away and Eugene had been annoyed with her. All that had been in his dream.

She was so charming, his little sister! Her babies were walking now, holding her skirts for support. They made a portrait, delicate as ivory with their pale silks and their heavy black silk hair. He could still remember Miriam in drab wool, cold and shivering in the stony kitchen on the Judengasse. He supposed she had forgotten most of that, for she had been so young.

It saddened him that he had been away from her for so long. He felt that he hardly knew her. And he wished he could like her husband better. He wished he could be sure that Miriam was content with Eugene. He wondered whether he imagined sorrow in her face; sometimes it seemed as though a gray veil had been drawn across it. And it came to him suddenly that

never, in all the quiet family evenings, at the dinner
table, or with the children in the parlor, had he heard
a word, or seen a touch, a glance, a laugh, between the
husband and wife that reflected any tenderness, any
bond. Perhaps it was only their way? And yet he began to wonder. The man was so unlike Miriam. He
talked business; he talked money. Even when he didn't
speak the word, money was what he was talking
about. When he spoke of the war with Mexico and of
high democratic principles, he was really speaking
about more land for cotton culture.

David had learned not to dispute these things at
anybody's table. It was important that he not be iden-
tified as a radical or "different." His manner of living
was already different enough. He must not be a
breaker of idols. Small eccentricities were permissible,
perhaps even, to a degree, interesting. But in essence
he must seem to fit into the society.

"Lucien," he called, "when you're finished in the
kitchen, will you see that my suit's presentable?"

He was off to the St. Charles Theater with some
colleagues that evening to see Edwin Booth. Get tickets for Joe Jefferson's performance the week after next,
he reminded himself. You're a young doctor on the
way up, you know, a trifle odd, but very pleasant.
"Lives like a monk," he'd overheard someone say recently about him. It had been said without malice,
only with a certain kindly amusement.

An instant's fear now darted in his chest. Had he
said too much to Gabriel this afternoon? No, no,
Gabriel was an honorable man, there was nothing to
fear. He must be more discreet in the future, nevertheless.

Gabriel Carvalho was troubled. He tried, as he
walked along the street, to recall the exact wording of

his conversation with David. Had he pointed out that even the most peaceable discussion, the most peaceable meeting, was dangerous? But surely David must know that! One couldn't live here without having some understanding of the way things were. So then, knowing all that, David was determined to go ahead. In essence, of course, he was right; the end was right, but one had also to consider the means, the cost of reaching that end. You could say that a man like David was still a boy, high-minded but thoroughly impractical, whose efforts would prove futile, if not fatal. Or you could say that he was one of those who throughout history had moved the world forward, sacrificing themselves very often in the process.

And with a tinge of regret he thought, Perhaps I am one of the too cautious ones, seeing what is right but counting the cost of achieving it as too high and the way too difficult, while we wait for others to do it. David sees to the essence of things. I see the complexities.

He was half aware of the opinion people had of him: that he was prudent, "lawyerish," and deliberate; that, in a word, he lacked spark. Some, he was aware, even thought he was chilly or snobbish; these appellations hurt, since he knew he was neither. He was reserved and had been since childhood, holding his emotion in restraint because, once having let go, he knew he would display too much. His head must keep control of a wild heart, perhaps even a wilder heart than David's.

Abruptly his mind went back to the voyage of the *Mirabelle,* so long ago. He had been in Europe twice since then, once for a summer in Scotland and once for a trip down the Rhine, but that voyage of the *Mirabelle* was more vivid in his memory than either of those other times. For it was then that he had found

and made the closest friend he had yet had. In spite of
all differences of background, of temperament, and
often of conviction, the admiration and the trust remained, so that each truly cared what happened to the
other. It was a rare thing, this caring, not to be explained, he supposed, any more than one could explain
the love between woman and man.

Again to the *Mirabelle;* to David, foundering, terrified, in the trough of the waves; to the dog's piteous
bobbing head; to the crying, grateful child. He had
quite forgotten that child, but now, however seldom
he saw her on some social occasion, that picture kept
recurring. The contrast between this recollection of
her and what she now was had come to seem incredibly strange, which was actually foolish of him, since it
was only natural, after all, that a child should become
a woman, a married woman with children.

Biblical phrases came to his mind: cedars of Leba-
non, the green bay tree. Supple as a young tree she
stood, with her creamy shoulders and her waist emerging from the absurd concealing bell of her skirts so
that one could only imagine the body beneath them.

He stopped himself. To linger over thoughts like
these! She was another man's wife—his client's wife.

One respected Eugene Mendes. Intelligent and
forceful, secure in his achievements, he commanded
respect. Yet something in his gaze made it an effort to
meet that gaze. Perhaps it was your feeling that he was
taking your measure, calculating your deficits and
strengths.

He seemed a strange choice for Miriam Raphael! It
did not seem as if those two could be united. Were not
a man and woman supposed to become as one? And
he thought again of the wistfulness about her lips. Unlike other women at a dinner table, who were so avid
of attention, she often sat removed in some gentle

dream, as though she were expecting something, or even as though she were not there at all. And yet once, passing the Mendes's garden wall, he had heard delightful laughter, gay as bells, and peering in, had been astonished to see that the laughter was hers. She had been playing with her children, throwing a ball. Her hair had come loose; her hat had come off and the little boy was wearing it, a huge white straw with blue ribbons.

An alligator killed the dog, he remembered suddenly. Why not replace it? And it seemed that the dog had been a link between them, as if his rescue of it had been a portent of—of what? A portent of nothing, he thought impatiently, becoming annoyed with himself. She's my friend's sister. A thoughtful gesture from me to her would be acceptable and pleasing. Had he not bought a doll a while ago for the child of a friend, to replace the one she had left out in the rain? So, he would order a puppy from New York; one of the men in the office where he had worked raised King Charles spaniels. He could have it sent safely by ship. And he imagined her face when he put the dog in her arms. She would blush pink with pleasure, he thought, recalling how easily she blushed, and how her smile bloomed.

It was perfectly proper, a simple gift to a friend.

Turning the corner into the Place d'Armes, Gabriel was jolted back to the present by the proud blare of a brass band. A crowd was gathering in the square, where among tents and flags, a regiment had formed into marching order. After a quick glance he passed through the square. The Mexican War was popular, especially in the South. I have no stomach for it, Gabriel thought, as the band's blare faded from his ears, no stomach at all. Oh, probably it's not "manly" to think that way. Yet on the Sabbath one prays: *Grant us peace, O Lord, thy most precious gift.* Nothing is simple. There are so many sides to everything. As one turns the prism, the purest light reflects now from here, and then from there; as one turns, turns . . . Anyway, I have responsibilities and couldn't volunteer even if I were wild to go.

Rosa was still tearful in black and jet beads. Always she had appeared to dominate Henry, but now that he was gone, it was plain that she had depended on him. He had not left a great deal of money, and understandably, she wanted to stay with her children in their comfortable house. So Gabriel must now contribute. Fortunately, his prospects were good. He had a new office in the Banks Arcade, a prime location. He had, for a start, a list of clients inherited from Henry, mostly prosperous up-and-coming men like Eugene Mendes.

I shouldn't like to be his enemy, he thought unexpectedly. And he hastened his steps to get ahead of the band, which had caught up with him.

Miriam, on her way home from the French Market with Fanny, caught the last of the trooping flags and drums as they swept out of sight and hearing. Silence flowed back. The side streets were empty except for the milk wagon clattering its brass-bound cans and the old Negro with the ice cream freezer on his head crying: *"Crème à la glace! Crème à la glace!"*

"Look," said Miriam, "isn't that Mr. Mendes leaving that house?"

"I can't tell from here, Miss Miriam."

"But surely it is, in his new maroon coat."

The maroon coat hurried down the street and disappeared at the corner. A moment later a woman came out of the house and waited for a carriage that was just emerging from the carriage house in the alley.

Miriam and Fanny came abreast as the carriage drew up to let the woman enter it. She was a magnificent quadroon. Strong daylight glittered on gold chains, twining in her hair, on pearl tassels and gold leather slippers. A coal-black servant followed her, carrying a basket like that which Fanny was carrying for Miriam.

The young woman's frankly curious eyes met Miriam's for just an instant; then, lowering her eyes at once, she stepped into the carriage and drove away.

"Who was that, Fanny?"

"Why, Miss Miriam, you know. One of those. I don't like to say," Fanny said primly.

"Of course I know *what* she is. I meant, she recognized me."

"How could she ever know a lady like you, Miss Miriam?" Now Fanny was shrill.

"But she did," Miriam insisted. "I even felt for a second that she was about to speak to me."

"She wouldn't dare! She wouldn't dare talk to a white lady. Queen's far too smart for that."

"Queen? Is that her name? And, Fanny, that was Mr. Mendes. They came out of the house together. You saw it as well as I did."

"I don't know what I saw, Miss Miriam. Please don't ask me what I saw," Fanny pleaded.

"You're trembling, for heaven's sake! Don't drop the basket or you'll have those berries all over the street. Now, Fanny, tell me, what are you keeping back?"

"Nothing, Miss Miriam. I swear I'm not."

"I don't believe you. Listen here, Fanny, did I save Blaise for you? We've grown up together. You owe me something in return."

"Miss Miriam," Fanny said desperately. She panted, keeping up with Miriam's hurried steps. "Listen, if I do know anything, it's nothing that'll do you any good. Nothing you'll be happier knowing."

"Let's not talk about doing me good. I don't want to be made a fool of, that's all. I have a right to know what's happening."

Fanny was silent and Miriam said gently, "I know you're scared to talk. So I'll talk and you'll just nod your head if I'm right and shake it if I'm wrong. Mr. Mendes and that—that Queen. He goes there all the time?"

Fanny nodded. Her frightened eyes were wet.

"And he has been going there. He and she have been—together a long time?"

"I don't know how long, Miss Miriam, I swear I don't. I only know what I hear. I didn't tell you anything, did I? You aren't going to tell Mr. Eugene that I told you anything, are you? He'll beat me."

"He won't do that, Fanny. He has never beaten anyone, you know that perfectly well. And I wouldn't let him even if he wanted to."

"But he'd send me away," Fanny wailed.

"I wouldn't allow that, either."

"But you're not gonna tell him?"

"No. Go wash your face. Take the basket to the kitchen and wash your face. I'll just sit here in the garden awhile."

The fountain goddess, goddess of love, stood in her marble calm above the double cascade. On the wall plaque opposite the bench where Miriam sat, the name of the young wife who was buried there had been obscured by the droop of the trumpet vine.

Had the girl Aimée been sick with strife and doubting as I am? Or had she known from the beginning where she was going?

Miriam frowned. What was she really feeling at this moment? She tried to get outside herself, to see herself as an observer might. Chiefly then, it was pride that she saw. But why should she mind? Why care? In fact, she ought even to be grateful to that woman for taking care of Eugene's needs. Rarely now, when he came in late to find her asleep, did he wake her as he had when they were away at Beau Jardin.

Liaisons of this sort were common. No girl, however sheltered, could have lived in this city without knowing about them. The weekly quadroon balls at the Washington Ballroom were freely advertised. The girls were so beautiful that often the white balls emptied out early and everyone knew that the young men were bound next for the Washington and its beautiful quadroons. Everyone knew, although no one talked except Rosa, blunt, chatty Rosa.

"Oh, those women are very well brought up," she had told Miriam. "You'd be surprised! A man never touches one before being accepted by her mother. Then he has to set the daughter and the mother up in a nice little house and take care of them. It's an expensive hobby. He has to promise to support the children, too, should there be any. But," she added soberly, "sometimes it really is a case of love and these girls are faithful. Lots of men keep right on seeing the mistress even after making a good marriage."

So that's what it was. Fanny knew and had known. Without a doubt all the servants had. She wondered whether Rosa had. She didn't want to know whether Rosa had. She didn't want to be angry at Rosa.

Presently Eugene's rapid heavy steps sounded from the gallery. The front door opened and closed. A moment later voices came from the open windows upstairs. He had gone to the children's rooms, where they would just now be waking from their naps. He would go there first to toss the boy into the air, to make mock fists and pretend to pummel him; the boy

would squeal, laughing with excitement over his father's lavish love; his round hot cheeks would go red
and his eyes would flash. Then the father would clasp
him, ruffling his hair. To Angelique, Eugene brought
proper tribute; a white lace dress, a French bisque doll,
or a chain with a gold heart; but to his boy he gave his
own heart.

Now Eugene came down to the garden. He regarded
Miriam curiously. "What are you doing here?"

"Thinking," she answered, flinging the word like a
stone.

"Well," he said dryly, "that's always a worthy occu-
pation. Of what are you thinking, may I ask?"

"Of why you pretended you didn't see me a little
while ago."

"See you? Where should I have seen you?"

"You ran around the corner of Chartres Street.
Please don't say you didn't. I can't abide a liar."

"I beg your pardon!" Eugene said furiously.

Miriam stood up. Her pulsebeat was loud in her
ears. "I know why you were there. I know about
Queen."

His eyebrows, those eyebrows that she hated, slid
upward. Black caterpillars.

"Where did you hear that name?"

"Does it matter? I heard it."

"I can't stomach a liar, either, I'm warning you."

"I shan't lie. I simply don't intend to tell you."

"Was it Fanny? It was Fanny, wasn't it? No?
Lucetta? Blaise? Some meddling snooper from your
father's house? That miserable pair, Maxim and
Chanute?"

"It makes no difference, I tell you. They all knew it.
Everyone did except me."

Eugene had removed his gloves; she saw that his

hands were trembling. He looked past her to the drowsing dove at the feet of the little goddess.

"Well," he said after a minute, "since you know what you know, you might as well hear the rest." He met Miriam's eyes. His own, so severe and sharp whenever he turned them to her, now had a tender shine. "I have—there is—a child. A son. My other son. He's seven years old."

She needed moments to comprehend the words. Seven years. So it had been going on that long. At the time of their marriage and long before that. Another child, another boy, not hers. Here was a bewilderment of possibilities. She was aware of them standing there like two people who had just met, who knew nothing about each other.

"Then why did you marry me?" she whispered. "Surely not for money or position. You have ten times more than I have of either one."

"I wanted a son who could be recognized as mine. A boy with my name who would be educated here and have a future in this city. That's what I wanted."

Now she began to feel. Tears stung in back of her eyes. She was furious with her stupid tears.

"Oh!" she cried. "I know I was ignorant when I married you, ignorant as no girl ought to be and as we all are, but now I think I was mad besides! To marry a man who didn't even want me, who wanted—a brood mare!"

"No, you're wrong. I wanted much more than that. I wouldn't have asked you if I hadn't intended to make it work. I wanted a refined and beautiful young wife to give me a son and make a family. What is unnatural about that? But you didn't give it a chance."

She could not deny it.

"At first I thought I understood. A modest young girl, I thought. It will take a little time. But the time never came. Of course a man doesn't expect his wife to be like—well, a wife is a lady, after all, and the man knows that. But you! You're ice. You're as cold as that statue. What is it? Am I dirty? I ask myself. No, I am not. What, then? Ugly? It's not generally thought so. Coarse, then? I don't believe I am. Why do you despise me? Why do you find me disgusting? Because you do, and you can't deny it." He waited for her answer.

She could only answer miserably and with reluctance, "I don't know." How tell him: I can't bear your slightest touch, my teeth clench when you come near me.

"If there had been the least response from you, if you had—well, what's the use? I might have ended that other affair. I probably would have. But as it was . . ."

Never could she have imagined Eugene Mendes as a supplicant; it was never his way to ask, only to require. Now he stood before her, this foremost citizen in his velvet waistcoat with his hands still trembling as they held his buckskin gloves.

"Why?" he repeated. "Tell me. What's wrong with me?"

She looked down at the grass, at Eugene's feet on the grass. His fine London shoes were covered in dust. There was something pathetic about them. Everything was very still. A locust drilled abruptly, and as abruptly cut itself off. She had not thought of Eugene before as a human being who could be hurt; it was always he who did the hurting. But of course he had been wounded in the very core of his manhood. To be rejected even by a woman one didn't love must make a man doubt himself, even when there was another woman waiting with wide-open arms. She remembered the flash of those black, startled eyes and all the golden glitter.

But it was nobody's fault. She saw that suddenly and clearly. It was only a fact that he repelled her, a thing that had happened, like having a taste for gooseberries or an aversion to milk.

"Why?" Eugene insisted.

Her mouth was dry with fear. It was like standing on a cliff; since one could not go forward and certainly not backward, there remained only to go to the right or the left, but where those ways led one didn't know.

She faltered, "I suppose it's just that some people don't suit each other. I tried. I did try."

"Perhaps," Eugene said, "someone else would suit you better, then? Gabriel Carvalho, perhaps? He can't take his eyes away from you. Would he suit you better, do you think?"

She slapped him. Without thought, without conscious will, her hand came up and stung his cheek. The scorn on his face changed to a furious astonishment. Terrified at what she had done, she stepped back. He grasped her wrists and they stood there staring, ready to strike.

"Because you have a trollop, you think that I must be doing what you—"

"I take it back. You haven't life enough in you!"

"My God, how I hate you!" she cried.

"Lower your voice. Keep your dignity if you can."

"Oh, you're the right one, aren't you, to speak of dignity!"

"I am. I have done nothing that other men in my position don't do. I told you, if you had been a proper wife to me, I would have done differently. But whether I did or not, a proper wife would know how to keep out of her husband's concerns."

"Then, I am not a proper wife!"

"You are not a wife at all."

"But she—that woman—she is."

Eugene released her hands. "Yes," he said simply, "yes. She is."

On the other side of the wall a vendor passed, calling, "Strawberries! Fresh and nice, nice and fresh!" The sound of his drawl will stay in my ears, Miriam thought. Such moments mark a life: that sleepy voice, the powdery hot dust and the scent of Eugene's eau de cologne—these will remain.

She thought of something else. "You should not have said that about Gabriel Carvalho. It was wicked and untrue."

"Perhaps I should not. Yes, you're right, I should not. He's a decent gentleman. And you're the mother of my children, the mistress of my house. Let us remember it. Let us live here in decency."

"In decency," she said.

"Do what is expected of you and I shall never touch you again. You have my pledge of that. Do you understand?"

"Yes."

"You needn't worry. I don't even want you anymore."

For a moment they waited as if they did not know what came next. Then Eugene said, "I'm sorry. I'm really sorry."

"We're tied together in such falsehood. Tied." She turned her palms up in a hopeless gesture. "Forever, do you realize that?"

He nodded. And there being nothing more to say, he turned about and went back into the house.

Late that evening Miriam was still out on the balcony. A heavy rain swept through the trees and dripped from the roof, splashing her dress and her hair. In the smoky light of the streetlamp at the corner she could see Blaise and the stack of wooden boxes with which he took people dry-shod across the flooded street. She wondered whether he was saving his earnings to buy his freedom. And it occurred to her how odd it was that Blaise had some possibility of freedom, whereas she had none.

"Miss Miriam," Fanny called. "I been looking for you everyplace. What you doing out there in this rain? Aren't you ever coming in?"

Miriam's dress had gone limp and her hair had been torn about by the wind. Emma always said a lady should never allow anyone to see her looking less than her best. What would Emma have to say about Queen?

"Oh, it's the way men are," she would say. Miriam could hear her voice, slightly embarrassed and slightly superior. "Men are like that, my dear. But a wife should never let on that she knows. It wouldn't do any good, only make him angry. Best to look the other way. And if he treats you well, what difference does it make?"

Yes, certainly Emma would say that. So would Pelagie. And Rosa, so totally different from either of those two, would very likely say it also.

Why do I care? I have no reason to care what Eugene does. And the answer came: because he is free to take what he wants from life, while you are not. That's why.

Impatiently she tore at her buttons.

"You're ruining your dress! Here, let me," Fanny cried.

"I don't care. It's ruined anyway." Wet petticoats dropped to the floor. "Fanny, tell me. You can talk truly to me now. Mr. Mendes has told me everything. The boy, Queen's boy, have you ever seen him? Tell me the truth. I won't be angry."

Fanny picked up the petticoats.

"Yes, miss, I know her boy. He looks like Queen, maybe lighter than Queen."

Then he must be a handsome child. And now Miriam felt a thrust of jealousy, not for herself, God knew, but on behalf of her own little Eugene, whose father's love must surely be divided between him and that other son. At the same time she knew this was not rational.

She thought out loud, repeating herself. "Then, he must be a handsome child."

"Yes. Smart, too." Relieved from secrecy and fear, Fanny now rushed to tell her what she knew.

"Queen belonged to Mr. Mendes's family. She some kind of cousin, I think. Then he freed her, but not the boy. He still owns the boy."

To "own" one's child! It was all so queer and strange! The silence, when Fanny stopped talking, thrummed and drummed in Miriam's head. The candlelight threw distorted goblin figures and mocking faces on the wall; the walls pressed themselves in and began to spin. . . .

"He crazy about that boy," Fanny resumed. "Ashamed, too." She sighed. "But that's the way it always is. Nothing new about that."

She must pull herself together, keep hold. Things must not fly apart; the solid house must shelter her children, no matter what it cost; she must keep herself sane, must—

"I know something you could do," Fanny said suddenly.

"Do? What do you mean?"

"I could get you a black candle. If you want to hurt somebody, you know, like hurting Queen or"—she came closer to Miriam, whispering—"or Mr. Eugene, you write the name on a piece of paper and pin it on the candle. When the candle burns all the way down, the person will have awful sickness and pain."

This foolishness broke the spell and Miriam righted herself.

"Come! You don't believe such nonsense! You're too smart for that."

Ashamed, Fanny laughed. "Well, you're right, I guess. Still, sometimes I'm not so sure. I've seen things. Shall I get you some tea? Laurel-leaf tea for stomachache?"

"Just plain tea. It's not my stomach that aches."

"Not your heart, either."

"No. What is it, then?"

"Your head is thinking what you're going to do all your life."

"You're right. That's what my head is thinking."

There was such a fluttering within her that she had to move. She went to the window. Thunder, moving westward, still rolled. By the weak light of the street-lamp she saw that Blaise had left, having found, no doubt, that there were not enough customers tonight to make it worth his while to stand in the rain. Eugene, as always, would come home by carriage.

She lit a candle and went to her desk, where a little stack of notices and invitations waited to be answered. Leafing through them, she read: the Society for the Visiting of the Sick; a wedding announcement; a birthday dinner for one of Emma's more distant cousins; a meeting of the Hebrew Benevolent Society for the Relief of the Aged. The annual ball was to be next month and every fashionable member of the Jewish community would be there. She would need a new dress. Things collapsed, but nevertheless one needed a dress.

Gabriel Carvalho was one of the officers. *He can't take his eyes away from you,* Eugene had said. She didn't believe it. Certainly she had never noticed. To begin with, he seldom spoke to her directly and then only to mention something about their long-ago voyage, or about the dog, or else some polite comment about how the children were growing. He was—well, stiff. Yes, that was the word, stiff. People who acted like that were often supposed to be shy. Yet how could a man as successful as Gabriel was be shy? True, he never talked very much, even among the men; it was always David or Eugene who had so much to say, Eugene commanding and David enthusiastic. But then, they always turned to him for the final say, didn't they? It was really puzzling, when you thought about it.

But she had no wish to think about it. For whatever the reason, Gabriel was aloof, so let him be so! Rosa thought he was handsome. Naturally. He was her brother. Well, perhaps he was. He had fine, thoughtful eyes, an austere expression. But what Eugene had said today was untrue. He had even admitted that it was untrue. Unconsciously, Miriam made a pretty shrug as she straightened the papers and prepared for bed.

But she did not sleep. She moved to the very edge of the bed, thankful that it was a wide bed, since Eugene, for appearances' sake, would surely sleep beside her until the end of their days.

It was so cruel! A useless woman till the end of those days! Two children she had, and now no more. In two more years they would be in school and would not need her to read stories to them, or go on morning walks. Indeed, they scarcely needed her now; their nurses did almost everything for them, anyway. Often she liked to send the nurses out and give them their baths herself; it moved her heart to see how tall and firm they were, how Angelique, young as she was, had already begun to show the graceful indentation at the waist which is so feminine, while Eugene was so compact and square. His sister was voluble, her talk a string of questions: *Why must we? Who was that lady? Where are those people going?* Eugene could amuse himself for hours. He had a tower of blocks in his room as high as his waist. *It will reach the moon,* he said.

And soon all this will be over; they will grow up and go away. Then what would be left for their mother? To spend her life making wax flowers to put in glass bells or embroidering dresses for other women's babies?

And her thoughts went to Eulalie, busy with christening clothes, exquisite as bridal veils; to the feeble body and the eyes so filled with misery even when she wore the "social smile" that was expected of her. Yes, Miriam thought, there is little you could tell Eulalie about suffering. One did not like Eulalie; a Jew especially could not like a person who in his heart despised a Jew; yet one could understand her.

Who am I? Mrs. Eugene Mendes. What is she? What does she do? If I had a talent, a voice maybe, like that girl Marie Claire, I know what I'd do. She wants to go abroad to study, but her mother won't let her, Rosa says. I'd find a way. I'd go. If I had a talent, I would, but I don't know anything.

It's not right! Men can learn. They earn money and dispense it as they please. We have to ask for it. A man can preach chastity while he keeps a mistress. He can do whatever he wants.

I could hate men, but I don't want to. I want to love one man. I want a reason to love him. I've been asking for that ever since I was old enough to know the meaning of the word.

Maybe I still don't know the meaning of the word.

9

It was late autumn, but still very warm in the courtyard at the Raphael house, where preparations for an
elaborate party were almost complete. True to his
promise to "look after" his late partner's daughter,
Ferdinand was giving a dance in honor of Marie
Claire's engagement to André Perrin of Natchez.

"It is remarkable, Mama says," Pelagie observed,
"that he will marry her with such a small dowry.
You've never met him?"

Miriam answered carelessly, "No, but Eugene has.
They've had some business dealings, I believe."

"He's quite handsome. Wait till you see."

There was a cheerful bustle under the piazza where
they were standing. Sisyphus was setting the great silver coffee urns in place, these being his special responsibility and pride; Chanute and Maxim carried in the
last of the potted hydrangeas. Paper lanterns trembled
in a mild breeze, and the orchestra, tuning, made the
expectant sound that said that the curtain would
shortly rise. Except for the absence of a bridal canopy,
it was exactly like Miriam's wedding scene. Having no
wish to recall that scene, she turned away to inquire of
Pelagie where Marie Claire might be.

"In the guest bedroom with Mama. They're all flus-
ered. Some of the ruching came loose on her skirt and

her own mother didn't even notice it. Mama did, of course. You can trust her," Pelagie said pridefully, "to be efficient about every last detail, can't you? She really has put a great deal of effort into this party."

"It's been two years since I saw Marie Claire."

"I haven't seen her in a while, either, except for the week she spent at our place last summer. This has been a quick romance. Only three weeks."

"Really? Is she very happy?"

"Oh, she never shows how she feels. I sometimes think she doesn't feel much at all unless she's at the piano singing. She accompanies herself, you know."

Miriam remembered a long, sober face. In spite of having seen it so seldom, it rose clearly before her eyes. And with it once more came a strange sensation that their lives would in some way cross.

"She certainly ought to be happy now," Pelagie resumed. "André's charming. He's of a good family. His mother's Jewish and his father's French. They've plenty of money, too." And she repeated, "It really is remarkable that he's marrying her with so little. Of course your father is being generous as always. He's bought her silver and all sorts of nice extravagant things."

Miriam heard herself quoting Eugene. "My father can be too extravagant."

"You know, I'll tell you something, but don't dare repeat it. Marie Claire told me that this was her only chance to get to Europe to study voice. André has business there for at least a year. Do you suppose she would marry him just for that?"

"I don't know. I do remember feeling that there was something desperate about her."

"Desperate? She thinks too much of having a great career."

"Her voice is marvelous, Pelagie."

"Not as marvelous as having the right husband. She wants to study with Manuel García in Paris. She thinks she has a voice like Jenny Lind's."

"Maybe she has. How will she find out if she doesn't try?"

"It all sounds very grand, I'm sure, but for myself I wouldn't change with a hundred Jenny Linds. It always seems to me that each of my babies is more miraculous than the last. My little Louie is already sitting up! And you should see how wonderful Felicité is with him, with all the little ones. Can you believe she's twelve years old? Such a good-natured child, a little mother already. In a few years, just think, she will be a real mother. Oh, you've brought the children! They're so sweet, Miriam. I think twins are so sweet."

The twins had appeared in the courtyard to stare at the musicians until Fanny should lead them away. Pink and clean, with their well-kept hair and starched sleeves, they belonged in a picture book.

All I have in the world, Miriam thought fiercely, her eyes stretching as if to encompass and devour them.

"Yes, Papa wanted to see them," she answered, "so we're letting them stay up late. He likes to show off his first grandchildren."

"First? Are you—?"

"No," Miriam said shortly. "I'm not."

"But, Miriam, the twins are already three."

"I know they are."

Dear Pelagie could be so exasperating! When Sylvain had bought a city house for the winter season, Miriam had been so glad, but sometimes she felt overwhelmed by Pelagie's platitudes and hovering, kindly presence.

"I've a headache," she said abruptly. "I think I'll go

to the yellow guestroom to lie down for a few minutes."

Instead of lying down she confronted herself in the mirror. Earlier that day she had cried again. Now two pink spots glared on her cheekbones and there was a glaze on her eyelids which even the ice that Fanny had brought could not entirely dispel. A fleck of sawdust from the ice still clung to her sleeve. She could not remember why she had cried.

When Eugene was in a mood, he made no effort to conceal it. He spoke to her with contempt.

"The soup at dinner last night wasn't fit to eat. Can you not supervise your servants any better than that?"

She had made a dignified resolve not to let his words touch her.

"Speak up! I can't hear when you mumble, especially with that German accent."

She tried to keep herself immune, removed and above him, so that her response to these attacks was to make no response. Unfortunately, she was not always able to control her eyes, which could brim on the instant to overflowing while she kept lips and forehead steady.

"Oh, my God, crying again!" he would say. "Tears, tears, the woman's weapon."

If only she did not have to share a room with him! If only there were one place in that large house to which a woman might go and be alone with herself! Only in the morning after Eugene had left for the day could she be certain of a time alone, pretending to sleep so that even Fanny would not disturb her until she rang. And she would lie there watching the pink light creep across the floor, thinking about nothing and everything.

Now he knocked on the door. He was irritable. He had been looking for her.

"Come. What are you doing in here? Your father's asking for you. Turn around. Yes, the dress is good enough. The color suits you for once, puts color in your face. Can you manage a smile? There are important people here, the cream of the city's business."

"I'm coming," she said softly. Her voice sounded to her ears like a sigh. But then it seemed to her that wives' voices often did. She had begun to notice such things. Even Pelagie, who was so much in love with Sylvain, seemed to speak in a tone of submission. And she followed Eugene's tall broadcloth back downstairs.

The hall was filling, as if everyone were arriving at once. It was like looking down into a kaleidoscope in which buttons and pins and scraps of bright cloth can be made to whirl into fantastic shapes. Across the hall a dozen candles, casting a ruby glow, had turned the red room into a jewel box. Around the piano Ferdinand's chosen string quartet had grouped itself to play and sing the old French folk songs, familiar to the house.

Ferdinand kissed his daughter. "Come, you've not met Marie Claire's fiancé. This is André Perrin. My daughter, Mrs. Mendes. You're acquainted with her husband."

Perrin bowed. "Yes, certainly. A brilliant man, Mrs. Mendes."

She saw first the top of a head of strong fair hair, then a lively, frank young face with laugh lines radiating from the eyes.

Emma came bustling from the dining room, where she had been inspecting tables.

"André! Where's your bride? I've been looking for her. Ah, there she is! Marie Claire, how are you, my dear? But you look adorable"—as though she had not herself been upstairs only a few minutes before attending to the girl's dress.

Marie Claire gave her earnest smile. She had not changed. Her tight curls were still the color of pale sand and she wore an unbecoming dress of the same dull color. She is so plain, Miriam thought with sudden pity, and he's so flashing.

The engaged pair was drawn away and the party began to split into groups. Old ladies, the married and the widowed, collected around the buffet tables. Why were old people so hungry? Miriam stood outside herself observing. When I was young, she thought, four years ago when I was young, I was inside things; now I am outside watching. There's Sylvain, being chivalrous with Eulalie on his arm. There's Pelagie's Felicité with budding breasts and long, still-childish hair. Eugene has disappeared to seek the most important of the important people who are here this evening.

She stood alone in the swarm. Then it occurred to her to look for David. She saw him too seldom. But a physician's hours were full. She understood, but wished there could be some long private times with him, uninterrupted; then perhaps she might talk to him about herself, talk as she could to no one else. And sometimes she fantasized about the two of them, taking the children and running away, running north to free air, released from every burden, every obligation. . . . Fantasy, indeed!

She found him in the small library, sitting over a carafe of wine with Gabriel and Rosa, who was at ease in the company of cigars and men.

"Come sit with us," David said. "We are having a friendly argument about the future of Judaism."

"I'm only saying," Gabriel explained, "that so many of the petty laws and superstitions of the Orthodox are not original elements of the faith. In the last three thousand years there have been more years when we didn't live in ghettos than when we did."

David took up the argument. "Yes, and the years when we lived in ghettos and observed what you call those superstitions and petty laws were the very years when we held on to our highest moral standards. The world around us was beset with bloody wars, but in the orthodoxy of the ghetto there was peace."

"You sentimentalize that life, David. These are different times. I would rather remember the free learned Jews of Spain than the imprisoned Jew of the Polish ghetto, in spite of all his piety and virtue."

"Perhaps," Rosa said, "if you had ever seen our services in Charleston, David, you would—"

"I know about them. You've simply thrown out the very structure that for centuries has held the family and the whole people together. That's what you've done."

"Not at all—" Gabriel began, and was interrupted by Ferdinand, who, carrying a drink, stopped at their table.

"What? What kind of a conversation is this? Young people, you ought to be dancing. You're all too serious."

"Oh," David said lightly, "I'm sure there are plenty of conversations about the stock market going on in the house right this minute. Isn't that serious, too, Papa? Or horse racing at Metairie? You can lose a fortune there, and surely losing money is a serious matter!"

"Or poker, or faro. Yes, yes, you're right," Ferdinand replied, only half hearing. And he progressed to the next group, doing his duty as a host.

A moment later Eugene came into the room. By the speed of his walk it was evident that he was on a search. When he saw them, he stopped.

"I'm looking for Judge Ballantine. I daresay he hasn't come yet. You look very comfortable here."

"We are. Please join us," Gabriel said.

Can he really like Eugene? Miriam wondered as Eugene sat down. And suddenly remembering *He cannot take his eyes from you,* she wanted to get up, but was imprisoned now between her husband and Gabriel Carvalho.

The latter now resumed the interrupted discussion. "Resistance to the new is understandable, of course. When Moses Mendelssohn translated the Torah into German, how the Orthodox attacked him! They forgot how sixteen centuries earlier the sages had translated it into Arabic and Greek. No, David, it is some measure of reform that will save Judaism for many who would otherwise abandon it."

"The way it's been saved here in New Orleans? What have you got? Shops open on the Sabbath, synagogues three quarters empty . . ."

"But we haven't modernized yet here. That's my point! What we have here is just a handful of Orthodox leaning a trifle in the direction of change. And the rest of the people are nothing at all."

"Like my father," David said.

"Don't be too hard on your father." Gabriel spoke quietly. "He has no choice here, as I've just said. And he won't accept the old ways anymore. The old ways remind men like him of Europe. What does he remember? Suffering and brutality. Humiliation and—"

David interrupted. "You're more tolerant than I."

If only David would learn not to interrupt so rudely, Miriam thought. Forgetting her embarrassment in his presence, she wanted to hear what Gabriel had to say.

"More tolerant of everything around you," David said emphatically.

Something compelled Miriam to speak. Part boldly, part shyly, her words came forth. Without looking directly at him, she was addressing Gabriel. "Things don't seem to have changed much since Josephus wrote. The problems were the same almost two thousand years ago."

"My wife is a reader," Eugene said.

He was angry that she had spoken. He himself was too prudent to offer an opinion on a controversial subject. One never knew which potentially useful person one might offend.

"There's my son," he said abruptly.

Children and nursemaids were passing through the hall. On seeing his father, little Eugene came running. The father took the boy on his lap.

"What's this, what's this on your arm?"

"It's a bee sting. Blaise put mud on it."

"A bee sting? This time of year? It happened just now?"

"It happened yesterday," Miriam said.

"You didn't tell me!"

"It didn't seem that important."

"Well, well, since it's all right—but I should be told." And, as if doubting the wholeness of the boy, Eugene carefully examined his face, his neck, and his fat knees.

For a moment conversation stopped. All were expected to give their attention to little Eugene. And he was a handsome child in his kilt, his badger sporran, and Glengarry bonnet with its sprig of heather, all à la mode. Eugene had ordered the outfit from Scotland.

"Soon you will be going to school," he said, dandling his son.

"You're sending him to France?" inquired Rosa.

"Oh, not yet, but when he's older, of course."

No, Miriam thought fiercely, you will not do that to

me. And although she knew the answer perfectly well, she pursued the question. "What about Angelique? Shall you send her to France, too?"

Eugene shrugged. "If you wish, but it's not essential."

She had not spoken to him so directly for a long time, if ever. But now she was driven by the sight of him holding her child, as if he alone were responsible for Eugene.

"Oh, I know it's thought that a woman needs no education," she said in a low, rapid voice. "Education will only make her discontented and unfit to keep a household! Yes, that's what's said." She stopped. It was no use.

Eugene put down the boy, who scurried away, then turned to David. "Tell me, is it from you that my wife gets these unusual tastes?"

"Not at all. Miriam has her own tastes."

"These discussions lead nowhere." Eugene stood up. His tone touched the edge of mockery, as if he were saying: What do ideas matter anyway? We all know they don't.

"Down with discussions, then," David said.

The group dispersed and Miriam found herself enclosed with Gabriel behind a wall of people.

"Your brother and I have our differences, as you see. I like to think they keep our friendship lively."

"Your differences are very small, I think. You don't disagree on principles. And they're really all that matter, aren't they?"

"Do come, they're making a toast!" someone cried, and Miriam was pushed forward in the general movement toward the dining room.

"So you have been reading Josephus," Gabriel said, hurrying beside her.

"Over my husband's objections."

He did not comment. Instead he asked gently, "How is the dog getting on?"

"Oh, he has got his land legs. You were so kind, I don't know whether I thanked you enough."

"You did," he said.

He had brought the dog, complete with a basket and blanket, one Sunday afternoon. Rosa had put a red bow on its head; the wobbling bow had fallen over one eye, so that the little thing had seemed to be winking. Miriam had laughed with delight.

"Gretel the Second! She's almost exactly the same! It's so good of you, Gabriel, such a beautiful surprise!"

"Very thoughtful," Eugene had added. "I daresay if you'd brought her a basket of diamonds she wouldn't have been as pleased."

And Gabriel had stood there on the verandah watching the event, saying no more, but watching as he was doing right now, with a gaze so intense, so serious, that in her confusion she could only pretend to fix the clasp of her bracelet, which did not need to be fixed.

Earnestly, as if to draw her attention away from the bracelet, he said, "I had planned to replace your Gretel as long ago as last winter. It took too many months to make the arrangements."

He can't take his eyes away from you, Eugene had said.

In the dining room a bald gentleman with raised glass was saying something about blessings on the young couple, on the friends, on the house, on everything.

Ferdinand spoke jovially into Miriam's ear. "You see what a brotherly spirit we have? All for one and one for all." He was not a drinking man and he had already had two glasses of champagne.

"This party must be costing a fortune," someone

remarked in Miriam's other ear. She recognized the voice of Sylvain, who was hidden behind a pair of broad shoulders. "It's rumored that Raphael's overextended himself most awfully. Of course, it may be only a rumor. I hope so for the sake of my mother-in-law." And as the broad shoulders moved away, he caught sight of Miriam. "Ah, Miriam, I want to introduce the bridegroom. You must meet André. Everyone admires him."

"I have met him," she objected, but had already been drawn away by Sylvain's arm to a group around another small table upon which a single supper plate had been laid. There sat old Lambert Labouisse, enthroned and erect; his expression under a crown of immaculate white hair was severely regal. A discussion of politics had apparently been going on around him.

"My son, Alexandre, is five years old," said Sylvain, at once joining in, "and I predict that he will grow up to fight in a war."

"Let us hope not," Gabriel answered soberly.

"In Congress they are already ranting about 'the sin of slavery,'" Sylvain continued. "John Slidell—a very good friend of mine—comes back from Washington with warnings of the sentiments in the Senate."

"Do you not think it's significant," asked the elder Labouisse, "that some of our most brilliant defenders in the Senate are not southern born? Slidell is from New York and, of course, Soulé is from France. Remarkable," he mused, and the others inclined their heads respectfully as though the old man had himself said something remarkable. "Soulé is coming here tonight, I've been told. I've not seen him yet. In my opinion this talk of war is exaggerated. Our civilization will not be undermined by a handful of fanatics," he concluded scornfully.

Startled, Miriam heard a whisper and turned to look into the face of André Perrin.

"Excuse me. Would I be depriving you of this discussion or might you like to dance?"

"I should like to dance," she said, rising.

Suddenly the talk had become too heavy. It was important talk, but she had had enough of it; guiltily she understood this was because she was too absorbed with herself.

"Such heavy talk on a night like this," said André Perrin as if she had spoken her thought aloud.

In the courtyard, where dancing couples were moving in concentric circles, he drew her into the outer one. At once they fell into step.

"I have just come back from the war in Mexico," he told her. "I don't want to hear any more threats of war. People think it's all parades and flags. But you enjoyed old Rough-and-Ready's victory parade, I hope? He was quite a sight, riding Old Whitey."

"Oh, yes, it was splendid."

"Your little boy was thrilled with it, anyway. You're wondering how I knew he was there? I saw you. Your girl was with you, too. They're twins, aren't they?"

"Yes, but they say forty thousand people were in the Place d'Armes. How could you have seen me?"

Perrin enjoyed her surprise. "Because when we stood at attention opposite the cathedral, I recognized Pelagie in the front row. You were next to her. You wore a gray velvet bonnet with a white plume. Your boy wanted to pull away from your hand and run with the soldiers. You had to hold him back."

"Incredible! What a memory you have."

"As a matter of fact, my memory is not all that good. But I remembered you."

He was not much taller than she, so that she could look almost directly into his face. His skin was ruddy brown from wind and sun. He was so close that she could see the blond roots of his eyelashes.

"You think I'm too bold, Mrs. Mendes? I don't mean to be."

"It's all right," she murmured. After a moment of awkward silence she could think of nothing better to add than "It was a stirring parade."

"It was a stirring war. All the way from Matamoros, where we landed, to Monterrey."

"But such terrible suffering! The heat and the flies—we kept reading the dispatches in the *Picayune.* Surely you must want to forget it all."

"I should like to." He laughed. "My mother won't let me, though. She has renamed our plantation 'Palo Alto,' after the battle in which I was almost wounded. She wants to think I was a hero, which I wasn't."

Miriam liked the way he could laugh at himself, liked the easy grace of the dance, liked the way she was feeling. Swaying and swinging, they drew an arabesque around the courtyard. The light played on his face whenever they passed beneath a lantern. His mouth was beautifully molded, and even when he was not smiling, the curve of the lips gave an effect of good humor. Like sunshine, she thought.

"Shall you be living at Palo Alto?" she asked, and remembered at once what Pelagie had said about going abroad.

"No, we're going to France for a while. But we're having a house built here in town for when we come back. It's in the Garden District with the Americans."

"So you're deserting us in the Vieux Carré!"

"Oh, we are all getting mixed up together these days. The old rivalry's dying, it's practically dead. Look at us here tonight. Everyone of us speaks both languages. The Creoles themselves are moving, spreading all over the city. It's a wonderful city. I shall love working here."

"You're an attorney?"

"A notary. Of course, we're all mixed up here between the Code Napoléon and the English common law. But you probably know all that already. Or else you aren't interested and don't want to know, for which I wouldn't blame you."

"But I am very interested," she said brightly, making her eyes larger and at the same time thinking, This is just common flirting.

The waltz crashed and whirled. Marie Claire flew past in the arms of the French consul.

"How happy she must be!" Miriam cried.

"Who must?"

"Why, your Marie Claire, of course."

"Dancing with the Frenchman? Oh, she is in love with France, with anything French."

"So you are to live in France."

"Only for a year or two. We shall be here first for a while, though, at the St. Charles Hotel."

The St. Charles Hotel. A suite with a balcony. Cream-colored roses, large as cabbages. A bed. White linens and a blue silk quilt. A bed. With this man.

His right hand lay between her shoulder blades, not pressing, but so firmly placed that its heat, even though the hand was encased in a kid glove, rippled down to the small of her back. She was not used to being touched that way, with such natural familiarity. It came to her mind that she had never been touched with any tenderness at all—not even as a small child. There had been no one to do it.

And now she was only aware of that hand as it moved an inch or two from side to side over her naked back. All the blood in her body seemed to be pouring into the place where that hand rested. She wanted him to move her nearer to himself, to obliterate the empty air between them. At the same time she was horrified by her desire. This total stranger! It was absolutely mad!

How queer it would be if a person were ever able to look through the flesh and the forehead's white bone to know what another was thinking! It would be like walking naked down the street, as sometimes one does in those frantic dreams where one seeks a place to hide and something with which to cover oneself.

All this time her feet were moving to the music.

He was saying something to her. He had pulled a little away, to see her more clearly. She thought she had heard his question, but was not sure, and he had to repeat it.

"Why are you so unhappy?"

The most burning tears came at once. Her lips quivered. He had seen through her skull.

"Don't look at me," she said. "Please don't, or I shall cry here in front of everyone. Please."

He was shocked. "Forgive me. Oh, my God, I don't know why I said that! Forgive me."

Like wheels revolving to a stop, the music slowed and Perrin danced them into the house. In a tall mirror she saw that he had indeed turned his head away. He understood, then, that when you stare at a woman's tears, you make them flow harder. He brought her to where Eugene was standing, thanked her, and moved quickly away.

I have made a fool of myself, she thought.

"So you were dancing with Perrin. Good. I want you to cultivate them," Eugene said. "Invite them often; they'll be living at a hotel for the next few months and they'll be glad to come. Marie Claire's a friend of yours anyway."

She said faintly, "We've never been close, I hardly know her."

"What difference does that make? It's a contact that I want to encourage. He has connections all over the country and in Europe. Everywhere."

Without knowing why, she was terribly afraid. Her control was ebbing. She had no hold on things, and she did not want to see André Perrin again.

By midnight the party was ending. Coachmen and footmen who had been playing marbles under the streetlamps now mounted the boxes and the carriages departed, leaving the quiet street under a murky sky.

"Let's walk," David said.

Gabriel fell in beside him. Sycamore leaves crackled dryly under their feet. There was a silence between them, carried over from the bickering of the early evening. When they passed the cathedral, soon to be rebuilt, Gabriel broke the silence.

"These distinctions between us mean very little in the end, David. It's the principles of the faith that matter." Saying so, Gabriel remembered that Miriam had used those very words only a few hours before.

"Principles! You talk of making changes in our form of worship, but you don't change the very society in which we live. All this piety, and still the leaders of our Jewish community, the honored and respected, own slaves!"

"I do not own slaves," Gabriel retorted.

"You live with your sister who does. And you are silent about it."

Gabriel said coldly, "I would advise more silence on your part. Right now, in fact."

As if to emphasize his meaning, a cat's poignant cry startled the midnight stillness.

"Excuse me. You're right," David said suddenly. "I

don't know why it is, but I always manage to turn the conversation around to the one thing that stands between us." He glanced at his friend, whose profile under the streetlamps stood out with the aquiline gravity of a face on an ancient coin. "The truth is, Gabriel, I'm irritable, I'm worried, I'm not feeling good about anything. My sister worries me terribly. She's miserable. You saw that tonight."

"I know."

David sighed. "A child, married off before she knows what living is all about, if one ever does know. Listen," he said, grasping Gabriel's elbow. "I shouldn't ask and I'm not asking for anything about your client that I've no right to know. But is there anything you can tell me about my brother-in-law that I should know?"

Gabriel considered. All he could say about Eugene Mendes was that he was hardworking and shrewd in business, that he paid his bills and was truthful in his dealings.

He said only, "Mendes will never do anything that doesn't befit his position in the community. He will follow the rules. He will maintain his house and family. He will be generous, but never extravagant." Gabriel gave up. "The truth is, I don't know anything more than you do."

And again he saw Miriam's Mideastern eyes, so passionate and mournful, eyes of Rebecca and Rachel, out of the biblical age.

"Have you ever thought," David asked suddenly, "that there is a kind of slavery for women, too? It seems to me it must be very hard to be a woman."

"Yes, I've thought so," Gabriel said.

They walked together as far as David's house, where they parted and Gabriel went on alone.

The fog, lifting, revealed a vast, mysterious oyster-colored sky. Over the flat, silent city loomed the dark cupola of Charity Hospital. He walked slowly, in no hurry to reach home. When he put the key in the front door, he sensed that his sister was not yet home. Always the last to leave, she would have lingered at the party. She had a need for close companionship, a need which was lacking in himself. He wondered whether among her intimacies she had learned very much about Miriam Mendes. Probably not. And again he saw before him those passionate, suffering, lambent eyes.

Enough of this, he said sternly to himself. For a moment he stood in the hall, staring at nothing, then shook himself as if he were trying to shake off a burden, and climbed the stairs.

10

She lies awake in the sultry night. She lies, as she always does, at the very edge of the huge bed. The vacant hollow between her husband and herself is symbolic, she thinks; they are now totally apart. Thus it is that he has not noticed what has been happening to her during these many months and, satisfied that her appearance and behavior are "correct," has looked no deeper. It comes to her mind that possibly something is really wrong with her, some poisoning of spirit, some seeping disease.

She is obsessed by André Perrin. He inhabits a permanent corner of her memory. His voice with its peculiar, slightly nasal timbre, repeats in her ear his most trivial phrases. Her eye recalls the blond hairs on his wrists, revealed by a too loose cuff. She remembers the kid-gloved hand on her back.

She reads a story to Angelique. Two plump, sleek curls dangle on either side of the child's face; the mother twists the curls, drawing the child closer to her side, thinking *How sweet she is.* In the same moment she is thinking of André Perrin. In the marketplace she feels the melons, gray cantaloupes, netted and veined in darker green; when the ends give under the fingers, the flesh will be juicy and rosy. In the same moment she is thinking of André Perrin.

She counts the times she has seen him since their first meeting: Five times he has come home with Eugene for two o'clock dinner; there have been eighteen parties here and at other people's houses; eight times they have met at the theater. Four times they have met on the street when he was walking with Marie Claire.

Isn't it disgraceful that he should fill her mind? She has no right to these thoughts! He belongs to Marie Claire! They lie together at night, he with the remote and dreary Marie Claire. They lie together; his hands move wherever they want to move upon her body. Their arms and their mouths move wherever they want to move.

In the same way Eugene must lie with his woman. He lies now breathing heavily into the darkness; his heavy shoulders twitch in a dream.

What if Eugene were dead? What if Marie Claire were dead? What might happen then? Miriam throws the sheet back; she is suffocating with the heat and with these terrible guilty thoughts.

Why are you so unhappy? he asked me. I might have answered: Because my husband is not like you.

What can you know of me? he might have asked me then.

And I should have answered: How can three bars of music tear the heart with sorrow? How can a slow gray rain infuse the heart with delight? You see, there is no reason for any of these things.

She does not want to be alone with him ever again. Suppose some thought forms on her lips and sounds itself against her will? And now a horror seizes her. Someday, surely, that will happen. She will put out her hand and touch his arm in a way that will tell everything, or else her voice in making some ordinary remark will betray her.

In her dining room she places him far from herself

at the end of the table. Yet perversely, whenever she knows they are to meet, she takes particular pains with her dress. For years she has forgotten to be vain; probably the last time she had delighted in herself was at her first appearance at the opera, when Emma had taught her how to flutter a fan. Yet last week, buying a white straw bonnet heavy with lilacs, she wished that he might see her wearing it.

Occasionally she has met his glance. She knows he must remember her tears. Perhaps he wonders why she cried, or perhaps he thinks only that she is a weak and foolish woman, a spoiled and silly woman who ought to know better.

After all, your husband does not beat you, he—or anyone—might say.

Your children sleep safely under the solid roof.

How many women would not gladly change places with you?

First light breaks through the blinds and lies in stripes across the floor, striking the basket in the corner where Gabriel Carvalho's dog lies still asleep, creeping across the marble tabletop where last night's pearls lie coiled, to strike her at last full in the face, with the glare of another day.

11

On the riverboat going upstream, David stood at the rail, sorting out his thoughts. More than ever it was his sister who troubled those thoughts.

The perversity of human affairs! That after all this time he had come back to the South, and now it was she who wanted to go north!

Only a few months before, she had told him about her fantasy—and fantasy it was—he thought now, ruefully. She had told him, on that mild winter night, so much that he had felt the burden of it ever since.

On the way home from a late call, he had passed the Mendes's darkened house and seen her sitting at a single light by the library window. He had stopped and mounted the steps.

"What are you doing up so late? And alone?" he'd asked.

"I couldn't sleep. So I came downstairs again, that's all."

Her face was turned away, deliberately; not wanting him to see it, she allowed her hair to swing across her cheek. But her hands were clenched in her lap.

"What is it? What's troubling you so that you can't sleep?" he asked.

"Nothing. Nothing. I'm all right."

"There's always a reason why a person can't sleep, you know."

"You're being a doctor," she murmured, still turned away.

"Yes, but also your brother."

Her shoulders shook; she was making an effort not to weep.

He hesitated. They might have had a simple quarrel, just a bad day; women were often oversensitive; what was a tragedy tonight could easily be forgotten in morning light and morning smiles; he might do better minding his own business.

Yet something made him persist.

"I wish you'd tell me, Miriam. How will I be able to go home and sleep while all sorts of thoughts about you go pounding in my head?"

For a minute or two she did not answer. A shutter swung and creaked in the night wind. Gretel, asleep on the carpet, whimpered in her dream, and was still. The silence was stifling. And suddenly Miriam broke it. She whirled up from the chair and flung out her arms.

"I want . . . I want . . ." She gasped. "I want to get out of here! I despise it! There is no freedom, not only for the Negroes, but for anyone! There is a line, drawn so"—she drew a line with her foot—"and so, and over it one dares not walk. You have a position, you are Mrs. Whoever-it-may-be, and there are rules. Rule number one: Put on a good face, never let anybody know the truth about the way you live. . . ." Miriam's lips trembled.

She frightened David. He stood up and grasped her hands.

"What are you saying? Is it as bad as that?"

"Yes, yes, you don't know how I dream. . . . I have a daydream. . . . I'll take the children, and then you and I . . . we'll run away from here, go north, into another world, and—"

"Miriam, there is no paradise in the North. True, there's no Negro slavery, but there are other ills. People can be unhappy there, too. Isn't that just common sense?"

She pulled away and covered her eyes, swaying a little as she stood, and then, as abruptly as she had flung herself out of the chair, she came to David and laid her head on his shoulder.

"I have been so unhappy! You can't know. . . ."

"I can't know unless you tell me, my dear."

"Why did I marry Eugene? Why?" she whispered. "A fatal mistake! For him, too! There's nothing— there's nothing *there,* do you understand? There's not one way that we belong together. Not one way! I don't say it's anyone's fault, it just happened!" And she repeated, "Do you understand?"

He thought perhaps he did, but out of delicacy—she was, after all, his sister—could not say. He could only ask, helplessly, "No way at all? Nothing that can be done?"

Miriam shook her head.

"Perhaps if I . . . if someone . . . were to talk to you, perhaps both of you together, and find out . . ." Find out what? That there was no love? Or how to put it there where there wasn't any? He did not expect a reply, and she gave none.

And trying to conceal his heartache, he said, "I don't know what you can do, but I know one thing you can't do. Miriam, my dear, you must put these thoughts of running away right out of your head, or they will fester and make things harder for you."

"I thought," she said weakly, "if Papa would give me some money—"

He interrupted sharply. "Papa would never give you

money to leave your husband, you know that. And how would you live up North? As a single woman, ostracized, and your children without a father? No, Miriam, you have to be practical."

He heard himself speaking platitudes; despising the sound of them, he still knew them to be true and necessary. He held his sister's hands, and went on with his advice, knowing it to be more compassionate to pacify her than to encourage her despairing rebellion.

"Read, educate yourself, work in your charities, tend to the children. Busyness is everything. . . ."

And all the time, as he spoke, he wondered whether by any chance there could be an even deeper reason for her misery, another man perhaps?

Now recalling that night, he sighed. His tiredness was not physical, he knew; it came from his nerves, vibrating like taut fence wire that sings in a strong wind. He was unable to help Miriam. More than that, he was leading two lives, one of them clandestine. He feared the risks he was taking.

Leaning over the railing, he let the breeze cool his flushed cheeks. The history of the South was written along these riverbanks. Here and there on a bluff, a great house stood like a proud classic temple, while in the fields below, the hoe gangs toiled. Between the great houses lay the holdings of the little farmer, a couple of acres with a log house for the family and two or three cabins for the Negroes, beside whom their owner could be seen bent over in the cotton. At this season the distant woods were all in blossom, the dogwood white as stars, the hawthorn pink, and the forsythia like melting gold. In the foreground the road followed the river. Blue innocents grew wild in trailing patches, and brown cattle lay under the trees chewing their noon cud. An English landscape artist, a Constable, would make much of the innocent rural scene, and for a moment David wished he could see it through such eyes alone.

Instead he saw the ragged yokels running to peer whenever the boat stopped at a landing with a delivery from the city. Out of wondering eyes they stared at the traveling Quality on the floating palace. He saw the poor "white trash" sitting on the lower deck among shabby boxes. A pregnant young woman had lost all her teeth. A child was covered with sores. And suddenly he was back on the *Mirabelle*. That voyage might have happened in another age, so long ago it seemed, and he so changed from the greenhorn boy! No, not changed, except on the outside. He ran his hand over the doctor's bag, the good brown leather bag. Only changed on the outside.

In the ballroom behind him someone was playing the *Moonbeam Waltz* on the piano, the little tune making a thin, sweet tinkle. How pleasant to travel the river, dining with friends under crystal chandeliers or making profitable business deals over cigars and brandy, while all the time the soft green shores slid past! The steamboat was an extension of the seductive city. For a man who could give himself up to them, the pleasures of that city were Elysian: food and wine, women and money and music. The French Opera's orchestra was one of the best—some said *the* best—in the nation. The cooking was renowned, the women resplendent.

He remembered girls, half a dozen or more, and every one a treasure, laughing, flirting, or lovely in gravity; he thought of perfumed silk and white shoulders, and coming home to a young wife. . . . But in this time and in this place he had chosen another way; he was bound and committed to the bottom of his soul.

He took further stock. Intellectually and professionally he had every reason to be content. He had been building a substantial obstetrical practice, having been among the first to use chloroform. He was a regular contributor to the *New Orleans Medical Journal,* having written on yellow fever and sanitation. In a short few years he had acquired prestige, a prestige which the business of this day could destroy forever.

"You traveling far?" A voice spoke at his elbow. The speaker, a middle-aged gentleman with a polite expression, tipped his hat.

David tipped his. "Getting off at the next stop."

The stranger extended his hand. "Name's Cromwell, George Alexander Cromwell."

"I'm happy to meet you, sir. I'm Dr. David Raphael."

"Practicing in New Orleans? I believe I've heard your name. I live in Baton Rouge."

The man seemed inclined to stay at the rail in friendly conversation, so it became necessary to make some agreeable remark.

"Nice way to travel. Better than risking highwaymen on the roads," David said.

"Yes, the roads are terrible. But I always liked the river, anyway. I was on the *Duke of Orleans* when it set the record in forty-three. Six days, eleven hours between Cincinnati and New Orleans. A great boat."

"I should say so."

"If you can keep from getting caught by the gamblers. The captain set three of them ashore on that trip, I remember. They should do so more often. Too many planters are being ruined."

David nodded. Last week Eugene had mentioned something about Ferdinand's having lost a large sum at cards on the way to the Labouisse place upriver. He had also said something about the Raphael firm being on shaky ground, which seemed hard to believe. David had thought of asking Gabriel whether there was any truth in it, but Gabriel would not have told him if there were. You could turn Gabriel upside down and never get out of him anything that you shouldn't. The lawyer-client relationship was sacred.

David's troubled thoughts were interrupted as the stranger exclaimed, "Of course! I know where I heard your name. Sylvain Labouisse—isn't he a relative of yours?"

David smiled. "In a very roundabout way. My father's wife is his mother-in-law."

"Well, that's good enough. A fine family, the Labouisses. Distinguished in the state. A long history."

"So I understand," David said with the proper courteous interest.

"As a matter of fact, I've just come from a meeting in the city where he spoke. Getting after the abolitionist curse. I was one of the speakers, too. I introduced Henry Hyams. Are you acquainted with him?"

"I've met him."

"A coming man. They say he'll be governor of the state one day. A Jewish gentleman. I take it you are, too?"

"I am, sir."

"Well, let me tell you I admire a man like Hyams or Sylvain Labouisse or any man who speaks up. Fence sitters I despise. Letting other men prepare the defense of their women and children. There's too much antislavery propaganda going about, you know. We need vigilance, just as another fine speaker said. Eugene Mendes. He's from New Orleans, you must know him."

"I have the honor to be his brother-in-law."

George Alexander Cromwell was impressed. "Well, we need more like him. I tell you, people don't realize how serious this situation is. Ever since California wrote its constitution barring slavery, people like Garrison have been encouraged. Why even the churches are infected! I'm a Baptist and we had to secede from our national convention."

With a concerned expression David shook his head.

"Yes, you have to keep your eyes and your ears open." The other man lowered his voice. "I don't know how true it is, but yesterday they were saying something about an Englishman named Dyson. He runs that school for free colored boys in New Orleans. They say he's teaching a lot of others things beside the three R's."

"You don't mean—"

"I do mean. Plots and uprisings, my friend."

"Dyson! Really!" David exclaimed. "I shouldn't think so. Of course I've only met him casually. He lives not far from me, but I'd say he was just a pedagogue. Rather dull at that. He doesn't look at all like the type to be doing underground work. These rumors can touch the innocent, you know."

"Oh, no doubt. But it pays to be alert all the same. You remember in thirty-seven when they broke up that insurrection in Rapides Parish? It was highly organized. Then again in forty in Lafayette Parish. Four abolitionists down from the North had a revolt well on the way. My wife's father's slaves were in it but we caught them in time and hanged the lot. Oh, it pays to be alert."

"I daresay you're right. I get so busy with patients I don't have time for much else."

"You see patients this far out?" Cromwell nodded toward the brown leather bag.

"Rarely. Sometimes I combine a consultation with a visit to friends. One needs a little recreation out of the city now and then. Well, I get off round the next bend."

Mr. Cromwell tipped his hat again. "Glad to have met you."

David tipped his. "The same to you, sir."

His knees were weak when he left the boat.

From the little dock a dusty path led through the woods to the main road. The woods were loud with birdsong. A goat grazing along the path skittered away through the brush as David approached. Three little boys came out of a cabin some yards back to stare and retreat. Otherwise, there was no one about. He walked on, summoning his nerve, trying to arrange his features into an expression of calm assurance.

They were to meet at Bartlett's Hotel, half a mile down the road. It was a family resort, crowded on weekends when people came to dine and be entertained with lawn bowling, fireworks, and balloon ascensions. For that reason he had chosen to meet in the middle of the week. On the other hand, it was to be hoped the place would not be empty, making them conspicuous and too easily remembered. I was not born to conspire, David thought. I do not have the stomach for it.

A man stepped out of the bushes abreast of him. "You're late," Lucien said. "I was beginning to worry."

"We had one long stop, a grand piano to hoist. Is everyone here?"

"Just about. There are two other parties, children's birthdays. I took a private room and ordered a birthday cake."

Half a dozen carriages stood at the hotel's entrance. A group of men were entering the bar. Good. There was activity, but not too much.

"You ordered a birthday cake? Whose birthday is it?"

"Why not yours?" Lucien's long, doleful face crinkled with amusement.

"Fine. But you should brush your uniform. You don't look like a fitting servant for an up-and-coming young doctor who is celebrating his birthday."

"Sorry. I'll take care of it. Also, I've an extra horse. You'll go back by road by dark. Later tonight some people will come to the city to collect the circulars. One will come to the office and bring them to the others at a place I have arranged."

David stood still. "Who's coming?" he asked sharply.

"A friend of mine. You don't know him."

"A Negro?"

"Who else?" Lucien threw his hands out, palms up. "What other friend would I have?"

"But you're crazy! A Negro coming to my office at night! Could anything be more conspicuous?"

"He'll be a patient, a free man of color. He has a right to come to a doctor. He'll have a sore arm, or maybe an injured eye would be better."

"All right, then."

As they entered the lobby, David raised his voice. "Lucien, see to my guests. Take their drink orders, they'll be thirsty. And hurry up."

"Yes, sir. Right away, sir."

In the private dining room a small group was already waiting. Except for two traveling men from Massachusetts, they were all familiar. James MacKenzie was a printer who still kept his Scottish burr after fifteen years in America. Randolph Blair, rebellious and elegant, was the son of a Virginia planter. Ludwig Schiff, small and fussy, came from a German-Jewish family in Memphis. In a corner sat a nondescript individual with a meek demeanor, the very sort who chooses a corner to sit in.

David went straight to him, extending his hands. "Mr. Dyson!" he said. "Mr. Dyson! Welcome."

Late in the afternoon they were still at table. Leaning across the remains of the cheerful feast, they spoke in voices hardly above a whisper.

"Well, I think we can say we've made some progress today," David said at last.

Schiff laid a purse on the table. "Any of you, each of you, take whatever you need. There will be more next time. The money is coming in so nicely, so easily."

"Not easily," David corrected. "Give yourself credit, Schiff. You work at it."

MacKenzie said, "I wouldn't take so much if I didn't need more money to buy paper. I've also had to get a small press."

"Take the money," Schiff commanded.

The two northerners persisted. "We've spent the last hour discussing flyers and leaflets. What about guns?"

Young Blair, leaning back from the table, stretched his long legs. "I've told you. On your next trip you will send me a carton of books. Be sure there really are books on the top. *Clarissa* is the name of my sister's place. I'm staying the year out, so you can deliver them any time. Naturally, I shall unpack them myself."

"This is the part that stops me," David said. "I have no liking for guns, as you all know."

The Yankee answered dryly, "No one here has a *liking* for them. But you have to be realistic. We shall use them as little as possible. But we have to have them."

"All right, then. When shall you send them?"

"There's no hurry," Dyson said cautiously. "We're

not nearly ready. We must have no slapdash affair that fails. Ten hangings and it's all over."

Schiff was impatient. "How long do you expect to wait? It's been long enough already."

"As long as it takes to be prepared," Dyson replied. "Another year or two, probably. We must have plenty of support in the countryside. That takes time."

"There's where you come in." David nodded to MacKenzie. "Keep the printing presses rolling. I'll keep writing and you keep printing. We must have pamphlets at the door of every country church, white churches—not the Negro, since the Negroes can't read. But there is great support to be mustered among poor whites. It is only a question of reaching them with the right message."

MacKenzie nodded. "I have a lot ready for tonight. It's stashed in your yard."

David got up and opened the door. The corridor was clear except for Lucien standing just outside. David beckoned him to come in.

"You couldn't hear our voices? Are you sure?"

"Nothing. Only when you sang."

"Good! It sounded like a real party, then?"

"Like a real party."

"All right. Now let's get this straight. We will all separate. I shall ride back alone. MacKenzie has material at my office—"

"In the yard, under the cistern."

"And someone will come tonight for it."

"He will come with his left arm bandaged and a red bandana covering the bandage to keep it clean," Lucien recited. "He will put the flyers in a sack of melons in his wagon. If he is stopped, he will simply be carrying melons to market, or peddling them as the case may be. But there's no reason why he should be stopped."

"Suppose, though, that the worst happens and they do stop him?" Schiff asked.

"This man is like my brother," Lucien answered gravely. "He will kill himself or allow himself to be killed, but he will not endanger me."

These somber words caused a moment's silence in the room.

"You know," David said, "I really don't see why we can't have all the men come right to my place to collect, instead of having all these hiding places you and MacKenzie have worked out. I'm beginning to think I've been too cautious."

"No, no, Doctor," Dyson cried. "Too many people would know who you are. It is enough that I risk myself by being open with my pupils. We can't risk you, too."

"Nonsense," David said. "If these people can't be trusted, what are we doing with them in the first place?"

"Trusted." Lucien's melancholy eyes went past them all, out past the window onto the dusky blue lawn. "You don't know what a man will say with his feet held into a fire or when he's buried up to the neck and the fire ants crawl into his eyes."

"Enough." David shuddered. "Enough."

12

In the middle of the afternoon, that flat windless hour
when the day is no longer fresh and dusk lies like a
dirty powder on the leaves, Miriam put *Lelia* aside on
the garden bench. All that passion and strife, all that
radical defiance! It wearied the mind. It was impossible to compare a woman like George Sand with herself. And she sat in a drowsy inertia, letting her mind
go blank.

At the side-street gate, which was rarely used,
someone lifted the creaking latch. Lazily, only half
rising, she turned to see who was there.

"I thought you might be here," André Perrin said.

She felt a chill fear of imminent crisis, a fluttering
between heart and throat.

"I am often here in the afternoon," she answered
coldly.

He sat down on the other bench. She wanted to get
up and run into the house.

"I was passing," he said, "and since we are finally
going away next week—you know we are leaving for
France on the *Mirabelle?*"

"That's the ship that brought me here, years ago."

"How strange! Well, I only—I wanted to say good-
bye."

"I hope you have a good voyage and will be happy

in France." The stilted words fell dully into the oppressive air.

"Thank you."

He was holding his hat, which lay on his knees. Now with his left hand he began to run a forefinger over the brim. Round and round it passed as she watched. In her own fingertips she could feel the smooth straw edge. Something in this trivial motion was asking for time, as if he were collecting himself for something else. His lowered head as he examined the hat looked helpless. She did not understand what was happening.

Suddenly he looked up. "Yes, I came to say goodbye. But before I go, I wanted, I had to—"

He got up. He stood over her. The tips of his boots stopped within an inch of her skirt's hem, which lay on the grass.

"For months, for this whole year past, I've been trying not to say it. I'm ashamed, Miriam. Ashamed and afraid of what you will do. You may never forgive me. And I wouldn't blame you." The words came rushing. "I have been thinking of nothing but you. Nothing. I don't know what it means. Do I love you? I scarcely know you. Yet you fill my mind all day. Every day. You fill my mind."

She fastened her eyes on a hummingbird whose long beak was sucking deeply from a creamy flower on the trumpet vine. No larger than a grasshopper and as green, it flickered. Its iridescent wings were beating the air too fast for the human eye to see, and she held her gaze to the bird.

"Are you very angry?" he whispered.

She could not speak. She was afraid to speak. Perhaps, as she had feared it might happen, this at last was the moment of transition from reality to fantasy;

speech would betray her and everyone would know. She had gone mad.

"When I started to speak just now," she said, "I thought in the very same moment that I must be crazy, and I wanted to stop, but it's already too late."

She steadied herself, forcing her eyes away from the bird to look at him, forcing her mind into reality. His eyes were anxious, questioning, soft. His hand went out to touch most tentatively her own hand, which lay in her lap with the fingers weakly upturned.

Then she felt her lips opening into a smile, felt her own warm tears.

"Oh," he said, "is it possible? You never spoke to me. I thought I had displeased you so terribly. You never spoke to me."

"I was afraid you would see," she said very low. "I was afraid you would know."

His hand tightened on hers, the fingers intertwined.

"Oh, God," he said.

Unashamed, she raised her face, letting him see the teardrops slide down her cheeks.

"I thought of so many ways to meet you alone. Always it was at those dreadful dinners. I tried avoiding you. When I made plans, they came to nothing. I thought of what I could say to you. I understand about Eugene and you, you know."

"You can't know," she interrupted.

"I know enough. Do you understand that I was afraid—am afraid—to begin this thing? Yet I can't help it, can't go away without speaking to you, and still it's of no use, my speaking, is it?" And taking her other hand, he lifted it to his lips to kiss it.

Her wedding ring, a wide band strong as a rope and solid as a stone wall, brushed his lips.

He looked about desperately. "There's no time, no place, and so much to say."

Above the splashing double cascade the little love goddess looked with her indifferent chalk-white gaze at the agitated lovers.

"You married Marie Claire."

"We were guests at the same house for three weeks. At the end of the time we found ourselves engaged. I don't know how it happened. I think our mothers decided it. I think Marie Claire was as surprised as I was."

"Who does these things to us?" Miriam cried. "Why do we allow them to happen? Eugene and I— we're all wrong for each other." And she withdrew her hands, clasping them in a kind of supplication. All the long sorrow, the senseless injustice, and now this intoxication overwhelmed her.

André took her face in his hands, turning it into the glaring light. Fearlessly she let him examine it; whatever flaw was there, he must see and accept, the eyebrows too close together, a little white scar on the chin, any and every flaw. Then his mouth came down on hers, the lips fitting together as though they had been molded that way, so pliant, so perfect . . . Her arms went up to pull him closer.

A door slammed in the house and they sprang apart. They waited, but no one came.

"There's no place to go," André said again.

"It would be no use anyway. You're going to France."

"I'll be back."

"When? How long?"

"I'm not sure. Perhaps only a year."

"Only a year. And then?"

"There'll have to be something, some way. I don't know."

"I don't know, either."

A flock of pigeons came swooping over the wall,

attacking the crumbs the children must have dropped on the gravel path. They surrounded the bench just as on crowded Sunday afternoons in the public parks they always surround young lovers who seek in vain for a private place.

And suddenly, not caring who might see, knowing how mad this defiance was, Miriam drew him back to her, kissing his forehead, his cheeks, and his mouth over and over, making little cries; then her head went to his shoulder and he stroked her hair, murmuring. All she felt was a need to press closer and never stop, never—

She heard her son's voice. "Mama? Where are you? Are you out here?"

She sprang up, calling, "Yes, I'm here, darling."

The child came around the shrubbery. His cheeks were flushed from his nap; his hair, freshly parted, still held the babyish curl around his neck. Helpless, tender . . . What am I doing? she thought, in sudden fright.

But she said brightly, too brightly, in a shaking voice, "Eugene, you remember Mr. Perrin. He is going to Europe. He has come to say good-bye to us all."

"I'm going to go to Europe, too," the boy said confidently.

"I'm sure you will someday," André told him.

Over the child's head he looked at Miriam. His eyelashes fell like curtains, then rose on a look of despair which plainly said: We can't end this, I can't leave you like this.

She was cut in two. The halves were straining apart, she was in agony. She saw herself caught between the man and the child, felt them pulling her, each one with all his strength, yet neither was touching her.

Piteously she appealed to her son. "Will you go inside to play, Eugene? Just for a little while, please. Then I'll come to be with you."

"But I've been inside! It's half past three and Fanny said you promised to read to Angie and me." The shrill voice ended in a wail.

Now Angelique came from the house with Fanny.

"Here we are, Miss Miriam," Fanny said. "It's half past three."

They were not to be dislodged. Miriam gave a hopeless shake of the head. And André, having no choice, picked up his hat.

"Shall you be coming again to say good-bye to Eugene?" The words were formal, but the voice implored.

He shook his head. "I can't," he said miserably. And he stood there already half departed, unwilling to go the rest of the way.

"I can't," he repeated, as if to say, The next time will be unbearable.

She understood. "Well," she said, "I suppose you'll write to us?"

"I am not very good at writing, I'm afraid."

She understood that, too. A proper, stiff letter would be the only permissible one, and that would be worse than none at all.

"Mama, read!" demanded Angelique, screwing up her eyes.

"I'll go," André said. "Remember me to the rest of the family."

Her face burned; her hands were cold.

"I'll remember," she said, and turned away.

So she did not see him go, only heard his footsteps on gravel and the click of the gate.

"Mama, shall we get the books?"

"Yes, get them, do. Go upstairs and get them."

And she sat down again to wait. Two or three pigeons were still pecking at Aphrodite's feet. A ladybug in its spotted red shell alighted on the back of the bench. A wren took a bath in a dusty puddle. Heedless little creatures, crawling and flying, foraging for their simple sustenance from one day's end to the next! Only man had such longing, such confusion in his heart.

To have been given in one incredible moment one's heart's impossible desire! To have been given it, and then to have it as quickly taken away!

Lelia had fallen to the ground. She picked it up, riffling the pages. A life like that might befit George Sand, that fearless, extraordinary soul. But Miriam Mendes was not George Sand. She was neither fearless nor extraordinary. And this was America, not Paris.

Take the children and go north, putting everything, even André behind her? For what good could ever come to them? Let him return here and not find her! It would be better that way. In due time he would forget —or almost forget—and she would, too, men and women being what they are. She had seen and read enough of life to know that much.

She would have to ask Papa for the money to go away, since she had, of course, none of her own. Her dowry was the possession of her husband. A woman had always to ask. Nothing was hers by right. Ask Papa? she repeated. He would be horrified; she could see him slowly removing the cigar; his mouth would make a circle of dismay. She could hear his admonition: Go back to your husband; remember that you're a mother; you have responsibilities and a position to keep.

"Here's the book," said Angie, placing it on her mother's lap. The beloved fairy tales had been read so often that the pages were beginning to fall out. Unerringly, the stubby little finger went to the favorite picture, the favorite tale.

Miriam moved the book to make room on her lap

for the little girl. For a moment she laid her cheek against Angie's warm fragrant hair. She was almost choked by her surging love for the child and by the crisis of the last hour.

"I always like this story because it has a happy ending, Mama."

"Ah, yes, that's a very good reason," Miriam replied. And in a clear, controlled voice, she began to read.

"Once upon a time . . ."

Often from the glass in the bedroom a hopeless face stared back at her, a pinched face with dry lips. The dark hair, loosened for the night, gave her a wild look of desperation. The old fear of madness returned. Perhaps some night she would smash the mirror, letting the shards fly. Her lungs would strain from a scream of outrage; then the wind would carry her scream through the walls of the house over the ocean, and into the racing currents of the upper air, as far as Europe, where perhaps André might hear her cry.

13

It was a matter of some pride to Ferdinand Raphael that he had weathered the long-ago panic of 1837. The English cotton market had fallen like a stone, and like a stone tossed into a pond, the panic had rippled across the ocean to engulf New Orleans in a wave of failures. Banks defaulted their bonds, credit was withdrawn, and some of the most prestigious business houses in the city fell into ruin. But the House of Raphael had come through unscathed, one of the very few which had survived. Somehow Ferdinand had maneuvered his way around all the hidden reefs and dangerous currents of the times; he had even been able to come to the aid of friends.

"Experience," he liked to say by way of explanation. "Caution. And a bit of daring, too. Yes, certainly a bit of daring." And his youthful smile would brighten his cheeks up to the temples.

So it was with a shock of sudden thunder that the House of Raphael collapsed.

The city had long ago climbed back out of depression. Ships laden with cotton and sugar crowded the port again and wealth from the seven seas flowed in. Christmas week was being celebrated with eggnog, poinsettias, and cathedral bells. The Raphael house was filled. Emma's aunts and uncles from Shreveport and her cousins from Mobile, with their nursemaids and children, filled the guestrooms, while the overflow was housed at the St. Louis Hotel.

"We shall have to take the children to visit for Christmas," Miriam said. "They know quite well it's not their holiday, but Papa has presents for them and it would be cruel to refuse."

"Very well, then, you take them," Eugene said as she had known he would.

The opulence of the Raphael house that year was dazzling. Christmas roses drooped their luscious heads in every room. Handsome gifts were given and received: Persian shawls, gold chains, Belgian lace, cashmere dresses, and Meissen porcelains. A new star sapphire glittered on Emma's hand.

After the collapse Miriam likened it to a fireworks display, the last explosion always being the loudest and the highest, the boom deafening and the stars shooting far over the trees, only to blaze and fall into a little heap of cinders.

She had walked home through holiday streets with the children. It was a slow walk. They had to stop to peer at every lighted tree, to admire every wreathed and garlanded door. The children, entranced with the music and color of Christmas, could not help but enfold their mother in their delight. So in high spirits they reached home.

"Look!" cried little Eugene. "See what Grandpa gave me." With Miriam's help he brought in a heavy music box on which carved horses rode a carousel. "He gave Mama a new bracelet, and Angelique a—"

Eugene laid the newspaper down. "Allow me to say that your father is a spendthrift and a fool."

Unwilling to reveal her own unquiet doubts, Miriam defended him. "He's a wealthy man and has always been generous. It's his pleasure."

"Generous he is, but he is not wealthy anymore. His house of cards is about to collapse."

"What do you mean?" she cried.

"That he will be going through bankruptcy very soon."

"I don't believe it!"

"You can believe it. Rumors have been all over the city for weeks. He's been reorganizing his companies to stave it off, but it's too late, it won't help."

Miriam put her hand to her mouth in horror. "I don't believe it!"

Shortly before noon on the second day of the new year, the Bank of New Orleans called its loans to the House of Raphael. Whisper to whisper at first, then louder and surer, from the tables at Victor's to the wharves, the news was spread. By evening there was not a house in the Vieux Carré which did not know of the disaster.

For once unaccompanied by guests, Eugene came home to confirm the news. "Well," he said, "this is what happens when a man gets to thinking he's infallible." His tone was somewhere between commiseration and superiority.

Miriam sat on the sofa. They were in the front parlor, the stiff, gilded room. Her voice was harsh with pain.

"What happened? Why did it happen?"

"He was gullible, for one thing. He endorsed bad notes for his so-called friends. Wanted to be liked, I suppose. A common enough story. And for another, he simply spent too much. And for a third, he speculated, building pyramids like Pharaoh. Only Pharaoh's lasted longer."

"Pyramids? I don't understand."

"Mortgaging your properties to get money to buy

more property. Take the cornerstone out and the pyramid falls. You see?"

Standing against the daylight, Eugene was a powerful dark presence. One hand jingled coins in his pocket. The gesture spoke of easy assurance. This sort of thing will never happen to me, it said.

"I have no mortgages on any of my properties, nor did I ever speculate in cotton futures. Why do you think Judah Touro came through the panic unscathed? Because he was prudent."

"You mean Papa has nothing at all?"

"What do you think bankruptcy is? No, there is nothing left. Not of his, nor of Emma's either."

"Of Emma's?"

"He had enlarged Emma's plantation, bought three thousand acres adjoining it by mortgaging the original land." A bunch of keys in the other pocket now made their separate jingle. "Next comes the sheriff's sale: the schooner, the office and warehouses, all the baled cotton waiting for shipment, the slaves, the house on Conti Street—"

"Not Papa's beautiful house!"

Now pity came into his voice, as if suddenly he had seen that she was crushed. "Yes, it will go, I'm sorry to say."

She stood up. "I'm going to Papa now."

"I'll go with you," Eugene said immediately.

She didn't want him—with all that power and competence. "You don't have to. I'll go alone."

"It's my place," he said firmly. "I'm his son-in-law."

Yes, she thought as she followed him, it's your place. There are people who go to funerals because it's their place, but really it's to congratulate themselves on being alive.

In his front parlor Ferdinand was reading a newspaper. Over his head hung a portrait of young Emma in her Empire gown, with her bouquet and the affable gaze of a person who has never known any trouble. He had been reading the *Deutsche Zeitung,* which, wanting so much to be American that he was ashamed to be seen with a German newspaper, he had always read in secret. He made no attempt to hide it now.

"Well, Papa," Miriam said, kissing him. Stroking his forehead, she felt the forked vein on the temple throb under her fingers.

He murmured something and she drew away, pitying his embarrassment, should he be seen with tears in his eyes. But he was not weeping. Instead he wore a look of surprise, as if to say: I do not—no, I do not understand how this could have happened to me. To me!

After the swift, steady rise, his daughter thought, straining with every bit of energy, tensed to the fullest, after all that skillful juggling and maneuvering through the first hard years, and finally the lovely lavish years—to end like this?

"Let's talk about facts," Eugene said, taking command. "Get pens and paper."

Hastily, Ferdinand obeyed, and the two men bent their heads over a sheaf of documents on the desk. This was man's work. Miriam scarcely understood the meaning of words like *mortgage, demand note,* or *bond.* Half hearing them, she could only remember irrelevant things: that last year Papa had taken her children to P. T. Barnum's circus and bought them balloons.

Presently Ferdinand looked up. "Will you go see Emma?" he asked. "Poor Emma. She's upstairs in her sitting room with Pelagie and Eulalie."

On her *lit de repos,* leaning against a mound of ruffled pillows, Emma lay mourning, while her maid applied eau de cologne to her flushed forehead.

"My land! My beautiful land! How can it be? Yesterday it was there, all those acres! And the finest staircase in the state, did you know that? A free-standing staircase. Yesterday it was mine and now they tell me —they tell me—"

Poor Emma! Such bitter tragedy for her to whom "position in society" meant, next to her family, all there was of value in the world.

"And two hundred slaves!" A falling tear made a wet spot on Emma's blue sleeve. "People who served my parents and my grandmother! What is to become of them all? What is to become of Sisyphus?"

Yet she had not one word of blame for Ferdinand.

"Those wicked bankers!" she cried. "All the friends he helped, the people we entertained, where are they? It's their fault, bringing a good man down to ruin."

"Nonsense, Mama," Eulalie interjected. "It's nobody's fault but your husband's, your greedy, gambling, spendthrift husband. But then, you might have known, Jews are always—"

Pelagie whirled upon her sister. "What can you be saying? Was he the only one? Half the city was ruined in the panic only a few years ago. Half the city spends more than it owns, gambles on the horses, on cards, on anything it can. And you talk of a Jewish vice!"

For a moment Miriam's outrage tied her tongue. A moment later, in the face of Pelagie's decency, the anger ebbed. And again she saw Eulalie clearly: the rejected woman, filled with fears.

My father was her male protector, the only one she had, and he has failed her. Yes, and failed me, too. Now I am condemned to stay with Eugene. And Miriam caught herself wringing her hands in a helpless gesture which she had made without thinking, and which she despised.

Downstairs on the verandah the Christmas roses were turning a mournful purple, dropping their petals to the floor. In the courtyard under the pallid winter sun it was quite still, with neither clatter nor chatter heard from the quarters. The news had reached the servants, then, and they feared what might happen to them. A pall had fallen on the house.

On the bottom step she stood just looking. She saw her father on her wedding evening, expansive with pride in his daughter and his house. She saw herself sitting in the arbor struggling to read French, then later, entering her childish thoughts in the white satin book. There came Gretel, the first Gretel, turning, tamping the earth down to make a cool place for herself under the mulberry bush. There much later, on another night, she had danced—danced with the husband of Marie Claire. *Why are you so unhappy?* he'd asked.

Fool! Fool! Still thinking of him when nothing will ever come of it. Nothing.

Eugene came down the steps behind her.

"I thought you were up with Emma."

"I was. But Eulalie was too much for me. She blames it all on Papa's being Jewish."

"Stupid old maid. Nasty old maid," Eugene said savagely. "Had you known that about her before?"

"Oh, there've always been little things here and there, mostly things unsaid."

"They all took from him. How they all took from him! Of course, the wreck is his own doing, but they helped it along. I always said he had no right to support her extravagant relatives. What a reversal now! And he too old to start again."

From inside the house they heard voices, first David's and then Gabriel's.

David was asking, "Is it really as bad as it looks?"

"Every bit and perhaps even worse." Gabriel's voice was somber. The two men descended the steps to the courtyard.

"What's Papa doing?" Miriam asked.

"I urged him to lie down on the sofa and try to sleep. He hasn't slept all night."

Miriam met David's sorrowful eyes. The eyes spoke to one another. Seeing again how their father had once come to them in pride and splendor; now the eyes mourned for him.

"I shall go right to the office when I leave here," Gabriel said. "Maybe, after all, I'll find a loophole, some way to salvage something." This was more a question than a statement.

"You won't, you know that," Eugene told him. "Not even a clever lawyer like you."

"You are undoubtedly right." Gabriel sighed. "Still, I can try."

There was, then, no hope. And yet, even so, there was comfort in just the presence of these two men, her brother and her stalwart friend. And Miriam felt their joint strength as if it were a wall to shelter her and to lean on.

Where, though, as Emma had lamented, were all the friends and relatives who only a week ago had filled the house with celebration? Then a second question struck hard.

"Where will they go when they leave this house? Where will they live?"

It was Eugene who answered with astonishing alacrity.

"We shall take them in."

"We shall?"

"Certainly. The only other possibility is the Labouisse place with Pelagie and Sylvain, which actually isn't a possibility. How would it look for your father to go there when his own son-in-law has a home? No, we shall have to take them in. As for Eulalie, she can go to the Labouisse place if she wishes. Although," he added somewhat grandly, "I'm willing to take her, too, in spite of her prejudice." A little satisfied smile flickered at the corners of Eugene's full lips.

Miriam said hesitantly, "Emma is worried about what will happen to Sisyphus."

"Oh, tell her I shall buy him for her. And while I'm about it, that rascally pair, Chanute and Maxim, too. Why not? If I'm going to do this at all, I might as well do it right."

Such generosity must be acknowledged. Eugene was waiting for it.

"You're very generous," she murmured, as Gabriel and David smiled in agreement.

"Southerners take care of kin. It is a tradition among us, an obligation," Eugene said. And he said again, "How would it appear to the community if I were to do anything less?"

"Still, it's so good of you." She sounded humble. Indeed, she was humbled under the weight of this enormous indebtedness.

It would have been so much easier to accept the gift if instead Eugene had said: I shall do this because I'm sorry for your father, because I'm fond of him.

The narrow channel of Bourbon Street overflowed with the Mardi Gras crowd. Costumed knights and noblemen, emblazoned, spangled, and plumed, riding in carriages or on beribboned horses, jostled and pushed their way among rowdies, prostitutes, and pickpockets under the crowded balconies.

"Haven't we seen enough?" David complained, stepping out of the press to a side street to avoid a trio of lurching drunks.

He had always held himself aloof from the Mardi Gras. In spite of his compassion for humanity, he disliked all crowds, and in particular, he disliked this one. Protected as they were by masks, these holiday-makers seemed always to hover on the far, thin edge of good-natured celebration; an accidental shove, a startled rearing horse, could push it over that edge into violent anger.

Besides, Mardi Gras was a Christian holiday. Why should it have such fascination for Jews? He supposed it was simply the normal contagion of gaiety. That was the only reason he had gone this year, to cheer his father, who needed to be cheered.

"By God!" Eugene exclaimed. "If I weren't with all you proper gentlemen, I'd know where to spend the rest of the night!"

They had come abreast of the Washington Ballroom. A crush of arrivals and departures spilled from the luminous dazzle indoors to fill the sidewalk and half the width of the street. A woman with sparkling beads laced into her long black hair ran out laughing on the arm of a blond masked youth.

"The most beautiful women in the world," Eugene cried, "bar none. I've heard it said a thousand times by men who've been all over the globe—"

From the darkness outside of the streaming light a man's arms seized him by the shoulders, jerking him off his feet.

"Goddamn you, Raphael! You ruined me, did you, you bastard? Now it's my turn!"

Eugene fell heavily to the pavement. There was a crash and tinkle of broken glass, then running feet pounded away into the darkness, and Eugene was screaming, screaming.

"My eyes! Oh, God, my eyes!"

The noisy night had gone dead still. The terrible cries were alone in the stillness.

"Jesus!" somebody said.

Now a tremendous hubbub arose in the circling crowd. "What is it? What happened?"

"A man threw something at him."

"He's bleeding."

"No, it's his eyes!"

"It's his eyes, for Christ's sake!"

"Get him up off the street!"

"Somebody call—"

Eugene's legs moved, kicking the cobblestones. David bent over him, pulling at the hands that frantically cupped his eyes.

"Somebody help me! Hold him still."

A man brought a lantern.

"Here . . . Here . . . Eugene," David murmured, straining to see.

When he straightened up, his voice shook with horror. "Lime! My God! Boiling lime!"

Ferdinand sank to his knees. "It was meant for me." He sobbed. "You heard it. Meant for me."

"I'll get a carriage," Gabriel said. "We'll take him home. Unless, David, you think we ought—"

Now a woman parted the crowd with her elbows. "Let me see! I want to see! They said it was Eugene Mendes. . . ."

On the cobbles, in her satin skirt, she knelt over the wounded man, then turned her dark, anguished face up to David. "I know him. Take him to my house. It's near, just down the street."

"That will be better," David said. "Never mind the carriage, it'll take too long. Let us carry him."

They laid him on a sofa and bathed his eyes.

"More water," David said. "Pour it on, spill it on. More."

"Let me," the woman insisted. "I see how it's done." Her hands moved tenderly. The water spilled out of the basin onto the garish pink brocade pillow. She wept as Eugene moaned, wiping his eyes on her embroidered sleeve.

"Oh, my dear, my dearest. Oh, my dear."

Over her head the glances traveled from David to Gabriel.

The woman appealed to David. "You're a doctor? Is there nothing else to be done?"

"For the moment just keep flooding the eyes until the burning stops. Then we'll see. You're tired," he said pityingly. "Let me do it."

Almost fiercely she thrust him away. "No, no, I will."

The fancy little room had by now filled with the curious; pale brown ladies and their black servants hovered against the walls. A light-brown boy with a scared expression stood silently at the head of the couch.

"Mama, what happened?" he asked.

"Darling, he's been hurt. Some terrible person has hurt him."

This, David thought, this is the reason for my sister's misery. This must be what it is all about.

"Where've you been?" he asked Ferdinand, who had gone out for a minute and now came back, panting.

"I gave a fellow on the street twenty-five cents to fetch Miriam, fifty cents if he ran."

"You what? You sent for Miriam?"

"Well, naturally I did. What's wrong?"

"You don't understand where we are."

"Do you mind telling me what you're talking about?"

"Look over there and you'll know."

Still kneeling, the young woman had taken Eugene's hand between both of hers. As though they were alone in the room, she kissed his palm, laying it against her cheek, cradling the hand under the heavy sway of her hair.

Comprehension came to Ferdinand. He said quickly, "I'll head her off. I'll stand outside and make some excuse that we're bringing him right home."

It was too late. Miriam had already come in.

"There's been an accident," David said at once. "We carried him in here, it was the nearest house."

"I know, the boy told me." She walked to the sofa, where the woman got up from her knees and made a place. She touched her husband's cheek.

"Eugene, I'm here. It's Miriam."

He did not speak. For a long minute she stood looking down at him.

What she might be concealing during that minute no one could tell; her immobile face showed nothing. Only the quick rise and fall of her breathing told her brother anything at all; the physician saw that she was agitated, as surely anyone would be, but David could only wonder at the complicated secrets of the human heart. And his own heart ached for her, standing there so young and alone in her simple dress and her dignity, bearing God only knew what sorrow within. Perversely, too, his heart ached for the dark voluptuous woman so agonized by her grief and unashamed of it.

Presently Miriam turned to the other woman. "Thank you for sheltering my husband," she said quietly. "Will someone please arrange for a litter or carriage to bring him home? It isn't far."

At the door she drew David aside. "How bad is it, David? Tell me the truth."

David considered and decided. Yes, she would meet this savage truth. Apparently she had already met some other truths. So he answered bluntly.

"He will almost certainly be blind."

Friends, servants, and doctors moved in and out, up and down the stairs, carrying gifts and trays of food, whispering their commiseration and their curiosity. For some days Eugene lay against pillows on his bed. Then he was moved to a chair at the window from which, with a critical eye, he had used to look down to see whether the flower beds were being properly tended.

One by one the members of the household peered into the room, the servants overwhelmed with horror, Emma for once struck speechless, and Ferdinand sickened by his sense of responsibility for the disaster.

The children came. During the worst first days they had been kept away. Now it was time to acquaint them with the change in their father.

"It was an accident," Miriam said gently. "Somebody threw some bad stuff by mistake." Eugene had insisted that, at six, they were too young to know that the world contained human beings evil enough to destroy another human being's eyes.

"They will find it all out in time," he had said.

He took one of them on each knee.

"It was an accident," he repeated.

The children, not understanding, were simply curious.

Angelique laid a finger on the scorched cheek below Eugene's glasses.

"Does it hurt?"

"Not anymore."

Little Eugene asked whether he could see with the glasses off?

"No, son," the father answered steadily.

Such courage! thought Miriam. He will not even allow his voice to waver, for his children's sake.

"Well, can you see with the glasses on?"

"No, son. I can't see at all."

Angelique put her hand up. "Can't you see my fingers?"

This was too much, even for a brave man, to have to bear. And Miriam interrupted, turning away from the light so that they would not see her wet eyes and blurt, *Why are you crying, Mama?*

"Your father will be going downstairs tomorrow or the next day. The doctor said so. And you two will keep him company, have breakfast on the verandah or in the garden, wouldn't that be nice? You could pick some flowers for him. You'd like camellias, wouldn't you, Eugene?" She chattered; the light, lying words rippled from her tongue. "You two can be such a great help until your father gets better."

"Then you'll be all better soon," Angelique said.

"Well, never *all* better," Eugene told her. Truth, he and Miriam had decided, but a gradual and easy truth; don't frighten them. "I'll be walking around again soon," he added. "I'll get along fine, you'll see I will."

Some weeks later David and Miriam stood in the quiet garden.

"And so the professor has given the final word," Miriam said bleakly.

"No improvement, as I told you from the beginning."

The fountain trilled, making a sound too sprightly, David thought, for a house as burdened as this one. He put his hand on his sister's shoulder.

"What is it? Tell me. It's not only Eugene, though that's bad enough, God knows. It's not good to keep everything in, Miriam. One needs to talk to someone. Do you want to talk to me about—about the woman?"

"I don't need to talk about her. I've known about her for a long time, as you may have guessed."

Mystery within mystery, the Chinese box within a box, within a box, within—

"What, then?"

"Oh, many things. Mostly I think of Eugene. How terrible never to see! Not even his children's faces. And I think of poor Papa. His life's been turned upside down. He'll never forgive himself because that man, that devil, whoever he was, meant the punishment for him."

"It wasn't Papa's fault."

"No, but he feels guilty, all the same. I feel guilt, too, you know. Eugene has been so good to Papa and I don't love Eugene, you understand that, we are nothing to each other—yet it's because of my father that he is blind!"

David sighed. In the sunlight the fountain splashed so prettily, with its graceful cascades so polished and smooth. The whole pastel city, polished and perfumed, was rotting underneath.

Miriam was looking at the ground. Her head drooped sadly.

He thought he knew what she was thinking. "You're thinking that now you will never get away. That's true, isn't it?"

"Yes," she answered, in a voice so low that he could barely hear her. "It was never realistic, anyway. I should have known that."

Still, there is something else, he persisted to himself. She has not told me all. He did not know how he knew, yet he knew. But if it was not the woman Queen, what was it, then?

He tried one more time. "You don't want to tell me anything else?"

"There isn't anything else."

"Well," he said, giving up, "well, I've calls to make. A gangrenous foot. I'd better go."

Miriam saw him first. Eugene had gone that morning for the daily drive with Maxim or Chanute that, after a season or two, had become his routine. Where he went, she had no need to ask. So it surprised her now to see him there on a bench in the square, with his blind eyes turned up toward the streaming light and a cluster of pigeons around his feet. Puzzled, she looked about for the carriage or a servant, but neither was in sight; something warned her then to go on past and leave Eugene alone.

Angelique cried, "Look! There's Father! What's he doing here by himself?"

"Leave him! He wants . . ." she began, but the children had gone running to their father.

Eugene was not there by himself. A few feet behind him stood a tall boy holding a sketch pad on a board; when, gracefully, with a motion almost feminine, he threw a handful of corn to the birds, Miriam knew at once who he was. That grim scene flashed again; the cramped, gaudy room, Eugene writhing on a couch, the woman passionately weeping, the scared boy hovering. . . .

She had no choice now but to face the moment.

"The doctors want me to exercise," Eugene was saying, "so Pierre took me for a walk."

His name was Pierre. She wondered what he used for a last name.

Young Eugene said stoutly, "I could take you, Father. Why didn't you ask me?"

"You're not old enough yet to lead me, son."

"I'm almost as big as he is! How old are you?" young Eugene demanded of the other boy.

"Thirteen." The voice was almost a whisper, deferential, as were the backward steps taken to give space to the thrusting pair of seven-year-olds. Yet the eyes were curiously bold, moving in turn from the twins to Miriam.

He knows who we are, she thought. He remembers me, of course. But he must have been told everything even before that. How strange it is that they always know all about us, while we don't even know they exist!

And she wondered what Eugene's eyes would have said had they been able to meet hers during this discomfiting encounter.

"Come, children," she urged brightly, "your father wants to rest. Come along home."

But they protested. Angelique could be especially stubborn.

"Why must we? Father, you don't want us to go home now, do you?"

"I think you should. Do what your mother tells you."

Little Eugene stood on his toes to see the drawing board.

"What are you drawing?" he wanted to know.

"The pigeons." And Pierre, lowering the board, faced it outward so that Miriam could see his work.

He had caught in simple charcoal, black against white, the myriad gradations of iridescent feathering. He had caught the heaving motion of the flock, the peck and rise, the flutter and strut. The little sketch had a startling beauty. Miriam felt a sudden softness in herself. The way he stood there, so shy of speech, so painfully conscious of the situation, and still proud enough to want them to see his work!

"It's lovely," she said. And something, some sense of pity or fairness, compelled her to give this perception to her husband. "Pierre is talented, Eugene. Professional."

He did not reply. His face was flushed.

"Where did you learn to do that?" asked Angelique.

"I have art lessons."

"You can't go to school," the little girl said.

Miriam could only wince at the cruelty of the remark. For, at seven, what could a child know? Only enough to know that color was status, to know without being told who was one of the Others, who was a servant in his proper place, which did not include school.

"Blaise can draw," said little Eugene. "Blaise belongs to my father and mother. Who do you belong to?"

"To Mr. Mendes," Pierre replied. The statement was flat, conveying no more than the fact. For an instant his hand brushed Eugene's shoulder, then was removed, as though he had quickly recalled the fitness of things.

Conceived, most probably, by accident, thought Miriam. And probably unwanted; at least, it was doubtful that Eugene had wanted this superfluous boy. . . . She felt oppressed, saddened, angry, and bewildered.

"I insist you come home now!" Her voice was so sharp that the children turned to her in surprise.

Abruptly Eugene stood up, seizing his cane.

"You will find Maxim at the carriage," he directed Pierre. "Tell him that I have walked home."

Miriam asked Eugene, "Are you sure you can walk

so far?" Her anxiety was affected, the question merely a thing of words to fill air and time as she guided him out of the square.

"It's my sight that I've lost, not my legs."

The children had once more run ahead. The incident in the square, which for them had been without significance, now lay behind them; they were having an argument over the ownership of a white cat that had recently strayed into the yard.

After a minute or two Eugene spoke again. "Go on. Say what you have to say. Get it over with."

"I'd rather not." Confusion was still in her. She wasn't even sure how she felt, or ought to feel.

"Well, it happened this way. I quite thoughtlessly accepted the boy's suggestion that we go for a walk." He spoke sternly, covering his own embarrassment over a situation in which a gentleman should not have allowed himself to be caught. "Quite thoughtlessly . . . a public place . . . It will not happen again."

No reply was needed. And Miriam concentrated her thoughts on her two, who were by now far ahead. It was lucky they weren't both boys, or both girls. There would have been much more rivalry. This way they really got on quite well, considering how young they were. So she consoled herself for her other lacks with her satisfaction in her children.

At the same time the image of that other child floated through her head and steadied itself there; his narrow hands on the drawing board, his lowered lashes, and when he raised them, the unanswerable question in his eyes.

14

"So life goes on," Emma said brightly, opening another invitation as she read her mail at the breakfast table. She had at last accepted her position in the Mendes household with remarkable grace. A valiant lady, Miriam reflected. It took real courage to learn the art of receiving when one had always been a dispenser of gifts.

"Do you suppose, Miriam my dear," Emma inquired now, "that you could persuade your cook to make *bière douce* sometime? My Serafina used to do it for your father. He loves it and it's quite simple, really, just a few pineapple peelings, brown sugar, cloves, and rice."

"I'll tell her, Aunt Emma."

"Thank you, my dear. Oh, my, listen to this! My cousin Grace writes about that awful Tremont business. The old lady was a cousin of Grace's on the other side, you remember. Murdered in her bed! By a crowd of savages whom she'd raised and fed from childhood!"

"It's said, though, that her son was a cruel man. He sold them away without heart and they were badly fed," Miriam began, but was stopped by a snort from Eugene.

"Rubbish! That's what they always say. Abolitionist rubbish!"

"Oh, see," Emma said, "here's a letter from Marie Claire. My goodness, she's given a lieder recital. Had a fine reception. Her teacher predicts increasing success. Isn't that amazing! I always knew she could sing, but I really never thought she would . . . oh, they have made some fine contacts in Paris. . . . The Baroness Pontalba . . . you knew she's from New Orleans, didn't you, Miriam? Yes, it was her father who built the cathedral, the *cabildo,* and the *presbytère.* They married her off to Pontalba when he came here from France, and it never worked out. It's just all wrong, I always say, forcing or coaxing a marriage—they're both the same when you come down to it—it doesn't work out."

"No," Miriam assented faintly. It was hard to believe what she was hearing from the same Emma who had—well, no matter now.

"There was such a scandal. Quarrels over money, you know. Her father-in-law, the old baron, tried to kill her, then shot himself. My word, Marie Claire writes that the baroness is coming back here to build on her property in the Place d'Armes. The Perrins may eventually buy an apartment there when they're finished. Goodness! They're planning to sell their house!"

"Who is? What house?" Miriam asked in the same faint voice.

"Why, the new house that they've never lived in. How strange!"

"Do they say when they're coming back?"

"Let's see. No. They are planning to stay abroad a while longer because of her progress. . . . Oh, but André must be disappointed. . . . To think he planned that wonderful house himself. . . . Well, if they move to the Place d'Armes, I know Pelagie will be pleased. They'll be around the corner. Pelagie was always rather fond of Marie Claire, odd as she is. And André is so agreeable, don't you think so, Miriam?"

"Oh, yes, most agreeable."

"The whole thing's disgraceful," Eugene said contemptuously. "Singing. I don't know why he puts up with it."

Eulalie nodded agreement, and then remembering that Eugene could not see the nod, repeated, "Disgraceful."

Eulalie, who had been staying in her sister's town house, had been spending most of her days with Eugene, reading aloud to him and waiting on him, moving his chair from sun to shade. A curious relationship had developed. Eugene is a Jew, but she overlooks that, Miriam thought, because he allows her to serve him. He accepts her and no other man ever has. They made an odd contrast, he with his lavish beard and she with her scanty hair, too thin even to hold her combs.

"Where's my son?" the father asked now. "I haven't seen him since this morning."

Eulalie stood up. "I'll fetch him for you."

The children, especially the boy—or could it, Miriam thought bitterly, perhaps be "boys," to include that other one?—were all Eugene still cared about. Except for them he had removed himself from everything that had once filled his life. He was a crumbling castle, falling into ruin. His long silences were almost more disturbing than his tempers had been. She tried to comfort him, to reach out to him in his disaster, to tell him he was not alone.

"Don't," he would say. "You don't mean it. We don't mean it."

She protested. "I do mean it, Eugene. What kind of a human being do you think I am?" She had suggested a club, the Pelican Club, where doctors and lawyers, bankers and brokers, met to play brag and eat dinners prepared by a superb French chef.

"The finest people in the city belong," she said, appealing to his snobbishness.

And he had retorted, "I already know the finest people in the city. Clubs are all right for Anglo-Saxons. I'm a Creole and we don't need clubs."

You're a Jew, she thought, not a Creole, but of course a Jew could align himself with whatever forces he wished. Very well, Eugene had chosen to consider himself a Creole.

She had suggested that he be driven to the office every morning. Someone there could read reports to him and he would make decisions as before.

He had refused that, too. "No, Scofield is a good enough manager. I'll leave things in his hands."

Miriam wasn't so sure. Last month Scofield had brought a note to be signed.

"What's this?" Eugene had inquired after his listless hand had been guided to write his signature.

"Nothing of any great importance," Scofield had told him. "I had to borrow from the bank. Just temporarily to tide us over the month until they pay for the last London shipment."

As he was leaving, Miriam had stopped the man in the hall. "Why do we have to borrow, Mr. Scofield? We never had to before, did we?"

And he had looked at her with insolence in his eyes, while giving a courteous answer. "Nothing to worry about at all, ma'am. A common business practice. A lady shouldn't have to worry herself with such things."

But she had burned with anger.

Now she tried to put these thoughts at the back of

her mind. "Shall you be coming this afternoon to the temple dedication, Eugene?"

"No. I can't see it, so why should I go?"

She had expected the refusal, for he had a dread of showing his infirmity in public places. She understood that.

When at certain angles the light struck his glasses, one could see the shriveled, dead-white eyes. Scorched flesh shone hideously pink from forehead to cheek.

She had a mixture of feelings: first pity, then shuddering horror, then shame, a shame all the more painful because Eugene had never with the slightest word alluded to her father's part in his disaster.

Spring sunshine fell on the crowd at the corner of Canal and Bourbon streets. It whitened six tall Ionic columns under the splendid entablature of what had once been Christ Church Episcopal and was now, through the beneficence of Judah Touro, becoming the Nefutzoth Yehudah Synagogue. The splendid organ was still pealing after the service while a crowd of the rich and famous, Jew and non-Jew alike, in flowered bonnets and silk hats, lingered on the sidewalk to watch the dignitaries.

"The choir was magnificent," said Rosa. Her eyes fell fondly on her sons. "Your father would have been in his glory today. Look, there's Isaac Leeser, come all the way from Philadelphia."

"He's staying at Kursheedt's house. He must have had a dozen invitations, but he wanted a kosher home," David said meaningfully.

"Isn't that Touro?" Miriam asked.

Encircled by admirers in rainbow colors, Touro stood starkly in his somber black suit. His deep eyes were black and the furrows running to the corners of his stern mouth were dark.

The conversation on the homeward walk made much of him, as they passed the arcaded Touro Block and the bark *Judah Touro* on the riverfront, ready for departure.

"Astonishing," Gabriel remarked. "He has even become a Sabbath observer. Turned his life upside down at his age. After that, nothing seems impossible."

And Miriam remembered that he was one of the people who had made it possible. Suddenly she wanted to tell him of the fear which had been nagging at her for weeks. He was the family's lawyer, after all.

So when Rosa, with David and her sons, walked ahead on the narrow banquette, she began, "I am worried. It's about my husband's business affairs." She related the incident of the note and the encounter with Scofield. "I fear for us, for my children. Of course, I know nothing about business. I try to talk to Eugene, but he has lost interest. He has lost more than his eyes. He has lost his will."

"I know that," Gabriel said quietly.

"I daresay it's unbecoming of me." She heard herself apologizing. "I'm certain Mr. Scofield is an honest man, but—"

"Are you? One can never be certain about anyone."

"Well, then, I don't know what is to be done."

"I'm only your husband's lawyer. I have no power to examine his books without his permission. I've tried to speak to him, too, but as you say, he's lost interest. He has affairs in Memphis, cotton and lumber, which should be looked to."

Miriam felt suddenly lost, as if a chill wind had blown through the warm afternoon.

And she repeated, "It's as if he doesn't want to think anymore."

"Then someone must think for him."

"But there is no one! Surely not my father! And

David knows less than nothing about business affairs. My children will have no one to protect them."

"They have you."

"I? What can I do? I'm a woman."

Gabriel stopped and looked down at her.

"You can learn," he said sternly.

"Who will teach me?"

"I will. But you must get Eugene's permission to act in his stead."

Eugene would not grant it. "What! You to sit in an office and deal with men? No, I'm hardly such a fool as that! Not yet. I will take Scofield over you any day."

In spite of herself Miriam was relieved. Eugene was right: How was she to sit in an office and deal with men?

Yet she was troubled all that summer. In the autumn Scofield came again to the house with papers for Eugene's signature. Again, having glimpsed a bank's letterhead, she was certain that they were loans. This time Scofield avoided her, almost running in the hall on his way out. Standing in the doorway, watching him rush down the front walk and slip out of sight around the corner, it seemed to her that she was being given forewarning of disaster. She had lived long enough in New Orleans to know that fortunes are lost far more quickly than they are made. And she kept standing there, staring into the street, seeing not the child rolling a hoop, not the fruit cart, not the two old women chatting on the walk, seeing only that specter of disaster.

That night Angelique had a bad dream. Her cry woke Miriam out of the heavy sleep in which an aching mind seeks relief from its pressures.

The child was standing up in bed holding a doll. The beam from the candle made black pits of her eyes.

"There's no place to go," she whispered, "no place."

Miriam saw that she was terrified. She sat on the bed, drawing her daughter down onto her lap.

"No place to go? Tell me what you mean, darling. Tell me."

"I thought I was standing in the street all alone and I didn't know where to go."

"No, no, you're right here in your pretty bed, with the pink quilt that Aunt Emma gave you, and your dolls, and your brother in the next room, and Papa's down the hall, and we're—"

"But Papa had no place to go! They took his table away!"

Puzzled for a moment, Miriam remembered then how Emma had mourned the loss of her furniture at the sheriff's sale, especially the loss of the grand mahogany dining table at which twenty-four had been able to sit in comfort. Much as they had tried to conceal the disaster from the children, apparently the children had felt its impact, after all. Poor little beings!

The chilly hand of foreboding passed over her flesh and the voice of fear whispered: There'll be no one to shelter all of you as we did Papa.

"You were dreaming, darling. It was a bad, silly dream. We're never going to leave this house. It's ours, with everything in it."

"But Papa—"

"Papa's here, too, quite safe with us." Her fingers moved in Angelique's hair and smoothed the ruffles around the small neck. "Anyway, you mustn't think of all that. That was different, Angelique."

"Why was it?" the child persisted.

"Because it just was. It's too hard to explain. You have to believe me. I never fib to you, do I?"

"No."

"Well, then. Go back to sleep, dear. Everything's really all right."

Back in her own bed, she scolded herself for having caught the child's fright.

"That was different, Angelique," she had said.

How could she be sure it was?

Oh, stop this, Miriam! Things are always worse in the middle of the night, you ought to know that. You're behaving like a child yourself. There may be nothing wrong at all. This is your morbid imagination.

Or maybe not.

So early one evening, having got the office keys from Eugene's desk, she went downtown to look over the books. The figures in columns and rows were absolutely meaningless to her, but a letter in Scofield's top drawer was very clear. It was a peremptory demand and warning from the Bank of New Orleans, about an overdue note. The thing shook in her hand.

And she walked home slowly, reluctant to face Eugene with a crisis which he was not ready to confront. At the same time, who was ready to confront it?

In the Place d'Armes, although it was almost dusk, workmen were still clambering and clattering on the Pontalba Building. Low light touched the bricks with rose and, lying on ornamental black iron scrollwork, turned it shiny as licorice. The best of everything was going into these houses for the most fashionable families in the city. Hadn't Emma said André and Marie Claire were planning to move here? Miriam stood still. Strange that she no longer *felt* the old pain, yet could so sharply recall that she had once felt it. She wondered whether it would come back when he returned. She hoped, almost, that he would not return, certainly not to live here. And at the same time she scanned the building as if to guess which of the windows would be his.

On a second-floor balcony a woman was kneeling to examine a window frame. That must be the baroness! She had been the talk of the city since she had returned from Europe to keep an eye on her property, climbing ladders in her pantaloons. Extraordinary woman! One couldn't help but wonder at the drive and daring of such a woman, who obviously had no care for "what people thought." Extraordinary!

Eugene was not at home. He had left no message; he never did; where he had gone was understood. The bank's letter would have to wait until the morning. She went to her room to read it again, then opened the *Daily Delta.*

At once the name Pontalba caught her attention, followed by something about "an intelligent expression" and "energetic movements." So Miriam read rapidly.

From her frank and unostentatious style . . . one of those energetic ladies who, thrown upon their own resources and compelled to lay aside much of their feminine reserve, devote themselves industriously and energetically to the support of their dependent families. . . . Her proper businesslike style . . .

Miriam laid the paper aside.

"The support of their dependent families," she repeated aloud. "Their feminine reserve," she said, frowning a little. "A proper businesslike style."

She stood up and began to undress, thinking all the while about the baroness. In the tall glass she watched her dress fall to the floor, then the white muslin petticoat, the pleated horsehair petticoat, then a corded calico skirt, the crinoline, and finally the winter flannel petticoat. And remembering the pantaloons, it came to

her that there was something humorous about all this
clothing. One couldn't very well climb a ladder in
these things, could one? Of course, she had no need to
climb a ladder, but—

She picked up the paper again, eagerly reading:
"Energetic ladies thrown upon their own resources
. . ." Something ran up and down her spine, light fin-
gers of excitement and fear.

Your children have you, Gabriel had said.

I will teach you, he had said.

Why not?

In the morning she went to Eugene. He was sitting
in his wing chair holding a small object, turning it
over as if to see it with his fingers. Hearing her come
in, he placed it carefully on the table, and she saw
what it was: a tawny clay figurine, painted and glazed,
a recumbent lion.

"That's very good, Eugene." For a moment she hesitated before questioning gently, "Is it—the boy's?"

He nodded.

"The color is perfect, a kind of sandy gold."

She saw that, for whatever reason, he did not welcome the subject. And she thought she understood the
complexity, the sad confusion, of his feelings.

"I have a letter from the bank," she said then. "I'll
read it to you."

"They sent a letter to you?"

"They sent it to your manager, Mr. Scofield, and I
took it from his desk. No, listen to me before you
explode. Listen to me."

When Miriam had read the letter, Eugene was silent. Shock and humiliation washed over his tired face.
But most of all what one saw was a weary, gray indifference.

So the course lay plain before her.

"Now will you give me permission to work? I will

do nothing without the advice of Gabriel Carvalho. I will learn what I need to know, as once I had to learn to speak your languages here. Now will you give it to me?"

His silence was assent.

Presently, he got up. "Get the carriage for me. I'm going out."

"The carriage is already waiting. You will be going to Queen, then?"

Eugene turned toward her without answering. She saw his cheek twitch.

"It's all right, Eugene! Don't you think I know you still go there?"

She followed him to the hall, where Sisyphus waited to help him down the stairs.

"Please tell Maxim," she instructed Sisyphus, "to take Mr. Mendes to the house on Chartres Street where he always goes. And to wait for him if he wishes."

The instruction was certainly superfluous, since the routine was always the same. But it was a fine relief to say aloud what had been secret. Oh, it would give them something to gossip about in the kitchen! She felt some pride in being able to acknowledge freely what other people might construe as a humiliation. In the public acknowledgment of this thing it ceased to be a humiliation.

Besides, she had more important things to think about now.

15

The city was barely awake when David turned his horse eastward into the gorgeous morning light. Lucien followed at the customary respectful master–servant distance, and the two horses moved at a nice trot. David's medical kit was slung over the saddle horn, and his pistols hung heavily from his belt. Having never in his life carried a weapon, he was acutely aware of them, and would not have had them if Lucien had not refused to accompany him again unless he was armed.

Arms, however, attracted no attention. A southern gentleman was expected to carry a pistol or a dirk or both. A violent people under the surface of courtesy, David reflected now, as he rode past the dueling oaks behind the cathedral where, only last week, he had been summoned to help two handsome boys who had shot each other to death in a silly argument about an actress. Not more than eighteen, they had been, when their blood had gushed away into the ground.

Lucien was apprehensive today. He "felt things in his bones." David, however, had no reason to think that today's meetings were going to be any different from the usual. First to come was a leader's policy meeting under the guise of a social celebration at an inn. Then, in the evening, the gathering with Negro leaders in the swamp hideout would be held. In neither place was there any need for weapons.

Weapons had never been what he wanted, anyway. Words and ideas were always far more potent, for in the end there was no defense against ideas.

Certainly things were coming to a head now in the political area. The Whig party was moribund and the burgeoning new Republican party was spreading through the North. More and more the slave power was having to defend itself. Defend itself! How, for instance, a man like Judah Benjamin could stand up in the United States Senate and speak as he did, David would never understand! Slaves are property, he says; there is no right in law to rob a man of his property. Well, Charles Sumner might call Benjamin the most brilliant orator in the Senate, and he might well be, but oratory and elegant manners have nothing to do with morality. For a Jew to talk like that! Not that Benjamin was much of a Jew!

Yet David supposed a Jew had as much right as anyone to be wrong. Even the rabbis, like the clergy of every other denomination, were in disagreement among themselves these days.

Up in New York Rabbi Raphall quoted Exodus as authority for slavery. Oh, says the rabbi, he himself is not a slave owner, but it is certainly not forbidden to own slaves, provided that one treats them with dignity and kindness. His sermon is praised and quoted throughout the South.

In vehement rebuttal, Rabbi Einhorn of Baltimore replies: It is the essence of the Bible that we must follow, not its primitive customs. Of course slavery is mentioned there, as were polygamy and royalty, both of which have been abolished in the United States!

Now, as they crossed the city line, the horses' hooves struck quietly on sandy ground. The autumn air was warm at David's back and cool on his face. Ahead of him the road ran to the railroad tracks and beyond. At the crossing he reined the horse in and stood a moment observing the double black gleam of the tracks. There was direct service now all the way to New York. A frown turned the lines on his forehead into furrows.

Lucien rode up to him. "You'd never make it," he said softly. "You'd be caught at the next station. Boat's the only way, I keep telling you."

"I'm not going to be caught."

"Let us hope not."

Fear trickled through his veins. It felt cold. Any man who says he can face a painful death without fear is a liar. I am terribly afraid, he told himself.

Yet there was something stronger than fear within him, a hatred of the enemy—the system, not the men who ran it—so powerful that it seemed as if the system would have to weaken in the face of such hatred; weaken, rot, and die before he himself could die.

His frown deepened. He clucked to the horse and called back to Lucien.

"Come on, let's move, we've a long day."

Out of the swampland rose a mist so heavy that, in spite of the moonlight, only the innermost ring of trees could be seen from the spot where David halted. Beyond lay the jungle night. A constant dripping from the trees came steadily, like drums or marching feet.

"Draw the cloak collar up around your face," Lucien advised.

"Will you stop whispering? I can't hear you," David demanded irritably. With nerves on edge, he was impatient.

Now Lucien was impatient. "I said, cover your face

up to the eyes and pull the hat down. You must not be recognized. Don't you understand that yet?"

"Thank God it's chilly, then," David grumbled. He strained to see into the blackness, but a rolling mist still screened it.

"This place reminds me of—" he began, and stopped, having been about to say something about Macbeth's witches, before remembering that the remark would have no significance for Lucien.

"I haven't the slightest idea where the road is," he complained. "Are you sure you know where we're going?"

"Have faith. Another five minutes' walk and we'll be there."

Soon their feet caught in a soggy muck, so that each step became a struggle against a strong downward suction.

"Sorry," Lucien apologized. "But the wetter it is, the better to foil the dogs. They can follow a dry trail for five miles or more, with enough strength left at the end of it to tear a man apart."

"I still don't know how you know where you are."

"Oh, you get to recognize your landmarks. My brother lived in the cypress swamp for three years after he ran away. He and a band of twenty used to raid the plantations at night for food."

"You never told me."

"I didn't want to talk about it."

"Is he in the group we're seeing tonight?"

"No. He was hanged." And as David had no comment to that, Lucien continued, "An abolitionist from Illinois got them into a big group, maybe two thousand Negroes, making cartridges and other ammunition. But the vigilantes found out. That's the trouble when the group's too big. There's bound to be somebody who talks too much—Stop! Listen!"

A muffled, stealthy swishing of foliage being carefully moved aside came from the left. The two men waited. A moment later a smudge of light emerged from the trees, like moonglow behind clouds, revealing first a lantern, then the man who held it, and finally a circle of ten men, each with his weak light, together making a pool of light in the cramped clearing.

Lucien held his arm up in greeting. "Listen. I've brought someone to talk to you tonight. Don't ask who he is. You don't need to know. He's a friend. That's enough. He wouldn't be here otherwise, because it's a great risk and you all know it. I tried to talk him out of coming, but he wanted to come. Draw in closer."

In total silence the men obeyed. David was ringed with ghostly white teeth and eyewhites glistening out of blackness.

"Where are the horses?" Lucien asked.

A man answered. "Two good horses, rested and saddled. Right there behind those trees."

"Horses?" David inquired.

"For us. For you if there's need. See where I'm pointing? Go directly south. In less than a mile you'll reach the road. Turn right onto it and from there it's straight to the city line."

"But," David objected, "what about our horses in the hotel stable?"

"Please. If there's any trouble you'll have to get out of here fast," Lucien warned. "Listen to me. You'll go the way I just told you. I've got another route for myself. It's safer like that. You understand?"

David nodded. Tonight, it seemed, the servant and master had exchanged places.

"I understand," he said somberly.

"All right. Now begin."

David stepped forward. "I've come to you because I

have the same wish you have, to make life better for you and for us all."

No one moved. His little speech, which he had not prepared beforehand, came without effort, came naturally and truthfully from the heart.

"Sometimes it must seem to you that the changes we seek will never come, or at least not soon enough for you who are alive today to get any benefit from them."

Someone shifted a lantern, splashing light upward, so that there fell into David's line of vision an old man's tender face, bright with worshipful concentration. This, finally, is my meeting with reality, he thought, with brave flesh and vulnerable bones. All things before this were only plans and talk, philosophy and paper. Yet at the same time he was standing outside of this reality, observing himself here in the eerie night, an actor in a fantastic dream.

"If thousands of you should refuse to work for anything but wages, which would of course mean freedom, that would mean winning without violence."

He paused. Dark as it was, he could sense the instant stiffening of bodies, could sense the tilted heads, the listening. The hair on his forearms prickled.

A dog barked; the signal smashed the waiting stillness. Almost at once the stillness exploded with a violent crash of hooves, and the clamor of voices.

The circle broke. In frenzy the men dropped their lanterns, scattering themselves in the shelter of the underbrush. A moment later half a dozen men on horseback waving torches and pistols plunged through the trees; crows, startled out of their rest, cawed and flapped; horses neighed; the woods came awake.

Lucien and David stared at one another as if questioning their own senses, as if dazed.

Then, "For Christ's sakes, run!" Lucien cried. "Go!"

Rearing horses went wild. The huge animals, quivering under the whip and the terror, trampled through the underbrush.

"Run!" Lucien screamed again. "David! To the road!"

A horse wheeled across David's path. "David!" the rider cried. "So it's David! You"—he raised a pistol—"you scum!"

Out of the torchlight blazed the furious eyes of Sylvain Labouisse. *Hate! Kill!* said the mad eyes. David drew his pistol. Sylvain's shot splattered in the leafage over David's head, while his own shot knocked Sylvain out of the saddle.

"Go!" screamed Lucien. "He recognized you."

David swung up onto Sylvain's horse. "Lucien, get to my sister's or to Gabriel Carvalho, either one, I'll need money. I don't want them mixed up in this, just some money!" And he spurred the horse into the swamp.

Ten minutes later, as he pounded over the empty road, that queer sensation came again, as if a voice were saying: This is a dream, you know. Things like this don't happen in the space of minutes. Why, not half an hour ago you got up from supper at the hotel, said good night to your friends, and arranged to meet again in a month. Yesterday you were seeing patients. Now you are fleeing for your life. No, it simply can't be.

A man like you doesn't pull a pistol out of a holster without even thinking. Why, you've never even held one in your hand before! And was that really Sylvain Labouisse, and did you shoot him? Kill him, perhaps? God forbid! But he wanted to kill you! Why should he want to kill you? You've never harmed him, never harmed anyone! Not you, who care so much about the world. Maybe, though, it's a little bit crazy to care so much about the world. Maybe you should mind your own affairs. Who do you think you are? The Messiah?

"Oh, my God," he said aloud.

And before his horrified eyes, hanging in the air between the laid-back ears of the racing horse, was the grieving, uncomprehending sweet face of Pelagie.

When the door opened, the draft caught the remains of the burning papers and sent a flurry of scorched fragments over the floor.

"There's no time to bother with that. Leave it," Lucien said.

"I'm ready." David picked up his traveling bag. Dressed in a topcoat with a dark woolen shawl over his shoulders, he looked like any gentleman about to go on a journey. "I've burned MacKenzie's lists so no one will get into trouble." Almost lovingly he looked about the drab little room. "My books. I hate to leave my books."

"I'll send them to you," Miriam said, "as soon as I know where you'll be." And she rearranged the shawl, which did not need rearranging.

"Don't linger, David. Every second counts." Gabriel nodded toward Miriam. "She's in terrible danger here!"

As if suddenly inspired, David grasped his sister's shoulders. "Listen—you shouldn't have come . . . but now that you're here, listen, you used to talk about getting away. . . . You could. . . . Lucien could get young Eugene and Angelique . . . only another couple of minutes. . . . We could all go."

"No!" Gabriel cried vehemently. "No! You're not thinking straight. How do you know you'll make it to the boat, or that the boat won't be intercepted? You can't possibly want to risk her any more than you already have."

"You're right, of course, you're right. But still—"

"I couldn't anyway," Miriam said. "How could I leave Papa now? And Eugene, blind? I'm just now putting things in order."

David put his arms around his sister. "So, again I leave you. When you need me, when I should be here at your right hand, I leave you." He mourned; his eyes, his voice, and his own right hand, as it stroked her hair, all mourned.

"Dear David, don't worry about me. It's only you we should be thinking of right now. Oh, take care of yourself! Don't, don't, do any more foolish awful things! I mean—oh, I don't know what I mean! Just take care of yourself, my dear."

Lucien pulled David's sleeve. "They'll be coming for you."

"When you get where you're going, you'll let me know," Gabriel said. "I'll send whatever you need to start up again. You've got enough money for now. The skiff is marked *Elsie Ann*. You're sure you know how to sail, Lucien?"

"Yes, yes, I know." Lucien was already out the door.

"Very well. Once you're over the state line in Mississippi, you'll manage." Taking David's hand, Gabriel propelled him to the door. "Good God, what a rotten business! But God bless you anyway. Now, go! Go, will you?"

When the hurrying steps had died away, Gabriel sighed. "What a rotten business," he repeated. "Now give me the key. We'll lock the house and I'll see you home. Does anyone know Lucien came to your house?"

"Only Fanny, and she doesn't know why. Besides, I trust her."

"You can't trust anyone. You shouldn't have been mixed up in this at all."

"You are, and you aren't his brother."

"One has one's reasons. Complicated reasons, sometimes," Gabriel said gently.

"This is the second time you rescued him, do you realize that?"

Gabriel smiled. How rare his smile is, Miriam thought; it spreads so slowly as if his face were astonished at the sweetness of its own smile.

The stillness was absolute. Not a leaf moved through the heavy air. And they stood a moment, savoring the silence, relieving the tension of the past half hour. Suddenly Gabriel flung his arm up.

"Listen. Do you hear anything?"

"No, nothing. Yes, yes, I do."

"Shh. It's horses. Coming this way. Down Royal Street, I think."

The beat and clatter of hooves grew nearer and clearer.

"Get back into the house. There's no time to get home now. They're coming for him here. Hide here. No, wait. Wait a moment."

From a roll of bandage on the shelf he ripped off a piece. "Tie this around my head, over my ear. Make a big wad, tight. That's it."

Wonderingly, her heart racing, her mouth dry with fear, Miriam obeyed.

"Now, outside. Get out in the courtyard."

"Where? Where?" she cried, in panic now.

The horses had turned into the street and voices were heard, men calling to one another.

"Anywhere. Don't make a sound, no matter what happens."

In the bushes behind the necessary Miriam crouched, huddling in her skirts. Gabriel had lit a candle. Through the window she could see him sitting with his bandaged head resting on the back of the chair. She could hear the pounding on the front door, could see him get up and admit three disheveled, frantic men.

"Where's the doctor?"

"I wish I knew. I'm waiting for him," Gabriel complained. "I've got the devil of an earache."

"Don't I know you? You're a lawyer, aren't you?"

"Yes. Carvalho. Gabriel Carvalho. And you?"

"Lloyd Morrissey. You been here long?"

"About an hour. What's wrong? What's happened?"

"Plenty. Sylvain Labouisse has been shot. Raphael shot him."

"Dr. Raphael did? Why, I never knew him even to carry a gun. A very gentle man, he—"

"It was Raphael all right. Shot Labouisse out of the saddle."

"I can't believe it. Is Labouisse hurt badly?"

"Badly? He's dead."

"But the servant who let me in," Gabriel persisted, "told me the doctor had been out for hours. A woman giving birth, he said, a bad case. I think he said it was on North Rampart Street, though I didn't pay much attention, my ear hurts so."

"The servant lied to you. He's not out on a call, he's getting out of town."

Someone called. "Come on, Morrissey, for Christ's sake, let's spread out, one of us is bound to get hold of him."

The door crashed shut and the silence rushed back. Miriam waited for some minutes until she heard Gabriel's low call.

"Come quickly. They'll be hunting up and down the city. Follow me, stay close to the building line."

Shreds of cloud sailed across the moon, darkening the street, and drifting past the moon, released bright silver to illumine the banquette.

"You mustn't be seen," Gabriel whispered over her shoulder. "Walk as fast and lightly as you can. You never know who might be awake even at this hour. Plots and deaths," she heard him mutter as they crept through the streets.

Stooping a little, unconsciously trying to make himself smaller, he nevertheless cast a tall shadow. How he must hate all this! Miriam thought. It's against everything in his nature. And it crossed her mind, frightened and tense as she was, that, although David's emergency, with its revelation of what he had been doing during the past few years, had come as a shock, it had, on reflection, not been a surprise, for it was in keeping with the character of David. But one could never imagine Gabriel doing anything so incautious, so imprudent! Yet here he was, forceful and strong in this moment of crisis; she *knew,* following his rapid walk toward home, that he would get her there safely. He would come through for her, as surely he had just done for David.

She heard his whisper as they turned the final corner.

"David ought to be on the river by now. He had just enough minutes to spare, I'm fairly sure. And thank God for that."

From the State House to the cathedral the grave procession marched in respect to Sylvain Labouisse, acknowledging his civic benefactions. All was still. All was black. Six horses, blanketed and plumed in black, pulled the black funeral car; the canopy above the cof-

fin was draped in black. Only the white chrysanthe-
mums heaped on the coffin and the white dove
perched on the canopy relieved the pall.

"It reminds me," Rosa whispered, "of the memorial
service for Lafayette. That was in thirty-four. Only of
course they had a bust of Lafayette instead of a coffin.
But this is just as solemn."

Annoyed by her chatter, Miriam moved forward.
Women—since women did not go to funerals—were
standing outside the cathedral on the steps. Properly
speaking, they ought not to have been even that near,
but Rosa was curious, and Miriam had gone as far as
possible with her father, to be there when he came out.

The poor man was almost ill from shock. She had
tried to ease the blow, in some way to counter his
awful shame, much of which she felt herself.

"Sylvain would have killed him, too, Papa. Remember that."

"It was David's own doing! If he hadn't been there,
if he hadn't got himself mixed up in these dirty affairs
. . ."

"Papa, try to think. This whole tragedy came out of
David's beliefs, his honest beliefs. It was not a dirty
affair. You have to admit he acted honestly."

She had been met with a look of such outrage and
agony that she had closed her mouth.

How men were disappointed in their sons! Poor
Papa! Once more to be brought to his knees, as if the
financial crash had not been enough.

Whether or not others, especially Emma, would
censure him for David's act—and except for Eulalie,
who was in a savage rage, Miriam felt confident that
they did not—Ferdinand felt that they did, and would
probably feel so always.

Now just past the open doors she could see her father in the back row. He had come in last to avoid

being seen. And she wondered what he would say if he could know the part she had played in her brother's escape.

Steady, steady, she said to herself. Think of something else.

Straight before her, far down the aisle, stood the jeweled glitter of the altar. Her eyes moved from gilded lettering on the arch. There on a mural St. Louis, king of France, proclaimed the start of the Seventh Crusade. Swords and blood! Burning Jews in their huddled streets as they marched across Europe.

Enough! Enough blood spilled here, without remembering all the centuries.

No, he had said that day at Beau Jardin when he first came back, no, a wife would not fit with what I intend to do in my life. And far back, long ago in Europe, their grandfather had said, with some pride and some vexation, How stubborn he is when he thinks a thing is right.

Who is to know what is right?

Flames tremble on the candle tips. The whole world trembles.

"You're taking it very hard," Rosa said kindly. "No one blames it on you."

"It's not that. I was thinking of Pelagie," which was also true.

Cascades of grief flowed from the organ. The coffin came first in the procession of men in mourning coats and tall hats. At the curb where Eugene and Ferdinand were getting into their carriage, Gabriel caught up with Miriam. His glance said: This knowledge we share. He spoke quietly.

"Are you all right?"

I must look like death, she thought, and said, "I'm going to see Pelagie."

"Catholic women here wait nine days before paying condolence calls," Rosa reminded her.

"I'm not Catholic and I have to see her."

Rosa laid a hand on Miriam's arm. "She may not want to see you," she said gently.

"That is what I have to know."

She was eight years old again, standing in the upstairs bedroom and Pelagie was saying, "Oh, you're going to be a beauty, darling, and your papa will buy diamonds for your ears."

The front door was hung with gray crepe, and Miriam, sounding the knocker, remembered that for married people, unless they were old, colors of mourning were lavender or gray. In the center hung a wreath of black beads containing strands of Sylvain's hair under a velvet bow. All these structures and customs, she thought. All of us keep them in our differing ways, to ease our sorrow. And do they ease it? How can I know? I have never had a sorrow like hers.

Someone opened the door and left her. Uncertain where to go, she stood in the hall. It was dim. All the shades were drawn, and the enormous mirror was covered with a cloth. The clock under the stairs read nine fifteen; it had been stopped at the hour of Sylvain's death. Nine fifteen in the night in a deserted swamp, my brother— She held her head up and walked into the parlor.

Pelagie was sitting on the sofa between Emma and Eulalie. Under her black skirt another baby waited to be born, this one surely the last, for who would marry a widow with eight children?

At the sound of Miriam's entrance the three women looked up. The mother and the sister spoke to each other without words: Why has she come here?

For a long minute Miriam and Pelagie waited. Unsteadily then, Pelagie stood up and Miriam rushed to her, opening her arms. Touched by the warmth of living flesh, together they mourned the dead and forgave the living.

Even before she opened the envelope bearing David's script and a New York postmark, the fear, which for the past month had lain like a cold stone in Miriam, broke apart. No one was at home when the letter arrived, so she was spared both the angry silences and the angry words that followed any reference to David.

She could not turn the pages fast enough; from line to line her mind's eye saw between each, written tall in flaming letters, the one word: Safe! Safe!

"In the harbor we found a sailboat," he wrote discreetly.

> For the first time in my life I had to take something that didn't belong to me. We cut the boat loose and turned downriver. Lucien is an excellent sailor and the wind was with us; but for all that, they would surely have caught me. Five minutes later would have been too late, and I would not be writing this to you. We were only a few yards out when we heard shouts on the levee. Torches flared. There is a terror in the sight of so many torches on a black night. There must have been a dozen men, to judge by the lights and the voices. They didn't see us. It was mercifully dark on the water and the harbor was crowded with ships at anchor. Still, it's a wonder they didn't hear the pounding of my heart. . . .
> . . . and having neither food nor water, began to worry. Toward midmorning, coming into the old pirate lair on Barataria Bay, I decided to take a small chance and sent Lucien ashore to buy enough to last us through the long sail to Missis-

sippi. . . . So we passed between Cat Island and Pass Christian, remembering how you used to write about your summers at the Pass. I was afraid to put ashore there, thinking I might encounter someone who knew me from New Orleans. . . .

. . . finally landed at Pascagoula, where Lucien got hold of some back issues of the New Orleans papers, and so learned that Sylvain was dead, which, although I had hoped he was only wounded, I had actually suspected from the first. I took my terrible sadness and guilt with me on the train to Mobile, where we changed cars for the North. . . . Lucien keeps telling me that a man who kills in self-defense need feel no guilt, which seems reasonable, and yet I do. . . .

So I am already back at work, having opened my little office yesterday. I hope my act hasn't brought too much trouble to the family. Our poor father! I seem doomed to keep hurting him. And you. I love you so and worry about you, who have troubles enough without my heaping more upon you. Forgive me. But I am the way I am. . . .

"I have a letter from David," Miriam told Emma later that day. "Perhaps you will tell my father that he's safe in New York. I can't talk about it anymore."

Later still Emma came to report. "He didn't say a word, but he looked very relieved. A father is a father, after all."

True. And the anger would pass. The pain might well last, but the anger would ease away. Ferdinand was not a man to hold on to it forever.

16

Gabriel Carvalho closed the ledger with a smart thud and leaned back on the sofa. Often they went over the quarterly accounts of Mendes and Company in the comfort of Rosa's parlor, combining this business with Miriam's social visit to Rosa.

"So," he said, "a job nicely done. Mendes is solvent. Very much so, I should say."

"Only because of you."

"Not so. You have caught on wonderfully well."

It was true. Miriam had astonished herself. With Scofield replaced by an honorable, bright young manager who had no objection to working with a Mrs. instead of a Mr., she had "gone back to school," as it were, and found it exciting. Having learned from Ferdinand's failure and from Eugene's prior example, she had as soon as possible paid off the debts which Scofield had piled up. Recently she had even begun to invest in real estate, prime vacant land alongside the railroad. Railroads will develop as the city grows; they are bound to, she had thought. And Sanderson the manager had agreed.

"I had an idea," she began now, and stopped.

It was far easier to express herself to Sanderson than to Gabriel. There was too much unspoken between herself and him: the affair with David, and Eugene's taunt, retracted, it was true, but not forgotten by her: *He can't take his eyes away from you.* Absurd! The truth was, he seldom looked at her at all; when his head wasn't bent over documents, his eyes were directed at the wall behind her head. She was quite certain that this behavior was not due to any shyness; he was too positive to be shy; rather, he was austere, kind but austere. One wondered whether he and any woman would—her thoughts stumbled, ashamed of themselves—what he and a woman would . . . But with André it was all clear, all vivid; one could imagine.

"You were saying you had an idea."

She retrieved the idea. "Yes, I was thinking, do you suppose we might offer Sanderson an interest in the business? He'd have more incentive than one can have with just a salary."

"And I was thinking of suggesting that myself. You're a step ahead of me. Soon I shall have to run to keep up with you."

"Oh, no, there's so much I don't understand! All that business about bank stocks, Sanderson was trying to explain."

"Why they're a sound investment? Because banks have to be exceptionally strong in this economy. Planters need big loans to keep themselves afloat between harvests."

"But why is it so hard to keep themselves afloat?"

"They have to modernize. It costs money to run a plantation. A cane-grinding engine alone costs five thousand dollars. Then there're all the slaves to be fed. And the owners live lavishly. They spend from crop to crop."

"Creoles are so extravagant!"

"Not so much anymore. It's not the Creoles, but the Americans, who have the real money now. Today's

Creoles are tightening their belts. Very few can recall the days of places like Valcour Aime's Versailles."

"And a good thing, too. I was there once and it disgusted me. I remember how annoyed Eugene was because I wasn't impressed." Miriam paused, as if to make up her mind whether to speak or not. "I would like to sell Beau Jardin. I never liked it."

"Oh, no!" Rosa cried. She had been working quietly at an embroidery frame. "Not that beautiful place!"

"Yes. I would like to free all the slaves and be rid of it. Every time I go there I despise it more. I drive past the fields where the people are working and I think, 'That woman there with the infant on her back was bought for a thousand dollars; that man driving the mule wagon was bought for fifteen hundred dollars.' And I cannot stand it."

There was a silence in the room. Rosa's, Miriam knew, was disapproving. Gabriel's might also be disapproving, yet there was something about him that gave her full freedom to speak her mind. And she continued. "It's hard to reconcile that feeling with the people I know so well. Eugene, after all, is not a villain."

"No," said Gabriel, "he is not."

"He's only like everyone else. Living here, he does what everyone else does. I understand that."

From the street a voice cried through the tall open windows, "Artichokes! Figs! Cantaloupes!"

"The Green Sass Man," Rosa said. "Have you been buying figs from him, Miriam? They've been especially good this season."

"That old man," Miriam said, ignoring the question, "has been buying his freedom as long as I've known him. His master must make a good two or three thousand a year out of his sales. Oh, how I hate it the more I see of it!"

Gabriel asked, "What does Eugene say about selling Beau Jardin?"

"Of course he doesn't see things my way at all. He won't hear of it. No one sees it my way except David, and even he writes to me now that we might need the place as a refuge when war comes. He's become more and more pessimistic in the two years since he left."

"When war comes!" Rosa cried.

With pity Miriam thought, Her sons will have to go.

"Yes," she said, "David believes there is no stopping it. He says it's only a question of when, not whether."

"Thanks to people like himself!" Rosa cried sharply. "How clever he was all the time he was here! Who could have had the slightest idea what he was doing?" Her words cut the air. "It's a wonder he got safely away."

"Feelings are very high. It's well to be cautious," Gabriel advised. And Miriam understood that this was a warning for her. "The other night at our meeting, our Jewish widows and orphans relief, some of the men almost came to blows."

"We Jews should stay out of politics," Rosa pronounced. "We have enough of our own affairs to keep us busy. Look at that mess in the Albany Temple in New York, with the Orthodox fighting Rabbi Wise over women's rights!" She was out of breath with indignation.

Miriam said, "I'm sorry, I can't agree."

"Agitators on both sides are whipping people up too high," Gabriel said soberly. "I go along with Isaac Leeser in the *American Jewish Advocate*. He thinks Jews ought to stay in the middle as peacemakers."

"It's very hard to remain in the middle when you have convictions," Miriam argued. "Have you read *Uncle Tom's Cabin?* David sent it to me from New York. It's sold over a million copies in the North."

"I glanced at it," Rosa said. "A sensational book, that's all. It's disgracefully exaggerated, and you must know that, Miriam."

"Probably so. Still, one often has to exaggerate to make a point."

Rosa's voice became shrill. "I should think you'd want to stay away from the miserable subject, Miriam. I understand you have convictions, but it seems to me you've had enough trouble and shouldn't want any more. If you don't mind my giving you some advice, I hope you don't talk this way in front of your stepmother's family. Frankly, I think it's wonderful that they've never humiliated you—not that it was your fault—but still, he is your brother, and just seeing you must be a constant reminder."

"Of course you must know I don't talk about these things except here," Miriam answered with some heat.

"Well, good," Rosa grunted. "We get all the blame for slavery, while the North raises tariffs and enjoys all the financial benefits from it."

"Benefits?" repeated Miriam.

"Benefits. Money."

Gabriel intervened. "All the talk in the world won't change the fact that the system is bound to end no matter who wins. I say that over and over."

"Then you take war for granted?" his sister cried.

"The handwriting's on the wall. The Republican party is being organized to oppose the extension of slavery into the territories. The next step is to eliminate it in the southern states."

Rosa was aghast. "And you think they have a right to do that?"

"No, I don't think the national government has a right in law to do it. It's meddling in business that belongs to the states."

"Then how," asked Miriam, "would you eliminate slavery?"

"The states must do it themselves. And in time they will do just that, if they're not interfered with."

"In time," Miriam repeated.

"Meanwhile," Gabriel said, "the law of the land is the law."

"Spoken, as David always used to say, like a lawyer." She smiled, wanting to quiet the charged atmosphere.

Gabriel did not return the smile. Instead he got up to stand with his hand on the back of a chair. He spoke softly, musing, as if to himself.

"Sometimes I wish I weren't a lawyer at all. I wish I were a musician or a mathematician, dealing in abstractions. Everything quite clear and clean. I'd erase" —he made a broad, harsh gesture—"I'd erase everything emotional. Just facts, just facts." He looked out of the window where a bee buzzed in the dangling wisteria. "And sometimes I think I'd like to strike out to California—not for gold, I'm not interested in that, just for something new. I'd take the *Sea Witch* around Cape Horn." A faraway smile fled across his face. He might have been feeling himself at the prow of the *Sea Witch* in high seas and gusting wind. "It set a record, you know: ninety-seven days from New York to San Francisco." He broke off to rest a hand on Rosa's shoulder; she had been looking anxious. "Don't worry, I shan't abandon you yet, not till I see your boys grown and on their way."

"Then let's talk of more cheerful things," Rosa responded.

"All right, my dear. You begin," said Gabriel.

"Well," she said brightly, "is either one of you planning to hear *Le Roi David*? I heard it once. Such lovely music! Imagine that boy, only fifteen years old! Louis

Moreau Gottschalk. His grandfather was some sort of
cousin to Henry's mother, I think."

Every prominent or prosperous Jew, no matter
where from, turns out to be "some sort of cousin,"
Miriam thought with amusement.

"That's a cheerful subject. And I do plan to hear it.
Now I shall leave you ladies to go on talking of cheerful things," Gabriel said as he left them.

"I like your hat," Rosa said by way of reconcilia-
tion. "I've given all my bonnets away. Only old ladies
wear them anymore. Yes, the hat's becoming. But you
look tired. Not bad, mind you, but I've seen you look
better. If you ask me, you're working too hard."

It is the work that saves me, Miriam thought, not
answering. If it were not for the work, I should be
completely without use or purpose.

Rosa filled the teacups. "How do you like my new
decorations? You haven't said."

On a trip to the Crystal Palace Exhibition in New
York, she had fallen in love with the Belter style. She
had refurbished the old parlor with plaster garlands on
the ceiling and a flowered carpet. Sofas and chairs,
covered in a pattern of golden bees on blue satin, stood
around a large table topped with white marble. Carved
flowers, grapes, and unicorns covered every inch of
woodwork, and from the four sides of the room, tall
mirrors reflected all this glory.

"You don't like it?" Rosa inquired, continuing before Miriam could reply, "You can be frank with me.
No, you don't care for it, I see that. It's not your taste.
Perhaps it is a bit show-offy, but I had to have it. I'm
happy in this room."

"That's all that matters, then," Miriam said gently.

"After all, one has to have something. I live alone,
don't I? My brother and my sons are wonderful to me,
goodness knows, but still, I'm alone."

"Forgive me for asking, but I believe we've known each other long enough and well enough for me to ask you: How is it that a woman as lively as you doesn't marry again?"

Rosa set the teacup down with a click. She looked significantly at Miriam.

"For the same reason my brother doesn't."

"Why doesn't he?"

"We're all the same in our family. If we can't have what we want, we don't take second best. You remember, I told you once."

"Ah, yes. He wasn't Jewish."

"Wasn't. Isn't."

"He's still living, then?"

"Yes, and he would still have me. He's wonderful, but I can't do it. Of course, if I should find another man of my own faith, as good a man as Henry—but I haven't, and as I said, we don't take second best."

"And you say it's the same with Gabriel?"

"Not exactly the same. You mean you don't know? You can't see?"

"See what?"

"That he has never loved anyone but you." Rosa regarded her with a curiosity that was almost prurient. "He could never obligate himself to another woman while he felt like that about you."

Unlike that old lingering taunt of Eugene's, this apparently was fact, and it was stunning.

"Gabriel has told you this?" Miriam whispered.

"Let's say I wormed it out of him."

Immediately, then, Miriam thought of André. That some other man should be entranced by her as she was —no, as she used to be—by André!

Suddenly Rosa was alarmed. She clapped her hand to her mouth. "You won't dare let him know I've told you? I don't know why I do these things. It just

slipped out. I swore I'd say nothing. He was sorry
after he'd said it and I promised him I'd never tell."

"Trust me, Rosa. I give you my word. Do you really
think I would bring up such a subject with Gabriel?"

"Oh, dear heaven, what an awful conversation this
has been! Let's talk about something else quickly so we
can forget it. Tell me some gossip instead."

"I don't know any. I don't hear much since I've
been spending afternoons at the office."

"Well, I know a bit. André Perrin is finally coming
home. What do you think of that? I was beginning to
think they had settled permanently in Paris. But I hear
he didn't get his money out of that beautiful house in
the garden district. Such an extravagance, to build it
and never use it!"

So Rosa chattered on about the new neighbor across
the street and the rabbi's wife and the dressmaker's
charges. But Miriam, nodding or shaking her head in
the right places, was only half with Rosa, the rest being divided, torn between forces of home and children,
of Gabriel, whom she would now dread to face, and of
André, who was coming home, having perhaps forgotten her entirely. And if he had not forgotten her, what
then?

Presently, she got up and left. The carriage was
waiting at the door.

"Maxim," she said, "there's some property I want
to see before we go home." And she directed him to
the garden district.

Past Urania, Thalia, and Euterpe streets they drove,
past towers, stained-glass windows, and serene lawns.
It was a different world from that of the Vieux Carré
—an American world.

"Here, Maxim, stop here for a minute."

It had been a long time since she had seen the
house. With a queer sense of satisfaction she noted

how it differed from the others on the street. White
and classical, it stood apart in an airy grove of mimosa
trees. For a few minutes she sat in the carriage just
looking at it, at a child who ran around from the back
of the house, and at the second-story windows at
which lace curtains hung in what must be a lovely
room, where a man and woman slept together.

The horse flicked its tail and stamped, recalling her
to herself.

"Home now, Maxim," she said.

"Very pretty here, Miss Miriam," Maxim observed,
feeling chatty. "I had to go past Adele Street this
morning for Miss Emma. She had an errand. You
wouldn't believe it's the same city as this, with the
slaughterhouse and all the smells. Those Irish sure is
dirty people."

Everyone wanted to look down on someone else.
Maxim in his fine suit, driving his owner's fine carriage, could feel himself superior to any poor Irishman
who had no fine suit, no fine carriage, and no master
to provide him with either. Curious indeed.

Ferdinand and Emma were having coffee on the verandah.

"You stayed a long time," Ferdinand said.

"Yes. Rosa and I talked after the business was
over."

"What did you talk about?" So long "out of things,"
he was eager for every crumb of news, however unim-
portant it might be.

"Oh, religion, home furnishings, war—"

"War!" Ferdinand was indignant. "There'll be no
war. We left all that behind in Europe."

"Gabriel thinks there will be. So does David. But,"
she ventured boldly, "I do think if women were to run

the world, there would not be. We'd find other ways to solve things."

"Women, my dear?" Ferdinand gave his daughter the same smile he gave to little Eugene and Angelique. "Women? Surely, if man with his strength and intellect can't manage affairs any better, what makes you think women can? Why not entrust affairs to children while you're about it?"

And who has been keeping this house together since Eugene lost his sight and you lost your money, she thought angrily. Vain, ignorant man!

But he looked so old, throwing his shoulders back with such pathetic bravado. Let him talk, she thought, and did not reply.

17

Now in autumn a cooler breeze swept in from the Gulf, and the sun, ceasing to scorch, poured out a benevolent warmth. In the side garden where Miriam sat with an unread book, the first yellowing leaves lay on Aphrodite's shoulder; on the dry grass an overripe persimmon fell, splashing its sweet thick juice, to which at once a bee came buzzing in a perfect frenzy.

The gate clicked. Mildly vexed by the intrusion, she turned to see who the intruder might be.

"Miriam. I've just arrived. I came as soon as I could," said André.

So often in imagination she had contrived this meeting, fancying a chance encounter on the street or at some formal, drawing-room occasion, or even, foolishly, a tryst in a forest as in a German opera—always toying with such fancies and discarding them, embarrassed at their futility. Now, as he stood there, she did not know what she felt other than dull wonder that he was there at all.

"So much has happened to you since I went away. . . . Your brother. Oh, Miriam, in my heart I cried for you."

"And you knew about Eugene?"

"Yes, long ago. Emma wrote to Marie Claire."

"Marie Claire" hung in the air between them. "And

how is she—your wife?" Whether in the saying of the
name there was any sharp intent to hurt either him or
herself, she could not have said.

"She hasn't come with me. She has had some recit-
als. Her teacher is enthusiastic. Well, at any rate, she
wants to stay there a while longer."

So they are drawing apart, she thought maliciously,
and was ashamed of the thought.

"But I had to come back. I'd been away long
enough. We've taken a house in the Pontalba Building."

"They are very handsome houses," Miriam said.

These perfunctory remarks—what did they mean?
He looked the same, with the same brightness about
him. Did he remember their parting here in this place,
how they had clung to one another? Perhaps not.
Time flows, changing, changing as each moment
passes.

"Would you like to see the house?" André asked
now.

She had a need to walk, to move, to do something
with the churning that was inside her.

But she spoke primly. "That would be very nice."

With morning church over, the streets came to life
as people streamed toward their Sunday amusements,
the cock fights, the horse races, the minstrel shows,
and the taverns.

"This much hasn't changed, I see," André remarked. "I suppose the Protestants still fume over
these merry Catholic Sundays?"

"I suppose they do."

"Well, I see no harm in amusing oneself, regardless
of the day. Gloom never made the world any better."

In the little square behind the cathedral children
clustered about the ice cream stand.

"That hasn't changed either."

"No," Miriam agreed.

They were making conversation. She felt the strain of stepping so gingerly around the only question of importance: Are we the same, or have time and separation left their mark?

André remarked on the new cathedral. "A sumptuous building."

"Yes, thanks to the generosity of Judah Touro."

"We read about his will in Europe. Most extraordinary! All those charities, the Jewish Hospital here, and orphan homes and help for the poor of Jerusalem. Remarkable."

"Gabriel says if Touro had died ten years ago he would have left nothing at all to any Jewish cause. Gabriel had great influence on him, you know. He was one of the people who brought him back to his faith."

"How is Gabriel? Still not married?"

"Still not married."

In some odd way she felt as though she were defending Gabriel, or as if, still more illogically, her very existence as the object of his love were her fault.

And she went on, thinking aloud, "He has been a great help to me, a right hand since Eugene's accident."

"Ah, but you've had too many burdens!" André exclaimed. "Far too many."

Pausing a moment before unlocking the door, he surveyed the square with obvious admiration. "Except for Andrew Jackson capering on his horse, one might think oneself on the Place des Vosges in Paris."

He led her upstairs into a tall salon with a Louis XV black marble fireplace. Automatically they walked to the windows; in these rooms one would always walk to the windows. Below, in the square, crepe myrtle spread pink autumn flowers. To the right, one saw the levee and the glistening river. They stood quite still; the silence ticked.

What am I doing here? Miriam thought. She began to speak in a high, unnatural voice.

"That's the wharf where Jenny Lind arrived. P. T. Barnum brought her from Cuba. There were ten thousand people waiting. Such a crush! She stayed here in the Baroness Pontalba's house."

"Did she?" André was behind her, not touching; yet in the air around him there was an aureole of warmth which covered her back and shoulders.

"Yes," she said, "yes, she was here a month. They sold the tickets at auction for two hundred dollars and more." The words rushed. "Perhaps Marie Claire will be like her someday."

Why speak of Marie Claire?

André replied, "Marie Claire has a pure voice, but it's a little voice. She will never be a Jenny Lind or an Adelina Patti, although she doesn't realize it yet."

"I'm sorry," Miriam said.

The grave, plain child sang her heart out in Papa's parlor. The drab young bride stood with André. Aunt Emma falsely chirped: Don't they make a handsome couple?

"Sorry?"

"Yes. Sorry that she will not have what she wants so badly. It's a terrible thing to want something you know you will never have."

"We didn't come here to talk about these things," he said.

She put her hands over her face. "I am all confused. I don't know."

He laid her head on his shoulder. His fingers moved in her hair, loosening the sturdy pins, undoing the chignon at the back of her neck so that the slippery hair fell to her shoulders.

Her heart slowed; she could feel it pulsing steadily and strongly. Something rose in her that she had never felt before; a flower opened and spread; a river ran; a wave lifted to a crest. His hands released the fastenings of her dress and she stood quite still, with closed eyes, allowing him to do what he wished. Wire hoops and twenty yards of yellow cloth fell to the floor. When she opened her eyes, she saw in the mirror the pale mauve mounds of her breasts swelling above the shift before it, too, fell. Her face was opalescent; it swam in the mirror; the shadows under her eyes were like tear stains, while her lips turned upward slowly, slowly, into a wandering, gentle smile.

Lightly he lifted her, easily carried her, and in a high, white lovely room, laid her down on the bed.

Now his head rested on her shoulder. With her free hand she stroked his cheek, on which the thinnest ray of afternoon light, having slid through the drawn blinds, tipped the fine hair with gold. What a beautiful thing was his hand, with its fingers lying loose in sleep! Each nail, smooth as glass, bore its pale crescent. Such tenderness, such skill in that strong hand!

In a wonderful languor she stretched her arm, smelling a lemon scent on her warm skin, feeling the bloom of her own health. A small quickening breeze swept in, waking André.

"You haven't slept?" he murmured.

"No, I was drowsy, but I didn't sleep."

"You were thinking," he reproached gently. "You think too much."

At this instant, at this reminder, anxiety shattered her peace.

"I was remembering how often I wondered how it would be when you came back."

"Well, now you know. You don't have to wonder anymore."

"I feel as if these years hadn't passed at all; as if you'd left only yesterday."

He kissed her eyelids. "I want you to be happy . . . happy."

"If only we never had to get up, if we could stay in this room like this."

"Dear Miriam, we're here now, don't spoil it."

"I don't want to, but . . ."

"But what?"

"If only there were no Eugene or Marie Claire!"

Two pairs of her stockings, the black net worn over the flesh-colored silk, lay over a chair. They reminded her of—of Eugene's woman. Am I then no better than she?

"You're worried about them? We're taking nothing away that anyone wants. Certainly not Eugene, after all you've told me."

"But Marie Claire?"

"It doesn't matter, I tell you. She cares about her voice and nothing else, certainly not about me! And if she doesn't care, why should I?"

"Do you know, you probably won't believe me, but it's true, I always saw my life touching hers one day?"

"Do you often 'see' things?" André teased.

"Not often," she said soberly. "But sometimes. For us I see only a blank, a dark blank."

"You've listened too long to the servants. Superstitions. Listen to me." He held her closely. "Always listen to me. Think of yourself going on a long, wonderful, dangerous journey. I'm the guide, I'll keep you safe, I'll keep danger away."

She sighed. "You do comfort me. Even your voice comforts me."

"That's what I want to do." He kissed her. "You'll

come again? I shall have to be away a great deal—my family's place, and business in the North—but never for very long. You'll come again?"

"Oh, yes, oh, yes I will. I will."

So it began.

18

Now in the last year of peace there were some who saw what was coming and others who denied it, even though it was scrawled across the sky.

John Brown had seized the federal arsenal at Harpers Ferry. Hailed in the North as a defender of human liberty, he was daily condemned as a vicious agitator when merchants and planters met over lunch at Maspero's Exchange. There they spoke, too, of men like David Raphael, wondering that he, for instance, could have come from so decent a family. And they were sorry for his relatives. They quoted politicians who were saying that secession was inevitable unless some "reasonable compromise" could be effected and soon. In lowered voices and somber tones they spoke of Englishmen murdered in the Indian Mutiny at Lucknow only a few years before.

The Mistick Krew of Comus organized a Mardi Gras parade that year as splendid as any; the French Opera House opened with a spectacular season of Donizetti, Massenet and Bellini; Adelina Patti sang; the new gaslights were installed in the grandest houses; and women, parting their hair in the center, madonna-style, had themselves photographed.

Yet perhaps it was not ignorance but the fear of war

which engendered this gaiety and roused Eugene from his indifference.

"It's too long since we had guests at Beau Jardin," he said one day. He frowned. "Why have we not done it before?"

"We were conserving," Miriam reminded him with some resentment. Not once had he given her any credit for what she had been doing.

"We'll invite people in time for the grinding season."

That meant a week of lavish entertainment, of escorting visitors through the sugar mill, drinking hot cane juice and rum, while the slaves toiled twenty-four hours a day until the cane had all been ground.

"We'll bring everyone upriver on the *Edward J. Gay,* do it in fine style while we're about it," Eugene said. He became enthusiastic. "I shall want a fine menu, chowders and turtle soup, pigeons, whatever you can think of. And very likely we're low on Madeira. It's so long since I've checked. Will you take care of that? And the guest list, too, since—since I can't write?"

She fetched pencil and paper.

"We'll begin with Gabriel and the sister."

"Rosa will be in Saratoga," she reminded him.

"Well, Gabriel, then. He's a cool sort, but he grows on you. Emma's people, of course, Eulalie, Pelagie, and any of her children who want to come. Oh, yes, put Perrin down, André Perrin. I haven't seen him since he's been back in town. He never comes to call; you'd think he'd be more friendly."

Miriam's pencil rested; she controlled her trembling hand. "If he's not that friendly, why invite him?"

"Oh, well, I've no grudge. I do know he travels a good deal, so maybe that's why he hasn't come round.

I always liked him, he's clever, goes all over the world, which I wish I'd done when I was still able."

"So he's very likely away somewhere. I'll find out for you."

"Don't bother. I can find out myself. Put his name down."

André Perrin. The letters shaped themselves into spaces on the paper. They looked up quizzically, startled and alarmed as the pounding of her frightened heart.

On the piazza after dinner the men smoked and talked. The drone of their voices coming through the long open windows was in competition with the harp, which Pelagie's daughter, Felicité, was playing in the parlor.

Miriam's thoughts moved like troubled wanderers looking for a place to rest. They moved from Angelique, who, pretending to be attentive to the music, was probably wishing she were as old as Felicité and could wear her hair up, back to André on the piazza. She strained to hear his voice among the others', but it did not come.

After three days they had still not been alone together. Men and women bathed separately in the bayou. In groups they went driving through the countryside; in groups they dined and played cards. Occasionally her eyes had met his; then, remembering how Pelagie's adoration of Sylvain had been so naked on her face, she had turned away.

She thought curiously: Gabriel's face is covered up. Nothing is revealed in it. Could Rosa have been mistaken? No, of course not. Then it must be very hard for Gabriel tonight. . . . How strange that two men who loved her should be sitting there together!

How strange to be having these thoughts at all! She,

Miriam, the proper-seeming wife of a respected gentleman; the mistress of this family home, gleaming and
orderly in its traditions; the mother of that manly boy,
already old enough to take his place with the men
after dinner; the mother to be an example for her
daughter . . .

What would the world—the world in which she had
to live—say of her if they knew? Her children . . .
she would stand shattered before them. How they
would suffer! And she passed her hand over her per-
spiring forehead.

"I'm thinking," Pelagie remarked, "of how Marie
Claire used to play for us. It's so strange that she stays
abroad. It must be very hard on a young husband."

"I suppose it must be," Miriam agreed.

"Yet he seems content! He looks very well, don't
you think so?"

"Very well."

"And you do, too, Miriam. I don't know when I've
seen you so blooming, so healthy and pink."

Miriam moved closer to the window, giving as excuse the heat, but needing really to remove herself
from Pelagie's remarks.

"I have enormous respect for Rabbi Wise," Gabriel
was saying. "He feels religion and politics ought to be
separate and I agree."

"Well, Wise," Eugene replied, "Wise is against slavery, and of course I don't agree with him there. But
when he says he'd rather break up the Union than go
to war, there I do agree."

"There's no question that if war comes, it will be the
abolitionist Protestant preachers who brought it
about."

Miriam recalled a time when she had thought constantly about those questions; yet at this moment they

meant nothing; she was thinking of André. She had become a woman with a fixed idea.

"I'm told that at the State House they predict crisis," Eugene was saying. "They say if a Republican is elected President we shall secede."

Another voice was heard. "Then there will be war."

Other voices joined.

"We are short of everything: wagon factories, ammunition, tents, everything."

"Can you imagine abolition here? It's enough to make your flesh crawl! Hordes of them taking to the roads with no place to go, nothing to eat, except what they can steal."

She felt a touch on her shoulder.

"It's a perfect night," André said. "Too beautiful for such depressing conversation. Would you like a walk or a row in the skiff?"

She raised her eyebrows, as if to say, We can't do this.

But André countered lightly. "Any lady who wants to come is welcome. The boat holds two. Shall we take turns? You first, Pelagie?"

Pelagie declined. Miriam's chair scraped abruptly as she stood up, reminding her how he had drawn her away from the talk on that very first night.

"We started out so cheerfully," André said. "But they always turn to politics. Let's look at the stars. They've been here long before there was a North or a South and will be here long after."

The moon, faintly red, bled pink into the white sky. In the middle of the lawn where the decorous sound of the harp almost faded out of hearing, it was met by the poignant thrum and twang of a guitar. Over in the cabins a man was singing of ancient longings and transient delights; one needed no words to recognize both longing and delights.

On and on André and Miriam moved with identical steps. She felt the motion of his legs in unison with her own. The path to the bayou was thick with a hundred years' worth of fallen pine needles, on which feet made no more noise than a breeze in the treetops. Live oaks spilled streamers of gray moss like old women's hair.

"The moss is sorrowful," Miriam said.

André was not to be drawn into her mood. "To begin with, it isn't moss at all. It's related to the pineapple family, and that's the symbol of welcome."

He helped her into the boat. So still was the surface that the trees along the shore made a motionless reflection, scalloping a deeper black against the opaque bayou water. André dropped the oars to let the boat drift and took her hand. For a long time they sat without speaking, joined by the tightening contact of their hands.

"I wish there were someplace for us to go tonight," André said.

She dared then to say what she had been holding back. A woman should never take the initiative; a woman should wait to receive.

"I wish for more than tonight. To see ahead." And when he did not answer, she cried, "What's to happen? Where are we going?"

"Ah, don't! I can't bear it when you're unhappy! Listen to me. Remember that every day brings something new. When we first saw each other you were choked with tears. You couldn't have foreseen, that night, what's happened between us since then, could you?"

"That's true," she admitted.

"I'm not a superstitious man, but I've seen so many curious and wonderful turns and twists that I never give up hoping."

He stroked her hair. More than his words, his fingers calmed her. His compassion made her want to believe that in some miraculous turn of affairs all impediments between them might be swept away.

Presently he took the oars and turned the boat back to the landing, soothing all the while in his bright vigorous voice with talk of New York and Washington, of theater and amusing personalities.

They walked back up the path toward the house. In deepest shadow, just before the path emerged onto open lawn, they stopped and he pulled her to him. She trembled and, leaning against him, gave him all her weight, so that, half lifted, her feet barely grazed the ground and she was held to him by arms and lips.

At last he said, "I haven't told you, I have to go north again next week."

"Again? Must you?" she cried, thinking, I sound like a wife. I cling like a wife.

"I have to. I have business that has to be taken care of quickly. The war is coming, you know. I couldn't stand any more talk of it inside there tonight, but they're right, it's coming."

"And who will win?"

"Who can say? The North has more men and more money. The South will have help from Europe because of cotton. But who can say?"

All thought of issues and principles, all private secret allegiances, washed away. What would war do to André and Miriam?

She controlled her voice. "How long will you be gone this time?"

"It depends how things work out. A couple of months maybe, but I'll be back, you may be sure of that. Meanwhile, when you pass the Pontalba, think of me, remember that the place is waiting for us. Do you promise?"

She understood that he was aware of her fear and

that he would admire her for covering it up with gallantry.

"I promise," she said.

"Good! Then, let's go inside."

The brush raked her hair, snapping sparks. Through the mirror she saw the bed waiting and thought with relief that she would be asleep when Eugene came in after a late night at cards, so that she would not even be aware of his entry. How many thousands of hours they had lain together in the dark intimacy of that bed without touching! And she thought that, but for the constraint of law and custom, it would be—ought to be—so natural and simple for André instead of Eugene to walk through that door and lie down in that bed.

Someone knocked.

"Come in," she called, expecting Fanny.

It was Eulalie. Her skirts flounced through the door with such speed that the taffeta crackled. At once she began to speak, like a child who had run to deliver a message and dared not forget it.

"I want you to know that I saw you! I saw you and him tonight. I heard every word you both said."

Miriam's heart slowed. A heart was supposed to beat faster from shock; nevertheless, she felt hers beat slowly, felt its hard pulse pounding. She laid the brush down and waited.

"I was sitting on the lawn when I heard your voices quite clearly on the path. I certainly didn't stoop to eavesdropping, if that's what you're thinking."

"I'm not thinking anything."

Cool. Icy cool. Say as little as possible. Above all, don't let her see that you're terrified.

"I think," Eulalie said, clipping the words, "that you are a disgrace. A disgrace." A spray of her saliva struck Miriam's cheek. "Perhaps there isn't enough decency in you to know that you are."

Miriam collected her thoughts. "If you choose to misunderstand—completely misunderstand—what you say you heard, then there's nothing I can do about it, is there?"

Eulalie's laugh was the victor's laugh, scornful and careless. "There's nothing to misunderstand. The Pontalba! So that's where you go on your afternoon walks, the fine lady with—with gold bracelets!"

She will cry this through the house and over the city. My children will hear of it and hate me.

"No wonder they moved the state capital away from New Orleans! A modern Sodom, they said. Not fit for legislators, they said, and it's true when women like you from respectable homes . . ." For the moment Eulalie had no more words.

There is a streak of madness in her, Miriam thought, as the red flush, like a burn or a disease, stained the woman's neck. Perhaps it was that, before all else, that had kept the young men away: a streak of madness.

"What do you think your father will say, your father who thinks the sun rises on you! And my mother, who has treated you like one of her own daughters! And this is how you repay them!"

Now I have gone as far as I can go in this life of mine, they will do what they want with me.

Still she held on. "Is that all, Eulalie? Really, there's no point in continuing this, since you have made up your mind."

"Do you know what people will think of you? That you're a—a whore! Yes, a whore!"

Surely this is the first time such a word has left her tight mouth, Miriam thought. She stood up and slapped Eulalie with a light, humiliating sting.

"Don't use that word to me! What do you know of whores? Or of love? Or anything else? You hate the world! You're a poisoned woman, you hate yourself. You've been my enemy from the day I came to your house. I was a child, but I knew it even then. So now you've got a weapon! Well, do what you want with it, I can't stop you—"

"I could hear you at the end of the hall," Eugene said furiously. "What the devil is going on?"

Suddenly the walls revolved and the floor tilted upward.

"I need air," Miriam said. She stumbled to the verandah; she could hardly speak. "Eulalie will be glad to tell you what's going on."

From below came the sound of music and the voices of men still at cards. Among them André, unsuspecting, had no idea what the last few minutes had done. She thought again of her children. They were Eugene's children; he could take their mother out of their lives; the law said so.

Life has its way of surprising us, André had told her tonight. Float with its current, it's easy, he had told her. But this current could dash her to pieces on the rocks.

And that hard beat of her heart resumed. How long could a heart beat like that without failing?

Later—how much later? Ten minutes, half an hour? —she became aware that Eugene was alone in the room.

"You can come back in now," he called. "Sit down."

She was thankful that he could not see, for she knew that terror was written on her face.

"Well," he began, "that was quite a story! Quite! The woman's a poor, sneaky creature, but still I suppose she could hardly have invented it all. So it must be true."

She could not bear to look at him; instead, she looked down at her nails, the pink shells of her innocent nails. She sighed.

"It's true." And she waited for his fury.

Instead, the door to the hall, which had been ajar, was flung wide open and the children came in.

My God, she thought, he has told them already! Or he will tell them. He will condemn me in front of them, and they will despise me. They will be disgraced. No man of family will want to marry Angelique. In the temple on the Sabbath people will turn to stare—Her mind raced, aching like a winded runner.

"Mama!" cried Angelique. "Why haven't you been downstairs? They're playing the piano, and we've been dancing!" The child's vigor illuminated her skin so that it glowed like ivory. "Mr. Perrin has been teaching me to waltz, he says I'm as light on my feet as any of the ladies in Paris!"

"Does he indeed?" said Eugene.

Tensed for his next words, Miriam expected storm. But he only summoned the child to himself.

"Come here, Angelique." He smoothed her shoulders. "Lace. What color is it?"

"The lace is white, of course. My dress is blue."

"Very pretty, I'm sure. We must get you a velvet one for the holidays. And have you been dancing, too, Eugene?"

The boy assumed a manly air. "No, that's for girls. I don't dance."

His father laughed. "That's right. First learn to ride and shoot. I must remember to find a good gentle mare for you. You're outgrowing the pony, Blaise tells me. Yes, you'll have time enough for dancing. Now, both of you, go to bed. And close the door behind you, please. I suppose," he said when the door was shut, "I suppose your children gave you quite a fright just now, didn't they?"

Miriam had sunk into a chair with her face in her hands.

"You expected me to rage." Eugene's voice was light, almost amused.

"Remarkable! You surprise me! I'd have sworn you didn't have enough blood in you! André Perrin. A handsome fellow, or was when I could still see. But I should have thought Carvalho more to your taste. I believe I told you so once, didn't I? No?"

This mockery was worse than a righteous, angry assault. So lightly does a cat play with a fluttering, shrieking bird before he kills it.

"On the other hand," Eugene reflected, "Carvalho's moral code would never allow him to tinker with another man's wife, however tempting. Too bad! It would be so much less complicated. He's a solid citizen, he stays in one place, whereas the other goes here, there, and everywhere, to say nothing of the fact that he has a wife, even though she is four thousand miles away."

"Oh, my God, tell me what you're going to do and get this over with!"

"What did you think I was going to do? Play the outraged husband? Make a dramatic scene before the children? Put you out of the house?"

She could not answer.

"So? I'll tell you what I'm going to do. I'm not going to do anything."

Miriam looked up in disbelief.

"Oh, of course, I could easily do any of those things. After all, the law's on my side, the whole society's on my side. But I don't choose to. I'm not that much distressed, not that concerned. You see, I probably understand more about the world than many men do."

Yes, you ought to, you with that woman. . . .

"My one concern is that this business not leak out. We have a name. Your son and daughter have a distinguished name, two centuries old, and nothing must soil it."

"Then they won't ever know? Ever?"

"Certainly not. They will grow up with dignity and standing. They are all I have. All I ever will have," he added bitterly.

The breathless thudding of Miriam's heart began to dwindle. *Thank God, oh, thank God.*

Then she felt a queer and totally unexpected moment of compassion: The man gave care to velvet dresses and gentle mares. . . .

But—Eulalie, she thought next. The fear came stabbing back.

"Eulalie?" The name came out of her mouth with a quaver.

"Eulalie is to keep still. Permanently still. Actually, I've nothing to threaten her with, but I've threatened her, all the same. She respects me, she's maybe a little afraid of me. She will say nothing, you can be sure of that."

Eugene got up. Suddenly his power filled the room as it had used to do. "Perrin, of course, will leave here in the morning."

"In the morning?"

"What did you expect? I don't want him in my house ever again. A man has that much pride where his wife is concerned, even when he lives the way we do. But the world doesn't know how we live, and no man is going to make an ass of me before the world."

"Will you—is there going to be trouble between you?"

"I'm blind, remember? If I weren't, there would be plenty." Eugene gave a scornful whistle. "And if it weren't pitch dark night, and if I weren't a gentleman, I'd throw him out right now. But he'll be gone before you come downstairs in the morning. You understand that?"

"I understand."

"And that his name is not ever again to be mentioned in this house?"

"Yes."

"Now go to bed, and don't snivel and toss all night. I want to sleep."

She did not "snivel," nor did she toss. Instead, she lay still with her hands folded between her breasts until, suddenly remembering that this was the position in which a corpse was laid, she brought her hands down to her sides. The midsummer air was thick and blue, hard to breathe, but she drew on it deeply, forcing it into her lungs, clenching her fists, forcing courage.

She must try to separate her feelings, to put some order into a murky tangle of despair. There was the aftermath of fear. There was the frustration of being at the mercy of the despised and pitiable Eulalie. Yes, and loneliness, looming and towering ahead: never to see André again? Never? And shame: Would I want my daughter to do what I have done? No. I want her not to have to do it, not to need to do it.

These thoughts of Angelique now brought her mind back to the most recent of her brother's hortatory letters, each with its message meant to inspire, but which succeeded only in arousing a futile restlessness.

He had a new cause: women's rights. He had enclosed a sheet of clippings about Ernestine Rose, rabbi's daughter, abolitionist, and vigorous champion of women's rights. Indeed there had been fury in her speeches, searing, unforgettable phrases: "A slave from the cradle to the grave . . . Father and husband, master still . . . The right to her person, her property, and her children.''

They had everything to do with Miriam, these searing phrases. And at the same time, as she lay there in the stifling dark, they had nothing to do with her. It would be better, she thought bitterly, if David would stop his bombardment of ideas. What did he expect her to do, leave home and go out preaching?

Eugene stirred, mumbling in his sleep. And down the hall, ignorant of the coming day, André, too, slept.

Long before first light Miriam got up and with soundless steps went out to the verandah. The chill that precedes dawn raised prickles on her arms and shook in the trees. A lone bird twittered and was still. Silent, mysterious, gloomy woods and fields lay in the muffling darkness. But for once they held no fear; no crawling things or swooping things or human enemies could threaten out there; fear and threat lay inside this house. And that old wish, the one she had felt on the first sight of this place, came surging back: to strike out across the fields, through the woods, over the hills, and go.

Suddenly dawn broke. The sky exploded with light. Cascades of amethyst and scarlet sprayed upward from the rim of the earth, scattering into shreds of lavender and tender pink. And now a choir of birds in fullest song gave proper praise to this magnificence.

But one small wounded creature saw nothing in the face of all this grandeur, heard nothing but the breaking of its own small heart.

Miriam was still standing there when the front door opened below and André came out. Without a backward look he stepped into the waiting carriage and was driven away.

19

Gabriel swept a little stack of documents into his stovepipe hat. Chinese silk had long replaced beaver for men's hats, but he still wore his old beaver.

"We've covered everything for the season. The sugar crop is paid for and the accounts are in good shape, as good a shape as anything can be in these times."

His gravity seemed uncalled for in the circumstances of this routine meeting. But then, he must be miserably uncomfortable in her presence, if what Rosa had said was accurate. Miriam herself was uncomfortable, as if it were somehow her fault that she did not return the man's feelings. One would never suspect him, cool and cerebral as he was, of having that much inner passion! So different from André, with his bright exuberance!

She had cried herself out. Now there was just a heaviness, a dullness, in her chest, as though her tears had frozen there. Nothing more had been said about the episode. Eugene had outlawed the subject. It was as though it had never happened, as though André had never existed.

Her hands were smoothing her skirt. Recently she had acquired this nervous habit, and she wondered what other habits she might have acquired without being aware of them, some dreadful twitching of the

eye perhaps, or licking of the lips. Emma had a friend
who always wet her lips, and it was disgusting. She
brought her hands to rest on her lap and held them
there, looking down at them. They looked forlorn in
contrast to the sprigged white lawn of her dress; the
dress was new, as were the paperweight green slippers.
The world saw a fashionable woman.

"Will you have another drink?" Gabriel asked.

Rosa's cook had made iced orange-flower water.
Miriam had barely touched the glass. Surely he could
see that.

"Thank you, I still have this. Really, I should leave.
It's almost four."

"Oh, finish your drink," he said.

She understood that he wanted her to linger, yet he
seemed to have nothing to say.

The silence grew too difficult, so that she had somehow to break it. "Eugene has freed his son. Did you
see the public notice yesterday about the boy Eugene
freed?"

"I did."

There was a tone of finality in the two syllables of
this reply, as if to shut off the subject. She did not
know why the subject had come to her mind in the
first place or why, now, she felt compelled to pursue it.
Perhaps it was only that ineradicable picture of the
boy surrounded by pigeons, of the pale brown hand on
Eugene's black broadcloth shoulder, of the long lashes
closing over eyes filled with questions. . . . Lost, denied, out of place, she thought again, while at the same
time rancor mingled with her pity. Having begun, she
continued.

"You may have heard that he's my husband's son."

Gabriel inclined his head. The motion said plainly:
One has heard, certainly, but one makes no comment
about these things.

"He will send him to Paris to study sculpture. He has talent. Of course, it is only right of Eugene."

Now Gabriel answered. "Of course it is. But I take no credit from Eugene when I say that the boy would have been free in a few years anyway, the way things are going."

The war, again. Always the war. But my son is only twelve, Miriam thought. And the comfort of this fact soothed like warm milk.

"When will the war come?" she asked. People had been asking that for the last year or more; always not whether it would come, but when it would.

"It depends on the election. If Lincoln wins, it will be soon."

"David writes that New York is a hotbed of southern sentiment. It's because of trade. Southern planters owe two hundred million dollars to the banks and merchants—"

Gabriel interrupted. "Do you hear often from David?"

"I do, but not Papa! Papa has not forgiven him and I don't suppose he ever will."

With an uncharacteristic gesture Gabriel drove his fist into his hand. "Fanatics! The newspapers—North and South—encourage this! A lot of warmongers, all of them. I should like to let them fight it out with bullets instead of in newsprint for a change."

Miriam heard her voice go prim with disapproval. "Then you agree with Rabbi Gutheim?"

"I agree in principle. But even their best efforts won't work. The South will not live under a Republican president, the secessionists will prevail, the North will not permit secession, and—there you have it." Again the fist struck into the hand.

She watched him intently. "What will you do?" she asked then.

"I shall go to war."

The portentous words were simply spoken, with neither dread nor enthusiasm. I shall go to war. He might just as well have said: I shall take a ride upriver.

She was curious. "You were so against the Mexican War."

"That was different. This is different. The homeland is threatened. If South Carolina especially should leave the Union, what choice would I have? My people helped build the state. Six generations of them are buried there."

These words, which in another's mouth could well have been bombastic, were in Gabriel's mouth entirely natural, so that she saw at once how true and essential they were for him.

"And as for Louisiana, am I to turn my back on her, on my friends and the life I have here?"

"So, like Lincoln, you will stand on principle." She glanced toward the window, where, not ten feet away, people were passing on the street, darkening the translucent curtains as they passed. And lowering her voice, she said, "You know, of course, that I should do otherwise. If I were a man, I would fight on the other side."

He bowed slightly. Then, turning his back, he went to stand in front of the fireplace to stare at the empty grate. Miriam stood up, gathering her purse and shawl. Hearing her movement, he turned around to detain her once more.

"I've something to say. It is very disagreeable to me. Your husband left it to me to tell you, and I have been putting it off too long."

In sudden weakness she sat down again. Surely it was something about André. He had gone back to Europe. He was dead. Yes, she thought, I have lost all. David. André. All.

"He has doubts about the affairs he has entrusted to you."

"Doubts?" she cried. "Why? Have we not prospered, pulled the loose ends together? You said yourself over and over that I—" She stopped. It was surely because of André. It had to be.

"Why?" Gabriel repeated. He spoke almost listlessly, as if the subject were one that did not concern him. "You must have some idea why, I should think." And he looked at a spot on the wall behind Miriam's head.

The high, thin hum of silence rang in her ears. He was not going to make it easy for her. Always he had that habit of making a person pull words out of him, or else submit to waiting in that maddening silence until he was ready to speak.

"Oh," she said, "I really think that since you were given this commission, you are obliged to tell me all of it."

Now he met her eyes directly, fastening on them with his strange, severe, sad gaze. "Very well. It is because, he says, he is no longer sure he can trust your judgment. He is afraid that you might, quite unintentionally, sign papers or do some other foolish thing that might in some way involve the family." Gabriel hesitated. "Because of various influences . . ."

It was like being found out in a theft. She was shaking. "Is that all he told you? Nothing more?" And she forced herself to ask, "Did he name this—this influence?"

"Yes, he did."

How could Eugene have done such a filthy thing? Still, it was his right to protect his property, their children's property. At whatever cost she must not flinch under this man's gaze.

"And do you believe that?"

"Believe that you would allow your family to be harmed? No. I assured him that you were a very capable woman and that you could be trusted completely."

"Thank you," she said.

"There's no need to thank me. It is only the truth."

She could not bear the shame in the room, the humiliation. All Rosa's marble statuettes threatened to spring from their pedestals with outspread wings and clutching arms. The swollen furniture threatened to line itself in battle array and barricade the door. She had to get out.

"I'm sorry," Gabriel said. "There was really no need to tell you all this, except that he wanted it. I'm his lawyer. I have to do what he wants."

"It's all right. Forget it. I understand." She tried to push past him, but he prevented her.

"Wait! Wait, Miriam. Don't leave without hearing me."

"I don't feel well. Please. I have to go."

"Only a moment. I shouldn't say what I'm going to say, but I've held it in so long, and now this—all this business—it's too much to hold in anymore. Listen to me," he said, putting his hand on her arm.

He never touched me before, she thought, and was afraid, although she could have given no reason for her fear.

"You must know I love you. You must know. A woman as sensitive as you. How could you have sat in this room with me these many hours, not knowing what was in the room with us?"

"I didn't . . . you never said," she whispered awkwardly.

"No, I never did. And why? Because one is civilized and I had no right. Even now I would never have spoken . . . what I feel for you . . . can't help feeling. . . . In all decency I had to keep still. While he, this man, this man who already has a wife, he dares to expose you, a woman like you . . . to the scorn of the city. He risks your ruin and your children's ruin! Oh, I would never—"

Miriam was stripped bare. It was as if someone had entered that cool, quiet room above the river and the square, where she had been with André through long afternoons, had flung open the door and come upon the bed where they lay.

"As intelligent as you are . . . but knowing nothing of the world . . ." Gabriel spoke in broken sentences, with fury, with passion, such as she had not dreamed he possessed. "Nothing of the world . . . It is like robbery, a desecration. . . . If I were eighteen, a hothead of eighteen . . . and if he were to walk into this room, I would be able to kill him. Yes, even now . . . perhaps I would be unable to stop myself from killing him. My God, how could he have done this thing to you?"

And suddenly this purity of emotion obliterated Miriam's shame. It made the fact of her shame a degrading thing in itself. He was not thinking of *himself,* but only of her! And without one single word of blame for her, only with a protective rage on her behalf, as though it had been André alone who had done what Gabriel called "this thing," only André, and not Miriam, too! She was intensely moved.

"Is it only his fault?" she asked softly. "It is just as much mine if one can talk of fault at all. Why, is it a fault to love? Can anyone help it? You said yourself that you—"

"I said I loved you, but I spoke also of risk and humiliation."

"Does loving count risk or humiliation?" she countered.

"If it is really love, then yes, I think it must."

"Perhaps it ought, but we don't always do what we ought." She bowed her head, which felt hot and dizzy. There would be red blotches on her forehead and cheeks, they came always when she was anxious, making her ugly; she did not know why at this moment she should care about looking ugly before Gabriel. Then she thought of something else.

"You speak of risks. Have you forgotten the risk you took for my brother?"

He bowed. "You are right and I stand corrected. I risked my sister and her family. I had forgotten."

The little bow, the formal words, put a wall between them. She did not let it stand.

"What I meant was, you did what you did for David because you loved him, you didn't think of yourself." And she added, "I'll be in your debt forever, Gabriel."

"I don't want that. I don't want thanks. I didn't then and I don't now."

She was dismayed at having hurt him by her choice of words, speaking of debt, when what she meant was something so different.

"Gabriel," she began again, "we go back so far . . . I was a child, you and David weren't long past childhood either, and love came to the three of us even then. David and I . . . we would do anything for you, you must know that. We were talking about risks just now. Love knows none; that's all I meant to say. That's all I hoped you would understand."

"All right. I understand."

She saw that he was very tired and that he had already begun to regret what he had said, because it would come to nothing. He would lie awake tonight, as one does after pouring one's heart out to no avail. She wanted to say that everything was senseless and cruel: the way Eugene and she had come together, the way André and Marie Claire had come together, even the way that beautiful dark woman loved Eugene— how queer and strange to love Eugene!

But she said only, "I'm sorry, Gabriel. I truly am." And if it had been permissible, would have added, "my dear."

Except for that hand, trembling on her arm, he had not touched her. Raising the hand now, as if to curve it somewhere, to caress her cheek or her hair, perhaps to take her face between both hands and kiss her lips, he let it fall back, turning the motion into a gesture of despair. Then, standing aside, he allowed her to pass through the door.

A breeze had come up over the river, blowing the flimsy, summer skirt about her ankles. Under the thin cotton cloth her body burned.

20

"Let us wait at least until after the Inauguration to see what Lincoln will do," Ferdinand ventured timidly, in response to Eugene's positive indignation. "Give him a chance. Jefferson Davis wants to. Sam Houston wants to."

"Nonsense!" Eugene said. "The Union is a compact between sovereign states, and it can be broken as easily as it was put together. Governor Moore said exactly that only last week. Do you really expect Louisiana to live under a Black Republican government? Do you?"

Whether Ferdinand did so or not, Miriam did not discover. She suspected that what Ferdinand feared most was war. His memories of violence were too sharp to have been forgotten. Anyway, there was no arguing with Eugene. Flaunting the blue cockade in his lapel, he liked to tell them—had told them a dozen times already—that both the words and the music to "Cockades of Blue" had been written by none other than Penina Moise of Charleston, the same Penina Moise who wrote hymns for Temple Beth Elohim in that city.

After dinner Eugene liked to call for a whiskey punch and make a toast.

"With Stephen Decatur we repeat, 'My country, may she be right, but my country, right or wrong.'

This," he proclaimed, "is the same as the struggle against England in seventy-six. It is a fight for freedom."

In the face of such sentiments Miriam, too, kept silent. She was living on sufferance and was quite aware of it. Of course Eugene knew where her secret sympathies lay; he had simply decided that this was one more subject better left unmentioned between them. It was just as well. She could not have borne his touch upon her wounds.

Every so often the dull ache of André's absence was pierced by a pain so swift, so shocking, that it bent her over in the middle as if she had been stabbed. He had vanished. The earth, or perhaps the ocean, had swallowed him.

And yet it was unthinkable that he should not return.

In this terrible time there was no one to talk to, not even about the war. Her children were still too young, and besides, they were southerners, like everyone they knew. It would be wrong—cruel and dangerous—to confuse them with their mother's doubts.

Young Eugene came home from school in a mood halfway between anger and tears. He flung his books on the parlor floor between his parents' feet.

"The boys were talking about Uncle David in school!" he blurted. "And I was so ashamed. I hate him for what he did to us!"

Miriam felt her heart lurch once before it resumed its beat. She asked calmly, "What did he do to us?"

"You know! He killed Uncle Sylvain."

"Now, wait a minute. He's not a murderer, Eugene. It was a political difference, a terrible, ugly thing, but a dispute all the same, not a murder!"

"A political difference! But he was on the wrong

side, a dirty abolitionist! I don't like being blamed for
having him in my family!"

The boy looked toward his father as if asking for
support. The father said only, "None of us is responsible for his relatives. That's all you have to tell them,
and keep telling."

"They say somebody in the family must have helped
him get away. They say he escaped with only a couple
of minutes to spare."

"That's nonsense!" After another breathtaking
lurch of the heart, Miriam spoke sharply. "Nobody in
this family had anything to do with anything David
did. He was always his own master and took care of
himself."

"Indeed." The senior Eugene's tone was grim. "Indeed. Let us hope he can take care of himself in the
war that he and his kind are going to bring upon us."

"I'll fight if it comes!" The boy made fists, adding,
in his ignorance, his innocence. "Maxim and Chanute,
they'll fight, too! You'll see, we all will!"

Poor baby, Miriam thought. Poor country. Thirty
million people rushing into war.

She said that one evening to Fanny, who had come
running out of breath because of the nine o'clock cur-
few, which had now been imposed on all the city's
Negroes—an indignity which, on the first night of its
imposition, had caused Miriam to lower her eyes in
embarrassment before the girl.

"Dark blood on the moon," Fanny had said, which
was as good a way as any to express an ominous fear.

Dark blood on the moon.

From the Senate gallery the applause poured like
gold rain on Judah Benjamin.

"The fortunes of war," he said, "may be adverse to
our arms; you may carry desolation into our peaceful

land, and with torch and firebrand set our cities in flames . . . but you never can subjugate us."

South Carolina was the first to secede. When Louisiana's turn came, the *Picayune* and the *Crescent* wrote in elegiac phrases of honor and the Union's death.

Fort Sumter fell and Lincoln called for volunteers.

Robert E. Lee, who had emancipated the slaves he had inherited from his family, refused the command of the Union armies and, in anguish of mind, went home to Virginia to stand with his kin.

The war had come.

Southwinds brought fine April rain and moist air from the Gulf, to curl Angelique's black hair and uncurl the new leaves on the jasmine bush. Sweet-olive scent drifted over the piazza. Redbirds were twittering and rustling in the gum trees when Miriam, always the earliest to rise, stood at the window waiting for the city to wake up.

The awakening came abruptly, as soldiers poured in from the country and streamed out from the houses, filling the narrow streets with the vigor of drumbeats. There was a shine on everything, on swords, gold lace cuffs, and handsome horseflesh. On every woman's shoulder fluttered the bright scrap of a Confederate flag.

Eulalie was first to remark that Miriam was not wearing one. She had grown bolder, as if it were understood that a bargain had been struck: her silence about André in return for Miriam's acquiescence in all else. The very next afternoon, visiting with Pelagie, Eulalie brought a flag and pinned it on Miriam's shoulder. A few minutes later Rosa came, and she, too, was wearing one. Miriam looked down at the alien scrap of cloth on her own shoulder. So it was that one was drawn in. It would have been impossible not to wear this emblem in this company.

"My sons have got their orders," Rosa announced. "Henry goes to Fort St. Philip and Herbert to the Navy. They are commissioned," she added, trying to sound casual about it.

Pelagie explained, "Alexandre and Lambert are too young for commissions, but naturally they've enlisted. Alexandre is in the Mounted Wildcats and Lambert is in the De Soto Rifles."

"I should be ashamed of my nephews if they had not enlisted," Eulalie said. "A woman who lives near us—I won't mention any names—her son received a package in the mail with a petticoat in it."

"In some towns," Pelagie related with a shudder, "I've heard they have been tarring and feathering young men who won't volunteer."

"Well, I should hope they would!" Eulalie cried.

"I have heard," Rosa said softly, "that there is talk of jailing people who speak in favor of the North." From under the pure white shells of her eyelids her quick eyes slid up toward Miriam, conveying an anxious warning.

"Oh, I am proud of my sons," Pelagie said. Her round cheeks were flushed with pleasure. "Lambert told me, 'It's for the defense of southern womanhood, Mama.' But all the Labouisse cousins will distinguish themselves. They have been organizing their own companies. Mama's cousins upriver have organized a company, too. Sons of the best families. Yes, we can all be proud. Even my cook, Belinda, has been baking boxes and boxes of cookies for Lambert and Alexandre. They are her boys."

Cookies and guns. Guns and cookies, Miriam thought. And suddenly a picture of one of Pelagie's children flashed to mind—which one she could not

remember, for there had been so many—but a blond
boy whom she had been pushing on a swing long before she had had children of her own. He had dropped
his cookie on the grass and cried. Now he was to carry
a gun.

Without deliberate intent her gaze came to rest
upon her own Angelique, who was sitting in the corner, sewing a pile of bandages. Even the schoolgirls,
who last year had been learning to embroider trous-
seaus, were now enlisted in the war.

Then through the open window came the voice of
young Eugene reciting Latin declensions to his father.
The voice deepened, throaty and husky, then cracked
and squeaked. How long before he, too, would take up
a gun?

Not to be outdone, Rosa was saying, "Do you know
that David de Leon has just been made surgeon general of the Confederate Army? He's a cousin of
Henry's. Such an enormous network of cousins!"

"My little Louie," Pelagie related with satisfaction,
"is so upset because he's not old enough to go!"

"Perhaps," Miriam told her, "the war will last long
enough for him to have his wish."

The irony went unnoticed. "Oh, they say it will be
over in thirty days. On Good Friday I walked to nine
different churches to pray for victory. I felt sure of it
by the time I got home."

A letter from David crackled in Miriam's pocket.

"I have joined a medical unit. . . . England will
recognize the Confederacy as a belligerent power.
. . . They need cotton for the Lancashire mills. . . .
Their aristocrats side with the South, anyway. . . . It
will be a bitter, hard war. . . . Perhaps years."

As always, she had treasured his letter, reading it
over and over so that every word was clear in her
memory.

"For the first time I am thankful you are so far away. I am no military man, God knows, but I really don't believe the war will reach where you are. So you will be spared that, at least. I wish you could be spared all suffering! You have such burdens . . . the things we've talked about still there, I suppose, and added to, confused by your pity for him since he lost his sight. . . . But you are very strong. I don't think you even realize how strong you are. Gabriel and I have always known it . . . you will keep things going for your beautiful children. I think of them always. . . . Someday, in a better time, I shall remind them that it was I who held them in their first minutes on this earth. . . ."

Pelagie's voice interrupted, saying now, "Eulalie has sewn the most glorious silk banner for the parade at the encampment next week." Pelagie had not looked so youthful or enthusiastic since before Sylvain's death. "It will be such a grand affair! I had to get a new dress for it. Have you noticed how much wider skirts have got this season? One really looks passé if one's dress is more than a year old."

I really do not understand anything, Miriam thought, as the women talked.

The choir stood up and sang, "Be merciful unto me, O God."

Psalm 57, it said, in the Form of Service. On this June afternoon in the year 1861, President Jefferson Davis having decreed a day of prayer for the government, Miriam sat in the crowded synagogue.

"Yea, in the shadow of thy wings will I make my refuge, until these calamities be overpast."

In the pew behind her a woman stirred the air with a palmetto fan. The heat was overwhelming, but it was not only the temperature that weighed upon Miriam; it was her own unrest.

Angelique was yawning. Catching her mother's glance of reminder she clapped her hand in its white glove over her mouth. A flush touched the girl's high cheekbones; a strand of slippery hair lay damp on her forehead. She began to play with her bracelets, making a jangle in the quiet. Miriam's frown vanished almost as soon as it had appeared: How could this child envision what was coming? Let her bracelets jangle! Soon enough she would find out, soon enough.

Now came the twenty-ninth psalm. The congregation rose.

"The Lord will give strength unto His people; the Lord will bless His people with peace."

The stately music came to a hushed end, and the Scrolls of the Law were returned to the Ark.

Prayers and petitions for mercy.

"You know that Gabriel is leaving with the Tenth Louisiana?" Eugene asked.

She had not known. She had not seen him since that day she would rather not, for Gabriel's sake and her own, remember.

"But Rosa said he was to have a government post of some sort," she replied.

"He turned it down. He wanted no sinecure. I admire him for it."

Emma wondered whether Gabriel was to be with General Beauregard. "Fine old French stock, the Beauregards. Mrs. Beauregard says he rarely speaks English, only when he has to."

"We must give a dinner on the day he leaves, a gala dinner," Eugene said. "You might as well send Maxim right now with the invitations." His animation increased; the war had enlivened him. "What does he like to eat? We must have all his favorites."

"It seems to me," Emma recalled, "that he had a special fondness for gumbo."

And Ferdinand contributed. He had always had the gift for perfect hospitality. "Yes, and lettuce with brown gravy, the way Serafina makes it. A roast with champagne sauce. And plum pudding. It's not the season for it, but that doesn't matter. And a vanilla meringue. He likes that, too."

A double row of gilt buttons marched down the front of Major Carvalho's gray frock coat. Carrying a saber and wearing his military boots, Gabriel was another man, a stranger.

Miriam had not wanted to seat him at her right, but Sisyphus, who was a master of protocol, had naturally placed the guest of honor there. Relieved that, after the first required greeting, he did not say anything further to her, Miriam addressed her conversation to the man on her left, who happened to be another of Emma's cousins, a garrulous ancient who asked of her only that she listen while he talked of nothing in particular.

Meanwhile, general talk ranged around the table, chiefly a recapitulation of the concerns that had filled every mind since the start of the war.

"If we don't ship cotton, the European powers will starve for it, and they'll have to come over to our side."

"No, no, we should produce as much cotton as we can, more than ever before, and send it to England now to build up credit."

"Burn it up, is what I say! A lot of planters in Georgia and South Carolina are doing just that right now.

What did the Russians do when Napoleon occupied Moscow? They burned the city."

"Nonsense! The Union armies will never get as far as the cotton belt."

Gabriel had been silent until now. "Don't underestimate them. They may even threaten New Orleans." His words produced a flurry of shocked denial.

"They will never pass the forts," Eugene objected. "We have redoubts with cannon for sixty miles, all the way from the forts to the city. New Orleans! On the contrary, we'll see them in Washington!"

And Ferdinand added, "They'll be too busy in the east to bother with us." Once unwilling to admit even the possibility of war, now that it had come, he had turned into an eager strategist. "Anyway, if they should try—*if*, I say—the attempt will come from upriver."

"The forts are impregnable," Eugene said again. "The British couldn't breach one of them in 1815, and now we have two. And you think they will even try to attack, Gabriel?"

"I think they will try," Gabriel said firmly, "and may possibly succeed."

"General Lovell will have things in hand," Emma said. "I know the family—a delightful man, a brave gentleman."

Ferdinand tried again. "We have fifteen naval ships outside the forts—"

Rosa interrupted, "My Herbert tells me nothing will pass the *Louisiana* and *Mississippi* ironclads when they are finished. I don't know how you can talk like that, Gabriel. It's not like you to be so gloomy."

"Realistic, not gloomy," Gabriel replied.

He shifted restlessly in his chair and his leg, in doing so, brushed the hem of Miriam's dress; apparently too aware of the contact, he moved hastily away.

She felt his discomfiture as she felt her own. The dinner was interminable anyway, stilted and prolonged. People should eat their food, get it done with, and leave the table, she thought impatiently.

"Have you heard," asked Rosa, speaking to the table at large, "that André Perrin is on a commission to seek alliances abroad? Especially with France, I believe. He should be perfect for that, he knows the country so well. He has such polish, I always thought, so persuasive in a diplomat," she added innocently.

"Oh, an excellent choice!" It was a man's voice, certainly not Eugene's voice, nor Gabriel's, but whose, Miriam did not know, having suddenly become engrossed in her plate, on which a chinoiserie border of cobalt and gold encircled a fantasy of pagodas.

So if that was true, he would be back in France. Back with Marie Claire, to drift with her as she did with Eugene? Now the tension within Miriam, the tension of the two dark years since André had left, became unbearable. She could not sit a moment longer, but would have to get up and move regardless of appearances. With the very edge of vision she was aware that Gabriel was looking at her. Afraid to return the look, she could only guess that he was punishing himself with morbid curiosity, to see how she had reacted to the mention of André. And she wondered whether the nervous blotches were already staining her forehead.

Eugene had risen, and Sisyphus was guiding him toward the door. The dinner was concluded.

"The train goes at eight. We'll have plenty of time if we leave now," he said.

Gabriel protested. "It's a long ride and very hot. Really, I hadn't expected anyone to go."

"We are seeing you off," Eugene said firmly.

Horses, carriages, soldiers, and families crowded

alongside the train which was to carry the men away to Camp Louisiana in northern Virginia. Some soldiers had already taken their seats in the cars and begun to play poker, while friends handed fried chicken and cold drinks through the windows. Some were already drunk. There was much laughter, brave talk, solemn admonitions, and tearful good-byes. Babies were hoisted onto uniformed shoulders, anxious mothers held on to their restless children, and lovers parted. Over all a brass band blared triumphantly.

"I've packed ice in a bucket for you," Rosa said. "Be sure to remind Lorenzo that it's among your things."

"I really don't need to take Lorenzo," Gabriel objected. "He has plenty to do at home for you."

"Nonsense! What do you mean? Every officer has his body servant. Who's going to take care of your horses and cook for you and wash your clothes? Now, remember that he's got your watch, and I've given him three hundred dollars in gold to keep in case you need to buy anything, although I do believe I've thought of everything."

Eugene sniffed. "Three hundred dollars! You'd better watch out that your Lorenzo doesn't run off to the Yankees with it."

"Nonsense!" Rosa said again. "He adores Gabriel. He would never do that. Besides, why should he run off? He lives as well as Gabriel does, as well as we all do. Where could he live any better?"

The engine shrieked three times. Men began to climb into the train. Abruptly Rosa's brisk and lively courage gave way, collapsing with her pride. "Oh, my sons, my brother, everything's falling apart! When will it all be normal again?" Her nose ran. She rummaged in her reticule for a handkerchief. "Oh, I'm ashamed of myself! I can't help it."

"Come," Gabriel said gently. "Come, Rosa. You'll manage. It will be all right. We men need your courage. Come, my dear." Above Rosa's shaking, bowed shoulders, his eyes signaled to Miriam that he wanted to say something. He drew her aside.

"No, don't be alarmed! I only want to speak about Rosa. Will you take care of her? For all her brave talk and her worldly wit, she's not nearly as strong or sensible as you."

Miriam could not resist asking, "You can't still really think I am sensible?"

"I think you haven't learned yet how sensible you are."

How like him to speak in enigmas!

"I promise you I will do my best."

"She will need a friend."

"You needn't worry. I am her friend."

"Thank you."

There seemed nothing more to say, but he did not go. Gravel and cinders burned through the soles of their shoes. Yet he kept standing, searching her face candidly and still revealing nothing of himself, as was so often his way. God knew what he was thinking, where his thoughts had been! Surely, being human, he must have imagined her with the other man, lying together in a silky bed, must have wondered about drowsy afternoons or dark blue nights. If that were so, he must be suffering still.

"I am your friend, too, Gabriel," she said softly. "I always have been. I always will be your dear friend."

It was the wrong thing to say. His face tightened.

"Just please be Rosa's. I am afraid things may be very hard for her."

The whistles, shrieking for the last time, caused a rush to board the train, and Gabriel was lost in the scramble. His little group stood among the crowd until the train was out of sight, and then, in the beginning dusk, went home.

Eugene said only, "I wish I could have gone, too," and after that was silent the rest of the way.

And Miriam understood that the man beside her was feeling a painful deprivation of his right to proclaim his masculinity in the great adventure of the war. She thought how strange it was that this tragedy could be at the same time exhilarating for so many. Why, even Gabriel had worn his sword with a flourish!

All up and down the streets of the city the state flag bloomed from balconies and doorways. Candles and gas lamps burned in the windows, gilding the night. From as far off as the encampment a distant cannon, crashing in some final departing salute, scattered the pigeons on the square.

On the front steps young Eugene and Angelique waited, still flourishing their little flags. The boy, at sight of his parents, came rushing. His eyes glistened, his voice was hoarse, he had been cheering in the streets all afternoon.

"Why didn't you let us go along?" he demanded. Like his father he was torn by disappointment at having to miss the war.

"There wasn't enough room in the phaeton," Miriam apologized. "But I promise we'll take you the next time there's a send-off."

The child could barely stand still. "Was it awfully exciting?"

She smiled at her son, her lovely, tender boy, and consoled herself again: He is only twelve, thank God.

"Yes, yes," she said. "It was very exciting. Very."

21

A year of war had made all the difference. Miriam walked home with Fanny from the market. She had just paid an outrageous price for a tough and greasy mullet, popularly known as "Biloxi bacon." Along the riverfront a three-masted schooner was being loaded with baled cotton; with covered lights it would run the blockade to Havana, then on to London or Paris.

Paris. Squares like Jackson Square. Had he not said it resembled the Place des Vosges? André walking there—he had a rapid walk, almost a run—she could hear the sound of his hastening steps on the pavement. There would be great stone official buildings, parks, cafés, young women with sweet mouths, perfume, pearls. . . . A chill went through her and she stopped, closing her eyes.

"Are you all right?" asked Fanny.

She had been in Paris, she had forgotten Fanny, over whose vigilant face there now passed an expression in part concern, in greater part inquisitiveness. How much did Fanny know or guess? One could never tell about servants, so fearful, so sly, trained as they were never to reveal, but always to calculate, lest they offend.

Miriam blinked herself back to the moment, to the street and the morning.

"Yes, yes, I'm all right. A little tired."

He had not written; of course, he feared to subject her to Eugene's wrath; or perhaps he had written, but the mail was not getting through.

The ships were not getting through anymore. The blockade was choking the city; it was a rope around the city's neck.

In the next block they were taking a church bell down from the steeple to be cast into cannon. Indeed, the war had made a difference! Strange to realize how one got caught up on the very crest of the wave of war when one had hoped to let it wash past. At the synagogue the women were giving a ball to raise money for poor families whose men were in the fight. The women were knitting socks and gloves for the soldiers; bags of gray wool stood in every parlor. One sent blankets to the army. One gave up drinking coffee and eating meat so that the army might have them. Strange, painful and strange, to be doing all these things, to be doing them with such a full heart, and at the same time to be hoping that the other side where David stood among the men in blue, would triumph!

Rosa de Rivera was crossing Jackson Square.

"I had a letter today from Gabriel. Shall I read it? Or perhaps you'd rather not?" she added, giving to the perfectly normal existence of the letter a significance which apparently she thought it must have for Miriam.

Why, she is enjoying this "situation"! Miriam thought instantly. Unrequited love for a married woman. Delicious, sad, and slightly scandalous.

"Of course I'd rather," she said calmly. "Sit down and read it. You go on home without me, Fanny."

" 'I have been in victories and defeats,' " Rosa read. " 'At Manassas Junction, where we won, and at Fort Donelson, where we lost. They were equal in horror.

For my first battle, I was enthusiastic. It seemed to be a sweeping thing, and, in spite of the evil that is war, a chance to show what individual courage, multiplied by thousands, can do. Perhaps, decisively, to bring the war to an end? At any rate, I went into it with no fear, to my great astonishment, and with a feeling of power. All of that ended very quickly.

" 'In the morning the truth hit me between the eyes. It was a summer morning; do not those two words convey enough meaning? Summer morning, and against the greenery the red earth of the breastworks made another wound to add to the sum of the human wounded, of whom there were so many. That fresh, blooming earth, and what we had done to it! All the young men and what we had done to each other! We had captured the Federal depot, but because there weren't enough wagons and we couldn't carry much away, we had set fire to it. It had been burning all night. Of this tremendous bonfire only a heap was left, a small hill of smoking ruins, with sparks like little red evil eyes popping out of hell.

" 'General Lee allowed the Federals to collect their own wounded. Theirs and ours were laid out as separately as possible, under the trees, as much out of the sun's glare as we could. The wounds are terrible, far worse, they tell me, than in the Mexican War. That's because of the minié bullet; it has a conical shape, a devilish invention, it rips the flesh to jagged pieces. Already flies and maggots were settling in these awful wounds. The men, lying in long columns, kept shifting in their agony, so that the columns rippled as if some gigantic serpent were sliding across the field.

" 'Perhaps I should not write these things to you. Yet it seems to me that people ought to know about such horrors, even though I see no way now to prevent them. Now that we are in this war, we have no other course than to continue. At any rate, as I know I shall regret having written this, I remind myself that I shall not write again for a long while, for there is neither time nor place to do so.

" 'But let me finish. How shall I describe a battle? Should I even try? Yet, again, it seems that people ought to know. It is a din, a pandemonium. Even the trees are wounded, as Gatling-gun bullets tear them apart. One is caught in a rain of leaves and twigs. It was the Williams repeating cannon that we used or the twelve-pounder Napoleon. Our men's faces are black with gunpowder. The noise of these things is indescribable. On a level below them one hears the racket of fleeing birds and the terrible screams of wounded horses. Poor, ignorant creatures whose once kind masters have led them into this!

" 'Often it is waiting for battle that is the hardest. The suspense is sometimes more trying and difficult than the real thing. Knowing what is to come and fearing it, one still wants to get it over with. We march in slashing rain, soaked through to the bone. Most of the men have no raincoats and often not enough tents. Many must sleep in the wet, without shelter. We are thick with lice; sometimes we cannot change clothing for weeks and the lice lodge in the seams, so that even washing the clothes doesn't get rid of them. The men are so ashamed of being filthy. Illness attacks many more than are wounded. Most people don't know that. Last summer it was typhoid that killed. Now in the cold, it is pneumonia. The cold and snow are very hard on southern boys. And all the time in heat or cold, there is scurvy to fear. Our diet is crackers, salt pork, coffee, and beans.

" 'I have seen a hospital camp abandoned to the enemy because we had to retreat and save ourselves.

We left our own to die as prisoners or, perhaps worse, to suffer without anesthesia.

" 'Oh, God, why do I write all this? Maybe in the morning I will not send it to you after all. But now as I write by candlelight, I feel as if the ghosts of all I have seen are looking over my shoulder and telling me that I must put this down.

" 'I remember the look of these deaths, so unlike the white and quiet deaths of our grandparents. These deaths are red and raw. But hear what I dread: It is that I am becoming used to them. I glance at a dead boy lying twisted among his poor belongings, his tin cup, his pistol and frying pan, his knapsack with its scattered photographs and letters from home. I glance and pass on.

" 'What is to become of me? What kind of man will I be when this is over?' "

Rosa put the letter back into her reticule. There was a silence, neither woman speaking until Rosa took the letter out again.

"I almost forgot. There is a postscript. It says: 'Remember me to Miriam. I hope she is well.' "

Erect as a general, Ferdinand stood in front of the map which had been pinned on the wall of the back parlor, reading dispatches aloud to Eugene. The two men, with Emma and her daughters and young Eugene, were all following the war. They had rejoiced and argued over Manassas, railing at Jeff Davis.

"We should have and could have walked into Washington," declared Ferdinand. "They couldn't have stopped us."

The exhilaration which had revived Eugene's spirits at the war's beginning was gradually dissipating itself. "No, no," he answered. "That victory came too early to do any real good. It has made us think we're unbeatable."

Ferdinand, on the other hand, clung to cheer, and Miriam reflected on the contradiction. Papa had denied the very possibility of war, but accepting it now, he played it like a great, stimulating game, a complex exercise.

"I never thought," Eugene observed gloomily, "that Grant would whip Johnston and Beauregard at Shiloh. The Mississippi is open now as far down as Vicksburg."

Yesterday General Johnston's funeral cortege had passed up St. Charles Street in visible proof of the terrible defeat. At the mouth of the river, one hundred fifty miles south of the city, lay the Union fleet, waiting for their cautious, deliberate push toward the forts. In command was Admiral Farragut, bitterly referred to as a son of New Orleans. Strange and stranger, Miriam thought, these interwoven, contradictory allegiances.

Pelagie's Alexandre, a messenger on Lovell's staff, brought daily news to the back-parlor strategists. His pink cheeks were moist with perspiration and the breathless importance of his tidings.

"The forts and the city are positively safe! You can't believe what's being done! We've got dismasted schooners, eight of them, loaded with logs, they're fastened together with cable and laid in a row across the river. Absolutely impassable! And in the bayous we've driven piles, sunk live oak trees, still green, whole bands of them, forty-five feet wide. You couldn't possibly get through them, either! And on the river we've got fifty fire rafts heaped with wood and tar oil and cotton; one wouldn't want to come up against one of those when it's burning, I can tell you! And on the riverbanks below the fort, General Lovell's setting troops of sharpshooters."

A few days later he came rushing to report that the bombardment of the forts had begun. This time there shone through his description the beginnings of disbelief, as if what he had seen were something that neither he nor anyone else could possibly have conceived of.

"The air is so hot from all the firing that bees come swarming, trying to get away. And the river is full of dead fish. They say it's the detonation of the guns that kills them, I don't know. You can't imagine . . ." His arms were spread on the table, where he leaned to rest, and his thoughtless young face was crossed for an instant by a shadow of thought. "You should have seen the smoke when the fire rafts came rolling down the river! From the turpentine and burning tar, you know. I had to watch very closely to bring reports back. Oh, it was like, like—the way one thinks of hell, the smoke so thick we could hardly see, and then the yellow flames when the ships exploded. They say dozens of men were drowned; first scorched, and scalded from the boilers, then drowned . . . Union men, mostly . . ." And he broke off, his eyes stretched wide, as if in just that moment he had understood that these were men, flesh like himself, scorched, scalded, and drowned.

"Rosa's Herbert is out there on the river," was all Miriam said.

The alarm bell sounded just after they had risen from the breakfast table on the morning of the twenty-fourth. Twelve bronze notes tolling from a church tower, and four times repeated, made a vibration that went through to the bones and caused everyone to stop in place, Sisyphus with a laden tray of dishes, Angelique halfway up the stairs, tilting her head with an unspoken question, the dog running to whimper under a chair.

Emma quavered. "The alarm?" Her eyes begged for denial.

"The alarm. Send Maxim down to the newspaper office," Eugene ordered with a spark of his old command. "He can read the bulletin."

In half an hour Maxim was back, gay with the importance of carrying a report. "They have passed the forts. The forts have held, but the gunboats are coming up the river toward the city."

"Then they will be here by tomorrow," Eugene said.

Emma's hand flew to her mouth, stifling what would undoubtedly have emerged as a wail. Young Eugene was exhilarated: Something different was about to happen!

And I, Miriam thought, what do I feel? Fear? Yes, of course. Hope that now, maybe, the war will end? But no, wars do not end so quickly. Then, her thoughts turning to the immediate: Shall we be occupied or will they destroy the city first?

Late in the afternoon Alexandre appeared. Having gone first to say good-bye to his mother, he had been asked by her to bear the latest news to the Mendes house.

"I'm going with General Lovell to Camp Moore. The general has decided to leave the city without defense so the enemy will have no reason to bombard it."

The young man's dash and vigor did wonders for Emma's morale.

"He does us proud," she cried as her grandson went swinging down the steps. "He does us all proud. With men like him, we can't be beaten."

Still, in spite of such sentiments, panic struck and hysteria ran through the streets. People walked up and down, back and forth, to the riverfront, to the evacuation trains, everywhere, without aim. Serafina left the roast burning in the kitchen fireplace. Even Sisyphus, the most dependable of all, forgot to close the front door when he went out. Emma went to Pelagie's house, from which there was a view of the river. Rosa came looking for assurance—and was given assurance —that no news of her sons was bound to be good news.

Ferdinand, unable to sit still, suggested taking young Eugene and Angelique downtown with Blaise to see what was going on.

"What are they wearing?" Eugene inquired.

The question puzzled Miriam. "Wearing?" she repeated.

"Yes, I want them to dress up. Show pride. Even if we do lose the city, it's not the end for us. We mustn't look beaten. Wear your best clothes. Blaise, too, if he's going. Have you got a new uniform, Blaise?"

"Yes, sir." A faint shadow crossed Blaise's mouth and fled.

"Have you got it on?"

"No, sir."

"Then put it on. Hurry."

"He hates his new uniform," Angelique said when Blaise had gone. "Fanny told me he thinks it makes him look like the organ grinder's monkey."

"Nonsense!" Ferdinand was indignant. "I saw to it myself, the finest quality broadcloth."

"It's the color he hates. Purple. And the brass buttons. I don't blame him. I shouldn't want to be made to wear something I don't like," Angelique protested.

"You are you, but Blaise is a servant. He can consider himself fortunate that he's here at all," her father retorted, "instead of complaining about his clothes."

The child feels, however vaguely, what the father rejects, Miriam thought as she watched the little group go down the street. All was changing, all in motion toward the time when Blaise would throw his servile uniform away. Eugene didn't, or couldn't, see it coming. And she remembered the morning when she had pleaded with him not to sell Blaise out of the house.

When Ferdinand came back, his anguish at the city's plight contradicted his uncontrollable excitement at the drama of events.

"Fifteen thousand bales of cotton burning!" he cried. "Cotton ships, too. And steamboats, the docks, everything! Sugar and molasses poured out onto the street, people are scooping up what they can—"

"Burning cotton!" Eugene was horrified. "Damn fools! We shall be needing it! Don't they know that?"

"Those are the orders. Smash machinery and anything the enemy might use. Thousands of people are down at the docks."

Miriam stood on the verandah watching black smoke rise and swirl over the levee. A crowd of women passed at the bottom of the street, poor shabby women, and others in silk, followed by a taggle of little black children who probably thought this was another sort of carnival.

"Burn the city!" shrieked the women. "Don't let them take it! Set it all on fire!" Some of them brandishing pistols. Miriam was almost sure she recognized Eulalie. The world had gone mad. It is enough to make one go mad, she thought.

Night came. As darkness plunged, so quiet came, as if the city had exhausted itself with the day. The household went early to bed. Miriam alone was still downstairs when Fanny appeared at the parlor door.

"Shall you be wanting anything, Miss Miriam?" she inquired after the nightly ritual.

"No, thank you, Fanny, you may go to bed."

"You're not going?" The keen face expressed concern.

"Not just yet, Fanny."

The door closed quietly. And Miriam had an ugly, fleeting thought that the concern might be nothing more perhaps than a clever mask. One would like to ask: What do you think of all this, Fanny? Since this is a war—at least in part—for your liberation, are you rejoicing tonight that this city may fall, or are you perhaps a little saddened by the thought of its destruction? This was the first time there had been a barrier between them, something they could not cross with honest speech. No, that was not quite true. The central question of their relationship, of ownership, had never been spoken of, either; it had been tacitly forbidden on both their parts, so this was not the first time.

Can Fanny possibly have any intimation of how I really feel about what is happening in the South? Probably not, since I have had to keep my feelings hidden. Still, there are subtleties of voice and manner, things not said as much as things said; Fanny's brisk cheer, on which I daily rely, must surely conceal many things; in repose, when she thinks herself unobserved, a thoughtful expression, almost melancholic, settles over her face, but on hearing her name called, it is on the instant wiped away.

So Miriam's own thoughts ran on this night of fear and change.

The tall clock in the hall coughed like the old thing it was and sounded once: Bong! Half past midnight. She took a book from the shelves, and finding that the words made no sense, replaced it to stand and contemplate the pleasant rows of leather bindings, of George Eliot, Dickens, Cooper, the *Contes and Nouvelles* of de Musset, the recollection of smooth pages and smooth words, rich images, making a delicious taste on the tongue and glimmering before the eyes. Civilized.

She walked around the room. Finding some candy left in a silver dish on the table, she finished it. Then in the dining room she took a peach from the bowl on the sideboard, eating too much and still hungry. Back in the parlor she stood and stared at the piano. It was square and made of rosewood. It had been built in Boston. There was a chip on one of the legs where once little Eugene had hit it with his drumstick. She ran her fingers lightly over the keys; their trill and tinkle, although barely touched, were too loud in the dead stillness of the house.

The dog stood whining to go out. She picked it up. Warm little creature, not understanding a word, yet sure to respond to human need. Listen to me, Gretel, I'm all alone, there is no one I can tell how I feel. And do you know, I'm not even sure how I really do feel?

In deepest stillness the earth waited. Against the milky sky the date palms drooped black as funeral plumes. Suddenly, the echoing, hasty footsteps of someone passing unseen sent Miriam racing back into the house, closing the door so hard that the crystal balls on the hall candelabra jangled in distress. She leaned against the door with her hand on her pounding heart. Then, ashamed of her terror, she remembered the night-latch and slid it all the way, that great stout iron bar, five feet long, bolted to the wall. Still, if they wanted to get in, they could do so, couldn't they? They could batter down the top half of the door and climb in, or they could smash the windows. . . .

Upstairs a stripe of light fell across the bed where Angelique was asleep. She looked like a woman, with her long legs extended almost to the foot, and her hair sprayed out upon the pillow. The little girl who had

slept with each arm curled around a doll was poised
now on the farthest edge of childhood.

Across the hall a candle was hastily snuffed out as
Miriam passed the door. Let the boy think she didn't
know he read half the night against his father's orders!
And she had a quick recollection of David, in that
dark village so many years ago, borrowing every book
he could lay his hands on.

Oh, what would the war—the victory or the defeat,
depending on which side one stood—what would it do
to these young lives? To all of us in this house, in this
city? To André?

There was not a ray of light that could begin to
penetrate the future.

"I want to go to the levee," Eugene said in the
morning, meaning, Miriam knew, but not finding himself able to say: I want to see the Federal ships arrive.

And Miriam, because of her own turmoil, both
wanting and not wanting to see them, looked overhead, where dark clouds were swirling and the first
drops raining, and sought excuse. "It's going to
storm."

"I am quite able to go without you," he retorted, so
that she felt foolish, for surely he had always gone
everywhere without her.

"I'll be ready in a minute," she said.

The streets, too crowded for a carriage, were filling
with a defiant mob, pushing on foot toward the waterfront, oblivious to the rain. At the levee, over the
heads of the crowd, the gunboats were plainly to be
seen, for the river had crested and the ships could ride
high, their guns reminding Miriam, as always, of
threatening beast-mouths, pointed down upon the city.

Impatiently, Eugene demanded a description of
events.

"Some ships are still coming round the bend." Miriam wet dry lips. "Six altogether. No, seven, eight. They're filled with men, all armed." Her voice began to tremble. She did not say that the Stars and Stripes were flying and that all around them on the levee Confederate banners waved.

"Down with the Stars and Stripes!" a man cried out.

The cry was taken up by hundreds of voices, including those of Miriam's son and daughter. Women wept. A man with a fife joined in, piping "Dixie," and the crowd began to sing, Emma with profound conviction, as though she were singing a hymn. In spite of all reason this unified outpouring of emotion stirred Miriam to the heart.

A small boat put off from the *Hartford,* and three officers came to land.

Eugene was more frustrated than ever. "What are they doing now? Do you mind telling me what's happening?"

"Some officers are landing. There are sailors. They have guns and bayonets, too."

They passed, the strangers—almost shocking herself, Miriam had thought of the word "invaders"—in dark blue, with their gilt eagles and their severe faces, ignoring the crowd. But they were frightened; of course they must be terrified of this menacing mob; they were so young, like David, who wore their uniform. Miriam stood staring as the strangers swung away in step down the street.

"They'll be going to the city hall," someone said.

The crowd surged after them, behind them, alongside of them, restrained by the sight of guns and bayonets, but giving voice all the way.

"Go home, damned Yankees!"

Then the heavens opened. The steady rain mounted into flood. Yellow clouds roiled furiously, snaking and twining through the black. The rain pocked the river, splashing upward from the pavement, slashed at the trees, and drenched the group still standing at the levee. Savagely, the rain attacked as though the fall of the city were not grief enough for one day.

"It is all over," Eugene said. There were tears in his blind eyes.

Ferdinand remonstrated with him. "Don't say that. The forts haven't fallen."

"What difference? They've passed the forts. And the forts will surrender. They're loaded with northern men. Come, let's go home."

And all the way back to the house he muttered, "The cable wasn't put in the right place. It was a good idea, but it should have been placed above Fort St. Philip, where there's a fierce current, instead of below Jackson, where they could creep in practically undetected and dismantle it. Fools, fools," he repeated. "And this is only the beginning. In a few days Butler will land with his troops, and then we shall see something."

At the front door Sisyphus stood looking up the street. When he saw them he hurried down the steps. His old face was solemn with the message he had to give.

"They sent a boy from Madam de Rivera's. News of her son. He was killed in the fighting on the river."

"My God!" cried Miriam. "Which son was it, did they say?"

"Mr. Herbert. She asks you please to come."

Emma crossed herself. "God's will. We have neglected him, and now he is punishing our righteous cause. We must pray all the harder."

Scalded. Drowned. He was a baby, not yet walking when I first came to Rosa's house. Now he is—was—a young man with a young wife and a baby of his own. Scalded. Drowned.

She spurred herself. "At once. I'll go at once." But what comfort could she bring, what words?

"I will go to her," she repeated, as the others stood watching.

Ferdinand was stricken. She could read her father's mind: I thought I had left all this behind in Europe, he was thinking, as he looked back toward the river and the guns.

Once, as a child, she had watched where some peasants at the edge of a pond had spread a huge net to catch migrating birds. And she had never forgotten the cries and the struggle, the beating wings and limp, broken necks. Now it seemed as though the city, the whole country, were caught in such a net.

22

Sharp voices came from the hall below, and Miriam hurried downstairs in time to see the front door closing on a blue-clad soldier and Eugene disappearing into the parlor. Maxim had a letter in his hand.

"A Union officer, Miss Miriam. He brought this from your brother. He say a friend of his, he asked him specially to deliver this. Mr. Eugene say no Union man to set foot in this house."

"Thank you, Maxim." And taking the letter, she went upstairs to read it in private.

So long since she had heard from David! Spreading the sheets on her lap, she thought, My brother's hands were on this paper. Her eyes skimmed rapidly.

Dear Sister, I write this in August. It may take weeks to reach you. I was at the battle of Antietam Creek. More than twenty thousand men, counting both sides, were killed or wounded. I hope never to see anything like it again. Yet I know I will before this is all over. Where armies go, horror is not confined to the battlefield. I hope you in New Orleans will be spared what has happened here. . . . People turned out of their homes, the abuse of young girls, the Rebels pillaging. That I should be in the midst of this, I who have hated violence all my life, I find hard to believe, as hard to believe as the fact that I should be cursed with the memory of the life I took. I can still see Sylvain, a man I never liked, but still I see his living face accusing me. I remember his delicate, trusting wife.

But enough of that. One good thing has come out of our victory at Antietam, because now neither France nor England will recognize the Confederacy. They see the handwriting on the wall.

But André, Miriam thought, André is there, and his mission will fail. There is a hollow ache in my head when I think of it all.

Once again the High Holy Days have come and gone. Our separation is always saddest for me then. I spent the New Year and the Day of Atonement with a Jewish family—and this will surprise you—southern sympathizers in Maryland, just outside of Washington. They were kind and hospitable, putting out a feast for me both nights, although they were not at all well off. We had some friendly arguments, but I wasn't able to bring them over to my side!

You may be interested in knowing what I was doing in Washington. I don't know whether your papers have printed anything about the chaplaincy scandal, the decree that only Christian denominations are allowed to have chaplains in the army. (Interestingly enough, there's no such rule in the Confederacy!) There's been quite a storm over that, as you can imagine, and I was in the forefront of it.

Still carrying the banners, Miriam thought, smiling to herself. *A stubborn fellow,* Opa had said. *When he thinks he's right, he will never give up.*

Well, when we finally got to the President, who had known nothing about the matter, he corrected the situation at once. So the struggle did have a happy outcome, but it was quite a battle against bigotry, let me tell you.

Sometimes, when I can't sleep and get to feeling philosophical in the middle of the night, it seems as if living is nothing more than going from one struggle to the next. Maybe, in a way, that's good for us, I don't know. But I would like a little longer rest in between! I'd like to sit through a summer evening with a pretty girl and nothing to worry about. I'd like to be with you and your children again, on a cool beach or a boat, or in front of a fire on a winter night. I'd like to have a long walk and talk with Gabriel, the way we used to. But I am wearing blue, while he's in gray. . . .

Dear Miriam, I understand at last why it was impossible for you to leave your people and your home when I wanted to take you with me the night I fled. But at least I hope, now that your city is in Union hands, that you will take the oath of loyalty. I hope Eugene will see it that way, poor helpless man that he is now. Surely you all must know, apart from convictions or any question of right or wrong, that the cause is lost, that the South is doomed? Save yourselves, think of yourselves, my dear—

"You had a letter from your brother." Ferdinand spoke from the open door. "Eugene told me it was delivered."

"Yes."

"You weren't going to tell me. You hid yourself up here to read it?"

"I didn't think you would want to see it, Papa."

There was a silence. Half in and half out of the room, Ferdinand stood undecided.

"Shall I read it, Papa?"

"Well, yes. Go on."

" 'Dear Sister,' " she began, and looking up saw a muscle twitch in her father's cheek. She read on rapidly. " 'I hope you in New Orleans will be spared what has happened here: people turned out of their homes, the abuse of young girls, the Rebels pillaging—' "

"No more!" Ferdinand cried out. "No more! I don't want to hear any more from my son! He writes—he says such things—while we are conquered, our home —" And the old man finished, choking on his own words.

The city writhed in defeat like a sufferer turning on a sickbed. As the bulletins fly out of a sickroom, rumors were passed and whispered. It was said that General Butler had declared that with one wave of the hand from where he stood on the balcony of the St. Charles Hotel, he could have made—and still could make—the streets run with blood.

"What irony!" Eugene exclaimed. "To think that Butler's father served with Andrew Jackson to save this city!"

The beloved Pierre Soulé was sent to prison at Fort Warren in Boston; he had been the very symbol of secession. Two of the city's most influential and fashionable clergymen were sent to prison in New York,

the one for preaching a secessionist sermon and the
other for omitting a prayer for the President of the
United States.

Emma wrung her hands. "In God's name, who will
be next?"

"For this—this stupidity, I've lost my son!" Rosa
cried, her voice cracking like an old woman's.

And indeed, she had aged; on the morning after the
news of Herbert's terrible death, she had awakened as
an old woman. It was queer, Miriam thought, pitiable
and queer, to see her like this without her quick
tongue, her bracelets, and witty advice. Queer, too, to
hear her in agreement with, of all people, Eulalie.

"Oh, I hate them!" Rosa repeated. "Hate them! I
could kill Butler and every man in that rotten blue
uniform that I pass on the street!"

"There are plenty more to be despised on our own
side," Eulalie said darkly. "People like Judah Benjamin and his—his ilk. Was he not to blame for our
disaster at Roanoke Island? And now they have made
him secretary of state! People like him and—and his
ilk!"

His "ilk," Miriam thought. He is a Jew, although
not much of one, it's true, but that's what his "ilk" is.
You want to say so, only you don't dare in front of
Eugene. And I don't dare say to you what I'd like to
say and once would have said.

Emma steered the subject away from Benjamin.

"I saw a nasty thing yesterday on Royal Street. Two
ladies wearing our flag had held their noses when a
Union officer went by. Well, you know that happens
all the time, we all do it. But this officer chose to take
offense, and he followed them across the street, at
which"—she giggled—"they pretended to vomit! I
was on the other side of the street and stopped to
watch. The man was really furious and threatened:

'We have had enough of this! Don't let it happen again, I warn you!'—at which they were scared to death and hurried away."

"You must warn Angelique," Eugene said, frowning. "She must do nothing to attract attention to herself. She is no longer a child to be ignored."

"If Angelique is like her mother," Eulalie remarked with some daring, "she will not insult a *Union* officer."

"What do you mean?" Miriam was hot with anger. "What can you mean?"

"Well, you have taken our flag off your dress."

"Certainly I have. I don't wish to end like Mrs. Phillips."

"What a terrible thing!" Emma said. "I knew her slightly. From one of the best families in Alabama. They claim that she laughed when the funeral procession of a Federal officer passed her house! Have you ever heard of anything so outrageous? Is this a sample of freedom under the Union? That a woman is not free to laugh? And prison on Ship Island! They say she has had a nervous collapse, and no wonder!"

"Butler is known to despise Jews," Eugene said. "That's why he gave her so hard a sentence."

"Oh, yes," Miriam said, her remark being not addressed to, but meant for Eulalie, "the North blames Jews for running the blockade and being loyal to the South, while some southerners do not find us loyal enough. Strange, is it not?"

Eugene spoke with contempt. "Butler! How righteously he can speak while he lets his brother milk the city and pocket a fortune for them both!"

Ferdinand looked personally humiliated. "Hard to believe. Hard to believe," he muttered.

Gloom stifled the house. With the blinds half drawn, its inhabitants moved through the long, dim hours. No one went out to the garden anymore, for it

was too exposed. The out-of-doors felt less secure,
though there was really no sense in that; it was just a
better feeling to stay behind walls.

Even Eugene, Miriam realized suddenly one day,
had not been out of the house for weeks, not even to
make what she euphemistically thought of as his "vis-
its." And, unashamedly, she asked Fanny what she
knew about that. Fanny, equally unashamedly, told
her: "Queen has been entertained at that Union major's who took the house, you know the one down
from General Twigg's, that Butler took for hisself?
They say Queen gave a dinner for a dozen officers, and
the plates were solid silver."

So Queen had gone with the winners! Poor Eugene!
Even the servants had been more loyal, although
goodness knew why.

Miriam was reflecting on these things while her
knitting needles moved through skein after skein of
gray yarn, when young Eugene asked, "Are you going
to take the oath, Papa? My friend Bartlett's father says
he's going to. It's only words, he says, and he plans to
take it without meaning it."

"Does he indeed? Your friend Bartlett's father is a
low-class scoundrel and you are free to repeat those
words."

"They say," Miriam ventured, "that eleven thousand people have taken it already."

"Let them! No decent citizen will have anything to
do with anyone who takes it, mark my words."

*I hope, David had written, that you will at least take
the oath. The South is doomed.*

"It's confiscation, unless you do," Miriam said
again, making her tone sound flat—without urgency.

"Confiscation!" Ferdinand echoed bleakly. "That
means the house."

That means, Miriam thought, the second dispossession for you.

"Read the oath," Eugene commanded.

She picked up the paper. " 'I do solemnly swear that I will render true faith and allegiance to the Government of the United States, that I will not take up arms . . . or encourage others to do so . . . will use my utmost influence . . . to put down the rebellion. . . . This I do as I expect to answer to God. Sworn to and—' "

"Get my notebook!" Eugene cried. "I want to make a list. I want you to copy down the names of everyone you hear of who takes that disgraceful oath!"

Ferdinand looked dubious. He would take it if he dared, if it were not for Eugene. At this point in his life he wanted only peace and comfort; all the early fire had gone out of him. And he stood there looking quite defeated, in his hands the head of a china doll, which he had been trying to mend for Angelique.

"One thing is certain, no one in my family will ever take that oath," Emma declared. "No one of the old French stock could bear to shame himself like that."

Miriam said quietly, "It is not only the old French stock. Our Rabbi Gutheim will not do it, either, and he is hardly French. Nor half, or more than half of our congregation," she finished positively.

But why the defiance, why the need to defend the wrong side yet again? And she wondered about Gutheim, a German immigrant only eleven years in the city, choosing such loyalty to the southern cause. Probably it was the influence of his wife, a lady from an old Alabama family, that moved him. Loving her, he had been persuaded. If I were married to André . . .

"At any rate, we have until October first," Ferdinand was saying. Hopefully, he added, "There might well be some changes by then."

"This is September thirtieth," Miriam said. "You will have to make up your mind today, Eugene."

"I have already made it."

"You're certain?"

"Read the damned thing to me again!"

" '. . . all persons who have not renewed their allegiance . . . are ordered to present themselves . . . to the nearest provost marshal with a descriptive list of all their property . . . and each shall receive a certificate from the marshal . . . claiming to be an enemy of the United States.' " She put the paper down, thinking, I cannot bear it.

"Go on," Eugene said impatiently.

" '. . . Any persons neglecting so to register themselves shall be subject to fine, imprisonment at hard labor . . .' " She flung the paper down.

A blind man, stubborn, immovable; Emma and Ferdinand, equally helpless, and two children; all of them I must care for. Yes, and Rosa, too, who has also refused to take the oath and will be turned out of her house. I gave my word to Gabriel that I would look out for her.

Ferdinand stood in the hall looking around at the house he had come to think of as home. His expression was tinged not so much by grief and apprehension as by astonishment. It was the look he had worn on the day of his bankruptcy, a disbelief that things could tumble and he with them.

"Hurry, Papa," Miriam said gently. "They've given us only until noon to leave."

"I should like to take that picture," he said, as if he had not heard her.

She followed his gaze into the front parlor, where
the rugs had already been rolled up for the summer
and sprinkled with tobacco leaves to keep out insects.
Over the mantel hung a portrait, made in earliest
childhood, of little Eugene and Angelique. The boy,
wearing a sailor suit with long white duck trousers and
broad-brimmed black hat, stood next to the seated
girl, whose little hands were decorously folded as she
had been taught to fold them, on the lap of her green
silk apron.

"We're not allowed to take anything of value," Miriam said doubtfully, feeling the weight of the gold
coins sewn in a belt under her hoops, "although I
don't suppose that has value to anyone but us. Yes,
have Sisyphus wrap it and put it with the servants'
things. They'll be less likely to look there. And I shall
manage to take some books along. We'll be away a
long time."

"Oh, do you think so?" Ferdinand responded.

The little parade of carriages formed on the street in
front of the house. The garden gate was ajar, so that
Aphrodite was in full view with her calm gaze fixed
upon the ripe pears espaliered on the wall. The double
fountain poured, stone doves pecked at the ground,
and nothing in that circle of sunlit peace was changed.
Miriam felt a profound and unexpected sadness, which
must be nothing compared with Eugene's, whose true
home and pride this was. Then Maxim, on the box,
having received the order from Eugene, started the
horses and the carriages rolled away. At the rear came
Rosa's.

At Pelagie's house on the corner the windows were
closed and the blinds drawn; with Eulalie and her children she had left some weeks earlier for the Labouisse
place in the country.

Ferdinand was murmuring something to Emma

about the first time he had laid eyes on the city and
then something about the first time he had laid eyes on
her. Fearing to intrude on his privacy, Miriam turned
away and put her arm around Angelique's shoulder.
The girl looked up, giving her mother a smile of such
sweetness and encouragement that Miriam felt a
quick, piercing pride in the bravery of this child.

They passed the corner of the street where Eugene
had met his tragedy, the street where Queen lived.
Able to gauge the distance, having traveled it so often,
he must have sensed where they were, for his fingers
drummed on the side of the carriage and he lowered
his head. What memories—regrets or joyous recollec-
tions—were in that head at this moment only he could
know.

One after one they passed the homes of people who
had been part of their lives. They crossed Canal Street,
where, over the tops of the young trees that ran down
the middle of the street, Miriam could see the windows of the Custom House from which "Beast" Butler
ruled the city. They rode through the garden district,
past the street where André had built his fine house.
She closed her eyes to shut out the recollection, but it
would not go away.

At the city limits they showed their passes and
emerged into a countryside where any soldiers one
might now meet would be wearing gray. In a long line
the carriages jolted over the furrowed road under the
mild autumn sky. No one spoke very much except
once when Eugene said, "You wanted to sell the place.
What would we have done without it now?"

She might have answered, "We could have taken the
oath," but of course did not, and nothing more was
said.

Even the children were still; Angelique slept, her
head sharing her mother's lap with the dog. Young

Eugene wore a thoughtful frown; perhaps it was the finality of this departure that made him seem suddenly so much older than the boy who had, not so long ago, gone about the city cheering and waving a flag. Now he had nothing to say, only stared straight ahead at the road.

And there were no sounds except the stirring of wind in high old water-oaks, and the plodding of tired hooves.

Late on the following evening they came at last to Beau Jardin.

Although their arrival had not been expected, it was pleasing to see that things were in order. Neat rows of green peas, asparagus, and strawberries ran the length of the kitchen garden. Beyond the near fence a dozen young lambs were at pasture among the cows. Hens kept up a peaceable, homely clucking all the day. So there would be milk, eggs, fresh vegetables, all the good comforts, in spite of Butler's despoilment. The war seemed very far away.

In the soft evening Miriam stood quite still, absorbing the feel of the time and the place. I never liked it here, she thought, never liked the idleness, the loneliness, and the useless grandeur. Beau Jardin! Ironic name! One is meant to be at ease in a beautiful garden. God knows, I never was. Yes, in this soft evening the war can seem very far away, but of course, it is not. We shall see more hard, terrible things before we're finished.

23

Eugene and Ferdinand were back at their maps, arguing and speculating, while Ferdinand guided Eugene's fingers from New York to Texas.

"This is the time to invade the North, I tell you. Lincoln's majority is decreasing; there have been draft riots in New York."

"The British minister in Washington wrote back to London that there is strong sentiment in the North to let the South go its own way and quit the fight."

"We've captured Galveston and got all Texas in our hands."

"Vicksburg is still holding, and as long as it does, we cannot fail."

That's what André said, as long as Vicksburg holds. But he is in Paris, for all I know.

At the far end of the library, through the tall windows, one could just catch a glimpse of the road on which droves of Texas cattle raised swells of golden dust on their way to the Confederate Army. Week after week they plodded through. All life, animal and human, was being fed into the armies.

They had taken the last horses for the army except for the three that had been hidden in the swamps. Angelique cried when they took her Angel, the pony

with the delicate white ears. She had just finished cur-
rying Angel in the stable when they came.

"Sorry, little miss," the sergeant had said. "I know
how you feel. But the army is short of horses."

Now there were more troubling thoughts.

"Blaise came back from New Orleans just now,"
Miriam said, drawing the two men's attention away
from strategy. "They are saying the Federals will be
coming this way soon."

"They can't break through," Ferdinand began.
"Our troops—"

Eugene swept him aside. "Blaise! I don't trust him.
He says it to taunt us, to scare the life out of us. I
don't trust him, don't trust any of the servants."

It was true, there were many one did not trust anymore. Some stole. One knew they did and was afraid
to make accusations. They neglected the animals, and
the fences. Yet they could have run away. Blaise could
have stayed in New Orleans instead of coming back.
Perhaps he remembers, Miriam thought, when I saved
him from being sold away.

"In case it is true, just in case it is," Eugene said,
"you should start hiding the valuables. Do it at night
when they are all asleep."

"My family's silver," Emma murmured. It was all
she had left out of Ferdinand's debacle.

"The quarry would be a good place," Ferdinand
suggested.

And Rosa advised, "We should tie the silver to our
hoops, so they won't see it. You can never tell who's
awake and watching."

To Miriam this was melodrama, faintly ridiculous.
And with a small perversity which she could not have
explained, she disobeyed Eugene in one respect alone:
The diamonds that had been his mother's she gave to
Fanny for safekeeping. Was it to be a test of Fanny's

integrity or of her own perception of human nature? So be it! If the diamonds were lost, they would only be one more loss on top of all the rest.

All week it was quiet. Only the Texas cattle kept passing on the road. Then, abruptly one morning, the dust clouds rose from the opposite direction. All rushed down the lane to the gate.

A string of riders, carriages, and wagons extended to the curve of the road some half a mile away. They were moving at great speed. A gentleman called down from his sweating hunter without halting.

"There's been a skirmish about ten miles back. We were way outnumbered! The Federals are pouring in, it's hell!" And he spurred the horse.

"They're burning everything!" A woman, surrounded by little children, spoke as she leaned out of her carriage without stopping. "Hide your clothes. They take your clothes and everything you own. Everything!" she screamed.

"Stop!" Eugene cried. "Stay. Eat and rest. Where are you going?"

But the woman was already out of hearing.

And all morning on the rough road this traffic, nervous and fast as rapids tumbling on a streambed, moved past the gate. Galloping, trotting, panting, lathered, terrified, pop-eyed, weeping, shouting, pushing, fighting, bewildered, hysterical and grim, it moved on past.

Toward noon came the stragglers on foot, the poor with their bundles and fragile carts loaded with furniture and quilts. With their old men and their pregnant women, limping and stumbling they came; their dogs, whose tongues hung limp on their chests from heat and thirst, came, too. A cow, whose clumsy belly swayed over frail legs, swung its enormous bag, on which, long past milking time, the bulging veins seemed ready to burst; falling, the animal was prodded with a stick; it bawled its anguish with the blare of a cracked trumpet.

"They've burned the Haviland house!" a woman cried from the road.

"Oh," Emma said, "I hope they've saved that marvelous portrait of her mother!"

"They've saved nothing."

Sickened and unable to help, Miriam went back to the house.

When the last of the fleeing horde had gone, a silence, in its way more threatening, came down upon them all. Even a momentary rush of wind was too loud in that waiting silence.

"Why are we staying here?" Emma wailed. "Everyone else has gone."

"Gone where?" asked Miriam. "We are certainly better off waiting our chances here, whatever they may be, than taking to roads that go nowhere."

Eugene felt for a pair of pistols in the cupboard. "Oil the guns," he directed Ferdinand. "You take one and give one to me."

What did he think he could do with a pistol and no eyes? But Miriam said nothing. Instead, she commanded Angelique.

"Go upstairs to one of the attic bedrooms. Close the door and lie on the bed. You're sick, you have a highly contagious fever." And, as the girl looked uncomprehending, "Hurry! Do as I say!"

Supple and fresh. Her wet, bow-shaped lips, curled lashes, clouds of warm hair, newly washed. Her breasts, rising with each quick breath, stretching the waist cloth . . .

First came a low murmur, like the sound of waves at night. Rosa, crouching in a window seat, leaned out.

"Do I hear something?"

"Shh! Listen!" The murmur became a roar. "Yes, unmistakably. They're coming."

"Papa, go upstairs with the pistols," Miriam said. "Please—you and Eugene. Guard the stairs to the attic."

Heaven forbid that they should flourish those pistols or, worse yet, discharge one! That much she knew. It was common sense, that was all. And those two men weren't showing much of it right now.

"I'm not going to leave you women down here alone," Ferdinand shouted.

"Will you listen? It's more important to protect Angelique! And, son, you go upstairs, too. I'll just wait here in front of the house."

She had walked as far as the verandah, when the first hooves clattered on the lane and the first shouts sounded.

"Halt!" A mounted troop, mingled in careless disarray with a ragtag following of men on foot, had come tearing up the lane. A rough lot, she saw at once, accustomed as she now was to the ways of armies; these were amok and inflamed, without an officer in sight who could possibly, if he were so inclined, control them.

Sisyphus came out of the house to stand with Miriam. His teeth chattered in his jaw, but his stance was brave.

The lead man, a sergeant, dismounted and stood a step below Miriam, looking up out of small, hard eyes, with his hands on his heavy hips.

His manner was scornful, with an affectation of languor. "Well, now. Who lives in this place?"

"The name is Mendes." To Miriam's satisfaction her voice did not shake.

"Mendes. You live here alone? You and that nigger there?"

"I live here with my husband."

"Then where's your husband? Off with Lee getting trounced?"

And still her voice stayed level. "My husband is in the house. He is blind."

"Well, that's too bad. You'll have to show us around, then. We want food and drink, plenty of it."

"You can have what there is, which isn't much. There are more than a hundred of you."

"No, more like two hundred, missis."

And indeed they were still coming up the drive in a rush of dark-blue jackets, boots, breeches, and forage caps. Their sabers shot off sparks of painful light.

The sergeant drew his saber, pushing at Miriam and Sisyphus with the flat of it.

"Stand aside. Let the men in. We'll help ourselves. Go ahead, men," he bellowed.

In an instant the men were off their horses, up the steps, and through the door. In the next instant the sound of crashing and tinkling glass told that the liquor cabinet had been smashed.

"Make camp out there," the sergeant directed.

"Oh, not there! That's the cornfield!" Miriam protested. "You'll trample it down!"

"You don't say! Listen, missis, never mind the corn. Just tell us where the silver is, and don't lie about it, either."

"The silver was sent away long ago to relatives in Texas."

"You think I'll believe that?"

"Whether you believe it or not is up to you."

"Listen, missis. I won't stand for any nonsense from you, and you better—" He laid his hand on Miriam's shoulder.

"Leave this lady alone!" cried Sisyphus. "Don't you touch her!" He thrust the large red hand away from her shoulder.

In the middle of the flat red face the mouth opened with astonished amusement.

"What! You poor old fool, sticking up for folks that have taken the blood out of your old sack of a body! Why," he said, turning to Miriam, "he can hardly stand up, the bag of bones, and he wants to protect you! What's more, you're damn glad to be protected by a nigger! Bah—" He spat.

The thick gob of spit lay on the step, and Miriam moved her foot.

"Go look for the silver, boys. Turn out the mattresses, dig up the yard, you know where to find it, you've found it before."

Two men brought Ferdinand downstairs, jerking him by the collar.

"This your husband?"

"No, my father. I told you, my husband is blind." Thank God, neither of them had tried to use the pistols.

"Where's the silver, old man?"

Ferdinand hesitated. "He doesn't know," Miriam said. "He wasn't here when we sent it to Texas."

To the left, at the foot of the slope, a stinging smoke streamed over the concealing border of young birches; a single flame shot up, sputtered, fell, and returned with a vigorous burst of orange and gold.

"The gin house," Ferdinand said forlornly. "The gin house. It's the cotton burning."

The spiraling flames were almost hypnotic. Helpless and dazed, the three stood on the verandah encircled by a crazy swirl of motion: mounting flames, men running, excited tethered horses stamping. The noise of destruction was maddening. With sabers and spades the men dug up the garden. With saws they hacked the century-old oaks. Miriam winced as though her own flesh were cut when the first heavy limb of Eugene's famous beech, laden with coppery foliage gleaming in the sunlight, came crashing down.

But when they began to chop away at the fences, she could not contain herself, crying over the din while Ferdinand tried to stop her, "Don't! Don't! The cattle will get into the crop! Don't, don't!"

"There won't be any cattle when we're through," said the sergeant. He had not moved from the steps, where he stood in command of all this activity. "So don't worry about it."

From the barnyard came the popping sound of gunfire. A huge dead sow, along with her dead young, was being dragged across the lawn to the nearest fire built out of the dismantled fences. At the far end of the lawn some soldiers chased a little flock of terrified, bleating sheep.

"You kill all the animals," said Sisyphus to the sergeant, "you only make us colored folks go hungry. You here fighting this here war for us, you say—"

"Shut your mouth, old fool. Go inside. We didn't come here to fight for you. Most of us hate niggers." And suddenly remembering his earlier demand, the sergeant bellowed again, "Where's the silver?"

"My daughter told you," Ferdinand began.

"Suppose we hang your father if you don't tell us? Hey?"

He's drunk, Miriam thought, but possibly he means it. So if it comes to that, lead them to the quarry and be done with it.

They were diverted then by a tremendous bumping and thumping behind them. Two men were dragging furniture through the front door, after which they shoved it off the verandah, where Eugene's Hepple-

white secretary, one of his particular treasures, fell
with a crash, split open on the grass. A moment later
it was attacked with an axe by a man wearing a red
silk hat, Rosa's best winter hat. He was bent over with
laughter.

It was like a hurricane in its senseless brutality and
waste, but far more terrible. The hurricane at least
didn't know what it was doing.

Miriam was surprised that she had spoken this
thought aloud, for Ferdinand replied to it.

"Like the Hep Hep looting. Different causes, but
the same savagery." He clenched his fists. "Here I
stand, old, weak and worthless, can't do a thing to
help you." His voice broke.

New sounds came now from within the house,
sounds of heavy pounding feet. Then came shrieks, the
thin, abandoned shrieks of women. Emma and Rosa:
What would those drunken savages do to them? Or to
me? Yes, I'll die, I'll die like my mother, violently—

But my daughter, my girl. If they find her—If Eugene pulls the trigger and one of those men dies, then
—Well, then it's all over with her, with all of us, with
everything. But he must know that. Eugene must
know that!

New sounds drowned the female shrieks. Furious
male voices came from just over Miriam's head.
Above, on the piazza, Eugene stood in violent alterca-
tion with three soldiers. He was waving the gun,
which they were trying to wrest from him. For a moment the struggle held; all of a sudden Eugene had
become again the powerful man he once had been, a
man who got what he wanted; no longer, at this moment, was he the wounded being who had seemed to
shrink from the world he could not see.

"We'll burn the God-damned house, we're not half
through yet!"

"God damned if you will!" cried Eugene.

And backing up to level the gun, he fell against the railing.

"Eugene!" Miriam heard herself scream. And, "Look out! Look out, Eugene!" she warned, she implored, but too late, too late. . . .

He fell. Backward he toppled over the railing, the defiance on his lips turning into a howl of horror. His body hurtled, his hands grasped at nothing—

And he lay twisted on the gravel at the verandah steps, at Miriam's feet.

"Dear Lord," said Sisyphus very softly.

For a moment there was a silence of disbelief. Then the silence broke into shock. Rosa and Emma emerged from the house, still crying. Young Eugene raced to bend over his father. Angelique knelt at his other side. Her hair, loosened in her terrified flight down the stairs, streamed over her face. Servants who, half curious and half afraid, had been peering out of hiding places in the quarters, now came running to view the disaster. The ragtag, roving mob of soldiery came, too. There, in a ring ten or twelve deep, they all stood, family, servants and enemies, looking down upon the still-conscious Eugene in his atrocious agony.

There was a babble of comment and opinion.

"Lift him! Carry him inside."

"Water!"

"Brandy!"

Sisyphus took hold of Eugene's feet, while Chanute and Maxim, grasping his shoulders, attempted a lift, but the very first tugging motion brought from him such a fearful cry of anguish that they at once withdrew their hands.

"Leave him alone!"

"Get a blanket!"

And amid the babble of directions and questions,

the breathless cries of Emma and Rosa and the sobs of her children, Miriam was as if paralyzed: Think, think, what's to be done? What?

A single horse bearing a Union lieutenant came trotting rapidly up the lane. Someone on the fringe of the frenzy must have told him what was happening, for he swung himself off the horse, came at once to Miriam, and removed his cap.

"Oh, ma'am, I'm sorry! Sorry." He looked around at the lawn, which was littered with broken furniture and bottles, with clothing, books and bric-a-brac. He looked at Eugene and shook his head. "How terrible . . . I don't know . . . don't understand this sort of thing." His voice trailed away.

This unexpected sympathy was as painful in its way as the savagery, and Miriam's lips quivered.

"We tried to move him. Perhaps, if you have a doctor . . ."

"None with us. Short of doctors. Armies always are," the young man apologized. "But I've had a lot of experience, seen enough, perhaps I . . ." And he went to bend over Eugene, examining with eyes alone.

He looked up at the balcony from which Eugene had fallen, and shook his head again doubtfully.

"I don't know," he told Miriam. "Can't say with any certainty, I'm not qualified, but . . ." His voice faltered into a minor key, with his eyes not on Miriam, but on the boy and girl who had taken their father's hands and were still kneeling on the gravel path.

"I think his back's broken." And he murmured in pity as if to himself. "Blind, too." Then he looked at Miriam again. "The truth is, I don't know what to tell you, ma'am."

She thought, I suppose it doesn't matter. He will die. Quickly, I hope.

"Does that mean he will suffer very long?" she asked. "Can you tell me that?"

"I shouldn't think so. And you're left with all this," the lieutenant said, gesturing toward the devastation.

"They were going to burn the house."

The lieutenant said quickly, "I won't have that. I'll have them out of here in half an hour or less. Sergeant!" he called.

The red face appeared at once. The red hand saluted.

"Put out the fires and prepare to leave. These people have suffered enough."

"Yes sir," the sergeant said.

It had been two hours since the last of the marauders had gone, and the dust of their bustling departure had settled. Eugene still lay where he had fallen. From somewhere Fanny had found a pillow that had not been ripped apart, and this had been placed beneath his head. His pain had ebbed into paralysis. Rigid, motionless, as if he were lying on top of the sea, he was floating away.

"I'm dying." The whisper was hardly audible even in the heavy stillness that had descended along with the fading day. "You know I'm dying."

Huddled in their skirts, the mother and daughter knelt and waited. Young Eugene's head hung to his chest. After all these hours his strength was used up; yet still he clung to his father's hand.

Suddenly the father made a faint movement to release the hand.

"I want . . ." His lips moved and stopped. Miriam leaned closer. "I want to talk to your mother."

"I'm here, Eugene. You want the children to step away, is that it? You want to tell me something?"

Miriam nodded toward the verandah, where in the

early fall of night a line of servants still stood, leaned, and sat, grouping themselves around Emma, Ferdinand, and Rosa.

"You wanted to tell me something, Eugene?"

"The boy," he murmured. "Take care."

Her mind went back to the parlor, when after school the boy used to report to his father. She could see him, so graceful, bright, and charming, as he stood before the proud eyes of the father before those eyes had been destroyed.

"What did you do today?"

The answers had come with equal pride. "Oh, Latin, geometry, penmanship, and grammar."

"Did you get a good mark on the map you did last week?"

"Yes, Papa, a good mark. I'll show you."

Take care of my son, he means. See that he is educated as I would have seen.

She swallowed hard against her tears. "Eugene, I promise you, I will do everything you would want."

No pretense now, no refusal to acknowledge that he was about to die. That much at least they had always had in common, a scorn of pretense between themselves; as long, she thought now ruefully, as long as the public image was kept unblemished.

"Yes, I'll see them through this war somehow. You can depend on it."

Suddenly Eugene raised his voice. "And Angelique . . . They tell me she is very lovely. Well, that's something to leave behind, isn't it?"

"I'll take care of her, Eugene, depend on that, too."

A small, quivering smile passed across his face.

And she cried softly, "I'm so sorry about everything! That we could not have been happy together . . . If I've hurt you, I never meant to. It was never what I wanted, as I'm sure you never wanted to do it to me."

"No tears," he said, but not as once he had used to sneer: *What, more tears, the woman's weapon?*

"No tears," he repeated, and again the light smile quivered and faded.

And into that queer little movement, that flicker, maybe, of some recollected pleasure, Miriam read the story of his years with that flashing woman whose dark passion had once made him happy. Perhaps, forgetting her abandonment of him, he was wishing she were here with him now. She ought to be with him! She had taken whatever good he had had to give her, and should be with him now!

Toward midnight Eugene died. In a profound stillness, in the starlight, old Sisyphus, Chanute, and Maxim carried him into the house and laid him on the ruined sofa in the parlor.

Many years before, the previous owners of Beau Jardin had turned an old Indian mound, used centuries before that for burying, into their own family burying ground. Here, then, in the morning, while birds were noisy in the sheltering live oaks, they buried Eugene in a homemade coffin which had been made that night.

A sorry funeral, Miriam thought. At least Eugene would have thought so! He would have wanted everything to be done correctly: the burial in the synagogue's own cemetery, with the men wearing striped trousers and top hats and the rabbi leading the Kaddish. But there was certainly no going back to the city now, and only young Eugene to say the Kaddish. He said it well, in the heartbreaking, boyish, husky voice which skips back into the soprano. Ferdinand, who barely remembered the words, joined with him. And, after that, Maxim and Chanute poured earth upon the coffin.

I'm glad Eugene and I had those last words together, she thought, with her arms around her children. At least he lies in his own ground that he loved so well. And maybe, she thought irrelevantly as they walked back to the house, maybe his beech tree will survive its injuries. He would like that.

Two dozen sheep lay dead in the pasture after the previous day's slaughter. The storerooms were wrecked; the food that had not been taken had been defiled with molasses; the entire crop of potatoes and beans was ruined. The smokehouse had been stripped of the meat supply for the coming winter. Nothing was left.

She walked about, looking things over. And wreckage stared back. There were no mules left, except for two babies. The wagons had been burnt. The cattle that they had not butchered, they had driven away to be sold at auction, no doubt, in New Orleans.

The overseer came out of his house. He was dressed for travel and carried a pair of bags.

"I was coming to give you notice," he said with some embarrassment.

"Notice, Mr. Ransome? Sixty seconds' notice?"

"I know. I'm sorry. But in the circumstances . . . There's nothing left here. The die is cast. I'm going back to Connecticut."

She wanted to say something about abandoning a sinking ship, or some other rebuke, trite but true. Then, thinking that it would, after all, make no difference, she swallowed her indignation.

"Good luck to you, then, Mr. Ransome."

He hesitated. "I don't know what you're going to do. You know at least twenty-five of the hands left this morning? Went off into the swamps to hide or else follow the army, I'm not sure which."

"Then I shall have to manage with the ones who are left," she said coolly.

The veneer of courage was not very deep. I really need someone; how am I ever going to bring any order out of this? All the familiar sounds were stilled: the quarreling and singing in the fields and the busy rumbling of wheels; the cheerful bleats and clucks from the barns. The silence was hopeless.

All these people to care for! Ferdinand was suddenly old. Emma was crushed by the melancholy debris of the house; she had survived cruel tragedy, yet dirt and disorder defeated her spirits. In the midst of general madness the two children had to be nurtured and somehow educated into some pattern of normality. Rosa, in these last hours, had disintegrated. All day she had been moaning: "Oh, if Henry were here, if Henry . . . We had such a good life together. . . . He loved the opera . . . Oh, we heard Jenny Lind . . . and we saw George Harby's *Nick of the Woods* at its premiere. . . . Such a beautiful life . . . he would never believe that I've come to this." She was quite out of her senses.

Fanny came down the lane to meet Miriam.

"Simeon's at the back door. He wants to talk to you."

Wearily, Miriam responded, "What about?"

"About a crop. And he wants to tell you, he saved four mules. Hid them in the swamp."

Well, that was a blessing. And Simeon was going to stay.

Fanny was handing her a velvet string bag. She couldn't think what it was, she was so tired.

"What's this, Fanny?"

"Your diamonds. Did you forget?"

"As a matter of fact, I did. Thank you, Fanny."

For a moment, as so often in the past, they stood looking at each other, and as so often, too, Miriam wondered what the other was really thinking.

Fanny said softly, "I'm sorry about Mr. Eugene. Miss Angelique's taking it very hard."

"I know." Then Miriam said, "I am, too," and thought, We made each other so miserable, and still I would bring him back this minute if I could.

Fanny turned brisk. "I'm going to stuff the mattresses with Spanish moss. Those men ruined them with their machetes, or whatever you call those wicked things."

"Sabers."

"Well. Shall I send Simeon?"

"Yes, send him around to the verandah."

Goodness, he must be seven feet tall! She didn't even remember having seen him before, but then, there had been so many of them, working acres away from the house.

But suddenly a name came to her.

"Jasper." Eugene had mentioned a Jasper. "Is he still here on the place? My husband always admired him, so I thought—"

"Yes, missis, he still here, but he much too old to run things. We all, there's about twenty of us left, we all decided I'm the one. Yes, ma'am, I'm the one. I got youth and strength, and I knows how to run things."

Miriam regarded him carefully and made a decision.

"All right, then, you'll take charge, Simeon. You'll plan with me, the way Mr. Ransome used to plan with my husband. You'll teach me. The main thing is, we all have to eat. What's to be done about that?"

"Well, missis, we got some vegetables coming up. They didn't see the back garden behind the barn. And

I saved a few chickens in the swamps, some hens that belong to me. If we don't eat them now, we can have eggs and pullets next summer. There are two cows left, one's ready to calve."

Around the corner came Chanute and Maxim with their brass buttons glistening. Miriam called to them.

"Come here. You know Simeon."

They raised astonished, lofty eyebrows.

"But of course you know him! You've seen him around, don't tell me you haven't. Oh, I understand that you've never done field or barn work in your lives, but everything's different now. No more fancy uniforms. If you want to eat, you'll have to work, you'll have to help out, you and Blaise. We all will have to help out. You understand?"

"Oh, yes, Miss Miriam," they said in unison.

To Miriam's surprise Chanute was grinning. And then Miriam did a reckless thing.

"Tell me, why haven't you all run off the way the others did?"

The disparate three looked at each other, suddenly united in the singleness of their intent. The wide, white grins spread humorously. Chanute spoke first.

"Because. The Secesh will be back," he said.

So it was as simple as that. They'd thought it all out. Well, no matter. Just take one day at a time, that's all we can do.

One day at a time.

24

Now began a series of unexpected visitations.

A milk-blue sky was turning white, the sickly white of a fish's underbelly, and Miriam was calculating how long it would be before the storm broke, when she saw a carriage turn into the lane. Four fine horses pulled it; a coachman rode high—and alone in the back seat sat a woman in a yellow dress so glossy that even at that distance it could be recognized as satin.

The carriage rolled nearer, the black wheels, bright as jet, coming to a smart stop at the foot of the verandah. The coachman jumped down and helped the woman to alight.

The woman was Queen.

In her manner, this time, there was neither deference nor avoidance. Her eyes, no longer lowering and flickering away as they once had, swept frankly over Miriam's country bonnet and cotton dress, faded from many washings.

"You remember me," she said. It was not a question, but a declaration.

"I do."

"I came as soon as I heard what happened. . . . He was a good man." The curve of the chin, lifted above three strands of marvelous pearls, was vaguely defiant.

It was hardly worth coming all this way to tell me that, Miriam thought, feeling a hot rise of anger. And do you think I am going to argue with you about it? But she merely nodded to indicate that she had heard.

"I brought you some things. I thought—I knew you would be needing things."

The trampled corn, the broken railing of the piazza from which Eugene had fallen, and the fences on which repairs had barely begun, stood in mute evidence of that need.

"His—your—children will be needing things, I thought."

To be the recipient of this woman's largesse! I should like to tell her to take her charity elsewhere, Miriam told herself. But Angelique's bright dresses had caught the fancy of the marauders, who had stripped her room of everything she owned.

"The boxes are in the carriage. Shall I have my man take them into the house?"

The floor and half of the back seat were covered with parcels, nicely tied. So long since the last time one had known that voluptuous anticipation in the presence of a well-wrapped gift! Greed widened Miriam's eyes. She felt them stretching open.

"He may put them in the front hall," she said. "It's most kind of you. . . ."

The woman watched her servant and Miriam watched the woman. Her eardrops were diamonds. Gold bracelets, heavy and sinuous, twined around her wrists, and her fingers were covered with rings. The Queen of Sheba must have glittered so.

This obvious increase in wealth, this new manner of assurance and reversal of their relative positions, cut Miriam sharply, while at the same time she understood quite clearly that the cutting edges were her own resentment, injured pride, and envy.

When the last of the packages had been stacked in the hall, Queen started back to the carriage. An impulse toward ordinary decency shot through Miriam's foggy distraction. The humid air was stifling, and the woman had made a long journey for the benefit of Eugene's children.

"Come in and rest for a moment. I have nothing to offer you except rest in a cool place."

Fortunately, she thought wryly, this was the time of the afternoon nap, so there would be no one about—especially not Emma—to be amazed at the sight of the lady of the house entertaining a free woman of color in the parlor.

Queen's quick eyes were taking in the damage, the empty spaces where obviously furniture had stood, the shattered mirror, and the portrait with the ruinous diagonal rip.

"I don't understand why they had to do all this," she said. "They have left you nothing."

"Yes, between them and Beast Butler, we have almost nothing," Miriam said angrily.

"Yet he did do some good."

"Butler did good?" Miriam was scornful.

"Oh, yes, he brought in food when the city was starving, and fixed prices. And he set men to cleaning the dirty streets. You know we've had no yellow fever this past summer."

"That's little enough to have given back to the city when he has got so rich from the city."

Queen smiled. "Yes, many have got rich by it. His brother has made a fortune. I know people quite close to him, and I know it's true."

I am quite sure you do, Miriam said to herself.

In the distant west thunder muttered briefly, signaling, to her relief, its own passing away, for she could scarcely have allowed the woman to start home in the thick of a storm. Then a silence filled the room. It ticked in the ears and grew more disconcerting with each moment, until at last Queen began to speak.

"I wanted to tell him that I was sorry I—left him when the city was taken." Into the depths of her round, hooded eyes, so newly, confidently, bold, there now came a sorrowing remorse. "It's too late. . . . People do things they're not proud of afterward. But circumstances . . ." The soft, rushing voice, suggestive of love-words and laughter, stopped and the hands were flung out, palms upward, as if to say: Surely you will understand how it was.

Luxury, gaiety, and going over to the winners, that's how it was. Still there was a certain dignity in the plain confession.

"I'm sorry he didn't live to hear you tell him that," Miriam said, remembering that flicker of a smile as Eugene lay dying on the ground.

"There's something else. . . . It's about my son. He's a sculptor, did you know? He has won a prize in Rome. I would have liked to tell him about that, too. He would have been proud."

No. He would not have cared that much. And she remembered the lion on Eugene's chest of drawers. Yes, he would be—he had been—touched with understandable compassion, but his heart and his pride had been the son who carried his name in the city. My son, she thought; that's the reason he married me.

But that was a thing one did not speak, and so the pair of them fell back into silence. There was, after all, no reason why they should have any more to say to one another. And yet, in a curious way they were bound to an unwanted, unspoken intimacy by their linkage to the dead Eugene.

What if I had loved him, too? Miriam asked herself, finding no answer.

We are all tied in a chain whose overlapping links are meshed into a tangled convoluted net without an end or a beginning: she to me and I to Eugene; I to André and he to Marie Claire and she—

The satin skirt whispered on the floor as Queen stood up to leave. With a sudden gesture of pity and shame—who am I, what am I, to judge?—Miriam put out her hand, only to feel in return a quick pressure and to see a small spill of tears, as quickly wiped away.

When the carriage was out of sight, she went back into the house and called Fanny to unpack the boxes.

The next unusual visitor, some weeks later, was a fashionable gentleman with fashionable whiskers and a faintly British accent.

"My name is Isachar Zacharie, Dr. Isachar Zacharie."

He carried a basket of oranges and, as they immediately learned, a letter from David. His manner had a courtly formality combined with friendliness.

"Then, you know my son professionally?" inquired Ferdinand.

"No, I only met him once, in New York. He, naturally, is in the Medical Corps, while I am a chiropodist. Also, if I may say so, a friend of President Lincoln's."

Emma's lips pressed shut in distaste, and Rosa's corsets creaked as she straightened her back in total rejection of this information.

"As a matter of fact, I am in New Orleans on a mission from the President."

Suspicious glances flitted about the circle of faces. Was this some sort of charlatan, a fraud?

"Your son, when he asked me to deliver this letter, thought that perhaps you were still in New Orleans, but I inquired and learned you were not."

"Beast Butler forced us to leave," Ferdinand said coldly.

Dr. Zacharie smiled. "I understand your feelings."

"Tell what you can about my brother, please," Miriam asked with polite impatience.

"Oh, he has been in the thick of battles, he told me, but he seems to have survived pretty well. We really hadn't much time to talk. Both of us happened to be in the city for a couple of events, when the facilities of the Jews' Hospital were offered to the government for wounded soldiers. And then again at the Sanitary Fair, a day later. Raised over a million dollars for war relief. When he heard that I was bound for New Orleans—well," Zacharie said delicately, "I have brought some things. I happened to mention to Rabbi Illowy in New Orleans that I was coming here, and he suggested that possibly—the devastation . . . There are a few things in the carriage."

Directing Sisyphus to carry in an armful of blankets and quilts, Miriam thought, Gifts come from strange sources these days—first from Queen, and now from this peculiar man. But God knows they are welcome.

When she came back into the parlor, the man was saying, "Yes, my family is in Savannah, and it's a terrible hardship to be away from them. But if there is anything I can do to bring peace about, I will go to any lengths to do it."

Emma grasped the arms of her chair. Her pink flesh drooped; she had lost many pounds and her eyes were heavy with anxiety. Pelagie's third son had now gone away to fight. As yet there had been no casualties in her flock, but each day increased the likelihood of one.

"Just how will you do that?" she asked skeptically.

Dr. Zacharie waved a hand, dismissing the question.

"With all respect, madam, these are official matters, highly confidential, of which I can't speak. Oh, I can tell you that I have something to do with readjusting exchange rates between the Union currency and the local, but that's a small matter, and common knowledge anyway." He lowered his voice. "Unofficially, though, I can tell you that I've made myself very helpful to many Jews—I am one myself, you see—both northern Jews caught in New Orleans and southern Jews who have left the city for the Confederacy. In dire straits, they are, because they refuse to take the oath."

"My God, how long will this go on!" cried Miriam.

"Too long. But the longer it lasts, the more certain the Union is to win. Well, you asked me," Zacharie apologized.

"Yes, go on, please."

"We all know the Confederacy hopes to gain the support of France and England, but their missions, supposed to be secret, have all failed."

André . . . Then, where is he now?

"For one thing, England found new sources of cotton in Egypt and India, and for another, the laboring classes, both of France and England, are so against the institution of slavery that their governments wouldn't dare at this point to do otherwise. It has become a moral issue, especially in England."

"A moral issue!" Rosa exclaimed. Her shattered nerves, now gradually piecing themselves together, had given her voice a grating tone. "Yes, for the Confederacy it is indeed a moral issue to protect ourselves against a foreign invader! You have attacked our homes. . . . You have only to look! My brother, sir, a lawyer, a student of affairs, a just-minded man as all who know him will attest to, even he always said it is not a question of morality in the North; it is money! Consider the wealth they get from our cotton, far more than we get, who raise it! Their banks thrive on the slavery they prate about!" she finished passionately.

Miriam was embarrassed. "Dr. Zacharie has come on an errand of kindness. Let's leave these subjects."

"I've come and I must go," the doctor said with unruffled good nature. "I have a thousand errands back in the city."

"What did you think of him?" asked Ferdinand when he had seen Zacharie out of the house.

Miriam considered. "He is either a clever imposter, or a high-minded benefactor. Take your choice."

Emma said disconsolately, "He seems sure we are beaten."

"Never believe it," Ferdinand argued. "Our forces will be back. You will see the men in gray ride up this lane again before very long. Mark my words."

A spurt of rain struck the windowpane, followed by a flight of wind that rattled them in their frames. The autumn storms had come. Rain and mud will hold up the fighting, Miriam thought with gratitude.

But Ferdinand had just said that the men in gray would be back. And that meant more fighting, more deaths of young men.

Also quite possibly, could it mean that André might be back, too? If he were still alive . . . and it seemed to her that to be told she would not see him for ten years, or even never again, would be the hardest thing to bear; but to be told that he was dead would be unbearable.

Dear Sister [David wrote], and Papa, too, if he has forgiven me enough to hear my letter. Since I have not heard from you in so long, I must assume that it is because your letters have not reached me. I only hope this reaches you through the good offices of Dr. Zacharie. I have been mov-

ing about the country and covered more territory
than I would have thought possible in so short a
time.

After the battle at Corinth I was sent northward to the Memphis area, where I have been
tending the wounded again. It is a kind of work
to which I shall never become accustomed. Pray
God I will not have to do it much longer and that
this war will end, because the suffering I see, unlike disease, is not a natural phenomenon but
man-made, to man's everlasting disgrace.

And then there are the wounds to the spirit.
Are they, perhaps, even worse? I'm thinking of
Grant's infamous Order Number Eleven, expel-
ling all Jews from the Department of Tennessee. I
take for granted that you've read about it and
read as well the good news that Lincoln once
more came to the rescue and has had it rescinded.

Maybe you couldn't believe it when you first
learned of it; I know I couldn't. But it was true. I
myself saw an old couple, a traditional, bearded
Jew and his shabby little wife, being bullied and
bustled by soldiers onto a train. The woman was
weeping so—

Miriam put the letter down. Her heart raced. *The
women were weeping.* So went the story, heard a hundred times over, of her mother's death. And she read
on.

In case you don't know what it was all about, I'll
tell you. There's been a scandalous traffic across
battle lines, speculation in cotton, bribing and
taking bribes for permits. Some of the people doing it are Jews, as some are not. But Grant pun-
ished *only* the Jews—and *all* Jews, not just the

guilty ones! And who was, who is, the most guilty, and the richest of all? Jesse Grant, the general's own father!

I still see that poor old couple, hardly able to totter about, much less run around gathering a fortune in cotton! It hurts me to see such brutality on *my* side of the war.

Now here's something that will surprise you. The very next day after I saw all this, one of the majors here offered me a connection with a man down near Vicksburg who has enough cotton on his place to supply a mill for a week. We could slip it out on one of our gunboats, he said; it's done all the time, which I know. And he said the man was a "real southern aristocrat"; the name was Labouisse. I must have looked startled because he asked me whether I'd ever heard the name before. Heard the name! Miriam, it will haunt me for the rest of my life.

The son, dead at my hands, and the grandsons, fighting for what they believe in, while the grandfather, the aristocrat, sells to their enemy!

And do you know, after Grant expelled the Jewish traders, the trade got bigger? Whom could he blame it on then? I'll tell you, as Opa used to say, it's a strange world!

Do you often think about Opa? I didn't used to, but now I find myself remembering that old life so clearly—I suppose because I'm so far from anything at all familiar. I suppose it's only natural, when you're afraid, to remember home. I think about that day when Papa arrived in the coach, and I have to smile at myself: I thought then that he looked like a prince! And how strange our village must have seemed to him after his years in America! I wonder whether at some time in our lives you or I may ever go back to see it again. I don't even know whether I want to. . . .

My thoughts are jumbled as I write here in the half-dark; it's late and in a few hours I shall have to get up, for we expect an ambulance train around dawn. How I long for a wholesome practice again, doing sane, good things like, for instance, bringing healthy twins into the world!

How are my healthy twins? I keep a calendar in my mind to estimate their progress. Eugene ought to be getting a good deal taller than Angelique about now. His voice must have changed. . . . I know you are now mother and father to them. It was a cruel thing for them to lose their father, and in such a frightful way.

But I know, too, that you will manage, and they will grow up well. Tell them how I love them. Tell them not to forget me.

For the present the war continues, and I with it. I am expecting to be transferred to the east, somewhere in Virginia, I think.

May we all survive and be together again.

Your brother,
David

25

All week the wind kept up its eerie howl and whistle, shaking the trees and blowing out the candles whenever a door was left ajar. One afternoon, long past its proper season, the ominous rumble of a midsummer thunderstorm was heard again.

"But that's not thunder!" Ferdinand cried. "It's cannonading. Listen."

Eugene rushed outside.

"Blaise, go get him!" Miriam shrieked. "Where does he think he's going?"

At once Blaise, followed by old, stumbling Sisyphus, went down the lane after Eugene. When they brought him back, it startled Miriam to see that the "little master" of the house, whom she had sent them to protect, was taller than either of them.

The discovery embarrassed her and she vented her irritation in a scolding.

"Do you want to get shot out there, foolish boy? Haven't we had trouble enough?"

"We sure has." Sisyphus sighed. "Trouble enough in this family. You listen to your mother now, hear?"

"I'll just sneak to the road to see what's happening," Ferdinand said. "I know how to be careful. You all stay here."

Rosa and Emma sat clasping the arms of their

chairs as if these objects could shield them, while the
servants, frozen into silence, stood against the walls.
And to Miriam came that old sensation which had
first beset her in this house, an awareness of its total
isolation among its lonely fields. Helpless they were,
not only before marauders from outside, but so helpless before these people who cowered at the wall, who
could turn at whim and will. . . . So they waited.

Presently the familiar dust puffs came floating in a
golden haze above the trees. Hooves pounded and
wheels rumbled, coming nearer. Ferdinand, skirting
the lane behind concealing shrubbery, went down to
the road and, returning a few minutes later, reported
that the Union army was fleeing. Its great hooped canvas supply wagons, each drawn by four horses, were
tearing down the road.

"What did I tell you? They're in full retreat! Tossing
their stuff away into the ditch, they're in such a rush!
Scattering canteens and overcoats, even rifles and
small arms. I'd've picked up some, but then I thought
I'd better not. You know what this means? Our own
men can't be far behind. Oh, I knew they'd be coming
back!"

"Then we'd better hide the mules we saved from the
Federals. Go tell Simeon," Miriam instructed Eugene.

"What?" Rosa said. "Hide the mules from our own
people?"

"Yes, of course," Miriam answered somewhat
shortly.

They came. With the rebel whoop and so much dust
upon them that the black braid curlicued on their
chests was as gray as the cloth and with their bare,
bleeding feet, they came pouring through the gate.

An officer rode at the head of the detachment. At
the foot of the verandah he dismounted and took off
his cap to Ferdinand.

"Such gentlemen!" breathed Emma into Miriam's ear. "God bless them, our southern gentlemen!"

Ferdinand rejoiced. His jubilation bubbled out of his throat.

"Can you give us any news? We've been starved for it all these months. God bless you," he said, echoing Emma, "but I knew, I knew we'd be seeing you soon again!"

"Well, we routed them. Been fighting since yesterday morning about twelve miles east of here. Had no rations, either. The men are starved. Thirsty, too. The worse thing's their bleeding feet. We've no boots," the lieutenant said grimly.

"Tell the men to go around the back of the house and help themselves to whatever they need. The servants will show them. They won't harm anything, I'm sure." And smiling, Ferdinand added, "I trust our men, God knows, our brave men." Miriam's raised eyebrows went unnoticed. For the moment he was the expansive host of long ago. "Miriam, get brandy for the lieutenant. We've only one bottle, but you're welcome to it," he said as they went inside.

Miriam sat Dr. Zacharie's bottle beside the lieutenant's chair. His long blond mustache, which almost hid the lower half of his face, could conceal neither his extreme youth nor his exhaustion.

"Very good of you, sir, this is most welcome." He sighed. "It's been hard. More than half our horses were killed in this last skirmish. And desertions—"

"Desertions!" exclaimed Emma. Her innocent eyes were astonished.

"Oh, yes, ma'am. The death penalty doesn't mean anything anymore, we have so many. So we flog them, we brand them or shave their heads, but still"—the young man suddenly seemed to remember that this was not the way a stalwart officer should be talking—

"but still, we have the good stuff of the South and enough of it to see us through. Yessir, enough to see us through. Of course, if the leadership were better in some places . . ."

"You surely don't mean Lee?" asked Ferdinand.

"Not Lee. But take our secretary of state. Why, Davis stays so loyal to a descendant of the people who crucified the Lord has never made sense to me, sir. Nor to many others."

Rosa had gone upstairs, for which Miriam was thankful, since Rosa would not have held her tongue. Ferdinand was too nonplussed to answer, and Miriam was too shocked, although when the moment had passed and it was too late, she was immediately ashamed of herself for not having spoken.

The lieutenant replaced the glass. "Thank you, ma'am," he said gracefully. "That was a lift to my spirits. I needed it. I'll be on my way. You people can rest more easily tonight, now that you're back on the right side of the lines again."

He saluted, swung onto his horse, and swept back down the lane. It seemed to Miriam as she watched him clatter away that there was something archaic about his gallantry, something out of an old book and another age, a manner that had endured past its time and would soon cease to exist.

She was still standing there not many minutes later when a new gray flood came pouring. This time there was no officer in command. Except for the color of the cloth, they were not any different from the men who had come once before to maraud. They were the same ragtag lot with their loose mouths whooping and grinning; the whiskey they had been given or had stolen had revived their spirits.

All that afternoon they kept coming, invading the house and the barns. Whatever had been taken out of hiding since the Federals had looted was now seized by the men in gray. Only once, when one of them began to hack at a fence rail that had just this week been replaced by Simeon and his helpers, did Miriam run out to protest. The man went about his work.

"You can get your niggers to mend it again," he taunted, "or go without, for all I care. You think we're fighting this war for you, do you?"

No, you are not, she answered silently, I know your sort. You're fighting in the hope that you'll take my place, the place of what you call the "quality."

By evening they had had their fill. A line of pack mules, chained one behind the other with a pair of baskets slung across their backs, bore away the last of the harvest which had been so laboriously coaxed out of the soil by every pair of hands on the place, including Miriam's own. Helpless, shading her eyes from the glaring sunset, she could only watch them depart.

So, Papa, there are your southern gentlemen. "Help yourselves, I trust you!"

Wearily, Miriam sat down on the front steps. The sun made its final plunge, leaving an afterglow streaked in amber and russet, the soft hazy colors of the dying year. The autumn evening was mild; now that the equinoctial storms were over, the earth was ready for a winter's rest.

Fanny came around from the barns.

"Come sit down," Miriam said.

All the rest of the household, worn out by the day, had gone to bed, leaving her alone. She wanted now not so much to speak of significant things as not to speak, only to feel the support of a living presence, or perhaps to say whatever trivial thoughts might enter her head.

"My shoes," she said after a while, glancing at her kid slippers. "They're all worn out. My last pair, too."

"Simeon's brother makes shoes. Leather uppers on a wooden sole. He made some for me."

"He must make some for all of us, then."

"I'll tell him. He's down back of the stables. They're burying the mule."

"The mule! Oh, no!"

"Yes, those men today found one of them and shot it."

This was the last blow, the last senseless blow.

"Now, in heaven's name, why would they do that? Steal the poor creature if you must, but why kill it?"

"They were drunk."

"As my father says, 'Our own people!'"

Fanny did not comment on that. She said instead, "There's a gang of the men who ran away when the Federals came. They've come back. Brought their women and children back."

It was Miriam's turn to have no comment. Any words she could have spoken would have been inappropriate before Fanny, unthinkable before her. They would have been too angry, too hot with resentment. Now that the "Secesh" have returned, she was thinking, and these people have no other place to go, they come back here to be fed and cared for. I wish to God they would all run away, the lot of them! We've not food enough for the ones who stayed, and now we have to share with these others.

"I'm going in to clean up," Fanny said. "Those pigs spat tobacco all over the dining-room floor. Oh, someone's coming!"

Oh, not more of them! Was this the crossroads of the world? Once it had seemed so remote, too remote, on those long days, those monotonous afternoons when only the occasional caw of a crow had broken into the stillness, when, almost frantic with need of a new voice or something new to see, she had walked to the end of the lane and scanned the meandering empty road where weeds grew between the ruts.

"What can it be now?" she cried despairingly.

Fanny stood tall and shielded her eyes. "A rider with a wagon following."

Miriam was too tired to get up. "Can you tell who?"

Fanny strained to see. "Miss Miriam! Miss Miriam —I do believe it's that Mr. Perrin!"

A fearful drumming began in Miriam's head. "It can't be!"

He's in Europe. He's dead. He would never come back, because of Eugene. He—

"But it is Mr. Perrin! Yes, Miss Miriam, it is."

She wore her joy and her desire like a cloak. It seemed to her as they sat after the evening meal in the sunny circle of wan firelight that surely it must be visible to all, this cloak of scarlet silk which had been laid upon her, so that she felt the glow of its color. Wearing it, she was content to sit quite still, just watching and listening.

The others had taken possession of André with their eager questions. Rosa wanted to know whether by any chance he had heard anything about her son Henry, from whom no letter had been had in months. No, he had not. Emma wanted to know the same about her grandsons. No, he had not.

"My brother, Gabriel de Rivera, is with the Tenth Louisiana. If you ever come in contact with them, please tell him that I, that we—" The words choked her. "You'll not forget?"

"I'll not forget."

Then Emma asked how dear Marie Claire was doing, and how recently he had seen her. She was doing well, as far as André knew, but he had not been in France for months.

What could that mean? Surely if there had been any great change in his life, he would have gotten the news to her. A chill draft penetrated the scarlet cloak.

"Are you sure you're not tired of all my tales?" André had asked a few minutes earlier.

"We here know almost nothing about what's going on in the outside world," Ferdinand had replied. "We've had no papers since the Federals came. Anything you tell us is bound to be news, especially about yourself."

Now André threw up his hands, continuing, "Well, as you know, diplomacy failed. It was a sorry failure, although God knows we tried everything. I was with Slidell when he offered Louis Napoleon a present of cotton worth a hundred million francs in return for recognizing the Confederacy. The Frenchman was tempted, all right, but too afraid that the Union would win. So when I saw that diplomacy wasn't going to work, I decided to make a practical contribution to the war. I've been doing blockade runs. Oh, I'm not a seaman, I just get the goods assembled and ride along for the adventure."

"Dangerous adventures," Ferdinand observed.

"Oh, not for the fainthearted, that's true."

Always there was that brightness about him! Some children have it, although not all of them; even some old people have it, for it has nothing to do with age, Miriam thought. It's something inside that shines through, something bold, a delight and cheer to the listener and watcher. All were enthralled: the two women, Eugene, Angelique, and, most of all, Ferdinand, who was very likely recalling his youth, living again his bravest moments.

"You ought to see the waterfront at Nassau! Cotton higher than your head piled on the docks. Then in comes the blockade runner, an ugly dark beast of a

ship, but fast. They're built mostly in England or
Nova Scotia, and made with a convex deck to go
through heavy seas. You can stand at your window in
the Royal Victoria Hotel and see the harbor crowded
with them. You don't sleep much the night before you
get on board, I can tell you that. But the trip over is a
whole lot safer than the trip back, when you're loaded
with ammunition."

"You must have had some narrow escapes," Eugene
said with awe.

And André, understanding the boy's eagerness,
smiled and went on, enjoying the telling.

"Oh, narrow, yes! We travel with great care, heading for Charleston or Wilmington on the return;
they're the only ports left to us. We try for the dark of
the moon and high tide. Otherwise, when the tide's
low, you can't get through the inlets to hide. And of
course, no lights! It's death, and I mean death, for
anybody who shows a light. No talking, either."

Eugene nodded wisely. "Because voices carry over
the water."

"Right. Oh, it's pretty tense sneaking past the
blockading fleet."

"Have you ever been chased?" Ferdinand wanted to
know.

"Certainly have. There was one time when a U.S.
Navy steam frigate chased us all one afternoon. Believe me, we prayed hard. Raced to keep ahead until
almost dark, when we put out a smokescreen, thick,
black smoke, low to the water. We made it, too, by the
skin of our teeth."

Ferdinand gave a long sigh. "I admit I'm envious!
Here I sit doing nothing." Then he remembered something. "We had an interesting visitor, a Dr. Zacharie.
Have you by any chance ever heard of him? He talks
as if everybody ought to know him."

"Oh, he's very well known! Lately, he's represented Lincoln in Richmond, trying to negotiate a peace. Spoke with Benjamin and others in the Cabinet. Lincoln was pleased, but nothing came of it. The Cabinet in Washington would have none of it. The radicals in the North want to destroy the South first before they make peace. At least, so goes the talk in Washington."

"How do you know so much about what's going on in Washington?" asked Rosa. "I thought it was almost impossible to get through the lines. Except for spies," she added sardonically.

André shrugged. "One picks up information of all sorts, here and there."

"I wish," Miriam said, "someone could pick up information about my brother." This was the first time she had spoken directly to André all evening. "We haven't heard from him since Dr. Zacharie brought us word."

"I shouldn't wish to hear about him if he were my brother," Emma said, sounding, to everyone's abrupt astonishment, more like her daughter Eulalie than like herself.

Nerves at this point in the long war could be expected to fray, and Miriam controlled herself enough to respond with nothing more than a cold question. "And why so, Aunt Emma?"

André interrupted to prevent Emma's reply. He spoke gently.

"The saddest thing about this war, ma'am, is the way it has split families apart. Do you know that three of Henry Clay's grandsons are fighting for us, while another three of them are in the Union army? And Mrs. Lincoln's brothers have been killed, fighting for the South."

At that Emma fell silent and Ferdinand—poor man,

always in the middle, thought Miriam—addressed André.

"I hope you'll stay and rest with us, for a few days at least."

"I thank you, but I must leave before noon tomorrow. I'm on the Texas route. The cotton comes down from Vicksburg, that's how I happen to be here. Then over to Brownsville and across the Rio Grande to Matamoros. We ship overseas from there."

"Then you've a long road, and you'll want to rest. Come." At Ferdinand's signal everyone stood up. "It's time to sleep, anyway."

"I'm not tired." André glanced at Miriam. "Or rather, I suppose, I'm too tired to sleep just yet. I think I'll take a walk or sit outside for a while to admire the warm night."

It was nine o'clock. In another half hour they would surely all be asleep. She felt the leap of her blood as she went upstairs, following her shadow, which shook on the wall as the candle shook in her hand.

Fanny was in Miriam's room, where she had unpacked the boxes André had brought. Piles of cloth and clothing lay on the bed.

"There wasn't room in here for that whole wagonload. I put the men's things in Mr. Ferdinand's room. Maybe this is for Master Eugene." Fanny displayed a brown sack coat bearing a British label, a silk cravat, and a red velvet waistcoat.

"They will be fine for him if we ever get New Orleans back so we can go home."

"And what a beautiful hat!" Fanny said of a shallow plate heaped with lilies of the valley.

"A Watteau hat. I seem to remember seeing it in a fashion magazine"—Miriam was about to say, "a hundred years ago," but said instead, "It will be quite a change from our palmetto hats, don't you think?" She giggled, thinking, I am being hysterically silly. "Shall I wear it on my next visit to the stables?"

"All these clothes! Look at this blue broadcloth, it would make a fine coat for you, Miss Miriam! And this yellow taffeta! Wait till you see what's in the pantry, too. Meats and wines and brandy, just like old times. He's a grand gentleman, that Mr. Perrin."

"In the morning we will go over everything and find some clothes for you, Fanny."

A pair of kid gloves slipped through Miriam's hands like satin. However had he managed to find all these fine things? The newness, the richness, the freshness of them seemed suddenly unnatural, as if she were not entitled to them at all; they were now so out of place, out of another world and another life. And at the same time she was perplexed by this feeling.

Fanny was looking closely at her with a strange, enigmatic smile, that twist of the lips that she sometimes wore when she was hiding her true thoughts.

Why is she smiling? Does she know about me and André? Sudden anger surged in Miriam.

"You can go to bed, Fanny. I don't need you," she said sharply.

She knows, she knows.

When the house was quiet Miriam went down the stairs and outside. He would be waiting in the summer house, on the bench behind the wooden-lace grille. Her feet danced over the lawn. Light as her footsteps were, he had heard her; dim as the night was, he had seen her. She had gone only half the distance when he met her, caught her, lifting her light feet from the ground, kissing her, over and over, sweetly, over and over.

She told herself: I have come home.

"I had to see you. I've ridden ninety miles out of my way, but I had to."

"You didn't know Eugene was dead and you came anyway!"

He laughed. "I took a chance. I thought if I came with my hands full, he would admit me. Greeks bearing gifts . . . Tell me, was he in the maddest rage about us? He was that morning when he sent me away."

"Not mad. Rather more reasonable than I expected."

And she was still, recalled to the shameful sting of Eugene's scorn, and sorrowing now over the abrupt intrusion of such a memory into this moment which should have been perfect.

There were no sounds except the soft thud of ripe walnuts dropping from the old tree. Then she spoke.

"It was a terrible death, André."

"It's all terrible, all the devastation. When I sat in there tonight and saw what had been done to this house and the torn shoes on your poor feet—but I'll be back, and I'm going to see that you have what you need, or as much of it as I can."

She heard nothing except the words "I'll be back."

"When will you be back?"

He led her to the summer house. The quarter moon came out from behind the clouds, so that she could see him in delicate detail, the thick blond lashes, the amber skin, and the crisp molding of the beautiful lips.

"When will you be back?"

"It's hard to say. I've got a partner, an Englishman. We bought a ship in his name. British registry, neutral, so they won't stop us at sea."

She didn't want to hear about affairs and ships, she wanted only his promise to return.

"It's a small boat with shallow draft; we can operate where the Union's deepwater ships can't go. But you don't want to hear about that, do you?"

"No, I want to hear about you."

"Let's go to your room, then."

She hesitated.

"I want to, but . . ."

"But what?"

Pressed together from shoulder to knee, it was unbearable not to go farther.

"I want to," she repeated.

"Can't we? What is it?"

"My daughter's room is next to mine. My father's and Emma's is across the hall."

Fanny's shrewd eyes, the innocence of Angelique, my son's respect, my father's dismay and Rosa's disdain, all flashed into her vision.

André groaned. "When, then? This is cruel."

"I don't know."

She put her head on his shoulder and thought of the room in the Pontalba, that high white room with the damp breeze flowing, the smells of heat, and voices calling in the square below. She gave a little sob of longing and disappointment.

"Ah, don't cry. If it can't be, it can't. It is possible," he began slowly, "it is possible that Marie Claire will get a divorce. . . ."

Against her ears she heard the slow beat of his heart.

"It is not as scandalous in Europe as it would be here, you see. And so then we, you and I—"

"And you want that, André? You're sure you do?"

"My dearest, how can you ask? You know I do."

"Oh!" she cried. "You don't know, all this time, so much time! And I felt there was nothing more to expect in my life. My children, yes, God knows they come first, long before myself, but one is human, too, one wants something for oneself, and I've been thinking there would never be anything, that you and I would never—and now, now you give me everything to hope for!"

He turned her face up into the light, now almost vanished as clouds rolled back over the sky.

"Lovely, lovely. Such eyes! Never, never such eyes!" He kissed her eyelids.

"Seeing you like this and not having you is worse than not seeing you at all," he said.

They turned back to the house. The bayou shone like dark glass, and last year's dried stalks stood stiffly on the lily pads. Beneath the cedars lay a spongy carpet, a century's wealth of needles. Suddenly she felt like talking, like confiding.

"Cedars. Did you know the Negroes won't ever cut them because they say each represents a human life? I often think of that when I walk past here."

"You think too much."

"Are you impatient with me?"

"No, of course not. But for your own good you shouldn't be so serious."

"When the war's over, when the killing's over, I shall laugh. I shall be very, very happy and blissful, I promise you."

"And so you should be."

"Right now I can't help thinking of all the young lives, of your life, André."

"Don't I always tell you I'll be all right? I know what I'm doing. I lead a charmed existence, don't you know that?"

"I hope so. When I'm with you, I believe whatever you say. You make me feel safe, you always have."

"Happy is what I want to make you feel. Life's too short. The first time I saw you . . . you were so beautiful and so sad. That's what lured me, I think, your sadness. I wanted to do away with it. I brought you that yellow silk; have it made up right away. I want to think of you in yellow, the color of sunshine and laughter."

A sudden gust of wind shook the trees, chilling the air; a gray mist rose and colored the night as if to say, The time of sunshine and laughter is not yet.

But he wanted sunshine, so she smiled.

"We'll say good-bye now, shall we? It's easier than it would be tomorrow with everyone standing around."

"Not good-bye. Try again."

"*Au revoir?* Is that better?"

"Much better. *Au revoir,* my Miriam."

26

Just past Vicksburg Plaisance had stood by the river in its pristine grandeur, a white wooden Parthenon on a green rise, sloping up from its private dock at which servants bearing torches had brightened the way for guests arriving by steamboat. Between the house and the wide curve of the woods at its back, topiary trees, shaped by the skillful hands of a French landscape gardener, still skirted the long parterre. In the octagonal conservatory, pineapples flourished. Peacocks fanned their tails and paraded on the lawns, pausing to startle the afternoon with their raucous cries. And on the pond a pair of swans drowsed, floating through a paradise of summer.

"As long as we hold Vicksburg," André had said, "we'll be all right."

But Vicksburg fell and the refugees arrived. Two carriages drawn by weary horses held the family, Pelagie with her two youngest children, Eulalie, and Mr. Lambert Labouisse. Two wagons held the household servants, along with a sorry load of random salvaged household goods. After six days on the road they were all equally exhausted, hungry, and despairing.

"They've burned our house to the ground!" These were the old man's first words as, almost toppling, he was helped down from the carriage.

Pelagie wore a black alpaca mourning dress, grimy and stained with sweat.

"You didn't know. . . . Our letters never reached you. . . . Yes, my Alexandre's gone! They killed him at Yazoo Pass."

Emma shrieked and clasped her daughter.

"Thank God my Felicité is married in San Francisco, that one's safe at least."

Pelagie was more visibly distraught than she had been at the time of Sylvain's death. "Now I have to worry about Lambert and Louis: Where are they? I don't know. Off fighting somewhere . . . dead, too, maybe. And these two young ones safe at home with me. I thought—this boy, child of my heart, who never knew his father, and now his home is gone. . . ."

Miriam led her upstairs to a bedroom, and knowing how fastidious she was, at once called Fanny to bring hot water.

"And a cold drink, too, please, Fanny. Water, if there's nothing else. Now tell me, tell me, talk it out," she urged Pelagie.

Pelagie lay back on the *lit de repos* and took a long breath.

"To be under a roof again! You can't imagine. Well, after Vicksburg fell—we had friends there, you know, and they fled to us, one of them even brought her piano with her, it was all she could save. Well, then, the Federal gunboats went down the river firing at the houses along the bank, but we were fortunate—they didn't come as far as Plaisance. So we thought we were going to escape. But last week, last week they came! The shells landed on the roof! It caught fire! Oh, it was horrible! The wind seemed to be pulling the flames up toward the sky with all its force, they must have been visible for miles, like a volcano, the way they said Vicksburg looked when it blew up." Pelagie put her hands over her face. "And the most awful thing. When the gunboats came to destroy us, our field hands went running down to the levee. They had their hoes in their hands, they were waving and singing. I sometimes think it's just as well Sylvain didn't live to see all this. He loved that place, it was his home, he was born there."

Pelagie gave a queer, sad laugh. "That very morning my father-in-law had made out a new will. He was discussing with me who in the family might want this slave or that one. And he actually went about telling each of them who was to inherit him! And to think that very afternoon it all came to an end."

Certainly she has no love for that old tyrant, Miriam said to herself. But he had been a symbol of a stable world. Now, after this blatant failure of his judgment and his perception of things, who was Pelagie to rely upon? For she had to have a man to rely upon.

"No home, no home," Pelagie lamented.

"You have a home here. Somehow, someday, I don't know how or when, we'll all get back to normal. We will." And Miriam gave banal comfort, all there was to give.

At the same time she was worrying: What are we to do with all these people? We have almost nothing for ourselves. Not enough seed for the planting, no repairs for the broken-down machinery. The slaves are unwilling to work. Why should they? The handwriting is on the wall. Actually, it's astonishing that as many of them are willing to work as much as they do. Maybe they think their masters will yet win the war?

"Oh, who could have believed it?" Pelagie wailed now.

"I could have," Miriam might have answered, but did not.

There were no more tallow candles, so that they sat around the table that night in the choking smoke of the terrabene lamp. Its sharp turpentine smell tinctured the dusk and clung to the food. Meals were growing visibly more meager every day. Only half hearing the flow of talk—for words, endless words, she understood, gave release to their fears—Miriam took stock of what was on the platters and calculated.

No more flour; the price was one thousand dollars a barrel, if you could find any. Tea cost fifty dollars a pound; Fanny had taught her how to make it out of blackberry leaves. There was no more coffee, but one could make a miserable substitute out of peanuts or potatoes. They would have to tend the vegetables more carefully. If only the shortage of meat did no harm to the growing boy and girl! Some said one could be perfectly healthy on a diet of vegetables. Of course, there were eggs.

Eugene is almost fifteen. How soon will they take him for the army? Pelagie is worried that there'll be no men left for the girls to marry. Marriage! That's the last and the least of my worries.

What had she been thinking just now? Vegetables, yes. Tomorrow she must get up even earlier than usual, take the little mare, and ride over the whole place. It had been easier for her to learn than one would expect of a city girl. Now Miriam's mind swept from the fields and kitchen to the upstairs, where there were not enough blankets and no more sheets for these new arrivals. Cotton cloth was fifteen dollars a yard—again, if one could get any. Out here in the country, how could one? There were no pins or needles. Well, Fanny had showed her how to use thorns instead. But you couldn't sew without thread, which cost five dollars a spool, and the Confederate dollar was now worth ten cents.

A small horde of gold coins remained, sewn into the lining of the dress which had been made out of André's yellow silk. It was the only presentable dress she had. She would have to hold on to them, the dress and the coins. God only knew what emergency might require either one.

Old Lambert Labouisse was making a declaration; his most simple remarks were declarations.

"Yes, I threw the entire gold dinner service into the Mississippi, rather than let the Federals have it. Service for twenty-four, and many a distinguished occasion it graced! Well, it's had a respectable death, anyway."

You old fool, Miriam thought. I wish I knew how and where to fish it out.

Since Eugene's death, Ferdinand had made only a halfhearted effort to keep the war map current. Still, he remarked now in a discouraged voice, "Yes, the loss of Vicksburg was the final blow, losing our bridge over into Texas and Mexico. Now only a trickle of goods can get in or out of here."

And how will André get back? God only knows. It's all so dark; the clouds fold over us and one can't see a day ahead. How will it be for him and me, if and when he does get back?

"Just thirty thousand men would have kept Vicksburg for us," said old Labouisse. "We have that many deserters, that many and more, damn their souls, all of them."

Eulalie made one of her rare comments. "What could one have expected? Pemberton is a Yankee, after all. He shouldn't have been trusted."

Her pale eyes had angry pink sore-looking rims. The fierce Virginia warrior, Miriam thought again, remembering her promise of silence. She could imagine the truth coming out, the careful tiny drippings of sly innuendo, stains spreading through the fabric of her children's trust in their mother.

They had endured enough and too much. Even as she herself carried in her mind that indelible scene of her mother's death, a scene which had only been described to her, so would they bear forever the picture of their father dying on the ground with his hands held in theirs. They spoke of it seldom now, for what was there to be said? But between his eyes Eugene had two vertical grooves which had not been there before. And Angelique, prone since early childhood to vivid dreams and nightmares, cried out in her sleep, so that Miriam had often to go in and quiet her. Yes, they had borne enough. If Eulalie were to add more . . .

Then, no, she decided, Eulalie will not talk. She knows I would put her out. I can't think where I'd send her, but I'd send her somewhere out of this house, and she knows I would.

"The trouble is," Eulalie said now, "everyone, all of you people, have lost hope. I have not lost hope." And she looked around the table, asking to be challenged, but no one challenged her. So she continued, "We, with our good old blood, have it in our power to do much better than we've done yet. Look at the northern ranks! Full of nothing but Germans and Irish and heaven knows what else! And that ape Lincoln at the head with his emancipation!"

"I wish emancipation could be applied here."

This remark came from the foot of the table where Eugene sat. Every head turned to him in astonishment. His face had gone scarlet, as if the sound of his own words falling so unexpectedly into the room, now grown so still, had terrified even him. His startled eyes appealed now to his mother for help.

Miriam was stunned. How and when had the boy got such an idea? She had been so careful to skirt the deadly subject! Nevertheless, the little thrill, whose cause was part alarm and part a kind of joyful pride, sparked in her chest.

"It's all right, Eugene. You may speak," she said softly. "Go on."

"Well, I was thinking, I've been thinking about what I've seen since we came here to stay and—and," he stumbled, "it seems to me we'd be better off with a few skilled men working for wages than we are with all these poor, helpless folks to feed and care for."

Lambert Labouisse appeared about to erupt and Ferdinand hastened to explain.

"My grandson is only speaking practically, as a matter of economy, given the present conditions."

"Perhaps he isn't," Miriam said. Something within her rose in quick resentment of having to placate Mr. Lambert Labouisse. "Go on, Eugene."

The boy's voice grew stronger. "Well, wouldn't this whole country be better off if all these huge places were cut up into smaller farms? If the owners could work their own places, I mean. It would be more healthy. More prosperous, too, I think. There's so much waste in the slave system. And it's not really fair, either, to have so much land in so few hands. What good do two thousand acres of unused land do for anybody?"

Mr. Labouisse actually rapped his spoon on the table. "I have spent my life, and my father spent his before me, increasing our holdings for the benefit of generations to come! We have paid and paid to keep our lands intact! Talk like your son's is more than I can hear with any equanimity, ma'am! I'm sorry to say it, but I must!"

"I don't understand." Ferdinand was flustered. "It's very troubling to me, I assure you. Where could Eugene have got such thoughts, Miriam?"

"I'm sure I don't know, Papa. But he is certainly entitled to his thoughts." And she gave Eugene a smile.

"He got them from his uncle, I suspect," Eulalie snapped.

"From my brother?" Miriam retorted. "He's had a lot of contact with my brother these past years, hasn't he?"

Then surprisingly, and before Eulalie could fuel the fire any more, Pelagie spoke. "Do you know, Father, when Louis was home on leave the last time, he said much the same thing?" She hesitated. "He's of the opinion that these large holdings must go and the slave system along with them."

The old man stared. "My grandson said that? My grandson?"

"Well, you have to admit," Pelagie faltered, "it is a costly system. The money that our children could inherit goes for the upkeep of all these slaves, their clothing, and . . . then with so much of the land being idle, as Eugene said . . ."

"Eugene! Idiocy!" The old man was furious; spittle shot from his mouth. "Claptrap! Wicked, stupid claptrap! Never produced ten cents' worth of anything in their lives, not dry behind the ears yet, and already giving away their birthright, the fools. Ought to take the whip to the lot of them!"

Rosa glanced nervously at Miriam. The glance said, What on earth can have happened to Pelagie?

To that Miriam could have answered, "Only that she, even she, has at last been jolted into reality."

27

Between the Rapidan River on the north and the wide, cleared fields of Spottsylvania on the south lay a wilderness some twelve to twenty miles long and six miles deep of sluggish, silent swamp and gloomy forest, a thick maze of vine and thorn and waist-high underbrush.

Now in the lovely blue days of early May the white-topped wagons rumbled over the turnpike and the Orange Plank Road, heading toward confrontation with Grant's Army of the Potomac.

Gabriel's body and the tawny body of his mare Polaris had, after more than three years of war, merged almost into one. Without directive or pressure the horse kept place in line, leaving the rider absorbed in his somber reflections.

Last year they had met Grant at Chancellorsville, where Lee had won. This year, passing the site of that victory, they had come upon its aftermath of silent, burnt-out ruins, rotting and mouldering in weedy fields. There'd been a farmer alongside a road; *I never owned a slave. With my own hands I cleared these fields, built this house; the Federals took it all, the hogs, the chickens, the cow for the children's milk, a lifetime's work.* What could states rights mean to him?

So I plod, so we go stumbling together, wading rivers, enduring in a weariness beyond belief, with no way of knowing where it will end.

He had a sense of fearful foreboding. It is the spring, he thought, it is the dogwood lying flat on the air like starched lace, white and pink; it is the wet gloss on the leaves, the south wind and the sun's warm touch on the horse's living neck; it is—it is knowing that I may never see all this again.

He straightened up. Enough! It's spineless and does you no good.

Yet all around him the others, officers and men, were quiet, too. His lieutenant, riding slightly behind him, had not spoken for an hour. The occasional snort of a horse was startling.

On either side the woods grew thicker, narrowing the road, throwing a gloom across the advancing day. Heat struck, heavy and stifling; it glossed Polaris's neck and stung the sweat under Gabriel's gray coat.

Far ahead the line could be seen turning off the road. He did not need to take the map from his pocket; he had memorized it; he knew where they were going and where they expected to take Grant by surprise. So he would rest his mind by trying to think of what lay in his past, rather than of what might lie ahead today.

It was so long since he had been home! And he wondered what was left of his city. They had taken Rosa's house, that he knew. Perhaps someone would be good enough to protect the precious treasure of his law books, a collection inherited from Henry and most carefully enlarged by himself. Such a pleasant room, the little square library with its comfortable chair and footstool! The windows, opened to the courtyard, took in the pungent smell of wet stone after rain, and the lazy sound of dripping from the banana leaves. Under the window there was always a leftover puddle where the pavement sagged; there sat the most minute green frog, bright as an emerald, a crown jewel.

So long since he had seen home! Or Miriam . . . Months after the fact, the news of Eugene's death had reached him, but Rosa never wrote about Miriam, wanting to spare him, he understood, and supposing herself to be tactful.

And he recalled, with a kind of half-sad humor, his sister's efforts, also meant to be tactful, to arouse his interest in one "eligible" young woman after the other. Her definition of "eligible" was young, good-natured, reasonably pretty, and, most important, of fine family background. Dear Rosa! The question of his loving the girl never entered her mind. Oh, there had been some —he remembered one, very charming, very willing, with burnished copper hair—he could very likely have gone farther with her, if it had not been for Miriam. Always the image of Miriam came between him and any other.

The hurt inside him was something he could almost touch, like a burn or a cut. The anger—not toward her; no, never toward her, but toward that man Perrin —was like fire. He tried to quench it, but it always flared back. Now that she was widowed and free, he supposed they would be married; Perrin already had a wife, to be sure, but a man like him would find some way, Gabriel thought scornfully. That man, that man —if he were here I'd run my bayonet through him, he thought, and I've never used my bayonet, not in spite of all the carnage, and I've been in the thick of it. But I've never had to use it, thank God. A bullet is bad enough, but to feel the weapon in your moving hands slicing through another man's flesh!

Polaris, following the line, stepped cautiously into the ditch that bordered the road and clambered up again, entering now a place where she must plow knee

deep through troughs of many years' fallen leaves,
struggling through prickers and stickers, catching herself in a jumble of saplings and vines. They had been in
places like this before. No, not like this, Gabriel
thought, as they picked their way more deeply into a
darkness that must be like the bottom of the sea. Tall
pines met overhead. A ravine, so steep and sudden
that an inexpert rider would pitch over the horse's
head, cut across the way. They struggled on. How can
a battle be fought in here where you can't see either
enemy or friend? he wondered.

The call to halt was passed up the line. A good
thing, too, for it was almost noon, and they had been
going since dawn. The heat was now so overpowering
that if the going weren't so precarious, one might almost fall asleep in the saddle.

Men crowded into the clearing where the halt had
been called. There, in a circle of patchy sunlight, hung
the dogwood again, a jubilant, exquisite white in an
ominous gloom. And Gabriel felt again that irregular
palpitation they called "soldier's heart," blaming it on
strain or heat. But it was more than just those: it was
fear.

"Conference up ahead," someone reported.

"Scout says Union forces are approaching."

"—said Grant's sitting on a stump, wearing dress
uniform and a sword."

Nervous laughter. The body is afraid to go ahead,
but the spirit, fearing cowardice, is afraid that the
body might really turn about and flee, to the spirit's
everlasting shame.

Polaris stamped, curving her head as far back as she
could, as if to communicate with Gabriel. She had the
haughty, delicate nose of an aristocrat, but her intelligent eyes were soft and mild. She knows me well,
thought Gabriel. We have been together a long time.

Someone was talking loudly. "Hell, this is no place for horses! How we gonna fight in here? Can't move faster than one mile an hour, if that much."

Nevertheless, they moved forward. They slid down the muddy banks of hidden brooks, climbed back up, and kept on going, going, until at last they heard the first spatter and crack of gunfire up ahead.

"Leave the horses. Get down. It's impossible."

Soldier's heart again. Gabriel dismounted from Polaris and stroked her muzzle. Would he ever find her again?

A corps of sharpshooters to the right went ducking under bramble bushes. Field artillery, with a great noise of dragging, crushed the underbrush.

Oh, my God! A whole blue division, so close, using grape and canister, came to life, erupting out of the woods and the murk. And a storm of lead exploded. My God! Whole sheets of it, like rain slanting in the wind.

"Forward, forward!" Who is that screaming, whose throat is that, torn raw with the screaming rebel yell as the men plunge, plunge, so close now to the men in blue and the bright silver of bayonets? My voice?

He fired. Covered by the trunk of an ancient oak, blindly he keeps firing at an enemy that is hidden in a mass of pungent, stinging smoke. The noise is shattering, a hammer on the eardrums and in the head. Bugles blare, summoning courage, giving signals that no one understands or can heed because no one can see or know where he is himself or where the enemy is.

"Fire! Fire! Load and reload." Bullets snap through the leafage, sending a shower of papery scraps to the ground. Someone screams not three feet away; it is a terrible high animal scream. There is no time to look. Still firing, Gabriel kneels, bent low, for nothing that stands upright in this hell can live.

Oh, God, it is the worst hell in a thousand days of hellish war that he has yet lived through!

A man collides with another, crawling on hands and knees, going toward the rear, the wrong way.

"Where you going? Where the devil do you think you're going?"

"I'm hurt, sir. Back to the rear, I'm hurt."

"Hurt where? Show blood or turn around, go back, God damn you, go back!"

"They're shooting at our own side, for Christ's sake!"

"Can't help it. They can't see. Get down! Down!"

And still, hour after hour, the thundering, the whistle before the crash, the roar and smash go on. . . . Will the night never fall?

It falls. The blackest night that Gabriel has ever seen smothers the woods. Shots dwindle, and in the darkness both sides, exhausted, fall to the ground wherever they happen to be.

All is still. They have taken the wounded to the rear. The ground is littered with the dead or silent. Silent and free, thinks Gabriel. They don't have to dread the return of the morning.

Once a whippoorwill calls. Its pure, liquid voice is heard for a few seconds, then stops. Even the birds cower, he thinks, they in their nests—those that have not been blasted away—and we on the ground.

He takes a deep breath. He is too tired to investigate anything; anyway, it is too dark; it is his function to stay here with his men or with what is left of them, and wait. He sleeps with his head between his knees.

Then, the second day, a day of rising wind. While bullets rain and rattle, the wind flows and little fires, flaring out of sparks in the underbrush, are carried from twig to twig, from skeletal stripped branch to the next leaf-stripped branch. Flames, like living creatures, slither over the ground. Probing and searching, they mount the tree trunks, murmuring as they creep. In seconds a scrub pine turns into a torch, one vertical billow of flame. Far behind the forward lines the log breastworks, so laboriously built, catch fire, too. Cinders whirl in this wind; the whole forest, all pitch and resin, roars with fire. The very air burns a man's lungs.

Now the flames come like racing surf, wave after surging wave. The helpless wounded scream in horror as the waves come near and nearer; some scream in anguish as the waves roll over them; they scream and die, while others shoot themselves in time, if they are strong enough to do so. Men in blue and men in gray alike rush out to save their own, some even saving the enemy's men.

Gabriel drags a man to safety, thinking, If Lorenzo were here, he could help, and for the first time, he misses him; but Lorenzo went months ago to the other side and is in New York or Washington by now. Incredibly, in all this chaos, Gabriel has a flash of amusement: Rosa had been so sure of his loyalty! *Why, why shouldn't he be faithful, he adores you?*

After some yards he lays the man down near a shallow ravine; with luck the fire just may not jump that ravine. He is too exhausted at any rate to go another step. There is a terrible pain in his foot.

He looks for a pile of leaves to lie on and stumbles again, this time over a body. The uniform is blue. He searches the face: young, younger than I, I am a million years old.

The eyes open, staring back at Gabriel, eyes too clouded even to recognize the enemy.

"I'm awfully cold. My sister Margaret, no, not Margaret, the other one, she says, you see, if I had a blanket, I was sick all over this one."

Gabriel leans closer, although even this slight motion stabs his foot. The boy babbles, makes a strangling noise, heaves a slimy vomit out of his guts, and having done so, falls back into silence.

Half a night later Gabriel knows that the boy is dead. The stars are thick in a sliver of sky between the treetops, and in their bluish light he can see the dead face. It is extraordinarily dignified, he thinks. He lies on his elbow looking at it, wishing he had a blanket or some decent cover for it. Then it occurs to him that something ought to be said to or about this dignified face, which seems to be expecting that recognition be given. So he says the Kaddish. It is a prayer in praise of God, a Jewish prayer, but it is the only one he knows, and surely suitable.

The pain is a cutting knife in his foot. He must have been shot. How queer that he cannot recall when! His head feels foggy. He lies without moving. From every direction the wounded are calling: Water! Help me! Mother! Christ! But no one comes. It is too dark, too far away.

Dawn comes. A fly has settled on the dead boy's cheek, and Gabriel shoos it away. The eyes are open and he reaches over to close them. It is a struggle to reach; the pain is growing worse. He wants to find a pocket with an address, and he thinks of the letter he will write to the parents about how their son died, but suddenly his leg gives way and he falls back on the ground.

Now he tries to get his boot off, but he lacks the strength to do it. He wonders whether he will lose his foot or his leg. It feels wet under the boot.

It is so quiet. The battle must have moved elsewhere. He wonders who is winning, or has won, but he doesn't really care. It doesn't concern him. High above the little space between the leaves, where the stars were just a while ago, the sky has turned to the most intense and marvelous blue. So it must be full morning.

She will not want a cripple, he thinks. Does not want me anyway. Wants that—other. He has—what? A gallantry that I have not, have never had?

Back and forth, ebb and flow; that's my life. Loving without wanting to. Fighting without wanting to. Yet I fight. Yet I love.

History is battles. How many fought, how many wounded, how many died. Someday they will write about this. Numbers and words don't matter, though. They will write, but it will mean nothing. If I live through this war and they ask me what it was like, I won't be able to tell them.

And now he hears that a low whispering has begun among the vastness of the trees. Swirling and spreading, it sounds like the moan of the sea. After a while he understands that this is the moaning of the wounded.

He lies quite still. He is spent, even the pain in his foot is spent, he is slipping away and out.

When he opens his eyes, he sees that the scrap of blue over his head is now iron gray. It must be evening again. Somebody is doing something to his foot; his boot is off.

"He may lose the foot," someone says.

"Maybe not."

"Be careful with that candle. Drop one of them and every man on the ground here goes up in flames."

These men wear blue! The Federal uniform, he thinks indifferently. He must be a prisoner.

He is picked up, carried out to a road, and put in a wagon. There must be hundreds of them stretching all the way down the road. He recognizes ammunition wagons, mustered into ambulance service. They have no springs. Now, as they begin to rumble down the corduroy road, each jolt sends a shaft of blood-red pain down his spine. He wants to ask where they are going, but it is too much effort, and besides, they will probably not answer. But he can tell by the fading light that they are moving eastward, toward Fredericksburg, he supposes.

"Lucky we got a place," a voice says. "There must be seven thousand men in this load alone. The rest of them will lie there two days till they get more wagons."

How many hours to Fredericksburg?

A man dies and the wagon halts for the removal of the body. At the side of the road lies a huge black bloated crescent, curved like a beached whale. A whale here in this place! He's seen one only once before, one summer long ago at Pass Christian. He remembers it well, that summer. All that blue and silver water, all the way to Cat Island! He thinks of crabbing, fishing, and the cool porch in the evening behind the trumpet vine, and music coming from somewhere down the beach.

He looks out over the side of the wagon at the whale. But it is not a whale; it has four stiffened legs, which project into the road, almost touching the wagon wheels. It is a horse. Enormous, iridescent flies cluster on its back, buzzing at its ears. And suddenly the legs flail; with a wild lunge the animal flips over to its other side, making a terrible sound of despair in the brutal heat.

"Oh, for God's sake," Gabriel cries, "kill it! Shoot it!"

"Shoot who?" The Yankee sergeant, cradling his gun by the side of the wagon, hears him and laughs. He has big, rotten teeth. "Not allowed to shoot prisoners, you know that."

Gabriel's tongue is thick. He points.

The sergeant looks. "Oh, the horse, you mean?"

Gabriel nods. "Your rifle," he manages to say.

"You know how many men died these last few days? And you're worried about a horse?"

But the horse, Gabriel thinks, more clearly now, as they move on, the horse doesn't even know why—the horse must ponder why. Polaris, surely she wonders where I am. Polaris needs somebody to take care of her so that she will not die in a ditch like this one.

In Fredericksburg they put him down in some sort of public building, a warehouse or mill. There are holes in the roof and puddles where the rain comes in. There's food, some hardtack and water, but never enough water. How long he lies there, he doesn't know.

"You won't need to lose this foot," someone says at last, a tired man with pouches under the eyes. As on our side, they don't have enough doctors. Wouldn't it be strange if David were to walk in here now? Wouldn't it be sunlight in the dark?

"No, you won't lose it. I've cleaned it out. Keep it clean, if you can."

More days, and then back onto the wagons, going north. Of course, where else but north? And they come to a stop near a river. There is a dock at which a steamer waits for the long line of wagons. Like a floating cavern, it takes him away from shells, smoke, bloody faces, and dawn attacks, away into a buried silence, a peace that is not peace. Yes, he feels relief as they move down the river, but more than that, a weighty guilt at this removal to the territory of the enemy, at being relieved of the struggle while others must go on fighting as long as they—

"You fainted," someone says, "but you're all right now."

He is lying down on solid ground. Something soft

whisks over his nose, a little clump of pine needles. He lets the sweet forest smell lie on his lips. They have put him under a tree.

"Where are we?" he asks.

The man steps back, and Gabriel sees him at full length; fat chest, bearded face, and medical insignia. For a moment, because of the touch of a German accent, he has thought of David. Why not? Stranger things have happened. But this is not David's acquiline face. This man is ruddy-round, and his beard is grizzled. Northern armies have so many Germans. Irish, too. Funny. But southern ones have Cajuns and Scotch-Irish in North Carolina. Funny, all of it. He drowses again.

His feet are in the sun, now, but his head and shoulders are still in the shade. Lucky. The things you're grateful for! A piece of shade. It is so bright out that even the grass looks white. There are rows and rows of stretchers in the white sun. The rows run as far as the flagpole. On the flagpole the Stars and Stripes flatten out when the wind pulls, and fall back again, drooping down the pole.

Someone comes to look at his foot, which has begun to bleed again. He bites his lip. Isn't going to make a sound, no, God damn it, not here.

"There, that's better. Can you get up and limp?" This is a different voice, not the German's.

He steadies himself. "How far?"

"Not far. Just a couple of steps to the train." The man is making an attempt at kindness. "Only as far as the train."

"I thought—this is Washington?"

"Oh, yes, but you're not staying here. Did you think you were staying here?" This is spoken with flat amusement, tired amusement. "You're off to Elmira to be locked up, you and this whole bunch."

The train lies glistening on its bed of cinders like a snake on a sunlit rock. The engine is the snake's head. Impatient, hissing noises come from its throat.

All along the path to the train stands a double line of soldiers with rifles and bayonets. Hell, do they think we're going to run away? Even the ones among us who haven't a scratch can't run away; where the hell could we go? Silently, shuffling, the wounded and the whole climb up onto the train.

"Here, get in. I'll hoist you."

"Elmira," someone says. "Had a cousin there. Alabama boy, my mother's kin. Died there last winter, too."

"Likely froze to death."

"Snow gets up to your belly button, I've heard tell."

"Shucks! And I forgot my winter overcoat." That's the humorous one; Gabriel remembers him from when they lay in Fredericksburg that first night. Sounds like him, anyway. Not more than seventeen, with a high, still-girlish voice, cracking jokes to keep from crying.

"Winter? It's only May! You don't think we'll still be there by winter?"

Nobody answers.

28

Where once a sweep of grasses, succulent and high, had covered it, the red Georgia earth lay bare, brick-hard, and brick-hot under the broiling sun. Within the stockade no tree gave shade to comfort a man's head. No brook ran to cool a man's feet. There were no tents into which men might crawl to seek relief, only for some the meager shelter, self-contrived, of a torn blanket stretched on four weak sticks.

In one of these David Raphael had established a claim to his share of space, about six square feet to a man, he estimated. Humanity swarmed and overlapped like clustered beetles. He fancied that if one could view the scene from above, it would appear as a single solid mass of flesh.

When he stretched his legs for length, they touched another man's back. It didn't matter, because the man scarcely felt the touch; he hadn't moved all morning and would soon die, might be dead already. In that case one hoped they would pick him up soon. The cart would be coming by sometime before noon, and if they should miss him then, they wouldn't take him away until tomorrow, God help us.

Someone stirred on his left, mumbling a question.

"Talk louder, I can't hear you."

"Turn around, then."

"I can't." It was too great an effort to turn.

"I said, I asked, where did they catch you?"

"Wilderness. Battle of the Wilderness. I blundered into the wrong lines in the dark."

"How long you been here?"

"Couple of months, I guess, if this is July."

"It's July."

Silence. The fellow stirred again, clumsily shifting. He sounded young. David sighed. It was too much effort to talk, but maybe the boy needed to talk to somebody.

"I'm David Raphael."

"Tim Woods. Artillery. And you?"

"A doctor."

"Oh. I've a wound. Fleshy part, back of the knee. How do you know when there's gangrene? I've heard—"

Oh, my God, son, how do you know. By the stench and the pain, enough to send you through the ceiling, if there were a ceiling—

"Don't worry, you haven't got it. You'd know if you had."

"I know I haven't yet. But will I get it?"

"Oh, I'd say not. Youth is on your side, you know."
No harm in a lie, and maybe some temporary use.

"They live long in my family. My grandfather was ninety-eight. I suppose that's a good sign."

"The best. Heredity is what counts."

"Say, Doctor, what do you think our chances are?"

"For what? Getting out of here?"

"Yeah. What do you think?"

"Oh, not long. War can't last much longer."

"God, this heat! How do folks live here?"

"They do."

They live in shacks under the trees and sleep in hammocks in the shade. Or they live in tall rooms on verandahs with palmetto fans and drinks in cold glasses.

"I'm from New Hampshire. We have hot summers, but this . . ." The voice trailed away. Suddenly it resumed. "This leg hurts me like hell."

"Don't talk, then. It tires you out. It'll heal better if you try to sleep."

"Thanks, Doctor, I'll try."

And now the wind, such as it was, a hot wind like the blast from the open oven when the meat is roasting, veered abruptly to blow the fetid air from a corner in which someone had vomited or soiled himself again. It brought a stench not like the natural smell of a manured field, which, though hardly perfumed as it steams in the sun, is yet so natural as to be almost inoffensive, but a stench so nauseating that the contents of the stomach must rise to the throat.

What contents? Moldy bread, some slops, indistinguishable warm grease, and yet, not enough even of these.

We are starving, David thought. He moved his teeth with his tongue. He had already lost three by last count. If he had some lemons, it might not be too late to save the rest. Or limes. His tongue moved over his gums, feeling the wet, clean sting of lemons. Or limes.

A man screamed. "Shit! Oh, you darling—"

"Shut up! Shut up, you crazy bastard!"

"Oh, you darling!"

It might be a lucky thing to lose your mind here. You wouldn't know, then, that you were here. There'd be no past to remember.

So far David's mind was sharp. Maybe abnormally keen, unnaturally acute? He worried, giving careful notice to a louse that crawled on the shoulder of the man on his right. That other man, standing up, had a dark patch of sweat on his ragged shirt. The stain made a fish shape; there the fins, and there the tail, curving when the man bent over. Was it normal to notice things like that, or a sign that his mind was going? God knew, an hour from now he might start to rave, to see things that weren't there.

That poor fellow in the hospital that time. I remember. The Christian chaplain tried to convert him before he died. Meant well, but it didn't work. If I die, I would like a Jewish chaplain to read services over me. There never are enough of them. I had to read for so many Jewish dead myself. I think I am dying. Can't last much longer like this. So filthy, I disgust myself.

Over the low drone and murmur of suffering came voices, not loud, but incisive, clear, and close by.

"Well, but Dr. Joseph Jones of our medical department spoke just last month about conditions here."

On the left New Hampshire whispered, "Inspection tour, for what good it will do."

With tremendous effort David raised his head a few inches. Two officers in gray and a man in civilian clothes were standing together. The blond civilian wore a suit of fine dark cloth. People still dressed like that and were clean. It was he who inquired how many there were in this place.

"About thirty thousand," replied the elder of the officers.

"Well, I do appreciate your invitation. I was just passing through on business. . . . Curious to see . . . Still, quite terrible . . . Sorry I came." The voice, borne to and fro by the hot wind, revealed distress.

"Well. A prison camp is hardly a pleasant place, I agree."

And the man in the fine suit repeated himself. "Yes, sorry I came to see it."

There was something familiar in the southern voice,

something from long ago. An easy grace. Sylvain? No, you killed him. Remember?

The men were still standing in the aisle.

"This heat is murderous," said the man who was not Sylvain.

"But on the other hand," the officer answered, "our men freeze in their prisons, in open box cars, in the snow, wearing cotton fit for New Orleans."

New Orleans. If not Sylvain, someone else, then? Someone I didn't like. Why didn't I like him? I do know. I do know. He was dancing—somewhere—he was dancing—where was it? And Gabriel was there, and my sister. I always thought Gabriel was half in love with her, or more than half. He must be dead by now, and she and all of us must be dead, or will be soon. But this man, who was he? Where was it?

And raising his arm, he struggled, got up, and lurched, pulling the blanket so that the stick shelter collapsed upon the New Hampshire boy's wounded leg. And at his cry the men, the officers and the civilian, turned around.

Look at me, David wanted to say. I'm not crazy, even though I know my mouth is bleeding, I'm only dirty, I'm disgusting, but look at me.

Instead he heard his own cry: "Raphael, David Raphael!"

On the bright, blond face of the civilian he saw astonishment. The man took a step, opened his mouth to speak, and was decisively pulled back.

"Not permitted," said the officer. "Sorry, but absolutely not permitted."

The three men moved quickly away.

And David sobbed now, crying over and over, "David, David Raphael. You know. *Kennst du mich nicht? Kennst—*" At the same time he knew he was raving.

29

Ferdinand had insisted upon going with Miriam.

"It's eleven miles to the store," he had objected. "I doubt they'll have much, anyway."

She answered with firmness.

"We can use anything that's there, since we have nothing. Thread. With any luck, some cloth. We don't even have a scrap for a bandage. And quinine. Poor Fanny is coming down with a fever, I think."

"You'll never get quinine." Emma was positive. "It's worth as much as gold these days."

Miriam did not say that she still had the few pieces of gold sewn into her dress. She said only, "We'll try. Come along, then, Papa, if you're coming."

Ruts where successive armies had torn along the road were so deep and crooked that the horse had to zigzag and weave; its hooves sucked up the mud of the autumn rains. In a ditch lay a mule's carcass being ravaged by buzzards; their naked black wrinkled heads buried themselves voraciously in the dead flesh. Through long stretches of abandoned countryside no other living thing, human or animal, was to be seen. Weeds stood tall in vacant fields. Trampled corn lay rotting. Only here and there was there a house fortunate enough, like Beau Jardin, to have been left standing.

This ruination silenced father and daughter. The
sound, even of low voices, would have been too loud.
As the least noise in an empty, dark house is eerie, so
it was in this gray, empty land. Miriam glanced at
Ferdinand's pistol, which lay on the seat between
them. She had objected to it, but probably he had been
right to take it.

"Can't be much farther," he said at last.

"About a mile more after the hill at the crossroads.
He used to keep a good stock, I remember."

Her fingers felt the lump of the six coins at her
waist. They had the shape and thickness of lozenges,
and just as lozenges hold the expectation of flavor and
juice, so did these hold a rich expectation.

"Place looks empty," Ferdinand said.

At the foot of the incline stood a small building of
unpainted board, surrounded by a yard and a couple
of sheds. Now the horse, relieved of effort, quickened
into an easy trot downhill and turned into the yard.
Here, too, was a heavy stillness, as though a dome had
lowered and enclosed the site. There was no one to be
seen. The door was wide open.

Ferdinand forced a hello. "Is anyone here? No one
here?"

Balls of gray dust ran like mice over the floor. Every
shelf and counter was bare. Not a box, not a piece of
twine or scrap of paper, were left to indicate that there
ever had been anything on these shelves and counters.

"He's left," Miriam said disconsolately. "Given up
and left or gone to the army."

Suddenly from the yard came a screech and
squawk. Jolted to the alert, they turned about to see a
young hound chasing a scrawny solitary hen, which,
flapping and bouncing, managed just in time to obtain
a perch above his reach.

"Has to be somebody here," said Ferdinand.

Around the corner of the shed there appeared a thin man, scrawny as the hen, and of no particular age. Removing his cap before Miriam, he spoke with a definite Scottish burr.

"You wanted something, did you?"

"Oh," she replied somewhat ruefully, "we wanted everything! Anything at all, and everything."

"They cleaned me out. Not that I had much to start with. Not Union troops, either. Scalawags. Women. I wouldn't have thought women could be so—begging your pardon, ma'am—women could be so savage. They had guns."

The sunken eyes made two dark holes in the grimy, unshaven face. One knew he had not spoken to another human being before now about this woe and disaster, and that he needed to express his anguish; out of compassion, courtesy, and the strength of the man's need, they heard him out.

"Said crazy things. That the shortages were my doing! That I had stuff hidden away waiting for higher prices! Likely you think so, too."

"No," Miriam said, and then on the off chance that this frantic creature might just have something hidden away, she added, "Although we have gold to pay."

"There, you see! You think so, too! But I have nothing! Nothing, I tell you! Everybody knows the South never had manufactured goods, everything came from the North, so how am I expected to have cloth or thread or medicines? Where would I get them out here in the middle of nowhere? Lucky they didn't kill me or burn the roof over my head."

Ferdinand said gently, "Of course, of course."

"We came from North Carolina. I'm a Scot, but my wife was born there. She had the rheumatism, and the winters got too much for her, so we came here, and she caught the fever instead. Died of it last year. And here I am. Here I am." The voice cracked and the arms flung themselves up toward the gray, indifferent sky. "Scalawags! Scalawags! Between them and the Jayhawkers, what's the choice? Attacking me, who never owned a slave in my life! I had all I could do to feed ourselves. Myself."

As delicately as they could, they retreated, followed by his voice which floated after them halfway up the hill.

"Cleaned me out, they did! Cleaned me out!"

Now, after this, the stillness on the homeward journey seemed more foreboding. The tired horse moved slowly. Ferdinand let the reins dangle from one hand, while his other rested where the pistol gleamed dully on the seat.

Once he looked over at Miriam, saying with a failed attempt at good humor, "It's a long time since I held reins in my hands. It reminds me of the old days, only in those days my wagon was full, and I wasn't afraid of anything."

Miriam had no answer. Her eyes, alert and quick, darted and scanned every line of trees; they reached down the road ahead and the road behind as she turned to look back.

A burnt-out mansion lay wrecked at the end of a long alley of chestnut trees. Its chimneys at this distance were a pair of gaunt giants, a threatening apparition in the wilderness.

"The Johnson Hicks place," Ferdinand observed, stating the obvious.

"They fled by our house that morning. I wonder where they went."

"Can't imagine where."

The silence thickened like fog. The horse's hooves went whispering now, as the track turned sandy. And enveloped again by the silence, they rode on steadily, tensed and without being aware of it, leaning forward with the motion of the horse as if to hasten him home.

Out of the underbrush a woman thrust herself, with the force of a hurled stone, into the road. The horse's neigh blared his terror, as though he had seen a snake, but before he could gather himself into a gallop, the woman jerked the reins at his mouth and pulled him to a stop.

She lowered a rifle toward Ferdinand and Miriam. Ferdinand rose in his seat.

"What the devil do you want?" he cried.

"What do you think I want? Money."

Ferdinand groped for the pistol. He had never fired one in his life, and certainly Miriam had not; they were no match for this attacker. And Miriam slid the pistol out of reach.

Ferdinand, as though he were not taking the threat seriously, sputtered. "Scalawags! Jayhawkers! Decent citizens can't even travel the roads—"

Miriam cried sharp warning. "Papa! No!" She lowered her voice, struggling to keep it even. "We have no money. We'd like to have some, too."

The woman came closer. The rifle was an extension of her skinny arm and her ragged sleeve. With them it lifted and trembled.

Now Miriam's heart shook under her ribs.

"I'd be obliged if you'd point that thing away from us. If you kill us, you'll surely get nothing."

"You went to the store. You must have money."

"We passed the store. It was empty. As empty as our house."

Under the poke bonnet was a young face, sunken and toothless. The blue eyes were mad.

"I know you," Miriam said in sudden recognition. "You used to come for food before the war when my husband was alive. We always gave it to you."

"Why not? You had more than you needed."

"That's true. But we surely don't have it now. Between the two armies we've had to go without."

"Time you knew how, then. You and your niggers that keep good men from getting work. You and your fancy children that never knew hunger."

Miriam wondered, looking at this woman probably no older than herself, standing there holding that gun in desperation, how a woman like herself must have appeared in those times of splendid pride, riding behind her coachman, holding not a gun, but a ruffled parasol.

"Maybe it is time," she said. "But killing me isn't going to feed your children."

The gun was lowered. Not far away in the swamps those pinch-faced, ragged children must be hiding from the southern draft with their father.

The suspicious, mad eyes searched the empty carriage.

"Killing you mightn't, but burning your house down might smoke out what you've got hidden away in it."

Just don't let her find these coins, Miriam thought. These I must hold on to. Without them I should be totally helpless in the world.

"Listen," she said. "Do you think I want your children to starve? I'm a woman, a mother. If you need some potatoes and meal, come to our place, come in peace, and I'll give you some." A surge of courage strengthened her voice and straightened her posture. "But I warn you, if you come to steal or burn, I will report your husband and all his friends to the Confederate authorities. And if you send your men to steal or burn, I'll have them shot. Do you understand me?"

"I'll come this evening. No tricks, now. If I don't

come back safely, my hus—some others will come and make you pay."

"You will go back safely. With food. Come tonight."

The woman moved back into the underbrush; it closed behind her without a mark. Ferdinand began to whip the horse into a gallop.

"No, Papa. Slow down to a walk. Don't show any fear, that's the worst thing you can do."

By the time they reached their lane, Miriam's momentary courage had passed, and she was shaking from the encounter.

A semicircle of expectant faces waited for them in the house.

"We've brought nothing. The man in the store had nothing."

"Oh, he must have had!" Eulalie's mouth was bitter with disappointment. "You probably didn't offer him enough. They always keep their goods hidden, that sort, they always do."

Miriam's nerves were as sore as though they had been scraped. She almost shouted.

"Who does? What sort do you mean?"

"We don't need to go into that," replied Eulalie, slicing each word carefully as one slices a thin loaf.

Miriam followed her out of the room, caught up with her in the hall, and grasped her elbow.

"I think we do need to go into it. Here and now. Of course I know what you meant about the storekeeper. Jews, you meant."

"Well, if I did, I'm not the only one who means it."

Miriam was almost breathless, tasting blood in her own mouth. "For your information, the storekeeper is a Scotsman. Now, listen, Eulalie, there's no sense going on like this. We're both here with no other place to go. I've got a son and a daughter, to say nothing of my father and your mother, neither of whom is any use at all." And as Eulalie's mouth opened in astonishment, Miriam countered: "Well, it's the truth, isn't it? I love them, but they're helpless. Facts are facts, and this surely is a time to face them, if ever there was one. So you see, there's enough to do around here, and it would be a whole lot easier to do it if we could keep our feelings buried. I don't like you, and you don't like me. You despise Jews, and you're shocked at what you call my sin."

"Oh, dear Heaven," Emma interjected tearfully from the doorway. "This is terrible, everything falling apart! I don't know what you could have said, Eulalie, but it's all so ugly. Everything is so ugly. I've tried, God knows I've tried, to bear up under one blow after the other. But is there no end to it? Can't we at least try to live in peace? I never thought I would live through such times."

Poor Emma! It was too late for her. She was too old. Her best years had been lived in a sunny garden.

"It's all right, Aunt Emma," Miriam said. She patted the quivering shoulders. "It's just talk. We're all overwrought. I know I am, and no wonder. It's been a horrible day. But it's all right. Now I'm going outside for a while to see Simeon at the barn."

When she came back Eulalie was in the dining room cutting the rug with a pair of long shears. Pelagie was horrified.

"An Aubusson! Eugene's fine Aubusson cut up for blankets! What can you be thinking of?"

"Eulalie is right," Miriam said calmly. "The nights are very cold and we have no blankets."

She was half out of the room again before Eulalie spoke. She did not look at Miriam.

"Your maid Fanny. You said she's sick. I have some blackberry root cordial. It might relieve her trouble."

"Why, that's kind, Eulalie. I thank you."

"Eulalie," Emma cried, "have you remembered to give Miriam her letter?"

"I forgot. I have it here." And Eulalie drew an envelope from her pocket.

"A man on horseback brought it while you were gone this morning," Emma said. "I hope it's not bad news."

Two crisp sheets rustled in Miriam's hands.

"It's from André, from Mr. Perrin—" At once she was silenced by the shock of the opening lines.

> Dear Miriam,
> I don't want to frighten you, but I must get straight to the point. Your brother is in a prison camp in Georgia. In quite the strangest way, among all the thousands there, I caught sight of him.

"Oh, call Papa! Papa, where are you? Listen! It says David is terribly ill . . . oh, dear God, desperately ill!"

She read aloud.

" 'But I am hoping that by the time you get this letter he will be on his way northward in a prisoner exchange. It is very hard to arrange, but I have been promised–'

"Papa! Imagine! André—Mr. Perrin—has probably got David out to a military hospital in Washington, he says. Oh, bless him for it! God bless his goodness!"

Ferdinand seemed not to have heard. His pallid face looked green, and he swallowed as though a large piece of food had lodged in his throat.

"He's been in Georgia, a terrible prison in Georgia."

Her eyes returned to the letter. This part she read silently.

> I shall be out of the country on personal business [What business? A divorce?] for quite a while. I would rather not tell you now what it is, except that when I come back to tell you there will be a smile on your face. Your smile is so lovely! But, through no fault of yours, it's been far too rare. Well, I intend to take care of that. We shall dance again, you will wear a ball gown, you will laugh and I shall love you. . . .

She felt the charm, the promise, of these beautiful hopeful words. Yet she had to know more about David and, speeding to the end, read aloud:

" 'My friends, the Douglas Hammonds, in Richmond, will help you and will have information about your brother.' "

She put the letter down. "Papa, I'll have to go. I'll have to get there!"

"It's impossible! You can't go. It's dangerous, it will take weeks, a month."

"I don't care. I'm going to Richmond. And from there to Washington, if David's really there. I don't know how I'll get there, but I will. God only knows what's happened to him!"

"Mama, don't," Angelique pleaded. Her face was so thin and white!

"You're afraid something will happen to me, too," Miriam said gently. "But it won't. I shall be very careful, I promise."

"You can't promise." Eugene corrected his mother. "How can you keep a bullet from striking through a train, or—"

"I know, I know. But tell me, Eugene, if, Heaven

forbid, it were Angelique who was ill and alone somewhere, wouldn't you go to her? Or she to you? Well,
then, this is the same! David and I . . ." Miriam's
voice quivered.

There they stood, solemn and fearful, these two, still
young enough to be in need of a mother. And there,
far off, lay David, if he were still alive.

"He cared for me," she said, "from the time I was
born. He was only a little boy, but so old for his years!
He saw our mother die, I have told you how that was,
how the looters and killers from the universities came
down upon us! Violence, always violence and war!"
Now it was her turn to plead. "Will you understand,
please? Will you try to understand why I must go?"

Ferdinand cleared his throat again. Eugene laid a
hand on Angelique's shoulder, a touching gesture
meant to give his mother the assurance that she could
depend on him. He had outgrown his clothes, so that
his narrow, knobby wrist was bare. His hand had outgrown the rest of him; it was callused and brown, a
large, manly hand attached to a still-childish wrist.
The sight of it made her want to cry.

There was a deep stillness in the room. Ravaged,
chilly, and comfortless as it was, it was still home.
Wherever her son and daughter were, there would be
home. She did not want to leave it, did not want to
undertake a long, hard journey. And still she knew
that nothing and no one could stop her from going.

Presently Rosa broke into the stillness.

"Will you try to learn something about my Henry
and about Gabriel, if you can?"

"And my boys?" added Pelagie.

"How will we manage this place while you're
gone?" Emma complained.

"You will have to manage until I come back. You
can. You will have to."

Slowly the train moved northward and eastward
into winter. Jolting over a crumbling roadbed and
shaky bridges, it moved seven or eight miles farther
with each passing hour. Occasionally it halted in the
middle of a desolate landscape, assailed by a fierce, icy
rain, and Miriam's eyes, bloodshot and strained from
the dust that sifted through the broken windows,
could observe the life of the countryside: overladen
wagons, the mules up to their bellies in mud; and cattle lashed as fast as they could be driven; and a farm
family sitting on a pile of ramshackle furniture, the
mother holding a baby, the littlest daughter holding a
struggling cat.

Women; always women, she thought. How many
widows would there be when this war ended?

She sighed, murmuring aloud, "One could almost
walk faster to Richmond," and hugging herself against
the clinging cold, sank deeper into the folds of her
shawl.

An old man and an old woman, strangers to one
another, had struck up a conversation some time before. The old man gave out scraps of information.

"Look at those half-starved cows! They'll be the last
meat the army will be eating, I'm thinking. I hear
most of the troops only have one day's bread supply at
a time."

The woman, who wore a widow's cap, clucked for
the tenth time in dismay.

"I hear," the man went on, "the Cabinet in Richmond is debating whether to melt down some of these
locomotives for cannon."

The woman stopped clucking, apparently too discouraged by his dismal enumeration to respond. Leaning across the aisle, she caught Miriam's attention just
as the train, with a shattering jolt, began to move.

"You going all the way to Richmond?" And, as Miriam nodded, she said, "The city's jammed, they tell me. One can hardly find shelter. Even the worst dirty room costs as much as a night in a palace."

"I have friends to stay with—or friends of a friend, I should say."

"Lucky for you, then. It's terrible, my cousin wrote me that people are trading their valuables, wedding rings, anything, right out on the street for cow-peas or rice." And like the old man whom she had just shunned, she recited her own litany. "My cousin says eggs are five dollars a dozen, if you can get them. And butter five dollars a pound. For us on the farm it's not been that bad. I've managed to keep a few hens, so we've had eggs, at least. But medicines, no. My cousin says quinine costs a hundred fifty dollars an ounce. Her baby died for lack of it. Sinful, that's what I call it. Sinful."

Miriam nodded again, and turning her head toward the window with eyes half closed, pretended to need sleep. The landscape, drear as it was with the rain blowing and the trees lifting bare old arms toward the iron-gray sky, was not as gloomy as the talk inside the car.

The train crawled north.

"You must be frozen, poor dear," said Mrs. Hammond. "You know, this is the worst cold in our history."

A genial fire crackled in the guest bedroom. Miriam, sitting close to it in a Queen Anne wing chair, held her blue hands out to the heat.

In spite of the gracious hospitality which these strangers were showing to her, she was stiff with embarrassment. Her traveling dress, shabby to begin with, was now stained and wrinkled from the journey;

it was beyond respectability. Once she would not have considered it nearly decent enough to give to a servant. She recalled the piles of good clothing which used to be collected for the servants in her father's house, and later on, in her own. Her mind traveled back to those long-ago houses, where fires had burned in every room and silver had been polished, and the gold damask draperies had hung in folds.

Her mind traveled farther, too, back to the meager home of her childhood.

She summoned herself to the moment and to the hostess, who was waiting for a response.

"Such a lovely house, Mrs. Hammond! And you are so very kind to have me here."

"It's a real pleasure to have you. Mr. Perrin has told us how charming you are, and I see that he did not exaggerate."

"I'm afraid I'm not very charming today. I feel rather unsightly."

"Not at all. You've come a long way under dreadful conditions. I'm sure you would like a hot bath before dinner."

"That would be wonderful." Miriam hesitated. "You dress for dinner?"

A stupid question! In a house like this, of course one dressed for dinner.

"As a matter of fact, tonight is rather a special night, my husband's birthday. We're having a little group of old friends." Mrs. Hammond sighed. "A very little group, unhappily, with so many of our men away. Now, please don't be shy, my dear. I understand quite well that you're not supplied with evening gowns. May I lend you one?"

"If I'm to be presentable downstairs, I shall have to say yes, I'm afraid."

"Of course. We are just about the same size. I'll go

send my maid Lettie with bath water and a dress. Let me see your feet. Yes, slippers, too. If they should be a little large for you, I'm sure you'll manage and no one will notice."

Miriam laid her head against the back of the chair. Left alone, she could have sunk right there into a long, grateful sleep. The room was warm and quiet. Light twinkled on the brass fender and on a photograph in a silver frame. It lay across the polished floor and on the great mahogany chest. The windows and the four-poster were hung in a sprightly red-and-white toile, on which a pattern of trees, leaping deer, and castle turrets repeated itself in framed medallions of twining vines. Across the foot of the bed a rosy silk quilt lay folded, promising a light, blissful warmth through the coming night.

And she thought how delightful these comforts could be, how lovely the quiet, orderly life with no intrusion of politics.

These thoughts were still soothing her spirit when the door opened and the maid came in bearing in turn bath water, lavender soap, warm towels, and a dressing gown.

"Mrs. Hammond says I'm to do your hair for you," she said when Miriam had bathed. "One minute, I'll bring your dress."

The dress, evidently quite new, had a French label. Miriam stroked the bottle-green velvet skirt and the white lace bertha.

"I didn't know anyone had dresses from France anymore, Lettie."

Lettie's strong arm pulled the brush through Miriam's hair, drawing sparks.

"Why, all the ladies get their dresses from France," she replied, as if that should be common knowledge.

"It's not what I expected. I heard that things were so terrible in Richmond."

"Wait till you go out into the streets. You'll see how terrible they are. People are starving. They have to burn their furniture to keep warm. The soldiers' wives are the poorest, they get the wages, but the money buys less every day. Doesn't buy anything anymore."

How odd to hear a black slave give sympathy to a poor white! Everything was upside down and inside out.

The dining room glittered. Many of the men were in uniform. The others wore proper evening attire, and the women were splendid. Grateful for the velvet dress, Miriam thought she had never seen, even at the opera at home, so many diamond parures and lavalieres. But then, probably she had forgotten. It had been so long.

She was unused to crowds of strangers, too. Half humorously, she compared herself with a farm wife on her first visit to the city, gaping and marveling at the five-story buildings, the carriages and crowded sidewalks. Yet everyone was friendly, making an effort to show southern courtesy, inquiring about her family and events in Louisiana. There were young faces and old ones around the long table, round Irish faces, two or three Jewish faces, and many that belonged to the oldest families in the city. What they all had in common was the handsome look of wealth. And this continued to astonish Miriam. Here in this high room with dozens of candles flaring, with champagne chilling in ice-filled buckets, oysters roasting on the hearth, crystal without a flaw and damask without a crease, it seemed as if the war did not exist.

Wild ducks, turkey, puddings, molds, and ices were passed and repassed on their silver platters.

"My goodness," a lady remarked, "the price of turkey is incredible. Thirty dollars! Who ever heard of such a thing?"

"Turkey!" someone said. "What about champagne? I paid one hundred fifty dollars a bottle for it last week. Heaven only knows what it will be next week."

"I want you to know," the host announced, "that the champagne we are drinking tonight is a gift from our friend. From André, of course. A generous friend to us all. And of yours, too," he added, bowing to Miriam.

She hoped that the hot color which rose at once would be attributed to the fireplace and the wine.

"He is a good friend of my family's, yes indeed." When this seemed to arouse no curiosity, she grew bolder. "He is in Europe, he wrote to us. I wonder when he will be back."

Mr. Hammond shrugged. "One never knows. He doesn't tell and we don't ask."

She felt rebuked. Possibly there was no reason why she should feel so; nevertheless, she did. Discomfited now, she resigned herself to listening. And she tried to isolate some common thread in the animated conversations that were passing around and across the table. What she heard was a mixture of cynicism and bravado.

"What's a planter, for instance, to do if the war should ruin him? There's nothing else he knows how to do but be a planter. 'Go to work,' they say. What work? He's never really worked in his life."

Yes, they have forgotten how, Miriam reflected. Their ancestors worked! She remembered Aunt Emma's description of her great-grandparents' first humble farm on the German coast: the cabin and the sparse acres. That had been the beginning, but that was long generations past.

"They say the Virginia legislature is going to request Davis and the entire Cabinet except Trenholm to resign. You know, it's a disgrace! The generals telegraph for reinforcements and artillery, but they get nothing from the Virginia government."

"They get nothing because there is nothing."

"Nonsense! I don't believe it. That's newspaper talk. They ought to stop attacking the Confederate government once and for all. By God, they're giving more aid to the enemy than the northern papers are."

"They aren't the only ones who are giving aid to the enemy."

Raised, disapproving eyebrows followed this sally, and from someone at the end of the table came quickly stifled, knowing laughter. It occurred to Miriam that one of these people's own community might have been caught out. There had been talk about women in the highest circles of Richmond society who were working for the Union; perhaps one of them in this room now.

Suddenly she was very tired and wished it were time to go to bed.

On Miriam's left a man was saying to someone, "I heard he made fifty thousand dollars a month running the blockade. He did in the beginning, anyway."

"Well, he won't do it much longer. That's all over. No more French wines. No more anything from Europe. So drink up now."

"I'm not worried. We'll get what we want from Baltimore, that's all."

Who made fifty thousand dollars a month? She had not caught the name. And was this what had been coming through the blockade? Champagne and velvet dresses—with quinine costing a hundred fifty dollars an ounce?

Now the man on Miriam's right spoke across the table. "Money will soon be worthless."

And someone answered, "So one might as well spend it."

Soon everyone went from the dining room to the music room. There, on all four walls, hung the usual fashionable gilt-framed mirrors, so that one saw oneself from every angle. Miriam's face had gone pale. The pink flush of the earlier evening had ebbed, leaving dark stains under her eyes. She looked alien among these vivacious people who were gathered at the piano singing and playing. "Annie Laurie," "Listen to the Mockingbird," and "Juanita," they sang. "My Maryland" stirred them to applause and brought everyone to his feet. Miriam stood with the rest, but she was hardly there. She had drifted away into some vague space where memories merged, where father and brother merged with Eugene, with Gabriel and André and colliding armies.

"You're very thoughtful," said her host, leaning over her chair.

"I'm sorry. I'm not good company. I've been thinking." She hesitated in this room among these people to speak of David, a soldier in the Union army. And yet was he not the reason for her being in Richmond? And did this man not know it was? "I've been thinking about my brother."

"Of course you have. I had meant to tell you in the morning, but since you mention him, I can tell you now. Everything has been arranged. You will see him at the military hospital in Washington. Your pass should be ready in a day or two."

In her fragile state this solicitude touched her almost to tears.

"How?" she asked innocently. "How have you managed to do this wonderful thing for me?"

The man was amused. "Dear lady," he said kindly, "nothing is impossible as long as one knows the right people. And André Perrin knows them. It's he whom you should thank, not me."

The most striking aspect of the streets, as Miriam went wandering through the city the next morning, was the number of wounded men. It was a city of wounded men. They limped on crutches. They walked with bloody bandages on hands, arms, and faces. Wagons bore them through the streets and stood before the door of the St. Charles Hotel, waiting until room could be found on the bare floor for yet another load.

Other wagons bore them away in coffins.

A woman stopped her, begging for a coin to buy milk.

"I know a place where they have some," she pleaded. "There hasn't been any in a week, and besides I didn't have the money."

Miriam gave her a coin. She walked on. Desperation hung overhead like fog; it had fog's clammy feel. A woman ran past in frantic haste, pulling a dirty, wailing child. Two boys fought each other to the ground over a bag of peas, which spilled on the sidewalk while they struggled. A cat whose every bone stuck out under its skimpy, worn fur stiffened and died before her eyes. She walked on.

A jeweler's window held a display of rubies: brooches, bracelets, and necklaces on black velvet cushions. Drawn to their deep glow, she stood there for a moment, when behind her back she heard what could only be described as a squeal.

"Oh, what a dazzle! Tell me, have you ever seen such rubies? Have you?"

The girl clung to the officer's arm. She was a handsome girl and he was a handsome man, twice her age. They looked confident. They looked like lovers. They went into the shop.

Farther on Miriam passed a display of landscape paintings, a shipment of French antiques, and a window full of imported lace. In front of a bookstore Miriam stopped. She had not bought a book in so long! They had once been a necessity for her. Here now was Blackwood's *Edinburgh Magazine,* an old favorite. And look here! *Les Misérables,* in French. Her fingers sought the lump of coins in her dress, a lump grown smaller since the start of her journey. But still, she thought, arguing with herself, enough for a book. She went inside.

Bookstore owners were usually old men, friendly and, naturally, bespectacled. This one was no exception. Watching him wrap *Les Misérables,* she felt a familiar pleasure and a desire to make conversation.

"Tell me, I see all these wonderful shops, so many beautiful, expensive things. And then all the wounded, and so many beggars. It makes you wonder . . ."

The old man gave a bitter laugh.

"It is 'why' that you're asking me? Why? I'll ask you: Was it ever any different in any war?"

"I don't know. I don't know enough history to answer."

"I'll answer, then. No, it was never any different."

"Why do they allow it? I saw a man buying rubies just now. And a shipment of French antiques just arrived. Is that what the ships are bringing in? Not food? Not medicines?"

"Oh, certainly the Congress has forbidden the importation of luxuries, but they come through all the same. There are always people to bring them and more to buy them."

Slowly, Miriam returned to the Hammond house carrying her book. Suddenly she was ashamed of it, as those people ought to have been ashamed who were buying rubies. The little sum that the book had cost might better have gone to some hungry child on the street. And she was tempted to return it, but thought then that the bookseller seemed to be rather in need, too.

"There's a wonderful theatrical tonight, *The Rivals,*" Mrs. Hammond said when Miriam came in. "And after that a supper at the Lloyds'. They've such a delightful house! Of course, you're invited."

"I thank you," Miriam told her, "but will you accept my regrets this time?"

"I do hope you're not worried about a dress. Is that the reason? Because there's no trouble about that," the woman said generously. "I have a satin, a taffeta, or a brocade to lend. You choose."

"No, no, you're so kind. It's just that I'm very tired, quite overcome."

"I understand. That journey must really have worn you out."

But it was not the journey. It was not the strong, still-young body which had been overcome—but rather the troubled spirit.

On the following day the pass arrived. She turned it over in her hand, this miraculous, flimsy slip of paper that permitted her to see her David again.

Allow the bearer, Miriam Mendes, to pass our lines and go north and return.

They said: "All you need to do is to know the right people, and André Perrin knows them."

30

The loss of his teeth had altered David's face, giving him at certain angles the sunken features of an old man. So thin was he that his cheeks sloped inward, and Miriam supposed, trying not to look too searchingly to reveal her pity and shock, that when he had first come to the hospital, their color must have been gray. A faint bloom now touched this meager flesh; the eyes were clear, so strength, she saw, must be on the slow return.

It was a mild day of thaw. All the benches which had been set out on the hospital's wintry lawn were occupied. Over the pale, soggy grass, the Stars and Stripes drooped from the pole in windless air. A steady dripping, like the tick of a metronome, came from the trees, and the weak sun was pleasant, falling like a benison upon this reunion.

"You're thinking I look like a skeleton. I'll look a lot better when I get some teeth," David said. "You ought to have seen me three months ago. No, I'm thankful you didn't."

She pressed his hand. "I'm just thankful you're alive."

"Yes, and to think I owe my life to André Perrin! A man I scarcely knew! When I saw him that day, you know, I'm sure I was running a high fever. I wasn't entirely sure I understood what was real and what I was dreaming. At the same time I felt it was real. It's hard to describe." He frowned with the effort of recollection. "Yes, when I saw that man, I knew—I knew I'd seen him somewhere before! He must have made a strong impression on me that first time, don't you think?" And in puzzlement, he shook his head. "One sees so many passing faces in a lifetime! Why should I have remembered his?"

She could have said, but did not, Because his is an extraordinary face; one remembers it as one remembers the flash and fire of an extraordinary jewel at a stranger's throat. Because he is ardent and vivid and never tired. . . .

Then, still showing that perplexed expression, David asked, "Why should the man have gone to so much effort for me? Just for me? That's what I don't understand."

She flushed. It angered her that she was never able to control this sore, red heat, which rose now from under her sleeves to flood past her collar and into her cheeks. David's sharp, curious look upset her further.

At last she murmured, "You don't know about André and me."

"Oh," he said. "Oh," and looked away, past Miriam to where other couples and families on other benches were revealing their own, their often secret, joys and griefs.

Then he brought his gaze back and focused it considerately, not upon his sister's face, but rather on her hands, which lay twisted nervously on her lap.

"So that was it! Of course, you were not well married. . . . Yet I always had a feeling that there was something else, too. I even asked you about it more than once, do you remember? But you would never tell me."

"Are you angry?"

"Angry? I've no right to say whom you should love or hate. I don't even know the man. To me he's only the man who saved my life. What can you say about someone who saves your life? Still, I should like to see him face to face." He looked up then with his old smile—wise, curious, and gentle. "Tell me, what *is* he like?"

Why should it be so difficult to find words for something which had so long filled every private recess of her mind? She could only stumble.

"He is . . . the way it is . . . he loves me. I am . . . was . . . happy with him."

And with the thought that David might be imagining what she had meant by "happy," the bed in the white room so long ago, so long—came a second rise of blood, burning her face.

"Tell me about him," David said again.

His kindly insistence made it rather easier to answer now.

"I should like to do him justice. . . . Well, to begin with, he's so very generous! He likes to be generous, as you see by what he's done for you. There's a softness, a gentleness, even in the way he speaks. . . . You feel cheerful when you're with him, glad to be alive! To wake up in the morning and know you're going to see him that day . . ." She clasped her hands in a passionate gesture. "It was so different, such a change for me, David, you can't know! To be so loved and praised! Do you understand?"

"I do, my dear. I do."

"I feel so much better," Miriam said earnestly, "now that you know! It's troubled me to have kept such an important secret from you."

David looked thoughtful, his forehead wrinkling into worry lines. But he spoke quietly, asking only,

"What is to happen? What are you going to do? You will have to do something, one way or the other."

"We were hoping, we were thinking—André thinks perhaps Marie Claire will want a divorce."

"It's an odd coincidence: Her name was mentioned to me some time ago. Some doctor I met had heard her in recital in Paris. He said she was making a name, she was glorious."

"Whatever brought up the subject?"

"He knew I'd lived in New Orleans and he asked, the way people always do, whether I happened to know this one or that one in the city, and then he mentioned this remarkable singer."

So Marie Claire, that odd, reclusive little person with the ambition that had always seemed much too large for her, had after all been right about herself! Miriam felt suddenly a singular admiration, a new respect, for the woman with whom her own life had been so peculiarly entwined.

"I can still see her quite clearly, although I never really knew her that well. She's clearer to me than the girls whom I sat with every day in school. She seemed so dull, and yet there was all that ambition inside."

"The outside and the inside are two different things," David said somberly. "One should remember that. . . . As for me," he said then, changing the subject with some abruptness, "the face I see is Pelagie's. I can't get out of my mind the way she must have looked when they told her Sylvain was dead, and how he died." He broke off. "How is Pelagie?"

"She's with us, as I told you. Holding together. Women usually do, don't they? Even the timid ones stand up after a while when they have to. It was horrible. They lost everything, that grand house, a treasure house, gone up in smoke. Even so," she said, "one should be ashamed to speak of houses and things after what you have been through. And all these men," she finished, lowering her voice as a man was carried past on a stretcher.

"You've had more than your share, too. The way Eugene died—he didn't deserve an end like that, either."

"That's true, he did not," Miriam said quietly.

They were still a moment.

Then David asked, "And Papa?"

"Papa's all right. I don't think he still quite believes what's happened to his promised land."

She looked away over the grass where a flock of pigeons were pecking bread crumbs at the feet of a soldier in a wheelchair. In Richmond, she remembered suddenly, they had told her there were no more pigeons in the parks; they had all been eaten.

"I haven't asked about the most important people of all, my twins. You know, I think about them all the time. I think, no matter how long I live or what work I may do, bringing them into the world will still be my triumph."

"Oh, Angelique is going to be beautiful! Sometimes I imagine she must look like our mother, she doesn't look like either me or Eugene. And my boy—oh, I am so afraid, if this war goes on any longer, they will take him."

"It won't go on much longer. It's almost over." And David said fiercely, "I think if I'd known what war really is, I'd have left things alone."

Miriam smiled. "You wouldn't have."

"Tell me, do you know anything about Gabriel?"

"No one's heard in almost a year. We don't know whether he's dead or alive. Rosa asked me to try to find out something in Richmond. They all want me to look for their men, for Rosa's Henry, too, and Pelagie's boys. But it's like looking for needles in a hay-stack."

"Perhaps not quite that hopeless. There have been prisoner exchanges lately. When you go back to Richmond, you might inquire at the War Department. Do you know which outfit he was in?"

He did not have to say he meant Gabriel. Gabriel was the one he would care about.

"The Tenth Louisiana."

The air had smelled of heat and dust, the day the Tenth Louisiana left. The delirium of noise had pounded in her head: the brass band and shrieking children, drunken laughter, weeping and clinging. He stood on the step as the train began to move. He had raised his arm in good-bye to the group, but his eyes had been on her. She could still see him distinctly.

"He hated the whole idea of fighting," she said. "And he didn't have to go. He could have stayed in the government. Yet he went. I don't understand it."

"Of course you understand! It's not that difficult. He always had his convictions, he acted on them, and I love him for that. I only hope that if he is a prisoner, he's in a better place than I was in, that at least they might have medicine and morphia for the dying." The vision of what he had lived through must have come flaring back, for David's face darkened in a grimace of pain.

The mention of medicines brought something to mind.

"The other night at dinner in Richmond they were talking about women, visitors like me, bringing medicines back under their dresses. It's dangerous, the Federals search you, but still some get away with it. So I was thinking that I—"

"What?" David interrupted. "You smuggling for the Confederacy? My sister, become a Rebel?"

"Do you know," she replied indignantly, "that fully a third of the men in the Confederate army are not slave owners at all? Why, even Gabriel—I don't know what makes you say such a thing."

"Come, I'm only teasing you. I'm well aware everything's all mixed up. Rabbi Raphall's son—remember Rabbi Raphall?—well, his son joined the Union army! Lost an arm at Gettysburg, too. Tell me, are you serious about"—he whispered—"about taking some medicines back?"

"I am."

David whistled. "It's very, very dangerous, Miriam."

She wanted to do it. She felt a need, a reckless one, perhaps, to take some risk, to have a part, however small, in correcting the overwhelming chaos of the war.

"Usually a lady sews the package in her bishop," she said thoughtfully.

"Her what?"

"Bishop. The little silk pillow that goes in back of your belt under your dress. It lifts up your petticoats."

"I can manage easily enough to get stuff out of the pharmacy, but it's dangerous," he repeated.

"I know. I've heard they stick a pin into the bishop to see whether anything is concealed. So I thought before I go back I could get myself a hat all heaped with flowers, and I'd hide it there. Oh," she cried, "if you could see what it's like in Richmond! So starved, so sick. I keep seeing the woman who asked for money to buy milk. And the wounded lying on the dirty, cold floor of the hotel. What do words mean then? 'Enemy.' 'States rights.' 'Contraband.' They don't mean a thing. Not to me."

" 'She reaches forth her hands to the needy,' " David said, and smiled and kissed her.

There were riots in Richmond. Hungry women, infuriated by the lavish displays which had so troubled Miriam, had now armed themselves with axes, and in desperation, had gone on a round of window-smashing so wild that only the government's threat to call soldiers out had scattered them.

Other crowds of women, consumed by another kind of desperation, had gone searching for sons and husbands among the ranks of prisoners in the last exchange.

"They brought a group in while you were away," Mr. Hammond told Miriam. "Came from Elmira by train, then took ship in Baltimore. It was a tragic outrage. They told me that even the Federal doctors were shocked that so many were in such terrible condition. On top of that they were seasick on the way south."

"There are so many thousands, I know that," Miriam said, "but just on the off chance, I thought I would inquire at the War Office. There might be a way, my brother said, of finding out whether some of the men I'm to search for have been brought back."

"No need for you to go. I'm there every day, and I know whom to ask. Just give me the names."

And, indeed, that same evening Mr. Hammond had news.

"I found one. Gabriel Carvalho. He's not in the hospital. He's apparently not sick. They've put him up in a boardinghouse. I've the address here."

He was thin, but he was whole. They had already given him a new uniform; its smartness contrasted sadly to the neglected, shabby room. Here, in a once prosperous home from which gentility had long vanished, the two sat facing an unwashed window which overlooked a grimy alley and a yard full of wet, rotting weeds.

"You're smiling," Gabriel said.

For some reason or other the image of Rosa's Belter parlor with its gold Napoleonic bees flying on blue satin had come to Miriam's mind. And the irony of that memory appearing to her in this place had brought a wan flicker to the corners of her mouth.

"I was remembering Rosa's parlor where we used to go over the accounts. And now here we are!"

"Her last letter—that was more than a year ago—was full of your goodness to her."

"She'll want to know more about you when I go back. You haven't told me very much yet."

He gave a little shrug, as if to deprecate his sufferings.

"There's not much more to tell. My wound healed and I survived Elmira. So many died there, one out of three, that I could almost feel guilty over being alive. One out of four had scurvy. Rats, cold, smallpox, the filth—but what's the use of telling Rosa all of that?"

"She'll ask me."

So, in the flat voice that conceals unbearable emotion, Gabriel continued.

"We got two meals a day. Wormy crackers and coffee for breakfast. A cup of bean soup and more crackers for supper. You know, I believe when the final tally is made, they're going to find that more men died in this war from sickness than on the battlefield. I do believe that."

"It sounds like what David went through in Georgia, except that there it was the heat. Perhaps that was even worse, I don't know."

"Neither side has a monopoly on cruelty. Thank God he got out before it was too late. Got out with all

his convictions intact, I'm sure," Gabriel added
fondly.

For some reason, not knowing even at the moment
of telling why or whether she ought to, she told him,
"You know it was André Perrin who did that for
David. It was a special feat, because there was no prisoner exchange going on then at all."

For a moment she thought he had not heard. She
followed his gaze. A military funeral was passing on
the street below. The riderless horse, with stirrups reversed, paced slowly to the sound of grave and muted
drums. Gabriel watched it as far as the corner. Then
he looked back at Miriam.

"A man of influence. Very fortunate for David."

The comment surely was a rebuke. She had made a
stupid, unforgivable mistake in mentioning André. A
cruel mistake. She had ruined the visit. And she
thought, I wish I could talk my heart out to him. Yet
she was not even sure what she would say if this inhi-
bition were to be removed. One knew this man, yet
always there was a distance, a space around him that
kept one away. Or was it only she whom he kept
away? What would she find if he were to open the
door, so to speak, and let her in?

Then at once she answered her own question: Of
course, he had long ago opened the door. She was the
one who had shut it again, so what could she expect of
him? And now she had reminded him so bluntly of
André, of the other—but then came the reply to *that*:
It is better to be honest. Gabriel is the first to want you
to be honest.

He said formally, "You're looking well in spite of
everything."

She regarded her chapped, uncared-for hands and
the scuffed toes of her homemade shoes, just visible
beneath her skirt.

"It's Mrs. Hammond's dress that improves me."

"Hammond? That's where you're staying?"

"Oh, yes, they've been so hospitable. It's as if they'd just turned time back in that house." She chattered nervously. "Everything is the way it used to be, they've anything you want to eat, and such cheerful gaiety, you can't imagine."

"Oh, yes, I can, very well," Gabriel said.

"Well, but if people like them have all that fresh meat and—and other things, why aren't there more of all those in the stores?"

"Very simple. Because it's more profitable to bring in liquor and imported luxuries."

The champagne tonight is a gift of André Perrin.

But no, there had to be something else. A trickle of inexplicable fear ran through Miriam, and she shook her head, as if to shake the fear away.

Gabriel stood up. He had grown older. There were two lines between nose and mouth which she did not remember having seen before; she supposed they would fill out whenever he was able to eat well again. But he was still the impressive man, detached and correct, that she remembered.

"You'll be home in time for Passover, I suppose," Gabriel said. He was making conversation, as if he had become aware of the cool atmosphere in the room and were making proper amends.

"Yes, between Rosa and myself, we'll try to have what holiday we can."

"I thought about it last year in Elmira. When you're hungry, you remember holidays, the way the table is set, and even the smell of the food. Two years ago we were in West Virginia fighting in the mountains. We got eggs and some chickens from a farmer and cooked them outside over a fire. General Lee sent matzoh and prayer books by a supply train; we rode thirty miles to the depot to pick them up. A great, good man, Lee. A tragic man, divided in his soul. I understand why."

The short afternoon was going. A misty twilight crept into the room, covering the stains on the carpet. And into this fading day Gabriel's voice melted; again he had retreated into himself, as if he were speaking to himself, not caring whether she heard or wanted to hear what he was saying.

"Yes, I understand. There is such loveliness here in our southern land! The pine hills, the gentle rivers, the way spring comes. The old houses and the sweet ways. It's been ours for two hundred years. How can a man turn his back on it? And yet—states rights are passé, I see that, too. There's to be a new age. One people."

"You believe that now?"

"Yes, yes I do."

"Then what are you going to do about it?"

"Do?" Gabriel repeated, not understanding.

"With yourself, I mean. Now. Next week."

"Next week? Why, I am going back to join my regiment," he said as if the question surprised him.

Miriam was more astonished. "After what you've just told me?"

"But of course. When you've set your hand to a thing, you finish it, don't you?"

"I don't know whether you do or not, Gabriel." A weight fell on her heart.

"But I know. There are times when one can turn away, but this isn't one of them."

She understood then. And she saw that this was a simple question of honor: one did not abandon a sinking ship. Honor. A little sigh came from her, without intention.

"Are you thinking this is some sort of theatrical grand gesture? I should be sorry if you were to think that of me."

"I could never think that of you. You are the last man of whom anyone could think that."

"I'm glad, then. You see, I went with Lee at the start, I gave my word. So now I'll stay and see what happens."

"You know what will happen."

She thought, If they kill you, what a waste it will be! To think that one bullet, one fraction of an instant, can destroy all that knowledge, all that quiet strength!

But she forced a little smile, thinking to take leave of him now with some smooth pleasantry, to end the visit in decent style.

For the second time that afternoon he asked her why she was smiling.

"Oh," she said, saying the first thing that came into her head, "I was thinking of Gretel."

"Which one?"

"Of both, I suppose. You gave them both to me, in a way. But this last one is an old lady. She sleeps most of the time. I hope she will still be alive when I reach home."

They had both stood up. Hesitating, they faced each other, caught in one of those uncertain moments of departure when neither wishes to appear abrupt.

"Gabriel. Tell me something. Tell me you're not too angry at me. I feel you're so far away! I don't want to leave you like this."

He went quite still, not merely quiet, but arrested, removed from the moment. And thinking that perhaps she had now really made him angry, she waited.

He put out his hand to touch hers, pressing lightly, withdrawing quickly.

"You're right. You've read me. I was locking myself away. But it's over now." And a compassionate expression of great beauty passed over his face.

"Will you tell my sister, please, that a letter will be

on the way? Now that I'm not a prisoner anymore, the mails should be more dependable."

"Do you know we have no writing paper? We turn old envelopes inside out and use the blank pages of books. But Rosa will find something to write on, you can be sure."

"And you? You have never written to me once since the war began."

It was true. Why hadn't she? Because of the memory that he loved her, and because of not knowing what to say.

"Why have you never written to me?" Gabriel persisted. "Was it because of André? Was it?"

"I don't know," she whispered, looking at the floor.

"You're still in love with him."

"Yes."

The sound of André's name caused a rush of feeling, painful and confused.

Only a few days ago, when she had been with David, she had had such a clear vision of André's bright face; in her mind's ear she had even heard his voice. Here, suddenly, all that had vanished; she could summon none of it back; all was vague and fearful. But why?

"I'm worrying you. I've no right. If you love him, that's the way it is. Forgive me. I only wanted to be sure in case there might be a chance for me . . ."

Before I die, he meant.

Without thinking, she laid her head on his shoulder. It was so comforting, this man's shoulder. His arms went around her and she felt his cheek against her head.

In her shyness, this strange shyness, she heard him say, twice—three times?—"Take care of yourself; be happy; I love you so. . . ."

She pulled away.

"Yes, go," he said quickly, "go home now."

"Home?"

"All the way home, I mean. Get out of Richmond. It may not be safe much longer. I want to know you're on the way home."

It had been no joining, but a touch; no, it had been more than a touch, more like a thing that happens in a dream, and like a dream, is only half remembered in the morning. Yet all the way back to the Hammond house, and afterward on the far journey home, it stayed with her, ebbing and flowing in turn and in time, with a long lament.

31

There was no hope left in the land of Louisiana. Governor Allen still sat in the capitol at Shreveport, but Union forces had spread almost entirely across the state, and Beau Jardin was on a shrinking little Confederate island in the midst of a rising sea.

The roads were thronged with deserters who had given up the fight. Three of these, to Miriam's astonishment, were sitting in the kitchen when she came home. To her further astonishment the kitchen helpers, busy over the iron pots that hung in the fireplace, were none other than Fanny and the ladies of the house—Eulalie, Rosa, Pelagie, and Angelique. Not one of these, to Miriam's knowledge, had ever done more in all her life than peek through a kitchen door.

"The cook has left," Fanny said, answering Miriam's question before she could ask it.

And Angelique said, "Go inside, Mama. Grandpa has something to tell you."

It was then that she learned of Emma's death.

"It was pneumonia." Ferdinand looked bewildered and somehow smaller than he had before. "The cold here was terrible. We couldn't cross the lines to take her body back to New Orleans, but the servants took her, Sisyphus with Blaise and a couple of young hands. They put her in the family vault. She left you her star sapphire, Miriam. And she dictated a will to me. There's a copy on her desk."

For long minutes Miriam stood in Emma's room before she could bring herself to read the document on the little desk. Every object in the room spoke of its owner: a heap of lace-trimmed pillows on the bed; pastel drawings, framed in gilt, of all her babies; her ruffled peignoir hung on the back of the door. And, with an unconscious gesture, Miriam straightened a ruffle, touching it as softly as if she were feeling Emma's own soft, powdered arm. With insight that only years can bring she felt for the first time the full measure of Emma's loving welcome when, as a child, she had come into the household. She smiled a little, remembering all the motherly injunctions about clothes and manners and family trees. She was a mother to me, Miriam thought, very different, I'm sure, from the one who brought me into the world, but in her way a mother, all the same, and I loved her. Suddenly the room, for all its tidy clutter, seemed very empty.

It was a minute or two before she could steady herself to read the will. Written in Ferdinand's pointed Germanic script, it made quick disposition of the few possessions left to Emma Raphael, née Duclos.

I know that Sisyphus, Maxim, and Chanute no longer belong to me, Mr. Eugene Mendes having purchased them from creditors in order to keep them with my family. Having no authority over their disposition, I yet request, and it is a heartfelt request, that my daughter Miriam Mendes keep them with her as long as they live and not dispose of them to strangers. They have given faithful service, and I consider them a part of my family. I have a bag of gold coins which I have saved and ask further that its contents be divided among the three aforementioned, the greater portion being given to Sisyphus, he being the eldest and the longest in service of my family.

This kindly, humane document, now soon to have no meaning or authority, touched Miriam's heart. Oh, possibly it was just as well that Emma had died when she had! The life that was coming would be too hard for her; it had already become too hard for her; she had not been able to understand it. And gently, Miriam laid the paper back in the drawer.

Outside spring had come streaming out of the earth as always. The far line of woods was edged with a fretwork of greenery, and in the middle distance the tulip tree that shaded the Indian mound where Eugene lay held its silky pink cups erect. Spring had no care for man's pains or joys or the dark iniquities of his wars.

Fanny opened the door and brought in a pile of clean wash.

"So, Fanny, you have been managing very well without me, I see," Miriam said, forcing herself back to practical matters.

"Oh, yes, everybody busy, Miss Miriam. Miss Pelagie, she's the same as always, cuts out baby dresses for the new ones in the quarters, gives medicines, busy every minute. Everybody loves Miss Pelagie. And Miss Angelique, she's grown up, she's learning, too. Miss Eulalie teaches her."

"Miss Eulalie teaches her?"

"Oh, yes, they're making sarsaparilla tea for spring, to purify the blood. And making dyes, blue out of indigo and red from pokeberry juice."

"I didn't know Miss Eulalie knew—I wonder how . . ."

"Miss Eulalie says she learned at home. Just watch the servants, she says."

Yes, that's how it would have been for her: a lonesome child, standing about, observing life, not in the parlors where a little girl was supposed to be pretty in her flounces, but in the hidden, back-door places where no one cared.

"Well," Miriam said, maintaining the cheerful, brisk appearance, "it's nice that my daughter is learning," and did not add, Because we have all been merely ornamental for too long.

"I must thank Miss Eulalie," she said.

"She works hard. Knits socks and things for the soldiers. Knits at night till her eyes ache."

"It sounds as if you've all been getting along very pleasantly together."

Fanny grimaced. "Well, most of the time. Of course, Miss Eulalie is—well, you know, Miss Miriam, how she is. But she's better than she used to be."

"I'm glad to hear that."

"I think she feels important," Fanny said wisely.

That was probably true. For the first time in her life, Eulalie had been needed.

I'm really not as clever about people as I thought I was, Miriam told herself when Fanny had left the room. See how Eulalie has surprised me! And what about the slaves? If they had revolted while all the men were away at the front, the Confederacy would have collapsed, there could be no doubt of it. Pelagie, intending no unkindness, believed it was because they were inferior and didn't have enough intelligence. Faithful oxen, she called them. Other people, though, including Miriam herself, were apt to say that their loyalty was a mask and that the revolt would surely come. But it had not come.

No, I am really not keen at seeing what is inside of other people. It is a serious defect, I am afraid.

Richmond fell.
A letter from André, posted in Richmond just before the fall, arrived at last.
Miriam's hands fumbled at it, while her heart's dull thudding sounded in her ears. Her heart was behaving as if it were afraid of something.

> I shall be in Louisiana again before long. I have news for you. Oh, Miriam, I can't wait!

The script itself was large and confident, commanding her to read it again. She read the few words half a dozen times, still with that dull thudding in her ears. And read on:

> Jefferson Davis says that the loss of Richmond will not be a hopeless calamity. The army is mobile and can keep on striking. They are saying that Lee will retreat to Danville to unite with Johnston, and following the railroad, will cross the Appomattox River, but I do not think he can do it.

This pessimism, so unlike André, had sounded like a doomsday bell in her ears, almost as if he had spoken the words aloud. Her sense of sorrowful foreboding astounded her: The defeat of the Confederacy was, after all, what she had wanted and expected! It had had to be. And yet there was all this pity, this regret in her.
I do not think he can do it. He had not done it. The letter had reached Miriam after Lee's surrender. She held it thoughtfully, then laid it down and picked up the newspaper again.

"Men," Lee said, "we have fought through the war together. I have done the best I could for you. My heart is too full to say more."

And she read about how Lee had asked that his men be allowed to keep their horses for spring plowing, and how Grant had assented; she read about the men in gray falling in line to stack their arms, and how some wept, and, again to her own astonishment, she wept, too. She thought of all the dead young men, the blue and the gray, now mouldering in the earth. And she thought about Gabriel, who had followed Lee to the end.

She put the paper aside. Why, she ought to be thinking of André! Soon he would be here. . . . But what had happened to the joy? Oh, it was because there were too many things to be decided! Her mind was too full, she told herself, tapping her nails on the tabletop. Yes, there was simply too much to do.

Last night Ferdinand had asked her where they should go, now that the war was over. He had made the question sound rhetorical, but in truth he was asking for his daughter's guidance; since Emma's death he had become more acquiescent, putting all decisions, without admitting that he was doing so, into his daughter's hands. Should they go back to New Orleans now? The house would be returned to them, surely. And she knew he wanted to go.

But how were they just to walk away from the land? Once she had seen this place only as a refuge, a kind of safe prison to shelter them through the war. She could remember her own shuddering dread of the long, useless days. . . . These last years, though, had been different years. Here the family had survived. The land had responded to their labor and kept them alive. It seemed as if now they must owe it something in return.

In the enclosure across the lane a small flock of new sheep, two ewes saved from the wreckage, followed by two lambs, ambled and grazed in peace.

Nearer, in the yard where they had been assembling for hours, the dark people waited for Miriam. For them, unlike the sheep, peace would be less simple than they probably expected it to be on this morning of their glory, their emancipation day. She tried to imagine, to feel how this must be, this fulfillment of a hope that had for generations gone unanswered; now that it was here it must be past believing! She supposed they must be dazed with the enormity of their rejoicing, as is the way when a grand wish comes true. In and out of the house since breakfast time, as she tried to prepare herself for the meeting, she had observed the differences among these varied individuals, as they jostled and argued among themselves, confronted as they were for the first time in their lives with choices, and uncertain which to take. She had seen many faces: ashamed and furtive eyes, sullen and defiant mouths, asserting themselves so that she would be sure to hear: "This land is mine, I worked it and it belongs to me now." While others proclaimed their plans for up North "to get my plenty, because there's piles of gold up there."

Simeon was prepared to leave, but his wife Chloe, so Fanny reported, had told him he would first have to get himself a job and her a house. Until then she would stay where she had a roof over her head. They had had a violent quarrel, and Simeon had departed, picked up a knapsack and stalked off down the road.

So it had gone since daybreak.

Having seen all this, Miriam's mouth went dry with apprehension. Yet it was necessary to face the people and get it over with. She went outside to stand on the verandah, looking down upon them, trying again to imagine herself in their places. Unable to do that, she decided simply to tell the forthright truth.

"Today there are no more masters, as you know. Today you're free to go wherever you wish. Perhaps some of you already know where you want to go, and if that's so, I will say good-bye and wish you good luck. But others of you may have no place, and if you want to stay here, if you feel this is your home, you may stay. I'll tell you what I will do. I will pay you wages. But you will have to work, to make a crop that I can sell. Otherwise, I'll have no money to pay wages, you understand that, don't you?"

Some nodded, while others looked perplexed. One young fellow stepped forward.

"How much, missis? How much will you pay?"

"Ten dollars a month," she said, and as a low grumble began to rise from the back rows, she said quickly, "You forget, you have a house and food and medicine when you're sick. You'll have everything you need, as you always have had. And money besides, if you work well. But if you don't work well," she said more boldly now, "I'll hire somebody else and tell you to leave. That's the way it will be from now on. That's all I have to tell you, except that—well, I should like you to remember that we, my husband and I, always treated you well. Some others didn't, but we always did. I should just like you to remember that. And now I'll wait here on the verandah while you decide, and come and tell me, each of you, whether you go or stay."

There was then a general movement on the lawn, a milling and clustering, a hubbub of palaver. Maxim and Chanute were engaged in what appeared to be a fiery quarrel under Eugene's giant beech tree.

Presently Maxim came to Miriam and, removing his cap as he always had, declared, "Missis, Chanute and

I, we've had a big fight. I think Chanute's gone crazy. All that big talk about gold, when anybody can see this whole country close to starving. Where's the gold coming from? So he can go if he wants, but I stay. I stay and keep this place for you. Then maybe after a while you'll raise my wages."

She had a swift picture of the two, as alike as twins in their lace-cuffed jackets, bizarre in their blackness as though they had come to the German village from another world, which indeed they had.

"You've never been apart, you and Chanute."

Maxim looked as though he were going to cry. "I know. Everything's gone crazy. But I'm not going to go crazy."

When Sisyphus appeared, he actually was crying.

"I stay, Miss Miriam. Didn't you know I would? I was born to Miss Emma's people, I came with her when she married Mr. Ferdinand, and I laid Miss Emma to rest in the tomb. Where would I go? This is my home."

One by one they kept coming, either to announce with timid relief that they would stay, or with a kind of defiance that they would go. Some even left in anger without a word.

When at last it was over, Miriam thought that this was the hardest day's work she had done in her life.

"Do you think this wage arrangement will work?" asked Ferdinand.

"Never," asserted Eulalie.

But Rosa had another opinion.

"I've heard that in New Orleans, under Union control, they found that free labor produced a hogshead and a half more sugar in a day than slaves produce."

"We shall see" was Miriam's only reply.

The hardest was yet to come. In the morning, when Fanny brought a basin of hot water to Miriam's room, she did not set it down and leave as usual, but paused instead with one hand on the doorjamb. Her dark eyes roved about the room as if she were searching or memorizing.

"What is it, Fanny? You want to tell me something?"

"I do. And I can't bring myself to do it."

"Say it. I won't be angry even if it's something bad. Is it something bad?"

Fanny's mouth trembled into the square, ugly shape of sorrow. "I don't know whether you'll call it bad or not."

All at once Miriam knew. She was stunned; others would leave, she had expected them to, but it had not entered her mind that Fanny might, any more than she could imagine Angelique saying, Mama, I don't want to be your daughter anymore.

She raised her head in a gesture of proud acceptance: "You're going away, that's it, isn't it?"

Fanny nodded. Her pleading eyes did nothing to assuage the hurt that lumped itself in Miriam's throat. She wanted to say, We were children together, does that mean so little to you? I thought you were contented here, happy here.

And suddenly words poured from Fanny.

"Miss Miriam, I have to go! I don't want to, but I have to. There's a part of me that says one way and a part that says the other. Blaise says we've never done anything, we don't know anything, and now we've got our chance. You can see he's right, can't you?"

I suppose I can see, but I don't want to, Miriam thought.

"I've a pain right here." Fanny put her hand on her heart. "A pain."

Miriam smiled sadly. "And in your head. It aches

with thinking about what you'll do with your life, I
know. You said that to me once, on a very hard day."

Fanny's eyes pleaded still. Like the eyes of an intelligent child asking mutely to be understood, they widened and shone. Suddenly the lump, the wound, in
Miriam's throat, dissolved. She could have said, You
will never again be as comfortable as you have been in
this house, but she did not say it. Instead, she held out
her arms.

"Of course you must go, it's the only way, and God
bless you, Fanny, wherever you go."

"I never thought, after all Lincoln did to us, that I
could feel sorry about his death," Pelagie said. "But
now that he's been murdered one thinks how good he
really was. And our southern papers call the crime
'barbaric,' too." She held the newspaper up to the light
of the terrabene lamp. "They call him a generous man.
They say Johnson won't be like him, either."

Ferdinand sighed. "Read David's letter again. Read
what he says about Lincoln."

" 'As you know,' " Miriam began, " 'the assassina-
tion came on the fifth day of Passover. Everyone went
into mourning. Here in New York the temple was
draped in black. What a debt we as Jews, let alone as
citizens, owe to that man! At the memorial exercises
fifteen lodges of B'nai Brith were in the march. I carried a banner myself. It was heavy for me, I'm still not
back to hundred-percent strength, but getting closer to
it every day, and so grateful to be alive, to know that
you're well and that the war, and the slaughter, are
over, that I'd have gone twice the distance if I'd had
to. So there was thankfulness, in the midst of the deepest grief.' "

"That was New York," Eulalie said. "There are
plenty of people in this country who are not mourning

that man's death, I assure you. And as for the war being over, the South was beaten only because of greater numbers and nothing else. The spirit was here and it still is, and what's more, always will be."

Ferdinand made haste to keep peace in the room.

"Courage! We have a new fight now, the fight with poverty." He smiled ruefully. "I feel as if I've been here before. Well, I was, back in Europe when I was much younger than any of you, and Napoleon had laid the continent to waste." He looked at Miriam, adding with some of his old jaunty confidence, "We'll manage. I did once. We'll do it again."

The confidence was pathetic. In reality Ferdinand was as helpless before this turn of events as someone whose boat is caught at the crest of a flood. But who has to appear able to keep it from capsizing. And in so appearing, Ferdinand was most touchingly brave.

In the very early morning a shredded mist hung like spiders' webs in the trees. Raccoons were still scuttling in the scrub swamp and birds were just waking up; the red sun was barely risen when Miriam went outside. Each morning, it seemed, she awoke earlier than on the day before, for sleep came hard. Where was life taking her? To stifle an anxiety like that, one got up early and filled one's hours with other problems.

Of these there were more than enough. Sunflowers, those great, gawky, hot-looking things, had spread themselves over into what should have been a flourishing vegetable patch and was not. The help were neglecting the work most disgracefully. The stables were never properly cleaned. Right now cows were moaning in the barn; it was long past milking time. Yards and yards of fence had not yet been mended. The big house needed paint. She sighed. The whole place prob-

ably wouldn't fetch more than ten thousand dollars, if
one could find somebody to buy it.

A door slammed as Eugene and Angelique came out
of the house.

"Go do something," their mother commanded.
"Maybe you can set an example. One of you feed the
chickens and the other bring some eggs to the
kitchen."

She watched them as in their clumsy, wood-soled
shoes they walked toward the chicken house, and saw
them disappear inside. When they reappeared, Eugene
was carrying the tub of grain. It pleased her that he
took the heavy work for himself without being told.
There was something protective in his manner toward
Angelique now that they were fairly past the age of
childish squabbles, something that reminded Miriam
of herself and David.

Oh, be fair! There's much of their father in them,
too! David's scowls don't cross young Eugene's forehead. Quite possibly the scowl is just not natural to
him, but if it were, his father would not have allowed
it. Disciplined according to their place and their social
class, these two are dutiful and compliant. Eugene is
affable and Angelique, in her dawning vanity, is
charming. She wants some proper clothes, and I wish
she had some. But if she had them, where would she
wear them, the way things are now?

The hens made a circular cluster at their feet, cack-
ling under the dusty shower of grain. A wry little
smile crossed Miriam's lips. What would their father
have said of such a rural vignette? Of his son, his
daughter, the Mendes' heir and heiress, in a chicken
yard? No matter, she told herself. Work won't hurt
them. They're lucky to have it, to have anything in
these times, to be alive at all.

And staring across dry, sallow fields on which the

morning's heat had already begun to quiver, she saw
through the white dazzle long rows of bloodied men
lying on the floor in Richmond, saw again the woman
whose begging hands had reached out for milk—

"What now, Mama?" asked Angelique.

"Find out from Maxim whether he needs you for
something. He's overworked, and he never asks for
any help."

"Sisyphus, too," Eugene said. "He was down at the
barn yesterday helping to lift a wagon while they fixed
a wheel. He's too old. I made him stop and took his
place."

"Tell me," Miriam said suddenly, "what changed
you, Eugene? When did you change sides in this war?
It's still not clear to me."

He answered, "I don't think I did quite that. I've
not been a traitor."

"I don't mean you are. I mean your thoughts."

"About the system? I don't know exactly. It just
came to me, when I had to work to keep things going
here, and I saw more of the way life was, how hard. It
just came to me."

A basic kindness, she thought gladly. A basic decency, that's all it was. But she wondered whether he
could have changed direction if his father had lived to
keep the old, strong hold upon him. Had that grue-
some death perhaps released the son to become what
he was?

She said only, "Here's Maxim. Maxim, these helpers want to know whether you need them for anything."

"No, ma'am, I'm doing fine. Shouldn't they be at
their books this morning?"

"It wouldn't hurt. Why don't you get to your German grammar, both of you? I'll test you on it later."

A pity she hadn't had more of an education herself

with which to help them through these lost years! German was about all she knew enough of to teach. Still, it was better than nothing.

Maxim reflected, as they walked away, "Seems like last week they were born in this house."

Last week, and a hundred years ago! So sweetly they had lain in their baskets. . . . David had come home to stay. . . . The river boat had whistled, landing guests and gifts . . . fruit and flowers, music and wine. . . . Gabriel had come home. . . .

"They're a real credit to you," Maxim was saying. "Kind young folks. Quality. Real quality."

"A credit to you, too, and to Blaise and Fanny and Sisyphus, remember. You all helped raise them."

A field hand, hearing Miriam's voice, came around the corner of the barn.

"Morning, missis. You're out early."

"I'm always out early. There's work to be done."

"I was thinking, missis, maybe we should shoot that old Pepper there. That used to be one feisty mule, but there's sure no pepper left in him now."

The old mule's tail swished casually, as with head hung over the fence, he crunched a sheaf of grass between his long yellow teeth. His wary, melancholy eyes regarded Miriam.

All of life's pathos was concentrated in the mule.

"Leave him alone. There'll be no more shooting," she said, and tearing another handful of grass, she thrust it into the soft, snuffling mouth.

"And listen," she commanded, "I want pine straw in the cattle barn this morning. Cows get sick lying in the wet."

"Yes, missis. Right away, missis."

No one had ever taught her how to care for cattle, but most things were only a matter of common sense, anyway.

She went back to the house to polish what was left of the silver. Only the week before she had gone with Rosa to retrieve the silver they had once so carefully hidden, and found half of it missing. The service that Eugene had given Miriam when they were married was safe in its place, but Emma's, buried with equal discretion, or so they had thought, was gone. Someone must have been watching them that night. Too bad it was Emma's! Miriam wouldn't have minded the loss of her own as much as the loss of Papa's; things meant so much to him.

In the dining room the coffee service waited on the table. Miriam sat down to work with the polishing rag. There was a certain satisfaction in making things clean, in bringing order with one's own hands, even though Sisyphus was still horrified to see the lady of the house at such labor.

Ferdinand came in to watch her. For a few minutes he waited without speaking. Then suddenly he interrupted the regular tick of the clock.

"You're getting to look like your mother."

"I never thought I did."

He had startled her. She couldn't even remember when he had last spoken of her mother.

"I've been seeing her lately. I hadn't in years," Ferdinand said. He mused. "She wore a plaid shawl the first time I laid eyes on her."

But that's the way I always see her! Miriam cried silently. Why do I always see her in a plaid shawl? I'm sure he never told me this before. Did anyone else ever tell me? She could not remember.

"She was lovely. She had an oval face, quiet and grave."

As he rocked, his chair creaked, blending with his even voice in a dreamy rhythm.

"Curious, the way a life unwinds. If it hadn't been

for a stone thrown by a hate-crazed lout, we'd all perhaps still be in the German village. Angelique and Eugene wouldn't have been born. Yes, you remind me of her, but David has her eyes. Exactly her eyes. I wish I could see David again. He made me so angry, but he's a good man, I know he is. I'd like to see him."

"Now that the war is over, he'll surely come to see you, Papa. I know he will."

She looked over at her father. He had started a beard, since it was the fashion again, but his beard made him look not fashionable, only like a patriarchal Jew, the Opa whom she could still see in her mind, rocking, rocking and creaking. The hair that had once been a crown of chestnut waves had turned quite gray. Oh, she thought, was it just today or was it last week that I saw he was old? Age comes like that; suddenly one day a person is old.

Ferdinand was staring out of the window.

"There goes Eulalie. She's got a bucket of water for the chicken yard. I can't get over the change in her."

"Maybe she feels important for the first time in her life."

"What? Tending chickens? From a family like hers?"

"That and all the rest she does. I never realized she knew so much. It's true she's sour, but we'd have managed here a lot less well without her. None of us knew how to preserve or sew or do anything properly until she showed us how." Something drove Miriam to talk, not so much in defense of Eulalie as out of a sense of fairness and personal indignation. "All her life she's been a failure because she wasn't good at the one thing you men expect us to be good at: being ornamental. I don't know how it is, but a man can be fat, bald, or buck-toothed, and it doesn't matter, but let a woman be even mildly plain and she goes into the discard.

Heaven help her, if she's not married, she can only cringe in shame. I don't want my daughter to be like that!" she finished sharply.

"Don't worry about Angelique." Ferdinand chuckled. "She's a beauty already."

Miriam started to say: *That's not what I meant at all,* but stopped. What was the use? He would never understand.

Gabriel would. It flashed across her mind that Gabriel had always understood, but she was kept from further thought by her father's next remark.

"I would like to see you married again, Miriam."

And I want it. . . . I have never been married, don't you know that? Married, with that comfort, that unity so warm, so trusting. How thrilling to belong, to have no secrets, to hold back nothing of body or heart! To know another so completely. . . . I try to see André, to hear his voice, and cannot anymore. Cannot.

"There's someone coming," Ferdinand said suddenly. He stood up to get a better view. "A man's riding up the lane."

She did not have to ask. She knew—she knew without asking or looking that it was André.

"This is a real celebration!" Ferdinand cried. "God help us, the war's over at last. And though our hearts ache for the sons who died"—glancing out of eyes gleaming wet with emotion at Rosa and Pelagie—"we give thanks that so many have survived and will come back. Now for the savior of my son"—Ferdinand raised his glass toward André—"for him a special thanks today, a toast drunk from the good wine he has brought us. Ahhh, excellent—nothing like a fine French wine, nothing!" he concluded, and sat down, quite overcome with sentiment and the heat of the wine. But he was not yet finished.

"Here's Sisyphus, good Sisyphus! We've not had a dinner like this in I don't know when, have we, Sisyphus? You mustn't think we've been living in such luxury, André. No, far from it," he declared, as Sisyphus brought the roast turkey on one of the rescued silver platters.

On the sideboard stood jellies which had been discovered in a forgotten cellar, and a floating custard, made under Eulalie's supervision, which had used up, Miriam thought with some concern, the last of the scarce eggs.

"Yes," André said, "the fall of Richmond was something to behold. Davis was in church, you know, when they came to tell him that the city was to be abandoned. People were absolutely shocked; they'd had no idea of the situation because the War Department had been keeping the truth out of the newspapers during the last few weeks. Instead, they'd been printing a lot of optimistic nonsense. So there was chaos in the streets. Church bells were still ringing for Sunday services while in government offices they were loading the archives into wagons to take them to the railroad. People were rushing to get on a train, but you couldn't get on without a pass from the secretary of war. And most people don't have access to the secretary of war, do they?"

André told the tale well. His rapid, resonant voice contained just enough dramatic emphasis. Miriam's avid, questioning eyes, which had not left him, attracted no notice, since every other eye in the room was on him, too.

His handsome features were unchanged. The war had left its mark on everyone else, laying its weight of gloom on some, agitating the brittle nerves of others, making voices shrill and tempers short; it had marked

Miriam with dark stains of fatigue under her eyes. But André glowed. He might have been at a ball.

"The city council ordered all liquor to be destroyed. You could see whiskey running in the gutters. What a waste!" André exclaimed, making a comic face. "But a lot of folks drank it up instead, and drunkards went lurching through the streets among the broken bottles with no idea of what was happening. Then the military ordered the burning of the flour mills. Stupid! The fire spread—well, it spread like wildfire! What did they expect? Or what can one expect of politicians and soldiers but stupidity?"

Something came into Miriam's head, a chance recollection: Once in her father's house an old man, a world traveler returned from India, had entranced his audience with his descriptions of the burning vats, the moonlight streaming on the filthy Ganges, and the morning sunlight uncovering the bodies of the poor who had died on the street during the night. It had seemed to her, child that she was then, that the man had been telling of these awful things with a thrill of excitement; he had been a spectator of the exotic, without any feeling of human kinship.

She blinked and the memory slid away.

"Naturally, the fire spread to the arsenals, so the munitions exploded. It was pandemonium, I tell you! People threw furniture from their burning houses, they made bonfires out of Confederate money, they crammed themselves into wagons and fled.

"I got on my horse and followed the railroad tracks out of the city. The last I saw of Richmond was cinders and smoke."

The story ended. André lit a cigar. Shocked into a mournful silence, all watched him tear off the band, bite the end, apply the match, and finally lean back to savor the first aromatic draw.

Lambert Labouisse broke the silence.

"Well, I always said Jeff Davis was never whole-heartedly with us. He tipped toward the Union, al-ways had. And this is the result. By God, this is the result." And he looked accusingly about the room, at faces and furniture, at ceiling and walls, as if one of these might have some other explanation for the disas-ter.

André observed cheerfully, "No use in recrimina-tions. You have to look at it this way: All's well that ends well."

"Ends well?" Miriam repeated somberly. "Without even counting the wounded and dead, one has only to stand at the foot of our lane and watch the men go past; they've been coming by for weeks now, carrying their paroles and nothing more, not a penny, and no work in sight. They're wiped out. The poverty is be-yond belief. That's how well it's ended."

"Oh, I understand." André's tone was sympathetic. "But that's not the case everywhere, you know that. Some, even in the South, have made fortunes they could never have dreamed of before. Why, up in Mem-phis and in Vicksburg—why, I assure you, as many bales of cotton went north on Union gunboats as went downriver to southern ports and overseas."

That was certainly true. Miriam was careful not to look at Lambert Labouisse except out of the corner of her eye, with which she could see him in his aging, but still correct, white summer suit, smoking one of An-dré's enormous Havana cigars.

"I'm sorry," André said. "This conversation has gotten too deep. A lecture on the frightfulness of war is not the right way to end a beautiful evening." His luminous smile asked them all to forgive him.

The words "end the evening" acted as the signal they were intended to be. Indeed, it had grown late, as

everyone was reminded by the hall clock's rattle and
bong.

"I thought they would never have sense enough to
leave us alone," André said when the others had gone
upstairs. "Come here! Come here!"

He stretched out his arms, into which she came
with automatic obedience, clasped her, kissed her, and
clasped her again. Her eyes, not closed in any ecstasy
of forgetfulness, were wide and alert, staring over his
shoulder toward the hearth, where a dozen tiny red
eyes winked back out of the gray ash.

Into her ear he murmured, "Sit down. I have things
to show you. First this. Read this."

From a clipping out of a Paris newspaper she read
the following:

> It is said on good authority that Madame Marie
> Claire Perrin, after her huge successes in the re-
> cital halls of Europe this past winter, will shortly
> obtain a final decree of divorce from her husband,
> who is said to be residing somewhere in the
> United States.

"Well, now, what do you think of that! She has di-
vorced me! Don't forget, this article is three months
old. I should be receiving papers any moment. But
wait, that's not all. There's this." And drawing a small
velvet box out of his pocket, André laid it on the table
before Miriam.

"Open it."

Her hands trembled, so that she was clumsy with
the catch. In his eagerness André reached over and
snapped up the lid.

"How do you like it?"

It was the traditional ruby engagement ring, but it
was no ordinary ruby. It was a splendor of splendors.

Many-faceted, it drew to itself all the light in the room and threw a rosy radiance into the shadows. She stared at it as though it were alive. And her mind went back—all evening her mind had been taking such backward leaps—to the moment when Eugene had given her his ring. She even recalled the dress she had worn that night, the way the skirt had spread; cream-colored lawn it was, laced with lavender ribbons. Yes, and she could recall that the ring had presented itself to her with no joy of possession, neither because of its symbolism nor its intrinsic beauty. It had frightened her.

And so did this ring now.

"It's very beautiful," she said.

"You don't like it?" André asked.

"How could I not admire it? But it's too magnificent for me." She stammered. "It doesn't suit me—or the times." And she made a half-conscious gesture toward her dress, which had been "turned," so that what had been the lining was now the outside.

"Ah, you're tired of it all, you've had nothing, that's what's the matter! You need new dresses, you need new pleasures. You're out of practice!"

He pulled her to him to kiss her again, but her position was awkward, and his mouth barely grazed hers. He smelled of wine. He was rough. The wine had gone to his head. And the ring still lay on the table.

"Here, put it on. Try it on."

She didn't want to do it. A terrible confusion, a weakness, overcame her, and without knowing it was going to happen, she felt her eyes fill. This caused panic. How did it look to cry, now, at this moment of fruition, of what was to have been fulfillment for them both? She squeezed, pressing her lids against her eyeballs, forcing the tears back.

"I must be very tired. There's been so much today."

Her lips formed the words just as they slid through her mind, phrases with no order or purpose. "I'm afraid . . . I don't understand . . ."

André was astonished. "What don't you understand? What can you be afraid of?"

"I don't know."

In the fireplace the little red eyes were winking out, one by one. It had begun to rain. One always heard the first slow, heavy drops on the verandah roof. They accelerated now. It would be a warm, gray rain, like tears.

"This place smells of defeat," André said abruptly, with a kind of scorn.

He waved his arm toward what she knew he had seen when he rode up that afternoon: the weathered boards rotting away for lack of paint and the dry, broken stalks of cotton in the fields. His scorn seemed to be turning into anger.

"Listen to me. I'm going to get you out of here, away from all this ruination. It's not worth building up again, anyway. What would you say to a small chateau along the Loire? Or a *mas* in Provence? It's a paradise in spring. We'll take the family, your father, too, of course."

Take Papa? Ask Papa to leave America and return to Europe? He doesn't know Papa, she thought.

"Or would you rather have an Elizabethan manor in the south of England? The choice is yours." And when Miriam did not answer, he added somewhat grandly, "I've a Sir Edwin Landseer painting of King Charles spaniels that I bought in London just for you. It would be splendid over the mantel in an old English house, or anywhere else. They look just like Gretel."

Gretel, hearing her name, raised her old head from the rug and after one weak thump of the tail, lay back.

*Gabriel brought the puppy; the soft, wriggling, tiny
thing was not much larger than the palm of his hand.*

"Are you so rich as all that?" Miriam asked softly.
"They were talking, your friends in Richmond, they
were talking about a man who made fifty thousand
dollars a month on imported goods. Was that you?"

"I don't know. I wasn't the only one. People like to
count other people's money, anyway. And I certainly
didn't do that sort of thing every month. It's an exag-
geration, although not too far off the mark."

When she offered no comment, he asked abruptly,
"What is it? What's wrong?"

"I was only thinking—"

But he interrupted, "Thinking again! It will take me
a long time, I can see, to train you out of all this
solemn thinking."

"I was thinking," she insisted, "of all the pain—and
fifty thousand dollars a month."

"That's what war is, Miriam, what did you think it
was? Pain and death! Don't take it so tragically, will
you? War is a damn-fool silly business, but people have
always had wars, they come and they go. This one's
over, so just forget it, forget the whole damn-fool business."

"Damn fool? You call it that?"

"Yes, and fools were the only ones who took it seriously. The smart ones took care of themselves. I was
scarcely ever in any real danger! Oh, I made a couple
of blockade runs during the early months, just for the
boyish thrill of it! But when it got too dangerous, I
quit. All the flags and slogans, what are they for? And
the glory that is no glory! Come back with a wooden
leg and a dirty rag with some stars on it—for what?
Stars and bars or stars and stripes—what difference
does it make? Is it worth a leg or an arm? Only fools,

boys"—André laughed—"thirty- and forty-year-old
boys, stir themselves up over that sort of thing."

She begged silently: Don't talk, don't. Every word is
a nail in the coffin.

He did not see that she was wretched. Pouring a
drink of brandy, he swirled the tan liquid in the
rotund glass and sniffed it sensuously. Miriam
watched the elegant ritual with a sinking heart.

"Listen! You want to know the truth? I never gave a
damn who won. I hedged my bets. If the South had
won—I knew it wouldn't, but if by some fluke, it had
—I would still have owned my land as before, but with
this difference. I'd have had the means to maintain it.
The other way, as it's turned out, I'm well supplied
with everything I'll need for six lifetimes. My cousins
can have my land here and are welcome to do what
they can with it, which won't be much."

Absorbed in this account of himself, he had forgotten that only a few minutes earlier he had been concerned over what might be wrong with *her,* and Miriam felt her body stiffening. She sat upright with her
hands clasped in her lap, with her nails cutting into
her palms.

"Wouldn't it have been a good deal more simple,"
she asked, "to have stayed in Europe where you were
when the war began? What made you come back to all
this trouble?"

And in the very instant of asking she was aware that
only a few months before she would have taken for
granted why he had come back: for love of her.

He answered, "How, after all I've just been telling
you, can you still ask that? Because there was a fortune to be made! Let me show you something in my
traveling bag." Out of a small bag which he had set
down in the corner of the room, he brought forth a
packet of photographs. "Here, look. This was when I

was running the blockade in sixty-two. This is a café in Havana called the Louvre. Everybody met there, northerners and southerners, to do business. Here I am, sitting with two officers in the Federal navy. They used to make contacts with northern merchant ships, you see, to bring down a load of manufactured stuff; the blockade runner would bring in the cotton and the middlemen would buy and sell. It seems complicated, but basically it was a trade and very advantageous to all. A shipload of cotton could bring in half a million dollars' worth in traded goods. That's how it worked."

Miriam examined the photograph. Yes, there he sat, squinting a little into what must have been a glaring tropical sun. But the smile was the old charming, vivid smile. He had been enjoying himself, while my brother —how he suffered! She saw David's sunken face, with the teeth rotted out. And Gabriel, who might or might not still be alive . . .

She said slowly, "It was like a play for you, wasn't it? A drama. Playacting. You didn't care, you say, which side was right or wrong, or even how it was all to end. You were scorning us all, weren't you? As long as you could have things like that"—and Miriam's arm swept toward the brandy and the pile of gifts still heaped on the sideboard.

"You enjoyed what I brought. That time I brought the yellow silk, and the shoes and hats, you enjoyed them, didn't you?"

"Yes. To my shame, I did."

He laughed. For the first time she realized that he laughed too much, too often. Now in this laugh there was faint incredulity.

"You're a silly thing. A silly, pious little girl, but a darling, all the same. Come here"—and he reached for her breast.

She moved out of reach. "André, I am neither silly nor little. And I am not a girl. I am a woman."

"Then, be one, and don't try to be like a man. Miriam, be yourself. Be what you were."

Was this André? What had happened to her? His words passed over her like wind. She trembled.

"André . . . We never talked about the war. The biggest event of our time, the biggest in our lives, and we never talked about it, do you know that? I'm just realizing that we never talked very much about anything."

"We talked about the only things that are important: you and me."

His voice coaxed. Still, she could feel her mouth setting itself into that downward curve of disapproval, that expression which, through observation in a mirror, she had trained herself to control; yet now this downward curve was on her face. She knew by his response.

"Most talk is blather anyway," he said. "What people really want to talk about, if they would only admit it, is survival. Ways to get on in the world and stay there."

She was still not able to believe that he could mean all these things.

"That's not so," she protested. "How can you talk like that? You who were so kind to my brother. That wasn't to 'get on in the world.' That was pure goodness."

"It was to please you! I hardly know your brother. And how do you think I was able to do it? Only because I had those contacts and dealings that seem to shock you so. Why are you so shocked, anyway? You were always a sympathizer with the North. You think I didn't know that?"

"Yes, I was. I am. But I had to live here with my

family, and I was loyal to these people, here where I live. At least I was loyal!"

"Your loyalty is rather ironic! Right in this house, a member of one of the so-called best families was playing both ends against the middle. I suppose you're not aware of that, though."

"Oh, I'm aware! It was old Labouisse. I knew about that long ago."

"And it didn't matter to you?"

"Of course I was shocked, but there was nothing I could do about it. Anyway, I've learned at last that people aren't always what they seem."

"A child knows that, Miriam."

"Not always. Girls brought up as they are here don't get to know much about the world, or what lies under smiles and courtesies." She took a deep breath. "What did I know about you, André? I'm beginning to think I don't know you at all."

"What the devil can you mean?"

"Oh, it's not your fault! No, it's not. Because you don't know me, either. We never opened ourselves to each other."

André's eyebrows went up. "Oh? I should have said we did, very much so."

She flushed. There it was again, that humiliating wave of hot red rising into her scalp.

"There are other ways beside just—"

"Just the body, you mean? Why don't you say it? Miriam, I don't understand what's wrong tonight, what's happening. You're different."

"Oh, yes, but you are, too. Or else I'm only seeing things I never saw before. You come down here to this ruination and talk the way you do! There's cruelty in it! Pelagie's home is burned and gone. She's lost a son. Rosa's lost one, and every cent she had in the world, besides. Gabriel had all their funds in Confederate bonds, and they're worth nothing."

"The more fool Gabriel," André said contemptuously. "If he'd had any sense, he'd have moved his money to a New York bank."

If you love him, Gabriel said, then that's the way it is. I only wanted to be sure, in case . . . She had felt his cheek against her hair. A military band played a glum march down on the dismal street. . . . I went with Lee at the start. I gave my word.

She almost screamed, "Don't you say that! Don't you call Gabriel a fool! He believed in something, maybe enough to give his life for it."

"Your face! Look at your face! Why, it's on fire! One might think you were in love with the man!"

"If you had *believed* in something!" she cried, ignoring his words. "What is life worth if you don't believe in something?"

"But I do believe! I believe in pleasure! In love and pleasure. They go together. We're here such a little time! I want to get as much as I can out of my time! It's as simple as that. Doesn't it make sense?"

The old caressing smile appealed for response. She met it thoughtfully.

"After all, Miriam, I've never hurt anyone, have I? Never in my life, not that I know of, anyway."

Not that he knew of. The hurt he was giving now, he would not understand, she saw that clearly; his comely blond face wore a look of puzzlement, with no comprehension of anything she had said all that evening.

Yes, a man for pleasure, welcome in dark times and places whether in a marriage without love or in the upheaval of a war. But he had nothing else to give. Nor had she anything left to give to him. The need was past. That's what it was. The need was past.

And she could have wept for him, wept for them both.

"Miriam . . . don't stare like that. You're frowning, as if I were some sort of villain."

"I'm sorry," she said quickly, "I don't mean to frown. Of course you're not a villain, you never were. It's just that, only that . . ."

There was a long silence, in which eyes searched eyes.

Then André said, very slowly, "Just that there's another man, I think. That's it, isn't it?"

In a lightning stroke everything is changed; one sees what one never saw before; desire is gone; the man who stands here is a stranger and always has been, although one didn't know it until now.

When she did not answer he demanded, seizing her hands, "Is there? Is there?"

She wanted so much not to wound him, only to make him *see* that they two had never been matched and never would be.

And she said, "There isn't anyone else, André. It's only that we're not—not *matched.* That's all it is."

He dropped her hands. "Not matched! I can't believe what I'm hearing!"

"I know. I can hardly believe it, either."

And again there was silence between them, while all around the sleeping home the rain fell, roaring.

"You always were a Puritan," André said at last. "A Bible Puritan, like your brother. Strange, because you don't look like one. At least, you didn't use to! Maybe that contradiction was the fascination. Who knows?" His voice roughened. "But there has to be more to this than you're telling me! Then it is another man. It's Carvalho. That's why you defended him when I called him a fool."

"You're wrong, André. Quite wrong."

She was drained. She suffered beneath his gaze, which kept studying her from the soiled hem of her old dress to her tired, bent head. A spark of light fell on the splendid ring which still lay on the table before her. It looked pathetic to her, a symbol of abandonment flung there on the bare wood. It had arrived so proudly in its velvet box.

André struck his fist impatiently into his palm. She knew the gesture. It meant that he wanted a solution, a quick answer.

"Is there anything I can do? You know me, Miriam. I can't stand all this vagueness, you with that mournful face. Just tell me whether there's anything you want me to do."

"There isn't anything," she answered miserably.

"Well, then, I suppose there's no point in my waiting here like this, is there? I might as well go the way I came. Fast." He swept the ring up and tucked it into his pocket.

Miriam touched his sleeve. "Don't hate me, André."

"I don't hate you. I couldn't, ever. I'm only sorry for you, Miriam, not even angry as I ought to be for this waste of my time, making this journey for nothing."

"I didn't know before. I really didn't know until today. Believe me."

"I believe you. It seems as though I didn't know you either, doesn't it?" He gave her a wry smile. "I just hope you're not making a terrible mistake that you'll regret when it's too late."

"If I am, so be it. I can't help it."

The rain stopped abruptly, and a humid wind out of the lonely night blew through the windows. André peered into the darkness.

"I'll take the night boat back to New Orleans."

She would have liked to bring order into this severance, to round it out diminuendo, as in music, to end
with a quiet chord.

"Don't," she said. "Don't go this way."

"How do you want me to go? I think I'm taking it
rather well—my first rejection."

"Don't think of it like that. I haven't rejected you.
We're rejecting each other, or we would have, eventually. It would have come to that, André. We're too
different."

He swallowed. She saw the hard contraction and
release of his throat; both pain and pride were stuck
there, then swallowed. Yet after a moment he was able
to summon up the old gaiety.

"No sense bemoaning, is there? We've some good
things to remember, after all, haven't we? If you want
to remember them, that is. And I do, Miriam. It was
lovely—while it lasted." His lips brushed her forehead. "So we go on to the next phase. . . ." He
looked at his watch. "I'd better rush. I've half an hour
to catch the boat."

She heard him close the door, heard his firm steps
crush the gravel. He was hastening away, putting this
night behind him as fast as he could. And why should
he not?

So the curtain comes down on the play. Sometimes,
though, the audience, deeply moved by what it has
just seen, pauses for a moment or two before gathering
wraps and departing. And Miriam sat quite still. Her
eyes filled up with stinging tears which did not fall but
swam there, blurring the dim room.

Presently she heard someone moving about. Eulalie
had come in to lock the brandy away from the servants. Curiosity was written large upon her, but she
did not speak.

"Yes, he's gone, Eulalie. It's over. And I was wrong,

you may be glad to know, or perhaps you don't care, but I'll tell you, anyway. I misjudged. I was wrong, only not for the reasons or in the way you're probably thinking." Then she remembered something. "I've never thanked you for having kept so discreetly quiet. So I thank you now."

"You've given me shelter," Eulalie said stiffly. "And I respect your husband's memory. I admired him. He was a southern gentleman."

"Yes, I know you did." Miriam put out her hand. "This seems to be a day of reckoning for me. So, truce, Eulalie. We'll never love each other, probably not even like each other very much, but truce anyway?"

They shook hands. Halfway out of the room with the bottle in her hand, Eulalie remarked, "I suppose he'll go back to his wife?"

"I suppose so."

There was no need to explain.

For a long time Miriam stood looking into the fire. Fire, like water, held one's thoughts. One saw a whole life in the flames. At the back of the hearth a piece of kindling wood had caught, renewing for a while the blaze that had been dying. She stood entranced before it. Years reflected themselves from the golden shimmer. The astonishing day just past reflected itself. Yes, she thought, he might have been a statue labeled: Grecian Youth. That's what he was, André, with all that glow to enchant a woman, but not to endure. There was not enough underneath, and he would burn away, as in a few more minutes this fire would burn away, too. There was not enough underneath to feed it.

Gabriel had said: *How could he have done this . . . an unworldly woman like you . . . a romantic, ignorant girl . . . to risk your ruin . . . if he were to walk in here, I would kill him.*

She passed her hand over her eyes, as if to wipe

away the recollection of Gabriel's wrath. She asked herself why she was crying and answered herself in André's words: Because it was so lovely while it lasted.

Yes, it was. But there was so little to it, and I took too long to find that out.

I don't cry for André; there will be someone else for him whenever he wants someone else. Wherever he goes, in London, in Paris, anywhere, they will be drawn to him. No tears for André.

After a while she was cried out. The ashes were gray, the house was silent, and she went upstairs feeling a subdued relief for having wept, as is the way with tears.

32

Day after day brought the homecomers in uniform and parts of uniform; walking or riding, limping or hale, they came straggling down the dusty roads from the north and west with the winding of the river, and over the hills from the east.

"It reminds me of Napoleon's troops returning when I was a boy," Ferdinand reflected. "Torn boots and no boots, some of them glad to get home, some of them scared of what they'll find. Same thing."

Surely Gabriel would take the train and would be coming to them from New Orleans, if he were coming at all.

Pelagie's boys arrived and submitted sheepishly to a tearful, unrestrained welcome, for they were ashamed, in their hard-won manhood, with their new-sprouted beards, to reveal how glad they were.

"How lucky I am!" their mother cried, when past the first tears and laughter. "Poor Mama lost eight of her eleven, but I've only lost two of my seven. And I have my boys back—with no roof to call their own, it's true, but at least they're alive."

Rosa's Henry came, incredibly untouched by the war, although he had fought his way through Georgia and surely seen the worst of it. Looking far younger than his thirty years, hardened and browned, he quite

obviously drew the shy attention of Angelique, who
came to dinner wearing Pelagie's only silk shawl and a
garnet necklace borrowed out of Miriam's jewelry box.

The girl had hardly ever seen an "eligible" man.
When I was her age, Miriam reflected, they were already maneuvering me into marriage, and I thought I
was ready for it, as no doubt she thinks she is, too. As
I did, she dreams of the bridegroom's body and the
marriage bed. I must tell her not to stare at Henry like
that, or Rosa will notice. No, I must tell her nothing.
Leave her alone. Let her make what she will of the
world. It's her world.

A dozen times Rosa asked Henry whether he had
seen or heard anything at all of Gabriel. Not satisfied
with his negative reply, she kept insisting that there
must be someone who knew and some way they might
find out what had happened after the confusion of the
final battle and the surrender.

Miriam, who asked no questions, now began to have
a series of strange dreams. They began with a suffusion
of longings different from any she had ever felt before,
even when she had longed for André. In this there was
a depth of tenderness close to sadness, something elu-
sive, so lightly grasped that the fear of losing it was as
marked as the thing itself. Halfway between sleep and
waking, yet aware that she was dreaming, she held a
man's head to her heart; she felt the weight of his
leaning. Oh, take care of him, never let anything hurt
him, never!

And then one day at last came the news, brought by
another of the footsore band that passed on the river
road, a farmer's boy from the hollow back of Beau
Jardin. Somehow in the welter of war he had come
into contact with Colonel Carvalho, and he had a message: Gabriel had "gone north for treatment of a
wound." He spoke in laconic monosyllables and had

no answers to any of their natural questions about the wound, and why Gabriel had not written, or when he would be home.

But Gabriel was at least alive. One could but wait.

Summer moved toward the zenith, bringing with it a restlessness and impatience to try other ways. The war was past; it seemed time to return to "real" life, which for Ferdinand's family, unlike the Labouisse connection, was urban life.

Eugene had lost too many years of education. Angelique had been hidden away in deep country silence; it was evident by her response to Henry de Rivera's presence that she was ready for the next phase. And now that the crisis, with its need for cheer, was past, even Ferdinand's eternal cheer had begun to falter.

Not so much asking Ferdinand's opinion as thinking aloud, Miriam remarked one day, "Sanderson writes that he's back in the city and has taken the liberty, as he puts it, of going down to the office and the warehouse. They're abandoned, but undamaged, he reports. I must say, in spite of Butler's horrors, they didn't destroy the city, which they could have done. Sanderson says there was an order in the mail from an old customer in England with a check in advance. He thinks we could start up again, very gradually and carefully, of course."

Her fingers folded and refolded the letter, playing with the crisp paper, recalling that first pleasure in mastering the mysteries of the ledger, in pitting her judgment against others', in building a little kingdom, if you could call it that, for her family.

"Commerce will thrive again," she said. "Someday, goodness knows when, but it will."

"I wish I could give you advice." Ferdinand sighed. The sigh was humble and wistful. "But I'm afraid to," he added abruptly, and laughed with embarrassment.

"Sit back now, Papa, you did your share in your time," she reminded him, knowing that he was only too relieved to "sit back."

Pelagie went with her sons to see what was left of Plaisance. Old Lambert, at his own behest, had been left behind. It would have been too hard for him to confront the ruination of the grandeur which had been at the core of his life.

"It will never be what it was, that we all know," they reported soberly on their return. "But just to get some sort of house up, a small place to live in while we try to clean up the devastation, maybe get a few hands to plant a few acres—that in itself will take a couple of years."

The prospect was desolate. It was then that Miriam got her idea.

"Why don't you all stay here until you can get a start at Plaisance? You could run this place while we go back to the city. Make a crop here, sell it, keep what you make and use it to help rehabilitate Plaisance."

Pelagie's tears, always so ready to rise, now rose in gratitude.

"You've been so good to us! You took us in, you fed us, and now this. I don't know how you managed it all."

"My daughter can manage anything. She has a man's head," Ferdinand said pridefully.

A man's head, Miriam thought with wry amusement. And she said to Pelagie and Eulalie, who stood waiting to be included, "You'll manage, too. You've a good heritage, both of you. Don't you remember how your mother used to tell of her great-grandmother on the German Coast? I think it was my very first time at table in her house when I heard her. Five hundred arpents of land, she said; the house was hewn logs and the hogs ran loose in the woods, hunting acorns. Yes, I remember. She was so proud of that hard life! Well, yours won't be that hard here. . . . So, it's settled, then."

Alone, Miriam went to take a last look at the land she had once so sorely resented. The cattle had been released from the barn and were moving through the gate with heads to grass. Already Pelagie's sons had begun to set things in order, regulating the milking times and setting firm schedules for planting and plowing. For them this was the natural way of life, rather than a way to be learned with struggling effort. The land and its creatures had been asking to be cared for, Miriam told herself, and she was glad to be leaving them with people who loved them.

Sisyphus was on the verandah supervising the family's meager luggage. And she recalled the flourish of their former arrivals and departures at Beau Jardin, the wagons piled with trunks, the coachmen in feathered hats and the glossy horses in brass-studded harness. Changes. Changes.

Downhill, out of the light, into the shadow of cypress and live oak, she went toward the bayou. The day was windless, so still that the tops of the tupelo trees caught not a breath of breeze, and the fluffy roseaux heads at the bayou's rim stood without swaying. The water lay thick as black glass, dotted here and there with silver or bronze where a shaft of sunshine pierced the darkness. Yet, in its calm depths the drowsing alligator lurked and the dreadful cottonmouth slithered.

Like life, Miriam thought. Danger hides in beauty and beauty in danger. Then, mocking herself: How philosophical we are this morning, Miriam! She walked back to the house. It was time to go.

Someone touched her shoulder. It was Angelique, holding a clutch of coarse, ragged zinnias out of the abandoned garden.

"We must put this on our papa's grave before we leave," she said solemnly.

Miriam's eyes lifted to the second-floor piazza, then lowered the spot on the grass where Eugene had lain.

"Of course," she said softly.

The son and the daughter laid the flowers on the father's grave. With soundless steps and muted voices they went, as if the man who lay behind the hedge of Cherokee roses could know that they were there. He was resting now in the place he had cherished, his Beau Jardin.

Standing a little apart from them, Miriam regarded her daughter and her son. They waited now, without knowing that they waited, in that short period of uncertain possibilities at the entrance to adult life. One had little way of foreseeing yet what they might finally become, but whatever it was would be soon. It was time. The boy, without schooling during these past years, had grown restless and awkward, almost as shy and raw as a backwoodsman. Blunt as a backwoodsman, too, she thought; or else, one might say, blunt and honest as David. There was no mistaking the honesty in his answering gaze, so much like David's.

Miriam's own gaze paused then at Angelique's bent head. Copper threaded her black, streaming hair; in one quick-moving curve she knelt to place the flowers, then straightened tall. Those odd tea-colored eyes, which in her father's face had seemed to hold such mystery and menace, were in the girl's face exotic and alluring. She had her father's pride, but none of his arrogance. And without envy the mother recognized a beauty greater than her own had ever been.

The boy was saying the Kaddish, his voice faltering with emotion, while Angelique looked down at the mounded grave over which two bumblebees pursued each other. How they loved their father! Miriam thought. They don't know we were unfaithful to each other. They don't know how they were conceived, how I had to grit my teeth to keep from crying out my rage. And they will never know. He fathered them and he cared for them. That's all that matters.

But how she had loathed him and been so sorry all the while! And she said suddenly to her children, "When you are twenty-one, you can decide whether you want this place. I do not."

Dear city, dear home! The house was in better condition than they had hoped it might be, although the curtains were faded where the rain had beaten in, the parquet floors were ruined, the garden was overgrown, and the fountain was filled with trash.

A letter had been left in the mailbox. From Gabriel, Miriam thought at once with a surge of hope, but it was not. It was from Fanny.

She wrote from Washington, where she was working in a fine household, caring for children and in general "helping out." No different from what she did here, thought Miriam, reading on.

"They are good people, this is a wonderful city, and I am happy, but I miss you all the same. I will never forget you, and always love you. Fanny." The signature made a nice flourish on the page.

I was a child myself when I taught her to write. I taught her and she, in her own ways, taught me.

"To life," Miriam said aloud. It was a kind of blessing, almost a prayer, if one wanted to think of it like that, an ancient Hebrew blessing.

"To you, Fanny," she said softly, and folded the letter away.

Summer slid into fall. Red haw and chinquapin ruddied the mornings, while a lively wind blew a thin filament of clouds across a sky as hard and blue as porcelain. Soon wild ducks would be hawked on the street and the shortening days would turn dark with rain.

Along the cemetery's wall the last of the hydrangea hung dry and brown, crisped by the final heat of the summer. Miriam and Ferdinand stood in front of the elaborate tomb which, in the days of his prosperity, he had bought at Emma's behest. For fully five minutes Ferdinand stood staring at the inscription.

> CI-GÎT EMMA RAPHAEL, NÉE DUCLOS.
> SHE WAS A GOOD MOTHER, GOOD FRIEND,
> AND MOURNED BY ALL WHO KNEW HER.
> PASSANTS PRIEZ POUR ELLE.

Miriam's eyes wandered down the long avenues of crypts set high and safe above flood water, to the tombs with their hovering angels, the glass cases of artificial flowers, and finally to the grave of Sylvain Labouisse, a few yards away. Old enmities! The terrible night of David's flight. Pelagie veiled in heavy black, and David, softest of men, in whose imagination the apparition of her stricken face would live as long as he did.

All the old enmities.

A man and woman bearing the unmistakable aspect of tourists came by. The woman spoke with a Yankee twang.

"Quaint, isn't it? I've never seen a cemetery like this. And everything in French—the whole city—it hardly seems American at all." They moved on.

"No," Ferdinand demurred, "it was the most American of cities. It was the American paradise. Oh, I remember coming downriver lugging my trunk off the boat. . . . Here there were no distinctions of any kind. Here if you worked hard, you could make something of yourself," he mused in his familiar way. "And, ah, the life, the sweet life!" He kissed his fingers.

"Well, yes, to be sure," Miriam replied patiently.

Ferdinand's hand smoothed the bas relief on which an angel with puffy cheeks and folded wings was blowing a trumpet.

Presently he sighed. "She was a good woman."

"She was kind, she was dear, and I loved her." Then hesitantly Miriam asked, "Will you lie here, too, Papa, when your time comes?"

"No. Have I never told you? I bought my grave in Shanarai Chasset Cemetery long ago." And at the unmistakable shadow of surprise in his daughter's expression, he added with a curious combination of shyness and pride, "Tomorrow I go to say Kaddish for Eugene. And for so many more. So many."

As they walked back toward the waiting carriage, he continued, "You know, there's something else about America that I don't think I ever really saw before."

"And what is that?"

"It's that you don't have to lose yourself in it or forget who you are. You can merge in the whole and keep yourself. Anyway," he reflected slowly, "you can't ever escape yourself, even if you want to, can you? This war and all the false—"

She interrupted. "But you don't want to escape anymore?"

"No. No . . ." And he turned on his daughter a bright, grieving look, almost youthful in its fervor. "I

suppose you might say I'm growing old and want to
make my peace. I think more and more of your
mother every day and of the things that meant so
much to her. But then, you've known that quite
awhile. . . . Then I think, strangely enough, of Judah
Touro, a man I scarcely knew, and how he came back
to his beginnings. Something happened to him. What?
Maybe it happens to us all in the end. Who can know
why? Maybe it's in the bones."

Once, Miriam remembered vaguely, Gabriel had
said something about people wanting to forget the old
fears and humiliations of Europe, and in the process,
discarding all else of value. Yes, Gabriel had said that.

And she thought, He is a long time coming home.

"I would like to see your brother, Miriam," Ferdinand said again, as so often lately. "I wonder whether
I ever will."

"I think you will, Papa, although I don't know
when."

"I would like to tell him that I understand more
than I once did. Oh, it took this terrible war for me to
understand my son! He was right, of course, although
the path he followed wasn't, God knows, the most
prudent! Still, he was true to himself, as you always
reminded me."

True to himself, she thought. As Gabriel was. And
reflections of Gabriel now crowded in upon her, vivid
scraps jumbled out of their times and places: the top
hat stuffed with papers, the flight from David's house
through the eerie streets, the room above the dreary
Richmond alley, and his arms around her.

Maxim started the horses, a pair of tired nags sold
cheaply by the occupying forces to save the trouble of
transporting them. The carriage rattled. Stuffing
bulged from the upholstery.

"They gave it hard wear," Ferdinand lamented. "I

remember the day I bought it and the day Eugene saved it for me from my wreckage. So good of him! It was a handsome piece of equipment in its time. I always liked bright things, red wheels, good leather. Expensive things." He laughed shortly and ruefully.

The shambling clip-clop of the horses was too loud in the too quiet streets.

"Oh, it will take a long time for this city to revive," Ferdinand said.

"But it will, Papa. And in the meantime things could be worse for us. At least we have a house, which is more than a lot of others have."

"True. A house. And your fine boy and girl. You know, I often imagine Angelique being married in the garden. Maybe to Rosa's Henry, what do you think? So the ancient stock will continue, the fine old Sephardic line go on?"

Strange comment from one who himself had not a trace of that fine old Sephardic stock in his own ancestry! But that was Papa, in spite of all reverses and defeats, still seeking grandeur, or his version of it! She suppressed her amusement.

"Heavens, I don't know," she said, and suddenly frowned, thinking, Marriage again, for Angelique barely sixteen! Oh, not that soon, not another mistake in the old style, not if I can help it!

"And I think of you, too, Miriam. You're a very young woman, too young to live alone. I suppose you're tired of hearing me say it. You know, for a while I thought there might be something between you and Perrin, if ever his wife should divorce him—there were some rumors of divorce, Emma always said. I'm rather relieved that there isn't."

"I thought you liked him. You seemed to enjoy him."

"Oh, enjoy, indeed! He has a way with him, good

humor that's catching. But there was something about him that didn't suit you."

Strange that he didn't see it when I married Eugene, she thought. She did not answer and her father, glancing sidelong, aware that some nerve had been touched, said no more.

Later that day Sisyphus, in the proper butler's garb that, old and frayed as it was, he insisted on wearing, was serving tea when a horse came trotting up the street and stopped at the curb. A man swung down, tied the reins to the hitching post, and came up the walk. Sisyphus almost dropped the cream pitcher.

"Why, that's got to be Mister Gabriel!" he cried. "Why, surely it is!"

All rushed, overturning a chair, clattering down the steps and the walk. But Miriam was first, first to call his name, first to fling her arms around him.

"Gabriel—"

His left sleeve dangled. The arm was gone.

She was horrified. She stammered, "Your arm . . ."

"In the last battle. At Five Forks, before Richmond fell."

"Your arm—" Her voice rose out of control.

"Don't, don't," he admonished her gently. "I'm alive and grateful."

They crowded back into the house, Angelique and Eugene, Miriam and Ferdinand and Gabriel, with Sisyphus, as overcome by his emotion as all the others, in the rear.

"Come inside, here, sit down, let's have a look at you," Ferdinand urged.

"Your arm . . ." repeated Miriam.

Ferdinand attempted heartiness, entering a masculine conspiracy to slide over the subject and spare the delicate woman.

"Where have you been? We have been waiting for months."

"I went north. About my arm—and other things."

Miriam composed herself, forcing her eyes away from the terrible empty sleeve to Gabriel's face. Attentive and courteous, he listened to Ferdinand's excited babble. The reticence was still there; his had never been a mobile or expressive face; what was within him was held in and carefully released, not spilled away. . . . She thought she had never seen so beautiful and masculine a face. She thought she had never really *seen* it before now.

"Will you have some brandy or wine? We've a bottle or two. They didn't leave us much." As always, Ferdinand was the anxious host.

"No, no, tea is fine, thank you."

"When I think of the old hospitality . . ." Ferdinand began, and asked then, "You're home to stay, of course?"

"Yes. I took the oath and I have my pardon."

For a moment nobody knew what more to say; Eugene and Angelique were obviously overawed by this hero of the war. Regardless of his altered judgment of the war Eugene would still revere a hero. His admiration shone.

Now his curiosity broke through. "What does the pardon say?"

Gabriel smiled. "It's very long. A lot of words."

"President Johnson's amnesty proclamation?"

"No, that only pardons those who have participated in what he calls the 'late rebellion,' as long as they were not high-ranking officers or didn't own taxable property worth twenty thousand dollars." Gabriel smiled. "Well, I surely haven't got property worth anything at all. But I was a high-ranking officer, so I had to apply for individual clemency."

There was a silence while all reflected on these facts.

Ferdinand asked, "He's not like Lincoln, is he, this Johnson?"

"No. I fear it won't go as well with us as it would have if Lincoln had lived."

Eugene said, almost timidly, "Lincoln was a just man."

"True. He was the best friend we had in the North."

"I never thought I'd hear you say a thing like that!" Ferdinand exclaimed.

"There are a lot of things I never thought I'd hear myself say."

All these words swirled past Miriam's head. She only half heard them. Why, it's so simple! she was thinking. Why did I not know it before?

He filled the room with his presence. All else fell away, along with the words they were speaking; the furniture, the very walls fell away, leaving only the vibrant afternoon light and Gabriel in the center of it. And she had the happiest, most foolish thought: I'm glad I changed my dress. I want to look perfect. He will see how glad I am.

"The war has changed us all. Do you know it would have cost less to have bought all the slaves and set them free? Yes, it would have cost far less. The differences between us weren't worth the war. It was the politicians who made it."

"Then why didn't they do it, then?" young Eugene inquired.

"Do what?"

"Buy the slaves and set them free."

"Why, that would have been too simple! No, seriously, there were many reasons. Money is one. It always is."

As though it were her own shame—and was it not in some part hers?—Miriam thought of the hideous profits out of blood. *The more fool he,* André had said, and laughed.

"Honor and glory," she murmured. The words came unbidden from her mouth. "They mean nothing, after all."

André had said that, too.

"Well," replied Gabriel, "there's no glory, that's true enough. But honor there is, and that's probably all we have left." His shoulders straightened. "We went in with honor and we've come out with it, as David says."

"David? You've talked to David?" cried Ferdinand.

"Yes, I met him in New York."

"Tell us. Tell us!" Ferdinand urged.

"I thought he looked pretty well. He's got his health back. The only things he won't get back are his teeth. Incidentally, I hear that that devil Wirz, who ran the infamous camp at Andersonville, is being court-mar-tialed for his crimes."

"What else? Is he coming home, did he say?"

Gabriel said gently, "I'm sure he'll come to visit, but home for David is in the North. You must know that."

"So he'll be opening an office in New York? Or where?"

"I don't think he's quite sure. He's the same old David, you see. . . ." Gabriel smiled. "Off to new wars again."

"Off to new wars!"

"Yes, wage slavery, he tells me, is only a little better than Negro slavery. It is selling oneself by the day and nothing more. So he's prepared to fight that, too, now."

"Fight it? How?" Ferdinand was aghast.

"Well, it's not fighting, exactly. He wants to raise wages, which really are disgracefully low in some places. Then the sanitary conditions in the tenements, the lack of safety in the factories, child labor, and a long list of abuses—he wants to tackle them all."

"Good God," Ferdinand muttered.

"Poor Papa!" Miriam said almost mischievously. There was something a little comical about her father's consternation. "It really is time we got used to our David, don't you think so?"

"He's our angry prophet," Gabriel remarked. And he said soberly, "The world needs people like him, miles ahead of the rest of us. And thank God America's always had people like him."

Ferdinand sighed. "And the Jews have. People like him are at the heart of our faith."

Miriam looked at her father with surprise.

"Oh, I'm getting old, Miriam, but I haven't forgotten everything yet."

Gabriel said quietly, "It's a democratic faith. Very American, when you think about it."

He stopped, looking toward the window, where some scorched leaves on a dead branch tapped the upper pane. He looked so long that the others turned their eyes there, too, but there was only the dead branch to be seen, and sensing his abstraction, they did not interrupt it.

"So," he said, turning back to them, "we build again. There'll be a new generation. In time it will be better for us all than it ever was before."

"That's what Rabbi Gutheim said last week," Eugene reported.

"And he was right," declared Gabriel.

Angelique, who had been studying Gabriel with her chin in her hands, blurted suddenly, "You know something, it's just occurred to me, you look like Lincoln!"

A flurry of laughter relieved the gravity. Gabriel made a comical formal bow.

"In many quarters that would not be taken as a compliment, Miss Angelique. But I take it as one."

Ferdinand stood up.

"I have things to do. Will you excuse me? Come, Eugene, come Angelique, you've things to do, too."

They had nothing to do, Miriam knew, but her father, with some thought in mind, had wanted to leave them alone.

She said the first thing that came to mind. "Your arm—does it hurt? I've heard that there's pain even after—"

"Only a little. But David tells me it will pass." He said ruefully, "The U.S. gives artificial limbs to its soldiers, but our side can't afford to. Well, I'll have to get my own and be thankful it wasn't a leg."

He leaned down to stroke the dog, who lay near him, keeping at it too long. And she knew he needed a reason not to speak, to cover the emotion that revealed itself by the twitching of his cheeks.

Questions, shreds of long-ago conversations, proud convictions, dark anxieties and doubts, lived on, humming in this silence. And remembering, Miriam knew that Gabriel, too, must be recalling these ghosts of the dead years, so that it seemed they were a presence in the room, like the genie in the box, awaiting the cutting of the string, the unpeeling of the paper, the lifting of the lid. She was afraid to cut the string.

After a while, forcing herself to speak, she made a soft reproach. "You never wrote. You could have got someone to do it for you."

"I can write," he answered quickly, evading the main issue. "I still have my right arm."

"Are you different—changed?" she asked, and at once would have withdrawn the absurd question if she could have done so. The words were unclear as she had spoken them, for what she had meant was: Do you feel the same about me?

He took a different meaning from the question. "Of course I've changed. One couldn't have gone through these last years without changing. I've seen men giving their last morphine to a wounded enemy, and—forgive me for this truth—I've seen men in savage rages cut out a wounded man's tongue. You ask me whether I've changed?"

She twisted Emma's sapphire round and round her finger, which had grown even thinner since the ring, too large to start with, had been given her.

"I'm sorry. It was a stupid thing to ask you."

"Yes . . . but I gave the wrong answer," he said quickly. "I'm sometimes too irritable. It will take effort. I'm trying . . ." His voice faded.

"What will you do now?" she asked quietly.

He did not answer at once. He had scarcely heard the question. She was sitting so near him that he could see every grain of her amber skin. Here she was, his Biblical Rebecca, just as he had remembered. Here were the fine, flashing eyes, the dominant, haughty nose, and the contradiction of a mouth as soft as a child's.

She opens her mouth with wisdom, and in her tongue is the law of kindness.

In Richmond she had come into his arms and laid her head on his shoulder. Oh, what a brotherly, mild embrace—not at all what he wanted, neither then nor now! Under the layers of bodice cloth, the foaming skirt, the silly hoops and wires, there waited . . . Not for him, though, but for that other, who wasn't worth her finger.

He collected himself. She had asked him what he was going to do. Bitterness, the most intense he had felt since the wounding, went through him. What choices did he have? He tried to flex the fingers that were not there, and a fiery, jagged pain went through the arm that was not there.

At least it is the left, he thought. But had it been the right, could he have learned to form the letters with his left? And this puzzled him, so that he frowned, feeling the pressure of the frown on his contracted forehead, and imagined the fingers of his left hand trying to form the letters of his name: the initial flourish of the capital *G*, then the downward stroke again, a short upward curve, and now the slanted stroke of the small *a*. The paper would be lying to the right of his hand as he worked the letters across it, trembling and awkward as a small child in his first attempt at printing.

He came back to the present moment. She was still waiting for an answer.

"Why, practice law," he said. "Try to pick up the pieces. And you?" He did not look at her, but at the floor on which the speckled light moved like confetti dots, as the sunshine quivered through the leafage at the open window. "David told me that he—that he will soon be free."

"André, do you mean?"

"André," Gabriel said, forcing the name.

"He is free already." She thought her throat would burst. "He's gone away. Gone back to Europe, I think."

For a moment Gabriel did not speak. Then he said very low, "I'm sorry, Miriam."

"Sorry? Why?"

"That you're hurt."

"But I'm not hurt, Gabriel! It's I who sent him away."

He looked disbelieving.

"Yes, yes, it was I! Because I knew, you see, oh, it took me too long to find out, but I knew it was all wrong, it was a delusion; such things can happen, can't they?"

"And so it is all finished," Gabriel said.

"Yes, finished! And I've so much I should tell you, that I need to say."

It seemed to her now that she must beg forgiveness of this man for her stupid blindness, for not having seen him as he was, for not having understood anything.

"Forgive me," she said, and wept.

She brought a footstool and sat before him; she took his hand, pressing its palm against her cheek, murmuring, whispering, letting the words rise to her lips without hesitation or shame, speaking to him in French for no reason other than that the words of love flowed softly in the lilting vowels of that language.

"*Je t'aime* . . . I love you. Oh, I've been so strange, not myself, I sometimes think; yet how can that be? But I love you."

He stroked her hair. She felt the warm cup of his hand smoothing, smoothing, and, in the sudden silence, could hear his breathing, yet he did not answer. She raised her head.

"I want to marry you, Gabriel. I want a long, quiet, wonderful life with you. I want to be with you for every day that's left to us. We're young, we can still—"

He turned his face away and covered it with his hand. She thought she heard him say, "Now! Dear God, now!"

Then, in a stronger voice, he said, "Oh, my dearest, I can't. How can I, the way I am?"

She sprang up. "What does that matter? Do you

think I care about that? Or care about anything at all except . . ." She could not go on.

"I know you don't. But I care. A one-armed lover, starting all over again at the bottom with nothing. That's not the way I used to dream I might come to you."

"You're wrong, you're stubborn, you're wrong! Tell me—is there some other reason? Because of him—of André—perhaps you don't trust me, don't believe in me anymore and don't want to say so?"

"I believe in you. I would trust you with my life."

"Well, then, trust me with it!"

Gabriel stood up. She came close to him, asking not in words alone, but with her eyes and her encircling arms, "Do you love me?"

"More than the world."

"Then take me. You can't just walk away and leave me."

The pressure of his arm was strong on her back. Yet, "See, I can't even hold you properly. I can't do anything for you. I couldn't even give you a ring."

"What do I care about a ring!"

"Don't torture me, Miriam. Oh, don't." He stroked her blazing cheek. "I want . . . I wanted . . ." His voice shook. "But the way things are . . . Let me go." And very gently, he pulled away.

She could not speak. All, all was unreal. Weak, almost faint, she held the back of a chair while Gabriel rushed into the hall. When the outer door thumped shut, she went to the window. Out of tearless eyes she watched him go down the walk and swing himself onto the horse. She could hear the clatter of the trot and see him to the end of the street. Then she let the curtain fall back.

From another window I watched another man depart, and it was sorrowful in its way, but this is different, this is my heart.

"What?" said Ferdinand, in his jolly voice. He must have been waiting in the parlor across the hall. "Gabriel gone so soon? Is anything wrong?"

She answered flatly, "Only that I asked him to marry me."

"You—wait a minute—you asked him, you said?"

"That's true."

Ferdinand's face wrinkled with astonishment. He threw back his head and laughed in pure glee.

"You asked him? You must be the only woman in the world with nerve enough to do that! You and your brother! The two of you will never cease to surprise me with the outlandish things you do. And David will be so glad, so absolutely glad! Can't you imagine? Tell me, when is it to be? Very soon, I hope."

"He refused me, Papa."

Ferdinand stared. "Refused! God Almighty! Rosa told me, she swore me to secrecy, she told me—"

Rosa and her secrets!

"—that he's been in love with you ever since—"

"Ever since before he lost an arm."

Ferdinand was stricken. "I don't understand. That shouldn't matter, if it doesn't matter to you."

"Pride, Papa. A man's pride, and he's got too much of it. It'll take a deal of talking to talk him out of it."

Ferdinand put a warm hand on his daughter's shoulder. His forehead wrinkled in distress. "I'm so sorry, dearest girl. You've been through too much in your short years."

"A lot of it was my own fault, Papa, though some of it wasn't."

"What are you going to do?"

"Do? I'm going to talk him out of it. But right now

I think, if you don't mind, I'd just like to be by myself awhile."

He stood aside to let her pass, and she went downstairs, out to the old side garden, that little spot where so much had happened in her life.

There, still, Aphrodite stood. The dove at her feet had been smashed, but Ferdinand had cleaned out the pool himself, and the water fell now as it always had, in two curving tiers, like flounces on a skirt. And she sat there, without moving, until her heartbeat slowed and her breath came quietly again. The water rippled and trilled; voices and noises came from the other side of the wall, as the life of the street resumed, the life of the old, old city on the brown enduring river.

Here her children had taken their first steps. Here she had made her first trembling visit to this house where her years as a woman had begun. And she remembered her father's house before that, lofty in her sight as a palace, when, clinging to David's hand and awkward in her fine new dress, she had come to this strange country. She remembered the strange languages learned on the heaving ocean, and the ship, and Gabriel the boy standing drenched on the deck with the shivering dog in his arms.

It had been a long, long way: up in the world and down, up again and down again.

"But I can do things," she said aloud. There was a thickness in her throat which she swallowed, and then went on talking to the air. "I can do things. I've done so much I never thought I could. And I can make him change his mind. Yes, Gabriel, I can."

A butterfly had settled on her wrist; its resting wings, erect as sails, were opalescent mauve. The common wood nymph, probably, she thought, surprising herself with this recollection from the frontispiece in one of David's enormous books. The lovely substance of the living wings was patterned like Oriental silk. All is pattern, all life, but we can't always see the pattern when we're part of it.

She was able to smile. Hadn't Fanny always said it was a good omen when a butterfly lights on you?

The little creature quivered, lowering its wings and fluttering from her outstretched arm. It flickered toward the shrubbery, wavered away, and was lost in the gold and silver dazzle of the afternoon.